AN APPEARANCE OF GOODNESS

A PRIDE AND PREJUDICE MYSTERY VARIATION

HEATHER MOLL

EXCESSIVELY
DIVERTED
PRESS

To the JASNA Capital Region group, who never grow tired of what I put their beloved characters through

CHAPTER ONE

July 1812

E lizabeth Bennet took a solitary walk, crossing fields and springing over puddles on her way home to Netherfield. The cold, wet, disagreeable weather had stopped for the present, and she took advantage of the chance for exercise and to refresh her spirits. She had felt out of sorts since she returned from Hunsford; and not even the joyful events that happened since could do away with her shame regarding her blind and prejudiced behaviour towards Darcy and Wickham.

If my mother ceased visiting the new Mrs Bingley every day, if the weather ceased to be rainy and cold, and if I ceased to think of Darcy's letter, how happy a summer I might have before me.

It had been a surprise to everyone when Bingley called at Longbourn the day after Elizabeth and Jane returned from London in May. His return could only have been Darcy's doing. After writing his letter, he must have decided his observations of Jane were incorrect—that she was not indifferent to his friend—and confessed his part in keeping Bingley from Jane last winter.

Perhaps Darcy even assured Bingley that Jane returned his affections with sincere regard, or perhaps he merely told Bingley that he perceived that *his* attachment was unabated. Either way, Bingley depended on his friend's judgment, and Darcy had given his permission. Bingley was invited to dine at Longbourn, stayed to supper, and the next day Elizabeth had allowed Jane and Bingley to outstrip her during a walk, knowing full well what could happen.

Darcy may have reunited them, but his letter had expressed no regret for separating them in the first place. Elizabeth stomped up a stile and jumped down. His letter was not penitent, but haughty. He had corrected his error, but she could not think well of a man who wrote to her—who spoke to her—with such pride and insolence.

His sending Bingley to Hertfordshire was a stroke of generosity she had not thought him capable of, but his promoting Bingley and Jane's marriage could not absolve him entirely. Was it not plain that Darcy had no regard for her if he could speak of her family in such a manner? She knew she had been weak and vain in regard to him, but that did not make him an amiable, civil man.

And whilst confessing his interference, did Darcy mention to Bingley our quarrel and his disastrous proposal?

In this perturbed state of mind, with thoughts that could rest on nothing, Elizabeth walked home. She had only called at Longbourn to pay her compliments to her parents and sisters. Mary could not be troubled to leave her instrument, Kitty had nothing at all to say, and Lydia still lamented not being allowed to follow the regiment to Brighton with Mrs Forster, although it had been nearly two months since the militia left.

"Lizzy!"

Bingley hallooed to her from atop his horse and came alongside her. "I see you are also making the most of this break in the rain." He dismounted. "We shall walk the last quarter-mile together."

When Jane and Bingley married, they had both insisted that she join their household. Jane wanted a female companion as she adjusted to her new position, and Bingley did not want Caroline to fill that role. Whilst he had forgiven his sisters for their contrivance and falsehood, Elizabeth suspected he knew that Jane could never be as dear to them as they once were to her.

"I meant to tell you congratulations on one month of marriage."

"Thank you! After everything that happened—well, I am a happy man. Last winter, I could not have imagined that by the middle of July I would be one month married."

It was no surprise to Elizabeth that the couple had returned from that walk engaged. Bingley's conversation with her father had been short and to the purpose, and it was settled that the wedding would take place in a month. But after dinner that evening, the two men had stayed in the dining room a long time after the ladies withdrew, and both appeared more solemn when they emerged than one might have expected given the happy occasion.

Neither man would answer for it, but the change at Longbourn following that private conversation was remarkable. The militia officers were no longer welcomed in the house, and her mother was forbidden from hosting the officers for a farewell dinner. Her father, far from giving unequivocal and vague answers—as was his wont—plainly told her mother that they would not spend the summer in Brighton, that Lydia could not accept Mrs Forster's invitation, and he was finished hearing about militia officers unless Napoleon himself landed on the coast. Elizabeth had had no luck convincing her father to speak of what caused such a change, but she hoped Bingley might say whilst they were alone.

"Did you make it as far as Longbourn?" Bingley interrupted her thoughts as Netherfield came into sight.

"I only stayed long enough to pay my compliments to my family. But my father teased that he had only consented to lose one daughter to you, not two, and still bade me to come home."

Bingley laughed. "And here I believed that you were home now."

"I feel as though I am." Bingley had, in a short time, become a dear brother to her. He was a sweet-tempered man who loved Jane. How could a man who was good humour itself have a steady friendship with Darcy, unless Darcy was more amiable than she had credited him with being? *I acted despicably towards him.*

"And how is your mother?"

She started and drew her thoughts from Darcy. "I daresay you will learn for yourself. Now that the rain has stopped, we can expect her soon." Bingley put on a face of practised patience. There was nothing Mrs Bennet liked better than to call on Mrs Bingley. "However, I did say that she ought not to call so early, so Jane will at least need not entertain her and her friends from breakfast to dinner."

Bingley thanked her, and Elizabeth wondered how many more daily visits would he stand before he would begin to talk of giving his mother-in-law the hint that she not call so often. The house was now near, and if she was to ask her question, she ought to do it now.

"Would you answer something for me? I have been curious—before the militia left, they had been welcomed at Longbourn, but then once you were engaged to Jane, there was a change."

Bingley stopped walking and busied himself with petting his horse. "It hardly matters. The militia is gone on to Brighton."

"Yes, but throughout May they were not so much as allowed to enter the village, let alone the house. My father even forbade Lydia to join Colonel Forster's wife in Brighton, and it would have been more comfortable for him to allow her to go. Charles"—she forced him to look at her—"I know it was your doing, but I cannot imagine what you said to cause such a change, or why."

He pursed his lips before speaking. "You are too clever, Lizzy, and I hope you are not determined to press the subject." He shook his head and said quietly, "He said you might ask."

Her stomach turned over as she realised her suspicion had been correct. "What did Mr Darcy tell you about what happened in Kent?"

Bingley looked surprised. "How do you mean what *happened*? Darcy only said that you told him Jane had been in town all winter."

Elizabeth hesitated for only a moment. "Yes! I asked if he had been fortunate enough to have seen her."

"Well, I suspect, given how discomposed Darcy was whilst talking of it, that you must have had a frank discussion. Somehow, you came to learn what he had done?"

She felt her cheeks turn pink. "His cousin boasted how he had separated—I, I accused Mr Darcy of ruining Jane's happiness—but we . . ." She hardly knew what to say.

"After speaking with you in Kent, Darcy reconsidered all of his actions and confessed what he had done. He was wrong, and did what

4

he could to right it. I do not think ill of him, although I was angry at the time," he added with a laugh.

"That explains why you returned, but what has Mr Darcy to do with what you spoke to my father about?" If Bingley knew nothing of Darcy's rejected proposal, there was one other reason why Darcy would suspect her questions. "Had it anything to do with Mr Wickham?"

His expression darkened. "And what know you about the history between Mr Wickham and Darcy?"

She had to tread carefully, for Darcy had not authorised her to make anything said in his letter public. *I dare not relate any particulars relative to his sister.* "I know the pecuniary transactions in which they had been connected."

"Then you already know the extravagance and general profligacy that Mr Wickham is capable of. I would hate to shock you, Lizzy, and I daresay *that* is reason enough to keep him, and any officer, away from Longbourn. I told your father, in general terms, about his conduct towards Darcy, and he agreed with me to sever all acquaintance with the entire militia."

Her father would not have gone to such trouble just because an idle man wasted three thousand pounds and forsook the generosity of his benefactor. But he was, beneath his satirical, eccentric manner, a respectable man with daughters to protect.

Darcy told Bingley about Wickham's designs on Miss Darcy, and had granted his permission to tell my father about Wickham.

"Lizzy? Lizzy, you look conscious."

Elizabeth sighed. Even given the acrimonious nature of her refusal, Darcy encouraged Bingley to pursue Jane and acted to prevent Wickham from injuring anyone she cared for. "I was only thinking of how I would keep my patience if my mother calls today. I hope I put her off until tomorrow, perhaps the day after if it rains again."

"Yes, well, Mrs Bennet does miss her eldest daughter, and you, as well. She is, of course, welcome any time at Netherfield." Bingley had been trying to keep his countenance, and now his smile faltered. "Lizzy, do you think that Jane might wish for a little relief from home?"

"You mean would she like to not be forced to entertain my mother, who brings her friends, most days when Jane is still learning how to be a wife and housekeeper?"

Bingley looked terribly embarrassed. "Jane's spirits are very good! I only wondered if a change of scene might be of service?"

Elizabeth smiled. "I think it a good idea. Where shall you take her?"

"I had thought to take her to Scarborough in August. I would like her to meet some of my friends, and I had planned to travel there this summer before we married. Caroline and Louisa and Hurst will go as well."

She wondered how reconciled to the match his sisters were, but Jane could be on good terms with anyone, even if they were never truly friends again. "Jane would spend the summer with them, I am sure, and she certainly wants to be known to anyone you hold dear. You shall have a splendid time."

"What do you mean 'you'? I intend for you to come as well. You are my sister, too, are you not?"

"Yes, of course. I think of us as brother and sister."

"As do I! It is decided, then. Jane wants you, and I want *all* of my sisters with me in Scarborough. Besides, I know how disappointed you were that the Gardiners had to cancel their trip to the Lakes because of your uncle's business. I would like you to have a pleasant summer, too."

Bingley truly was a considerate man. "I would like it very much!" Even with Caroline and Louisa's company, she would see the Yorkshire coast, check the sand for stones and shells, and take country rides to see the other natural beauties. "I promise when I visit the Scarborough shops, I shall find things that I need, not only things that I fancy that I want."

"You cannot fool me," Bingley cried. "You will find a pair of thick shoes and a spyglass, and explore the cliff, regardless if this cold, rainy weather persists all summer."

Elizabeth laughed at this picture of herself. "You and Jane need not join me."

"Perhaps some of my other friends shall walk with you, Balfour or

Utterson, perhaps. You are inclined to company, so I need not fear for you in meeting anyone new. So, we shall travel north, stay with some of my friends along the way, and go to Scarborough. And you are certain that Jane will enjoy it, even, even if my sisters are amongst the party?"

Her lightness faded, and she felt for him in that moment. Bingley knew that his sisters had not wanted him to marry his beloved wife. "Charles, Jane will want to go for a change of scene and to get to know you better, away from Meryton. She has travelled very little, and I know that your wanting to make her happy, and *your* company, will conquer any reservations she has about Caroline and Louisa."

"You truly think so?"

Still relying on others' judgment. "They will at least grant her the appearance of civility, and Jane will be kind to them for your sake."

He smiled widely. "I shall propose it to Jane immediately, and then write to my friends to arrange everything. I want everyone to meet her! I know several who can host us as we travel north, and a score who would join us at the seaside."

Elizabeth nodded, and they parted. Perhaps the rainy weather would improve, and she could leave Meryton and any reminders of the militia behind and pass a pleasant summer after all. She would have the opportunity to meet new people and see new places.

I should also like a means of distraction from thinking about what I owe to Fitzwilliam Darcy.

~

August 1812

DARCY LOOKED OUT THE INN'S WINDOW, SPLATTERED WITH RAINDROPS, and felt relieved to be so close to Pemberley. One hundred and forty miles from London, and he was finally back amidst rocks and hills and luxuriant foliage. The cold winds from the north and the east spent their chill on the hills around Matlock Bath, but rarely swept down through the valley. Still, it had to be the rainiest, coldest summer on record.

A fitting stage setting for my mood as of late.

He had passed the rest of the spring and early summer feeling a contrariety of emotions following his rejected proposal. Anger, resentment, and a wish to avoid Elizabeth Bennet for the rest of his life filled his heart for a while. That was soon replaced by a heartache that he avowed to never mention to another human being. Guilt and shame for his role in separating Bingley from Miss Bennet then became his focus, and he did what was necessary to alleviate the suffering he had caused them.

And confessed enough of Wickham's vicious propensities to help Bingley persuade Mr Bennet and all of the neighbourhood to draw back from that man.

Soon, angry pride had vanished, and the suffering of disappointment had lessened. Solitude and serious reflection had led him to consider Elizabeth's reproofs, and that naturally kept her close to his mind. His behaviour towards her had been unpardonable; his conduct and manners to everyone, ungentlemanly. It was some time before Darcy was able to be reasonable to the justness of her remarks. So whilst Bingley courted and then married his wife, Darcy had remained in London and learnt a hard lesson about his pride and selfishness.

"The rain has stopped," Georgiana said, peering through the window next to him, "but through the mist that hangs in the air I cannot see the flowers at the spring that Mr Balfour and his sister mentioned."

They were in a private room in Saxton's hotel to have an early dinner with his friends. Darcy sat at the table whilst Georgiana and Mrs Annesley stayed by the window to await the others. The sky, which had been clear when they departed, became clouded this August afternoon as his party travelled north, and then a heavy shower of rain forced them to stop in Matlock Bath rather than press on to Pemberley.

"It is too wet to look at them now; you shall ruin your shoes, my dear Miss Darcy," Mrs Annesley said.

"If it is dry tomorrow, you and Mrs Lanyon can ride the rest of the way to Pemberley," Darcy said. His sister enjoyed riding and had little opportunity in town. "I think her brother and Utterson intend to finish our final stage in a post-chaise."

"I prefer to ride in the carriage—I am out of practice to ride again so soon—but you could ride with her. You and Mrs Lanyon rode together two days ago, before it rained."

Darcy nodded, but said nothing. Georgiana was not one to forward a conversation, but Mrs Annesley instructed her charge by example. "Mrs Lanyon sits very well, sir. It must be pleasant for a horseman such as yourself to ride with a woman who has such a heart for it."

"She does sit well," he agreed.

"Does Mrs Lanyon keep her brother's house since she is widowed, or does she live with her father in Scotland?"

"She has her own home in Harley Street, not far from where her brother lodges." His friend Balfour would eventually inherit his father's estate in Scotland, and until then seemed content to spend the season in London, and the rest of his time gadding from one friend's home or watering place to another. Balfour was an earnest, affable man and would get on well with Bingley and his new wife when they all met at Pemberley.

Mrs Annesley now gave an emphatic look at Georgiana, who had been watching, but not speaking. Darcy waited whilst his sister thought of something to continue a conversation he had no interest in.

"I understand Mrs Lanyon brought ten thousand pounds to her marriage, and her husband left her well-provided. Did you know him?"

"No, but Colonel Fitzwilliam did. Captain Lanyon died in the year nine. Battle of Corunna," he answered their silent question.

Georgiana had nothing to add to that, and whilst Darcy wished for the appearance of the friends to end this line of interest, Mrs Annesley began anew. "She has been widowed three years, but she cannot be much older than you, sir. I would not call her handsome, but she has a general prettiness. She is still blooming."

Darcy only nodded, and Mrs Annesley swiftly took the hint. "Mr Utterson and Mr Balfour have a steady friendship, but I understand from Miss Darcy that Mr Utterson has not seen Pemberley either?"

"No, I have not known him as long, or rather, as well as I have known Balfour. Mrs Lanyon and the new Mrs Bingley have not stayed before either."

Georgiana came from the window to sit near to him and said softly, "You shall have a large party at Pemberley."

"No larger than I typically do for some part of the summer. Bingley and his family shall stay only a fortnight before they go on to Scarborough." Bingley had written that he would bring all of his sisters and Hurst—and, naturally, his bride. "When Bingley's party joins us, we shall only be eleven altogether."

Mrs Annesley pressed her hand to Georgiana's shoulder before she took her seat, and Darcy realised what she already knew. Georgiana was sixteen now, and would be expected to mix more with his friends, but she was still devastatingly shy. He took his sister's hand. "Do you fear that I shall force you into company from dawn until candlelight? And then I shall demand you perform every evening and play every game?"

Georgiana blushed, and Darcy thought she might well have believed him capable of such a thing. *Elizabeth was right about my selfish disdain of others' feelings.* He ought to have done more to put his sister at ease before now. "Georgiana, I promise that your time shall be your own, and if you spend only half an hour in the evenings with us, I would be very glad of it."

His sister relaxed her shoulders. "I do not like being forced into constant exertion, is all. I do well enough in a small group with those I am intimately acquainted with, and who I like, of course," she added, looking down.

Georgiana could refer only to Miss Bingley and Mrs Hurst. Perhaps now that Bingley was married and *that* particular chance for a nearer connexion between their families was gone, Bingley's sisters might not force themselves upon Georgiana's notice. "Whenever you wish to be alone, whenever the company is trying, you may mount your horse and be gone!"

Georgiana and Mrs Annesley laughed, and he considered that he ought to show more kindness to those outside of his circle, as well as to those within it. "Mrs Annesley, you have not said whether or not you ride."

That she was surprised by his question was obvious, but she recovered and said, "Not since I was younger. In my last position, I was governess to four girls and saw them all brought up, but not one of them enjoyed riding. I once rode every fine morning," she added with a fond smile.

"Then you must have a horse whilst you are at Pemberley." There was no sense to stable a horse in town for even his sister, but Mrs Annesley ought to ride whenever she wished whilst in the country. "I have two horses that can carry a woman."

"That is not necessary, sir."

"It certainly is, madam. You cannot always be inside or without exercise, even if the weather is cool." It was the first Tuesday in August, but it felt like April. "This rain is bound to end, and you and Georgiana must escape the confines of the house on the first dry day. I shall have you seated at the first opportunity."

A post-boy from the inn yard ran in to deliver his party's letters, scarcely managing to touch his hat before depositing them, pocketing the coin Darcy gave him, and running back out the door. He saved Bingley's letter for the last, since it was likely to be the greatest strain on his eyes.

Bingley wanted his friends to meet his new bride and wrote that he had left London the twenty-second of July with his sister. He then joined the Hursts at a friend's home in Birmingham, and they were all now on their way to Pemberley. *His ideas flow so rapidly that he writes that he left with his sister, but then later mentions meeting the Hursts and Miss Bingley at the home of another friend.* He also wrote that he intended to arrive on Wednesday, August 6.

Damn it. Today was Tuesday the fourth; Bingley had mistaken the dates. If Bingley left Birmingham yesterday, he might arrive at Pemberley tomorrow—Wednesday the fifth—or he could break his trip and arrive on Thursday the sixth. He might arrive tomorrow before Darcy's party did.

The door opened, and Balfour entered with Mrs Lanyon and Utterson. Balfour and his sister both had pleasing countenances and the same black hair and amber eyes. But whilst Balfour was cheerful, affable, and talked a great deal, his sister had a quiet dignity that scarcely made her conversable.

"You were not waiting long, were you?" Balfour cried as he pulled out a chair for his sister. "Hester needed to arrange her hair and change her shoes after we got wet. It is possible her behaviour may arise from vanity." His voice raised in mock outrage, and he winked at her.

"Lewis, you will give Miss Darcy and Mrs Annesley a poor opinion of me." Mrs Lanyon's voice was calm as it ever was. "You should not represent me in such a light."

"If any of us is vain about their appearance, it is you, Balfour," Utterson drawled out his words in a long, slow tone. "We might have been down a quarter of an hour ago if not for you."

Utterson was not an ill-humoured young man, but as their acquaintance furthered, Darcy noticed that Utterson often found other people provoking. A difficult quality for one studying the law. There might be a similarity in their dispositions as he came to know Utterson better, but Balfour was easier to get on with.

"I *do* wish to appear to my advantage," Balfour said, smiling to everyone around the table. "You will notice that I added a cravat pin and exchanged my waistcoat for another. One cannot allow travelling and bad weather to prevent a gentleman from taking care of his appearance."

The servants brought in the meal and Darcy passed out the letters, with Utterson taking his eagerly and ignoring everyone to read them. "When we are finished with dinner," Darcy said, "I intend to ride ahead to Pemberley tonight." After hearing everyone's exclamations of surprise, he explained Bingley's letter.

Utterson shook his head. "Bingley is too careless for my liking. He has put you to an inconvenience."

"Perhaps his new wife is a delightful distraction. We ought to make Mr Bingley some allowances," said Mrs Lanyon. She then turned to Darcy. "Although I shall miss the opportunity to ride with you tomorrow."

"When the rain has stopped and we are all at Pemberley, you need only name the day."

Mrs Lanyon thanked him and gave him a contented smile that he returned. She was near his age, widowed, wealthy, and, as Mrs Annesley said, still blooming. But she had little conversation, and nothing in her character that could be described as liveliness. He simply enjoyed riding with a woman who rode well and left him alone to his thoughts.

"You may all take your time in the morning," Darcy said. "It is only ten miles. If I leave after dinner, I shall be there before eight o'clock."

Balfour leant closer once everyone resumed eating. "Dinna say you only want to be there to greet Miss Bingley," he whispered. His vowels were shorter, and a few "ayes" and "naes" crept in occasionally, but in general an Oxford education and London society had stripped Balfour of his Scottish accent, unless he was being particularly mischievous.

Darcy threw him a look that earned him a knowing smile. "I am riding ahead to be a good host to my friend, and whomever he brings with him."

Darcy pushed his food back and forth on his plate. He had not been a good friend to Bingley, and he had been too full of pride, too capable of being selfish with anybody outside of his circle. He was fortunate he had preserved Bingley's friendship, and grateful that Jane Bennet had forgiven his friend and they were now happily wed.

What a horrid state of selfish vanity I was in when I proposed to Elizabeth. He had learnt the lesson, but he had learnt it too late to marry a woman he loved.

Going home would be the final restoration of his peace. He would survive his disappointment, especially since Elizabeth thought no more of him, the last man in the world she could be prevailed on to marry. He had done what he could to rectify his errors, and whilst she may not hate him, in the event that they ever met again, he had no reason to believe she would renew their acquaintance.

Balfour brought up a hand to conceal his mouth from the others, and leant nearer to provoke him again. "You want to ride ahead to be certain that Pemberley looks its best for its new mistress? Be sure the grand staircase is polished. Shall you offer your hand to Miss Bingley in a fortnight?"

Darcy scowled. "Spare me from ever offering for Bingley's sister."

CHAPTER TWO

"We have only one stage remaining," Bingley said as their party stood in the inn yard whilst the horses were exchanged for fresh ones. "We ought to be there by noon."

It felt good to be released from the confines of the carriage. Elizabeth shifted her shoulders back and turned her neck from side to side. Every turn in the road varied the gorgeous prospect and exhibited new beauties. Here in Derbyshire, the picturesque-loving tourists would have all of their wishes gratified. The dales must be explored through their various windings, and the hills scaled to their highest points of elevation.

Such a beautiful place!

Elizabeth and Jane and Bingley had been travelling for a fortnight, staying several days with this friend or that so Bingley could proudly introduce his bride as they travelled towards Scarborough. Bingley's circle seemed to know no bounds. He said that they would next meet his friend and his widowed sister, and their friend who was studying the law. Elizabeth understood that at this next home they would stay a fortnight, and it would be good to have the opportunity to cultivate a new acquaintance and have a break from always sitting on the fold-down seat in Bingley's chaise.

"The reception you meet with at inns is exactly proportioned to the style in which you arrive," Caroline was saying to Louisa in a low voice. "One who travels in a post-chaise is treated with more civility, but of course must pay for it."

Louisa looked around the inn yard in distaste. "Indeed. The stage traveller passes unnoticed."

Elizabeth moved farther away to avoid hearing more and to take in a better view of the valley. The charm and character of this place, the green of the rugged environs, lifted her spirits.

Elizabeth was grateful that she had been spared much of Caroline's company since they joined the Hurst party yesterday to travel into Derbyshire. Caroline rode in the Hursts' chaise whilst she rode with the Bingleys. The two groups met only briefly in inn yards or at meals. In the morning, Caroline was too tired to be supercilious and, in the evening, only complained about the nuisances of travel. In general, Bingley's sisters were civil, and their kindness to Jane, such as it was, was due to their affection for their brother.

And enough of their civility spills over onto me to make our journey tolerable.

For once it was not raining, and whilst it was not a hot day, Elizabeth tilted her face up to feel the sun's warmth. This escape from Meryton, the novelty of travelling and meeting new people, and now this beautiful country had been good for her equanimity. The events of the spring did not press on her mind as often as they once did.

"If not for the rain, we might have made it last night," Bingley said, "although I cannot say that Darcy would have been pleased to have his dinner interrupted."

"What!" Elizabeth turned so quickly her bonnet slipped off and dangled from its ribbons around her neck.

Caroline and Louisa stopped listening to Jane as she, too, cried out in surprise and came nearer.

"Charles dear, what did you say?" she asked. "What did you say about Mr Darcy?"

Bingley gave his wife a confused look. "We might have arrived at Pemberley last night, but—"

"Pemberley!" Elizabeth cried. She had not misheard, and now

Bingley's sisters were looking at her in confusion. She had to control her emotions before she was forced to explain herself.

"I thought we were to stay with your friend Mr Balfour and his sister, Mrs Lanyon?" Jane asked.

Elizabeth shook her head. "And I thought we were to stay with your friend Mr Utterson."

"Oh, Eliza! How can you be so mistaken?" Caroline had joined them. "Mr James Utterson does not have an estate." She laughed as though this was absurd. "He is a younger son, although an honourable. He is keeping the term at the Inn of Court." She turned to Jane. "And Mr Balfour will inherit Hyde House in Haddingtonshire on his father's death. How did you think a Lowland Scot had a home in Derbyshire?"

Jane turned to look at Elizabeth with an expression of horror. "Oh, Lizzy, I did not . . . Charles, you led us to believe that—" Jane took a calming breath. "What great confusion we are all in. We have met so many people and been travelling so long that you have not been clear as to where we shall stay."

"I am sorry, my dear." Bingley gave her a concerned look. "I daresay I have been as careless with this visit as some of the others. Remember when we arrived in Birmingham and I forgot entirely that Danvers—"

"Charles!" Jane cried. Elizabeth's stomach was churning horribly. "Charles dear," Jane began again in a tranquil tone, "you said we have one stage left. Tell us where we are staying for the next fortnight and who will be there."

"At Pemberley with Darcy, and his sister." Elizabeth gave a soft whimper, but no one save Jane appeared to hear. "He shall be very glad of it, too. He was eager to give you notice, my dear, to show you a kindness after . . . well, when I said we were travelling to Scarborough and visiting friends, he insisted we stay with him."

Elizabeth could only just collect herself to be pleased to know that Darcy wanted to cultivate an acquaintance with Jane. But nothing could remove her alarm at the thought of residing for two weeks with Darcy. *How does he feel about my coming?*

"My friend Balfour is there, amiable man—his father is a Scottish nabob and his mother an Indian. He talks more than I do and has even less ambition." Bingley laughed. "His sister is a wealthy widow, a year older than Balfour and Darcy, and an elegant woman. And Utterson is a few years older than me and will be a barrister, since his brother will inherit the baronetcy."

"Charles dear, does Mr Darcy know whom you are bringing with you?" Jane asked. "Does he know that Lizzy is with us?"

Bingley shrugged. "I said I was bringing my sisters and Hurst. I did tell him that Lizzy lives at Netherfield, and if I did not explicitly put her name to paper when I mentioned my sisters and me coming to Pemberley, and he is surprised to see her, then he is a greater simpleton than I thought possible. How could it matter? He *knows* Lizzy. And Darcy is a generous man who would welcome anyone I brought."

Oh, he will hate the very sight of me. She watched husband and wife exchange a look, and Bingley then asked softly, "Is Lizzy not wanting to stay at Pemberley?" He dropped his voice even farther. "Why does she dislike Darcy so much?"

Elizabeth had to say something because Jane was struggling for an answer. "It is not that I dislike him. He . . . he appears to have"—*how can I explain the cold reception that awaits me?*—"a coldness under his courteous demeanour that is not congenial to my mind." She quickly added for Bingley's benefit, "I am sure those on familiar terms with him would say otherwise but . . . we hardly know one another. I doubt that Mr Darcy wishes to strengthen any connexion with me."

Bingley looked confused. "You are the most cheerful woman of my acquaintance. He is a little reserved at times, but he is an amiable man. You have tastes in common, I think. You and Darcy are certain to be on more familiar terms in a fortnight."

Elizabeth felt horribly distressed. She had no business at Pemberley. She blushed at the very idea of residing in his house, at seeing Darcy at all. Would he think that she was throwing herself in his way?

Caroline and Louisa took notice of her behaviour. "Eliza, do you dislike the idea of staying at Pemberley?" Caroline asked. "George Wickham, who I recall was a favourite of yours, passed his youth there."

Rather than pierce her, Caroline's barb strengthened her. Elizabeth took a breath and answered, with a proper air of indifference, that she had not really any dislike to the scheme. "I am merely excessively surprised."

The horses were ready, and she climbed into Bingley's chaise with what she hoped was a calm and cool air. For the remainder of the journey, she tried to keep her eyes on the scenery, the hills and valleys, and all the rich varieties of nature that had previously captivated her. In truth, the only thing she saw, in her mind's eye, was the expression on Darcy's face when he had said, "Will you do me the honour of reading that letter?" That haughty composure was certainly the best she could expect from him.

Darcy might be taken by surprise, or he knows I am coming and could not refuse my company for the sake of his friendship with Bingley. Either way, his resentment would be exceptional.

As they drove along, she watched for the first appearance of Pemberley Woods with some perturbation and, when at length they turned in at the lodge, her spirits were in a high flutter. Although in agony at seeing Darcy's reaction to her, she could not help but admire the beautiful wood. Jane and Bingley talked about every point of view, but Elizabeth's mind was too full for conversation. She silently admired every remarkable spot until she saw the house. It was a large, handsome stone building, a beautiful family seat near the stream, situated on the opposite side of a valley. It was a stately centrepiece on high and commanding ground, and she gasped at the sight.

"What do you think, Lizzy?" Bingley asked, knowing full well that anyone of sense must admire it.

"I have never seen a place for which nature has done more." Elizabeth wished she could be warmer in her admiration—for the wood and the house deserved it—but she was struck that if she had said yes in April, she would have arrived here as Darcy's bride. She could not feel regret, but to be Pemberley's mistress might be something.

They drove to the door, and whilst examining the nearer aspect of Pemberley's tall columns, fine stonework, and many windows, all of her apprehensions about seeing its owner doubled. The carriage stopped, and a footman opened the door and folded out the steps. The Hursts' carriage was in front of theirs, and Elizabeth drew back from the side-glass enough so all she could see was a long pair of legs descending the stairs to greet them.

She heard his voice, welcoming the Hursts and Miss Bingley with his usual reserve, then a markedly warmer tone as he welcomed Bingley and congratulated him on his marriage.

I cannot hide in here for two weeks. Never had her embarrassment and her hesitation been more extreme or distressing as it was when she descended the carriage.

PEMBERLEY WAS A MENTAL SANCTUARY WHEN HE WAS GONE FROM IT, AND after only one evening at home, Darcy had begun to feel better. Greeting Bingley naturally reminded him of his own errors, and he was grateful that Bingley had forgiven him. He ought to show Mrs Bingley every courtesy because it was her due, but also because Bingley may have told her his role in separating them. *I have much to make up for.*

After receiving his kind welcome, Mrs Bingley deigned to offer her hand, and Darcy took it gratefully. She was not so mean as to resent the past, if she knew what he had done. "I am very pleased you accepted my invitation. Please come into the—"

Another woman descended the carriage, slowly, and with her head down and her bonnet concealing most of her face. He did not need her to lift it because he recognised the pleasing figure, the purple pelisse she had worn whilst walking Rosings park, the tan gloves he had last seen when he passed an envelope into them. And yet as his mind considered these facts, Darcy's heart still stopped and his stomach plummeted when she raised her head and he looked into Elizabeth's eyes.

Her manner was nervous. When she looked on him, her shoulders fell and she opened her lips but said nothing. Her cheeks were pink, and he felt his own grow warm. She looked terribly embarrassed, and he felt hardly composed himself.

"Mr Darcy? Mr Darcy?" Mrs Bingley linked an arm through her sister's. "I am afraid that Charles was not as clear in his letters as he could have been. When he said his sisters would join him, well, you can imagine how he thinks of Lizzy as his sister, especially since she is living with us."

He looked at Mrs Bingley, but was not ready with an answer.

"I did tell you that Lizzy was at Netherfield," Bingley added, his voice raising in question.

He must say something, speak politely, acknowledge the woman who—rightfully, painfully—rejected his hand. *Do not betray what you feel to everyone present.*

"Miss Bennet, I—you are . . . I welcome you to Pemberley." He stretched out a hand to take hers, but she curtseyed instead. Swallowing thickly, he then said, "I did not know you were travelling with the Bingleys."

Elizabeth pressed her lips together and nodded, looking anywhere but at him. "Thank you for allowing me to stay," she whispered.

Did she think him so resentful that he would turn her out? He had to act civilly, to show her that she was welcome, but every idea failed him. Darcy remembered the others, and said to them all, "It is not raining at the moment, but I daresay you would all still like to come into the house."

He escorted them inside, with Miss Bingley taking his arm, and he realised that Elizabeth entered last, and alone. He turned to look at her as they crossed the entrance hall, but her eyes were drawn up to the plasterwork on the ceiling.

"Are the others here?" Miss Bingley asked him. He nodded. "Did Mrs Lanyon leave her friends after all to join us on our travels to Scarborough?"

"Mrs Lanyon joined Balfour and Utterson, and they arrived this morning with Georgiana and Mrs Annesley. Georgiana is desirous of seeing you again and meeting your new sister."

Miss Bingley made a noncommittal sound. Clearly, she had not changed her opinion of Jane Bennet, unless she was irritated at the presence of Mrs Lanyon. He knew she would prefer it if Mrs Lanyon—a wealthy, eligible woman near to his own age—had gone elsewhere this summer.

Who would be the recipient of Miss Bingley's jealousy: Mrs Lanyon for having a fortune and for being the sister of his friend, or Elizabeth since she witnessed his admiration of her last autumn? It would likely be Mrs Lanyon, because Miss Bingley would not see any signs of his previous admiration for Elizabeth. He could hardly distress Elizabeth further by showing her any warm approval that might hint to his regard.

Do I still hold her in regard?

He tried to look at her, to see if she appeared at ease, but Miss Bingley tugged on his arm. "I hope I shall see dear Miss Darcy before dinner," Miss Bingley said heavily.

"Perhaps after you have all seen your rooms and washed off the dust from the road, the ladies can meet in the saloon. Balfour and Utterson have cried off to go fishing, even though I told them they would miss the pleasure of greeting Bingley's bride. Although I am certain he has written at length on your merits." He gave Mrs Bingley a smile, and was relieved that she returned it. "Your family have all stayed before, madam, and will know what chamber is to be theirs. I shall leave it to Bingley to show you."

Darcy then realised the housekeeper did not know Elizabeth had arrived. As the others filed out, he gestured the footman by the door to come near. "Find Mrs Reynolds and tell her that another bed must be made up."

Elizabeth looked miserably wretched, and he felt guilty at being the cause of her pain. Despite what happened at Hunsford, he could not have her think that she was unwelcome in his home. "So long as you do not mind being farther from Mrs Bingley, I shall have one of the principal bedrooms opened and aired in a few minutes. I believe it has a four-poster and new bed curtains. You do not mind that the furniture was not polished this morning? It shall be done tomorrow, of course."

He stopped his unimportant rambling and felt all the awkwardness of their situation. How could he have imagined when he awoke this morning that he would chance upon being alone with Elizabeth?

After a stretch of silence she said, without looking at him, "A daybed will suffice. Perhaps a sofa in the library." She tried to smile.

"It is no trouble. Just because you were not expected . . . there is plenty of room." He turned away to hide a wince. He now sounded boastful, rather than welcoming. *How am I to show her that I attended to her reproofs if I say such things?*

"Mr Darcy? I am all gratitude to you for your kindness to Jane." Darcy looked at her, and before he could refute anything remarkable in his notice of her sister, she added, "And your notice of me. You cannot have wanted, let alone expected to find me to be one of the party. I am certain the sight of me must be . . . distressing. What you must have felt when—"

"I assure you I felt only surprise." She pressed her lips together and looked away. "You—so—your sister said you did not know that you would be staying at Pemberley?"

She shook her head. "Until this morning, I thought we were staying at the home of Mr Utterson, and Jane thought we would be at the home of Mr Balfour." Elizabeth looked around the room, shaking her head.

"You appear unhappy, Miss Bennet," he said softly. "I assure you that you are welcome at Pemberley."

"Thank you," she murmured.

He was very much concerned with the idea of making her stay at Pemberley a pleasant one. "You are naturally a cheerful person, and I hope that the next fortnight will pass happily for you."

She tried to brighten, and she finally looked him in the eye. "Yes, I am determined to be happy and cheerful in whatever situation I may be. Happiness or misery depends on our dispositions as well as our circumstances, after all."

"Misery!" he cried. *The idea of staying at Pemberley, at spending a fortnight in my company, makes her miserable?* He had thought it was merely overwhelming surprise that caused her distress, that the awkward moment might be passed over and he could be secure in the knowledge that his civility would be noticed, that she might think better of him.

"I, no, I hardly meant . . . I am sorry—"

Mrs Reynolds entered the hall, and Darcy gave her a nod to show that he had seen her. She waited by the door, and he turned back to Elizabeth. It would be a long and difficult fortnight, but he would show her that her admonitions at Hunsford had worked a change. Any other wishes were best to be disregarded.

"Let us hope," he said so only she could hear, "that since they are not a permanent situation for you, neither my company nor my home should occasion misery to you."

He bowed and left her to the care of the housekeeper, more wounded than he had a right to feel.

ELIZABETH HAD BEEN PLACED IN A YELLOW BEDROOM, WITH CHINESE paper, mahogany furniture, and silk drapery on the bed. It was like the other rooms she had seen into today, lofty and handsome, with furniture suitable to Darcy's fortune. Words like "beautiful" and "charming" failed to do justice to Pemberley's merits.

But more striking than the house or the grounds was Darcy's manner. He showed particular notice to Jane, and he was concerned for *Elizabeth's* happiness whilst at Pemberley. Elizabeth felt amazed that he should even speak to her.

When she had met the other ladies in the saloon, her eyes were drawn to the magnificent plasterwork on the ceiling before she sat in what she assumed was a Robert Adam chair near to Miss Darcy. There had been a formal introduction between her and Jane and Miss Darcy, Mrs Annesley, and Mrs Lanyon. The latter was refined and reserved whilst Miss Darcy was uniformly silent.

"This is a marvellous chamber, Miss Darcy," Elizabeth had said to her as soon as Caroline stopped monopolising her attention. "Did you select the furniture?"

She had shaken her head and, at Mrs Annesley's prompting, answered something or other about it being her mother's favourite room and not wanting to change it.

Her conversation with Mrs Lanyon had been even more commonplace. They had exchanged a few words, that "the weather ought to be more settled for this time of year," and "the roads were good, and the travelling pleasant despite the rain," and "let us hope that August would not be rainy and cool like July and June."

Elizabeth moved aside the pelisse she had tossed on the chaise lounge in her bedchamber and sat. It was time to dress for dinner, although it would put her back in Darcy's company. She had hoped her summer travels would distract her from all of her confusion about him since Hunsford, and here she was, in his house. The minutes in which they were alone in the entrance hall were some of the most uncomfortable of her life, and he did not seem at ease either.

And he now has the impression that I am miserable here. She had seen the flash of sorrow in his eyes when she said that. What followed was an uncharitable rebuke, but she had deserved it. Still, she had always known that he was not a good-tempered man, and his words in the entrance hall showed how angry he still was at her rejection.

There was a knock, and a servant entered and immediately opened the wardrobe to sort through her gowns. "Good evening, Miss Bennet. I am Carew, Miss Darcy's lady. She sent me to help you dress."

Elizabeth stood in surprised silence whilst Carew swiftly selected a gown, and then put away her pelisse and began to organise her toilette table.

"I admire your purple pelisse, but you ought not to let merino wool lie about. How unfortunate the weather is so cold that you still need it in August."

This young woman, who was scarcely older than she, was bustling about her room and handling her things with authority. "Carew, you don't—that is, I thank you, but your help is not necessary. I can see to myself and my own things. And the lady who waits on my sister comes whenever there is an evening party or a ball."

Carew nodded before striding towards her and untying her gown. Out of habit, and a small amount of trepidation, Elizabeth raised her arms and let the purposeful woman go about her work. "Yes, ma'am, but Mrs Bingley's lady won't want to tend to both of you at Pemberley, not if she wants her new mistress to appear to an advantage. Mrs Hurst, Mrs Lanyon, and Miss Bingley all have their own ladies, and it won't impress anyone if it seems as though her duties must be shared."

"And will not Miss Darcy feel the same slight? Is she not as concerned with rank and appearances as her brother?"

The maid tugged too sharply on her ties, and the ring she wore scraped Elizabeth's skin. "No, she has no such pride, and neither does he. And it was the master who asked her if she could spare me for your sake when he realised you did not have your own. Odd that he asked Reynolds if your maid's chamber would be too far if you were put in this room. Anyway, neither of them wanted you or Mrs Bingley to appear at a disadvantage."

Elizabeth felt the unexpected compliment and consideration of Darcy's insistence. "You must thank Miss Darcy for me. I will try to do it this evening, if she will speak with me."

"You ought to thank the master, too."

Elizabeth smiled. "I am not certain I ought to, since he has demanded extra work from his sister's servant. You will not like me or him the better for it."

Carew's prim, pursed mouth relaxed into a small smile. "We all like Mr Darcy. He is a thoughtful master and a considerate landlord, and liberal to the poor."

"Still," Elizabeth said as she was firmly led to sit before the glass to have her hair brushed, "you ought only to answer to Miss Darcy."

The maid's large blue eyes met hers in the glass. "I grew up at Pemberley; my father is the carpenter and my mother was a maid, so it is only natural that I listen to Mr Darcy."

She thought of how angry he was and how hastily he had left the parsonage after their quarrel. *He was so certain I would say yes.* "Mr Darcy does like to have his own way."

Her hair was pulled taut as Carew said sternly, "Every servant would give him a good name, from Mrs Reynolds to the scullery maid. He does not take advantage, nor does he let the girls earn favour with him by trying. We have no *women of all work* at Pemberley."

"Oh! Heavens, no! I did not mean to imply anything improper." *Good God, since I arrived inside the house, I have said everything wrong.* "I never considered Mr Darcy would—I never thought him irreligious or . . . I only meant that he is a man who likes to have the power of choice, not that he . . ."

Carew's stern gaze softened, and the brush moved more gently through her hair. "Every maid knows that offering Mr Darcy anything more than folding back the shutters or lighting the fire whilst he is still abed will have you on the first mail coach. He is a generous master. He had me placed with his sister two years ago, and anyone on the estate is guaranteed work or a reference. And you ought to see the dinners and dances he puts on for the tenants, labourers, schoolchildren, and the people in the village."

"He seems an excellent landlord for a man who likely only spends half of his time here."

"If he marries, he might be more often at Pemberley, but, as Reynolds says, I do not know who is good enough for him."

Elizabeth watched the colour drain from her own face in the mirror, which led to Carew frowning and turning her face roughly to apply some application sure to brighten her under the candles this evening. "It—it is to your credit that you should think so of Mr Darcy," Elizabeth managed to say.

"'Tis the truth. I grew up in the park, and he is only a few years older than me. He was a sweet-tempered boy, good-natured as he grew older, also. Never cross, never abusing his position."

This was praise most opposite to her ideas. That Darcy was not a good-tempered man had been her firmest opinion. As Carew moved about her room with authority, tidying up and laying out her nightshift for later, Elizabeth asked, "Is Miss Darcy very like her brother?"

"Mr Darcy, as you seem to know, is sure of his place in the world and all the responsibilities that come with it. His sister is the opposite. Whilst the master will walk into any room and command attention, Miss Darcy creeps in as though she fears she might break something. Mr Darcy does his best to encourage her."

Carew finished putting the room in good order, and Elizabeth thanked her and Miss Darcy for their attention as she left.

Darcy is a caring master, a responsible landlord, a devoted friend, and an attentive brother. She did not regret refusing Darcy's offer of marriage, but she did regret the hateful things she had said to him. It was disgraceful how she had misjudged him and trusted Wickham. As Elizabeth went to the dining room, she had a more gentle sensation towards Darcy than she had ever previously held.

CHAPTER THREE

Despite Darcy's fears of an awkward evening, dinner proved a lively affair. He noticed that Mrs Lanyon was well entertained by bits and scraps at Bingley being so lovestruck by his wife that he was inattentive to others, and that Balfour was amused by Miss Bingley's affected refinement directed towards him. Utterson clearly found Mrs Hurst dull, and Mrs Annesley prompted Georgiana to tell the story about her dormouse that got loose in the drawing room when she was a child. Every laugh was indulged, and the entire scene was one of ease and good humour.

However, Elizabeth was quieter than he had previously seen her. Granted, she was seated next to Utterson, and he could be silent or severe in what he said. Still, Elizabeth was typically cheerful in mixed company. *Is she truly miserable at the thought of staying with me for two weeks?* Or perhaps their conversation in the entrance hall was an embarrassing encounter not to be taken seriously, and best forgotten.

"I understand that you did not know where you were to rest your head tonight, Miss Bennet," Balfour said across the table before turning to him. "And you did not know your table would have an even twelve after all?"

"I did not, but it is of no consequence." He kept his eye on Balfour and did not turn his head to see Elizabeth's expression. "I know Miss Bennet, and she can go no place where she will be more welcome than at Pemberley."

"Yet you might have known if Bingley was considerate of your time and your home, and wrote to you," Utterson said drily.

"I did write!" Bingley cried, with a smile. "I swear that I did. Darcy, what lies have you been saying of me?"

Darcy smiled. "I do not complain of your *not* writing, but of your writing so illegibly that I am half a day in deciphering one page, and then guess at most of it."

The room laughed, and then after a lengthy comparison on everyone's hand and style of writing, Balfour said, "You can tell how close a friendship you have with Darcy by his salutation. Shall we compare? Who amongst us lately received a *Sir*? Lift your hand." Utterson raised a hand and everyone groaned and shook their head in mock disapproval. "What about *Dear sir*?" Balfour raised his own hand and looked around. "Bingley?"

Bingley's hand raised and lowered and hovered near his head. "I have, at times, been *My dear sir*, but since most of Darcy's letters open with a complaint of having received my last and not being able to make sense of it, I am often only *Dear sir*."

Everyone laughed again, and then Bingley asked the table, "None amongst us have so steady a friendship that they *always* are *My dear sir* or *My dear madam* to Darcy?"

"Enough of this quizzing!" Darcy cried, laughing. "I think now that you are married, I shall correspond with Mrs Bingley instead, if she will answer?" Mrs Bingley nodded her agreement. "Then perhaps she will allow me to address her as *Dear madam*, and all of this unpleasantness can be avoided?"

"I promise to be a reliable, and legible, correspondent," Mrs Bingley said.

"I can think of one who must always be *My dear* to Mr Darcy," Mrs Lanyon said softly, drawing the attention to her end of the table, likely because it was nearly the only time she had spoken all evening. "Miss Darcy is certainly the deserving recipient of a letter with a warm salutation."

Georgiana turned pink as everyone looked at her and smiled. Darcy warmly agreed, and then noticed Elizabeth, who was seated at the centre on his sister's side of the table. Her eyes were downcast for a long time, as though she was either avoiding looking at anyone or intent on some inward reflection.

Be not alarmed, madam . . .

"And how does Darcy close his letters?" Balfour continued, when Georgiana did nothing but look embarrassed by their attention. "I suspect Miss Darcy receives *Your affectionate brother*, but shall we go round to learn what valediction he uses? I most often receive *With respect and affection*."

"*With greatest affection*," answered Bingley.

"*With respect*," said Utterson.

"What about you, Hurst?" Bingley asked his brother, who had his fork halfway to his mouth.

"Oh? Have I received a letter from Darcy?" Hurst turned to his wife as though she were his secretary. "I think I received a letter once when we asked to arrive at Pemberley early. I believe it closed with *Your servant, sir*."

"And there we have an accurate representation of how dear we are to Darcy!" cried Balfour, looking pleased with himself.

Elizabeth raised her head and looked at him, briefly. *I will only add, God bless you.* He had begun the letter in anger, but ended it in charity. What did she think of everything that he had written in between the salutation and the valediction? Did it make her think better of him? Or did some of the expressions make her hate him?

"I hope that all of you who are only *Sir* or *Madam* might raise yourself in Darcy's esteem." Balfour raised a glass in salute.

"I shall do what I can," Utterson muttered, lifting his eyes and taking a drink.

Mrs Lanyon took this quip as a sign that the ladies might go to the drawing room. The men stood as the ladies murmured to each other as they left. As Mrs Bingley and Elizabeth crossed in front of him, he heard the former say softly, "I like your hair tonight, Lizzy."

Elizabeth was near to Georgiana, who turned when she heard this.

She gave Georgiana an expressive smile. "It was a style Miss Darcy kindly suggested."

Georgiana gave her a shy little smile of acknowledgement before leaving. When she reached the door, Elizabeth turned to look at him. She gave a half-smile and the slightest of nods before she left.

～

THE NUMBER OF CHEERFUL VOICES, THE CLAMOUR OF LAUGHTER, HAD MADE a din of an extraordinary nature at Darcy's table. Elizabeth had been surprised by how Darcy behaved amongst his friends. He was a charming host. He was esteemed by everyone, he tolerated their sporting with him—to a degree—and was even considerate of *her*. He had a commanding air, but a patient demeanour amongst his friends.

"And with it she wore a turban of gold-spotted muslin, with bows and curls of white ribbon," Louisa was saying to Mrs Lanyon, who avoided answering her as she made the coffee. Miss Darcy was making the tea, often looking over her shoulder at Mrs Annesley to see if she was making it correctly. "Did neither of you see Lady Enfield in town this winter?"

Miss Darcy shook her head, and Mrs Lanyon ignored her.

"Her gown was the invention of Mrs Gill of Cork Street. She always has a distinguishing taste and unique invention of dress," added Caroline. "Does she provide gowns for you, Mrs Lanyon?"

"No."

Caroline and Louisa exchanged a look at this short reply. "I know your husband left you a house in Harley Street. Perhaps you have not had occasion to be fashionably dressed by a lady at Burlington Gardens? I would be happy to introduce you."

Elizabeth thought this amusing coming from a woman whose only claim to a house in town was her brother-in-law's leased house in Grosvenor Square.

"I cannot consent to anything so needlessly troublesome to you." Mrs Lanyon turned away, but Caroline would not be dissuaded.

"It is no trouble. We took our dear Jane to Mrs Gill, did we not?" Caroline gestured to Jane, who was compelled to rise and join the others by the tea table. "One of her gowns is a French frock of muslin, with a demi-train and bishop's sleeves. Perhaps you shall see it one evening. It is sure to do Charles credit."

Jane flushed, but smiled. Mrs Lanyon scarcely looked at her and said, "I am sure Mrs Gill's style and elegance is superior to most and inferior to none, but I shall see to my own gowns."

Mrs Lanyon began to walk away when Caroline added, "Do you prefer India muslin, Mrs Lanyon? Or do you only wear muslin from an English mill? One must choose a favourite, you know."

Mrs Lanyon stared for a long moment at Caroline before saying, "When there is no occasion for expressing an opinion, it is best to be silent." She then went to sit with Mrs Annesley, and Caroline came near to Elizabeth whilst Louisa and Jane stayed at the table. Elizabeth had begun to notice the two married ladies were more often together.

"Well, Eliza, Mrs Lanyon does not invite pleasant conversation, does she?" Caroline said.

"It was a rather dull reply, but perhaps she did not care for your comment on the street she lives on."

Caroline shrugged. "It was kindly meant." She lowered her voice. "Mrs Lanyon is the sort to think highly of herself. She scarcely spoke to any of us at dinner or in the saloon this afternoon."

Elizabeth nodded and looked at Mrs Lanyon, who quickly turned from watching them to look back at Mrs Annesley. She was perhaps thirty, with a brown complexion, amber eyes, and black hair, very like her brother. But where Mr Balfour was earnest and eager in conversation, Mrs Lanyon was cold.

I have misjudged reserved people in the past. "I think I shall try to get to know her a little better." She asked Caroline to excuse her, and joined Mrs Annesley and Mrs Lanyon. Mrs Annesley appeared to be forty, and was a genteel, agreeable-looking portly woman with a double chin. She greeted Elizabeth with an open countenance; Mrs Lanyon scarcely nodded.

After comparing her impressions of Pemberley with Mrs Annesley, as it was a first visit for them both, Elizabeth addressed Mrs Lanyon. "Your brother is a lively young man. Has he been friends with Mr Darcy for long?"

"They met six years ago."

"And you? From dinner, I gather that your friend Mr Utterson is a newer acquaintance of his, but how well do you know the Darcys? This is not your first visit to Pemberley, is it?"

"It is."

When she did not elaborate on their friendship, the visit, or even share her opinion of the house, Elizabeth said, "And have you known Mr Darcy and Miss Darcy as long as your brother has?"

"No."

Elizabeth turned to look at Caroline, who shrugged and rose to get a cup of tea. She tried again with Mrs Lanyon. "I am looking forward to joining Caroline and Louisa as we travel north with Jane and Charles. I understand that you and your brother and Mr Utterson also intend to be at Scarborough in September?"

"We do." When Elizabeth shifted in her seat, Mrs Lanyon added, "Lewis and I will then go on to Haddingtonshire."

"I thought I detected a hint of a Scottish voice, although it is more pronounced in Mr Balfour." Elizabeth smiled.

"Yes"—Mrs Lanyon's eyes flashed—"my father is a Lowland Scot, and I grew up in Scotland. I spend every autumn with my father and brother at Hyde House."

Elizabeth could not understand her defensive tone, and tried a different course of conversation. "You pass most of your time in town, then?" A nod. "Were you educated there as well, as your brother was, rather than in Scotland?"

"I was."

When she said nothing further, Elizabeth added, "I believe Caroline and Louisa were also educated in a seminary in town." Mrs Lanyon only nodded. "I did not have the pleasure of such an education. I was not placed in a school, nor did I have a governess."

Mrs Lanyon widened her eyes and tilted her head. "I am sure you were instructed to show yourself to advantage, the same as Miss Bingley," she added with a tone of frustration.

Elizabeth sought for something pleasant to say. "I shall have to hope that my accomplishments pass muster amongst such fine examples as Miss Darcy, and Caroline and Louisa. I have not heard the former, but she is often praised in my hearing. Do you play or sing?"

"I play."

When it was certain Mrs Lanyon would say nothing further, Mrs Annesley praised Miss Darcy, who they learnt played and sang all day long, and Elizabeth and Mrs Lanyon said everything that was appropriate. *Mrs Lanyon is cold and has nothing to say beyond the most commonplace inquiry or remark.*

Elizabeth parted from them, certain that Mrs Lanyon would not miss her, and returned to Jane and Caroline.

"Jane, when you are next in town," Caroline said, "I think a Parisian mob cap of fine lace with a silver-grey ribbon would be more the thing."

"I am happy with my cap. I think it rather similar to your turban, and yours is handsome," Jane said.

Elizabeth was duly impressed with the way her sister managed Caroline, for the latter smiled smugly and patted Jane's hand. Jane had the patience and sweetness of temper to get on with anyone if she chose to. Caroline then asked Elizabeth in a low voice, "How did you find Mrs Lanyon? Mrs Annesley is more genteel, is she not?"

Elizabeth had to agree. "For a woman of her age and situation, she has astonishingly little to say for herself."

Caroline took a sip from her teacup and looked at Mrs Lanyon, who was now standing on the other side of the room with Miss Darcy and asking about the dormouse mentioned at dinner. "She is familiar with dear Georgiana for someone so little acquainted with the Darcys." Jane and Elizabeth exchanged a look. *Caroline would not dare call Miss Darcy 'Georgiana' in her own hearing.* Caroline shook her head. "She tries too hard; it is unseemly. Some might consider it a fair match, but I think it would be offensive for her to marry a second time."

"Mrs Lanyon?" Jane asked. "Why?"

It was the words *fair match* that brought an unsettled feeling to Elizabeth's stomach that she could not rightfully explain.

"Her first marriage was one of affection, they say. I see no reason for her to seek a second with Mr Darcy. It is not as though she is in narrow circumstances, and there are younger women who would have him, ones whose fortune did not come from India."

Jane looked to Elizabeth, although whether it was from the idea of an alliance between Darcy and Mrs Lanyon, or Caroline's forgetting where her own fortune came from, she could not say. Jane asked, "What would Mr Balfour say to the match?"

"Mr Balfour would not mind it—what man would not want his sister to marry his friend?—but what right has a widow to marry another eligible young man?"

"Has, has Mr Darcy distinguished her, that . . . that you have seen?" Elizabeth asked, looking at Mrs Lanyon and better understanding Caroline's dislike of the stern widow.

Caroline shrugged. "I have seen no particular mark of attention, although they often ride together. A well-situated widow should abjure all second attachments. Still, I ought not to mention it." Caroline checked the clock, likely awaiting the return of the gentlemen. "A man of Mr Darcy's situation and independence must marry, and a man of sense would prefer a . . . a younger woman than Hester Lanyon."

The door then opened, and as the men advanced, Caroline immediately rose to help Miss Darcy with the tea and coffee. When this was done without any notice from Darcy, she offered to play, but this had an unintended result: whilst Caroline played on one side of the room, Darcy—rather than listen attentively—sat on the sofa in conversation with Mr Balfour and Mrs Lanyon about their father's home and health.

Elizabeth might have spoken to Jane—if anyone could distract her from her confused thoughts, it would be she—but Bingley insisted that Jane join his conversation with Mr Utterson. Upon seeing Miss Darcy alone, Elizabeth took pains to know her.

"You have been praised by all of your friends and relations, I am afraid," Elizabeth said, smiling. "It is an inauspicious start to our acquaintance, for how shall we fill the time? You cannot attempt to impress me if I already know all of your merits."

Miss Darcy looked embarrassed. "I would never boast of my own talents."

"No, you are too well bred for that, but good breeding does allow for aunts and brothers to boast on behalf of their beloved relation."

"I suppose," she said not unkindly.

"Lady Catherine once asked after your skill with the instrument in my presence, and your brother was quick with affectionate praise as, I suppose, all good brothers ought to be. I had no brother whilst growing up, so I can only guess if the practice is a common one."

"Fitzwilliam is ever so good to me."

Miss Darcy was not as quick to speak as her brother. She was very unlike Darcy: embarrassed, not assured, and there was not a tincture of hauteur about her. Elizabeth heard Darcy laugh at something Mr Balfour said; she turned to look in time to see him then ask a question of Mrs Lanyon. He was going out of his way to include her in his conversation. Darcy had the same noble bearing as she had previously seen from him, but he now had an easy manner.

Had it not been there before, or had I simply not seen it?

"I have been wanting to meet you." Miss Darcy's soft voice surprised her, and her face must have shown it because she added, "Fitzwilliam has spoken highly of you."

Elizabeth had to suppose that any mention of her stopped after April. "Well, I guess if a man is particularly well bred, then he is allowed to extend his praises beyond his sister and to the sisters of his friends' wives."

Miss Darcy tilted her head in confusion. "He wrote and spoke of *you* specifically, and before your sister married Mr Bingley."

He cannot have spoken so since. "I am not insensible to such a compliment from Mr Darcy, but"—she forced a wide smile—"we must not waste our time discussing what others have said of us when we finally have the chance to find out for ourselves if we have been lied to."

Miss Darcy gave a little laugh. "I see what he meant now. I think he admires your liveliness."

"We shall be superlatively stupid if we cannot find something of substance to talk of! Are you often at Pemberley?"

"Every summer except for—I . . . am down for the summer months."

Their eyes met, and Elizabeth saw all the shame and grief Miss Darcy was feeling. *I wonder if she knows what her brother told me.* Regardless if Miss Darcy was aware that she knew the extent of Wickham's actions against her, she had to put the modest girl at her ease again.

"If you are not often at Pemberley, you cannot want to have all of these guests occupy your house."

"It is my brother's house," she said plainly.

Elizabeth looked towards the sofa and saw Darcy watching them with a gentle smile on his face that she had seen him give her before. "I refuse to believe that Mr Darcy does not consider Pemberley your home. Tell me that he does not do all that he can to make you feel as much at home here as you felt when this was your father's house."

She turned pink and nodded. "He had a sitting room that I took a liking to at Christmas fitted up in a lighter style I prefer."

"There! It is proved. Whatever can give you any pleasure is sure to be done, and he wishes for Pemberley to be your home."

"Yes," she agreed pleasantly. Elizabeth felt pity for a shy girl of sixteen who hardly felt at home in her own house and who now must share it with guests.

"I suppose, with your temperament, you cannot like to have so many people here," Elizabeth said gently. "Friends or strangers, you must still always be dressing to appear in company or come into a room in a dishabille, or be as a prisoner in your own chamber to avoid us."

Rather than laugh, Miss Darcy said only, "My brother is fond of good company."

"He has not forced you to remain with us this evening, has he?"

"Oh no!" she cried. "He would never." After a pause, during which it was clear Miss Darcy was deciding whether or not to speak, she said, "In fact, yesterday he said that whenever I found the company tiresome, I was to mount my horse and be gone."

Elizabeth laughed, and Miss Darcy joined her. "See, he is a good brother! And when I find the company trying"—Elizabeth scarcely shifted her eyes to where Caroline played a duet with Louisa—"perhaps you will save me and join me on a walk on the grounds? I am no horsewoman, but I am an active walker. If we do not have a great deal of rain, I expect to walk the park often."

Miss Darcy made her promises, and then struggled with what else to say. Mrs Annesley and Mr Utterson then joined them, and her new acquaintance was spared anyone's undivided attention.

Over the course of the evening, Elizabeth looked now and then at Darcy, who was currently making a circle of his guests. He spoke more familiarly with those he knew best—those who could claim *My dear* or *Dear* salutations—but he was courteous to everyone. When he, at the last, approached where she and Jane were at the tea table, he said to Jane, "How have you enjoyed travelling, Mrs Bingley? Your husband has a tendency to press on at a breakneck pace, and I hope this is not the first time since July that you shall spend two nights in the same place."

Jane gave a little laugh. "I suspect his enthusiasm for Scarborough and the society of a watering place to be a great motivator."

"I think it rather Bingley's enthusiasm to show you off to his advantage to every friend he has ever known."

Elizabeth watched her sister blush prettily. "You are very kind, Mr Darcy. And I thank you for allowing us to stay for more than a few nights."

"The pleasure is entirely mine, and I have nothing to say against a house full of good company. Bingley has been my steady friend, madam. It is nothing less than what is due to him and you that you stay for as long as you like."

"Pemberley is a beautiful home, and your offer is tempting," Jane said kindly.

He bowed, and then gave Elizabeth a wary look. "How do you like what you have seen of Derbyshire through the rain?"

"I think the Peak scenery to be the most beautiful in the kingdom," she said warmly. "A true and natural beauty pervades the character of the county."

Darcy's countenance brightened, and he looked as though he might speak more on the subject, but he then looked back at Jane and said, in his usual way, "Are there any excursions you would like to take before Bingley leads you north? Any bath, druidical stone circle, dale, or fine home is a morning's carriage ride away."

Elizabeth watched him court the good opinion of the woman he had previously thought it a disgrace for his friend to marry. When she saw Darcy thus civil, not only to herself but to her sister, and recollected their last scene in Hunsford parsonage—the difference, the change, was so great and struck so forcibly on her mind that she could hardly restrain her astonishment from being visible.

When his and Jane's conversation reached a natural conclusion and Jane left to join Bingley, as Darcy was about to move away, she could not help but say quietly, "Thank you." This was neither the time nor the place, but he deserved to be thanked for telling her the truth about Wickham, for sending Bingley back to Jane, for sharing his sister's history with Wickham with her father, for welcoming her after their acrimonious last meeting.

He gave her a look of confusion, and his lips formed the word "Why" as they were then joined by Mr Balfour.

"Darcy, some of your guests wish to play cards, and I just put your name forward contrary to your desire, as I know you are no card player."

"I thought you called yourself my 'dear friend'?" he said wittily.

"Aye, I am, but you are also my host with an obligation to entertain me, and I shall be more entertained by forcing you to play cards with Hurst and Miss Bingley and keep your patience than I will be watching you talk to this pretty young lady." Darcy gave his friend a dark look. "Besides, you can afford to lose the money."

Darcy gave Mr Balfour a mock scowl, bowed to her, and continued to walk amongst the room whilst the card tables were placed.

"You appear eager for Mr Darcy to lose his money and have an unpleasant evening because of it," she said playfully.

"I wish that were the case," Mr Balfour said as they both watched Darcy walk away, "but, to my annoyance, the man is both too rich to notice the loss of a few coins between friends and also rather good at cards. He wins more often than he loses."

He did sound genuinely annoyed by Darcy's good fortune. "What a nuisance to have a wealthy friend who wins at loo. I had no idea your situation in life was so undesirable to make you jealous."

Mr Balfour arranged his features into one of complaisance. "You are quite right; I am not so poorly off. I will inherit an estate worth five thousand a year, but in the meantime, like Utterson, I must shift about on an allowance granted by my father." He gave her an appraising, admiring look. "You have a frank and open nature. What is your situation in life?"

"I know very well it will not support a son who is waiting to inherit and eager to spend."

Mr Balfour laughed. "I admire you, Miss Bennet! We understand each other, I see, and now we can avoid any unpleasantness over the next fortnight and simply talk at length and then part as amiable acquaintances until our paths cross again."

He was eager in conversation, almost indefatigable. She had a good opinion of him that was in near-direct opposition to her opinion of his sister. Elizabeth had a friendly but forgettable conversation with Mr Balfour until Mr Hurst demanded he help settle his argument with Mr Utterson over horses and how many miles it was from Matlock to Pemberley.

Elizabeth sat alone near the fire, grateful for a quiet moment. The idea of detention here for a fortnight had filled her with anxiety twelve hours ago. She had feared Darcy would be cold and reserved and she would be mortified, and that would lead her to being vexed and half-angry as she had no right to be.

I misjudged a good man, and I am grateful that he is still kind to me and my family.

She found herself noticing how Darcy spoke with Mrs Lanyon, and then how he spoke with Caroline later when she was telling some anecdote to him and Mr Balfour. He did not seem disposed to admire either of them, but then Darcy's proposal to her had been the greatest surprise of her life.

Elizabeth could not believe that the man who had burst into Charlotte's parlour four months ago with the words "You must allow me to tell you how ardently I admire and love you" would so soon be willing to commit himself to another woman. *What does it matter if Darcy marries?* She had no right to expect his constancy after she bitterly refused him. Whether it was Miss de Bourgh, or Caroline, or Mrs Lanyon, it could not matter to her since she had misjudged him and told him he could not have made her the offer of his hand in any possible way that would have tempted her to accept it.

CHAPTER FOUR

Although it had rained all night, the morning was favourable since the clouds were dispersing and the sun frequently appeared. Darcy sat at the breakfast table with Georgiana, Mrs Annesley, Balfour, and Mrs Lanyon, and was alternating his gaze between his coffee and the door. The Bingley party and Utterson had not yet made their way down.

"Are you hoping to catch the first glimpse of Mrs Bingley?" Balfour asked quietly as he added more food to his plate. Darcy narrowed his eyes in confusion. "You keep watching the door. She is a handsome woman. I dinna think Bingley would mind an admiring glance, so long as your admiration was limited to that."

Balfour could be intolerably rude in his teasing. "Mrs Bingley *is* handsome, but I was only wondering what could have made them so late." Balfour returned to his breakfast, and Darcy stopped looking for Elizabeth.

He had only spoken a few words with her last evening. After an admiring comment about Derbyshire that gratified him more than it ought, Elizabeth had thanked him after he spoke with Mrs Bingley. Did she think he still opposed the match, even when it could not be undone, even when he had all but placed Bingley in a carriage back to her? Perhaps it was gratitude for arranging for Georgiana's maid to look after Elizabeth when Reynolds told him that she did not have her own.

Last night, they were all in high spirits and good humour, eager to be happy. If Elizabeth had not often been silent, he would have deemed the evening a successful one. Was this how he would feel for the next two weeks, always wondering what Elizabeth thought of him? He must do what he could to temper that feeling, and still show her every courtesy that she deserved.

Every courtesy I previously neglected to show her.

"If this open weather holds," said Mrs Lanyon, "I hope to ride today, Miss Darcy, if you would like to join me?"

Darcy looked from the door in time to see Georgiana give an eager smile. He knew she disliked being in a large party, and Mrs Lanyon's quiet manner would suit his sister's shy temperament.

"Might your brother like to ride as well?" Mrs Lanyon asked Georgiana.

"Good morning," Mrs Annesley said, and Darcy looked up to see Bingley and his wife enter, followed quickly by his sisters and Hurst, and then Elizabeth and Utterson. She was smiling at him and had said something just outside the door to make the stern Utterson laugh. Whilst greetings were exchanged, Darcy did his best to quell the inexplicable sinking feeling in his stomach to be civil to everyone.

After Darcy was assured that his guests had slept well and found everything in their rooms to their liking, Utterson said, "Miss Bennet and I accidentally overheard you an hour ago, talking with your steward as we admired the paintings in the gallery. You must have met him in the lobby below us."

Darcy nodded, remembering. "Did I say anything worth noting?"

"You sounded resolved that an account of the stock—actually, every occurrence that happens in the course of the week be detailed to you on Saturday. Is this your usual practice?"

He nodded again, noting how Elizabeth was paying attention. "It is."

"Then we heard correctly and I was right about Darcy, Miss Bennet.

Not a cow calves nor ewe drops her lamb but is registered, and Darcy knows of it by the week's end."

"He is a controlling man," Balfour said, laughing.

"I did not say that," Utterson cried in his usual impatient manner. Darcy doubted Utterson would have called him controlling, but he hoped that Elizabeth did not believe him to be so.

"Aye, but does Miss Bennet think it, given what she now knows of how her host oversees the Pemberley estates?" Balfour asked.

The lady in question looked at him, her cheeks pink. Darcy held her gaze, uncertain of what she might say. She then smiled at him and said, whilst addressing Balfour, "I think he delegates well and that he cares deeply about Pemberley. Mr Darcy is a capable landlord." Elizabeth's eyes met his, briefly, before looking back at Utterson. "He is *perhaps* fastidious, as you said earlier, but certainly not controlling," she added firmly, giving Balfour half a smile.

Whilst Darcy's heart beat faster, Bingley said, "Think of how much paper will be saved now that you are home and need not write twice weekly to your steward."

"Twice weekly?" called Balfour from the other end of the table. "More like daily. Waste of time, paper, and ink, I say."

"You will not say so when Hyde House is *your* responsibility," Darcy said drily.

"That will not be for some time. My father is hale and hearty. If all of those years in India did nothing to weaken him, spending the twilight of his years in Scotland certainly will not." He popped his last bite of food into his mouth. "In the meanwhile, I cannot afford a quire of paper and ink to write daily letters about sheep or tenants or rents."

"Do you spend so freely that you cannot afford a few shillings' worth of paper?" Elizabeth asked in disbelief.

"Indeed, I cannot," Balfour said with mock seriousness. "You would think that with all the wealth he remitted from India to Scotland, my father might give me more of an allowance, but I am scarcely better off than Utterson here."

Utterson was at that moment reading his letters. "Oh yes," he said in a sullen drawl, "your life is as spare as mine. You shall inherit an estate, whereas I have an older brother." He turned towards Bingley's wife and added, by way of explanation, "My father pays my fees and expenses to enter the law, but has recently decided to reduce my spending allowance. He fears that London life will ruin me." Utterson turned back to Balfour. "And *you* are not in such dire straits."

"My father holds the ends of the purse strings, too, but I shall not argue with you at breakfast. Especially since I have ordered a new carriage and it ought to arrive any day."

This was met by exclamations of surprise from everyone, with questions as to who made it and what did it look like, along with a subtle shake of the head from Mrs Lanyon.

"What is it, Hester?" Balfour asked when the others had finished. "You look as though you do not approve."

"You bought a high-flyer phaeton last season—"

"*This* is a travelling chariot. I am weary of hiring a post-chaise. Do not dare to say that *you* would happily pay for it. No man wants to hear that from his sister. Why do you frown? Now we shall all be comfortable when we go on to Scarborough!"

"Yes, Mrs Lanyon, why scold your brother?" asked Miss Bingley. "I do not know what is proper where you are from, but I would never dream of sharing an opinion on my brother's choices. A gentleman may do as he pleases."

Darcy threw her a look that she pretended to not comprehend. He had been complicit in helping Miss Bingley share such an opinion that Bingley gave up Jane Bennet entirely. Shame made him pour more coffee into his cup to avoid looking at Elizabeth or Mrs Bingley.

Mrs Lanyon was silent a long moment. "Lewis may do as he pleases, of course. I shall be satisfied that whatever he decides may be judged decent and proper."

With this, the table's attention fell from Balfour, and talk amongst small groups recommenced. Darcy noticed Elizabeth watching Mrs Bingley and Mrs Hurst's conversation without joining it. Miss Bingley talked with Georgiana and Mrs Annesley, and Mrs Lanyon was again as silent as she typically was. *Is Elizabeth left out only by the arrangement of the table, or was she being slighted?*

"Darcy? I said, Darcy, what think you of Balfour's purchase?" Bingley asked him in a low voice, leaning across the table towards him.

He shrugged. "I shall have to see it, I suppose, although in general I think a coach like that a needless expense for a single man."

"No, I mean, ought I to have bought one for Jane? My chaise was new last autumn, and I hate to be wasteful. She said she did not need or want a new carriage, but—"

"You ought to trust your own judgment," he said quietly, "and not compare yourself to your friends." Darcy then laughed. "If you cannot do that, at the least trust your wife's judgment."

"Are you talking of me, Bingley?" Balfour called down the table. "You do not approve of how I spend my money?"

"You may do as you please," Bingley answered good-naturedly. "No matter how you complain, you seem to have the means, and you do travel amongst your numerous friends a great deal."

"He travels a great deal, but then he accomplishes so very little," Utterson added drily.

Balfour pretended to be affronted. "That is no striking resemblance to my character, I am sure! Mrs Bingley, Miss Bennet, do not believe a word they say about me. I am as determined as Utterson and as industrious as Darcy. I am a talented man, all ambition."

"All ambition?" Darcy had to interject. "You have *no* ambition. Your talents are unequal to great exertions."

"Yes!" agreed Bingley. "You have means, but what do you do with your time and talents?"

Balfour did not so much as blush when he said, "Like any young heir come a little prematurely into an inheritance from his mother's side, I run wanton and run riot until I bring my reputation to the brink of ruin."

The ladies blushed, laughed, and looked away at this matter-of-fact statement. Utterson lifted his eyes and shook his head. They did not know Balfour as well as Darcy did. He was a dependable friend, and an invaluable one in the days after Darcy's father had died. Balfour could act like a superficial, self-conceited coxcomb, but he was generous and loyal. He teased a great deal, but he mocked himself more than anyone else.

"If this is your manner with only a small legacy from your mother, what on earth shall be the state of your reputation upon the death of your father?" Elizabeth asked, a smile pulling at her lips. She appeared to have sketched Balfour's character accurately.

"Hmm, I have not given the matter a thought. Perhaps my debauchery ought to be in direct proportion to my inheritance? I am off to a fine start, at any rate."

Elizabeth only laughed politely.

"You have that look on your face, Darcy," Balfour said to him. "Do you not remember your own days as a young heir about town, or were they too long ago?"

"We passed those years together. You are the same age as me, lest you forget, and those days were not half so wild as you pretend they were." He and Balfour had met around the time they reached their majority, and had had a steady friendship ever since. "But you have not inherited yet, Balfour—that is the difference between us."

"Aye, my father is in excellent health. And so I am living on a small allowance like Utterson since I have wasted my mother's legacy on frivolity. I am in poverty compared to you. How unkind of you to call it to mind! You ought to think more on the cares and concerns of those who have less than you, my dear Darcy."

This was said carelessly, a way to tease an old friend, but painful thoughts intruded: *". . . your arrogance, your conceit, and your selfish disdain of the feelings of others . . ."* Did Elizabeth still think him proud, selfish, unfeeling? She clearly thought him an admirable landlord, but did she truly think better of him since Hunsford?

He must devote himself to the business of being agreeable to her. The visit could not pass without some moment to show her the kindness she deserved. *Would it be enough for me if she only thinks better of me?* Based on her manner and expression when she exited the carriage yesterday, it felt like there was no hope that she could love him.

Perhaps he would find a reason to speak with her alone after breakfast. The party rose to leave and were talking to one another. Darcy walked around the table to reach Elizabeth before she left, wondering if she would walk the grounds with him if he asked, or if she would refuse or insist someone else join them.

"Darcy, shall we kill all of your birds?" Balfour asked whilst he and Bingley were settling how to spend their day now that breakfast was finished. "I may not be a good shot, but I am eager to see what your gunroom has to offer."

"Today is the sixth; we cannot shoot until the twelfth," Utterson said with the utmost impatience. In a gentler voice, he then said, "If we are to amuse ourselves today, then perhaps Miss Bennet will finish admiring the paintings in the gallery with me?"

"Yes, but I say again I know nothing of art. Only one portrait held —" For some reason, Elizabeth's eyes flitted towards him for a heart-beat. She then said, in a hurried manner, "Can we look at Miss Darcy's work? They might be more intelligible to me."

Darcy wished he did not feel as though he had a greater claim on her attention than did any other gentleman. He was not of a jealous nature, and he had no right to feel slighted, but that did not stop the disappointed feelings from coursing through his veins when he saw Elizabeth and Utterson standing together.

"Mr Darcy," Mrs Lanyon called his attention. "You never did say if you wished to ride with Miss Darcy and me."

It would not do to spend the morning considering how reasonable or unreasonable were his own regrets, and he was resolved, after all, to be considerate of Mrs Lanyon for the sake of their mutual friends. "Yes, I should be happy to spend the morning with you."

"Do not waste your time, Eliza; he is the younger son. When he is a barrister and has briefs, he might earn only six hundred a year. After his brother inherits the baronetcy, I suspect Mr James Utterson will no longer receive an allowance, either."

After hearing about their earlier tour of the picture gallery, Caroline, for such reasons as Elizabeth could not comprehend, was inclined to share her thoughts on Mr Utterson. Before breakfast, Elizabeth had asked after Jane, but she had been with Louisa, as she more often was now. Elizabeth had walked through the house, and whilst she admired Pemberley, Mr Utterson, returning from a ride, offered to keep her company in the portrait gallery until breakfast.

I suppose I could be grateful that Caroline thinks well enough of me to wish better for me than a competency of six hundred a year.

"We spoke only of the house and the paintings," Elizabeth patiently replied. *And on how considerate a landlord Darcy is.* "Mr Utterson did not propose whilst we talked about Miss Darcy's drawings."

She could not give attention to what were likely good paintings, except for one portrait that she had stood several minutes before in earnest contemplation. Had Mr Utterson not asked if she thought it a striking likeness to Darcy, she might have still stood there, realising that the arresting smile he wore in the portrait was like how he used to look at her.

Although the expression of it was all wrong, she now remembered the warmth of his former regard every time that she looked on Darcy. She was certain the words "You must allow me to tell you how ardently I admire and love you" would stay in her mind for the rest of her life.

"In any event," Caroline continued, "you would do better to set your cap at Mr Balfour. Although his wealth comes through the East India Company, his allowance appears to be larger than Mr Utterson's, *and* he will inherit an estate. It could be a proper match—for you," she added.

"I cede any claim to Mr Darcy's single guests to you." Elizabeth wondered why she had not simply said she ceded claim to *all* of the single men at Pemberley, and then pushed the thought away.

"I thank you for the compliment, but no," Caroline said whilst pulling a face. "Mr Balfour is half—well, he has no ambition, and Mr Utterson thinks too often of his own complaints. Besides, I could little marry a man who has a lesser fortune than my father had."

Elizabeth, Jane, Caroline, and Louisa were taking advantage of the clear afternoon to walk in the park. There was a grandeur and beauty to Derbyshire, in the valley with all of its glory diversified by woods of various green hues, the windings of the stream, and the grey-coloured rocks. The only rival to the scenery she had seen was in the size, elegance, and beauty of Pemberley House itself.

Even Caroline's sharp conversation was not a distraction from admiring the beauties before her, although Elizabeth preferred to walk alone. They had fallen behind Jane and Louisa, and this seemed to be by design. Since they had joined the Hurst party, Jane and Louisa were often in conversation together. New duties were put before Jane that now likened her to Louisa. Household cares and husbands, and likely soon children, would pull Jane down a different path.

If only that did not put me more often in Caroline's sole company.

It seemed that in the absence of Louisa, Elizabeth would do for a substitute to hear all of Caroline's jealous, artful, or snide comments. Caroline's vacuous talk about "did she not think this style of gown would do better for Jane" and "had she met Lady Such and Such yet" was taxing her forbearance.

Elizabeth had a sudden thought and stopped walking. "I have grown tired. I should like to rest."

"What? Here?" Her voice rose to a shrill cry. "You cannot mean to sit on the ground."

"I do, here, by the stream bank. Would you care to keep me company?" Elizabeth kept a smile from her lips, and sat and settled her skirts around her.

Caroline looked at her own gown and shook her head. "No! I shall find the others and bring them back to you, and we can return to the house together after you have recovered." She gave her a pitying look and left.

Having succeeded in ridding herself, however briefly, of unwanted company, Elizabeth grinned and took in the scene. There was an immensity to the landscape, both in the park and what she had seen of Derbyshire on her way to Pemberley. The house itself gave variety and animation to a scene of wonderful beauty, and also seemed at home in the wilds of Derbyshire.

After contemplating the stream—another object of beauty, circling the meadow—she saw Mrs Lanyon walking her horse across the meadow towards the stable. She was on the other side of the stream, and only reined in when Elizabeth rose to greet her.

"Good afternoon, Mrs Lanyon!" Elizabeth called to the other bank. "I am surprised to see you back so early. But where are your companions?"

"Miss Darcy's horse lost a shoe," Mrs Lanyon said. "Mr Darcy led them back to repair the loss, and I rode as far as my own knowledge. I am now to see if the farrier has seen to it and if they still wish to ride."

"I was just admiring the noble stream and how it winds through the valley. You shall see more of this fine country by horseback than I shall see by my own two feet."

Mrs Lanyon had been about to signal her horse to leave just as Elizabeth replied, and had to pull on the reins quickly to stay its progress. Elizabeth watched her sigh and set her shoulders. *Mrs Lanyon is not inclined to chat.* She was unsure whether to laugh or be annoyed at how soon Mrs Lanyon wished to be gone from her.

"I suppose that I shall, if you do not ride. However, Mr Darcy tells me that there are lovely walks in the park."

Elizabeth felt the building wind and wondered if it would rain tonight or tomorrow. She gathered her purple pelisse tighter across her. "I hope to find time, in between the rain it seems likely we shall have, to visit all of Pemberley's principal walks. I have had just as much pleasure going over the grounds as I had the house."

"Aye, 'tis a handsome and spacious building . . . standing on elevated ground and commanding fine views over the adjacent country."

Something in her manner and the way she took in the house made Elizabeth ask, "Do you draw?"

Mrs Lanyon raised an eyebrow. "I have years bestowed in learning the typical accomplishments, the same as you, the same as any proper gentlewoman."

This stern reply surprised Elizabeth. "Ma'am, have I said or done something to offend you? I did not mean to imply that you are not accomplished. I do not draw myself, although I take pleasure in seeing the performance of others."

Mrs Lanyon's cheeks turned pink, and her horse seemed to feel her agitation and tossed its head. "I spoke unkindly. Please forgive me for being rude when you were being amiable. I assumed—I thought you rather like . . ." Mrs Lanyon's self-possession appeared shaken. "I am sorry."

She wondered how the cheerful Mr Balfour, with his easy manners and sanguine nature, could be the brother of such a severe woman. It would be a long ten more days if she could not be comfortable with Caroline, if she could not often be with Jane, and if she was always to feel awkward in Mr Darcy's company, *and* could not be on pleasant terms with Mrs Lanyon.

"After you tell me what I said to provoke you so I do not repeat the mistake, we shall say nothing more about it."

"You said nothing wrong." Mrs Lanyon's shoulders fell. "I presumed you were educated the same as your sister . . . and that you share similar views."

What similar views? Elizabeth narrowed her eyes. "Jane and I had no governess, but—"

"I meant Miss Bingley."

She drew back. "Oh, I suppose she is my sister, but Jane and I had to shift for ourselves at home with masters now and again."

The silence stretched out, and it was clear Mrs Lanyon, although wishing to be agreeable, did not know what to say. Elizabeth could part feeling awkward, or she could sustain the conversation and try to put them both at ease. "You leave me with the impression that you are fond of drawing. Do you ever take a likeness?"

"Only when a friend insists." She looked around her at the wood across from the meadow, and then back towards Pemberley. "I prefer to use my watercolour and pencils out of doors."

"You can have no want of subject here," Elizabeth exclaimed, looking around at the verdure herself, smiling. "You could fill your house with a dozen pictures of this stream and meadow alone."

Mrs Lanyon gave a small laugh, and when Elizabeth looked inquiringly, she said softly, "There are rooms in Hyde House that are rich in specimens of my landscapes and flowers."

"Your father must be proud of your talents. I would like to see your drawings of Pemberley, should you take any and are inclined to share them," she added hopefully.

"I do not think they would be worthy enough to be praised."

"What would Mr Balfour say if I were to ask him about your drawings?"

She smiled and patted her horse's neck. "Lewis has always said they are so good he is going to sell them off because they will fetch a good—"

Her eyes shifted over Elizabeth's shoulder, and when she turned, she saw Caroline approach the bank of the stream.

"Eliza, Jane and Louisa have already turned back to the house. We may as well return." Her voice dropped. "How do you do?"

Mrs Lanyon only nodded.

"You of all people must be careful in the sun, Mrs Lanyon!" Caroline called across the stream. "You can ill afford to grow coarse and brown. Should you join us on a walk, perhaps Miss Bennet shall lend you her parasol."

Mrs Lanyon only gave her a cold look. Elizabeth said, in an attempt to end their silent glaring, "If my parasol is wanted, she may certainly have it. Mrs Lanyon, would you like—"

"I must find Mr Darcy before it is too late to ride."

Mrs Lanyon did not bother to take leave, and her horse trotted off. After they had finally been speaking agreeably, it surprised her that she left abruptly. Elizabeth gave a questioning look to Caroline, who only shrugged before carefully making her way up the bank.

When they were both on the gravel path Caroline said, "Mrs Lanyon's seeking Mr Darcy out is a certain sign she intends to marry again."

Elizabeth was now confident Caroline was simply saying the same things to her that she might otherwise have shared with Louisa. "I have seen no sign of admiration between them, and she might still be too attached to her husband's memory to consider the subject."

"Captain Lanyon has been dead three years. Widows may think themselves in earnest when they say they shall never marry again, but those declarations are meant as compliments to their dead husbands. Do you not think it nearly scandalous for her to ride after Mr Darcy?" Caroline scoffed. "What does that imply?"

"I would transgress the duty of woman by woman if I made any insinuations against her."

"I should be loath to disoblige the sisterhood of ladies," she cried, "but Mrs Lanyon thinks the right of flirtation belongs to her alone, as a widowed woman." Caroline needed no encouragement to continue this rude subject. "She ought not be open in her pursuit of Mr Darcy."

"Assuming there is no romantic attachment on either side, there can be no harm in their friendship."

Caroline raised her eyes. "The most upright man alive is still subject to passions that can mislead reason."

Elizabeth was not equal to any reply, and they walked in silence to the house. She knew she had not been much in the world, but she knew enough to mark its shades. Still, it was difficult—no, *impossible*—to imagine Darcy indulging in licentious behaviour. Seducing a widow, his friend's sister, in his own home? It was more the actions she might expect from Wickham.

Caroline's dislike of Mrs Lanyon was from her jealousy of any woman Darcy esteemed, and apparently riding together was enough to make her suspect the woman in question of an improper attachment.

I had wondered why they did not get on, given how similar their back-grounds seem, and how their brothers are friends. Both were from trade, fashionably educated, accustomed to associating with people of rank, accomplished, and agreeable when they chose to take the trouble. Caroline might be jealous because she thought Mrs Lanyon a rival for Mr Darcy's affections, but it did not explain the widow's dislike in return.

Caroline Bingley might never take the hint that Darcy did not wish to be agreed with or deferred to. He would thoroughly despise any woman who assiduously courted him. Mrs Lanyon's simple request to join in an activity with him and his sister would have greater appeal than all the flattery Caroline could show him.

A sense of disquiet filled her as she made her way to her room to rest before dinner. Elizabeth was not jealous of Mrs Lanyon, but she did have a new regret that she had never learnt to ride and could not accompany Darcy on a long ride across the countryside.

CHAPTER FIVE

E lizabeth was still thinking about what it might be like to spend an afternoon in Darcy's sole company when Carew strode in. Miss Darcy's maid had her standing in her shift in seconds. Any belief that she had the power of choice over what she wore this evening was swiftly set aside as Carew selected a gown, and then moved behind her to lace her stays. Every tug jolted her off balance, and Carew's hoop ring scratched her skin.

"Have you anything to distress you today, Carew?"

"No, ma'am." Her voice rose in surprise. "Why do you ask?"

She had thought being pulled about was an indication of distraction, or a dislike for the task, but perhaps Carew was simply too intent and swift to notice how she jostled her. Miss Darcy did not seem the sort of mistress to speak up about such things.

"'Tis no matter. Miss Darcy is fortunate to have someone as skilled as you. And I am grateful to have your help in the evenings."

"The master thought you might be glad of better help than an upper housemaid's," Carew said before turning her roughly and tugging the gown up. "But I do not mind agreeing with you. None of the other maids waiting on the ladies here can arrange hair, remove a stain, or sew as fine a seam as I can."

Carew tied her gown swiftly, turned her, and pushed her by the shoulders to sit before the glass. "I understand you walked the park today." She wore an aspect of stern displeasure, but Elizabeth realised it was only the lady's natural expression.

"It was a delightful walk. I hope to see more of it if this clear weather holds."

"It was cold today for August. I suspect you had to wear your purple pelisse, ma'am?"

"I did. I had it made before going into Kent in March, and had no notion I would still be wearing it in August. Were you outside today yourself?"

"Yes, ma'am. I visited my father." Elizabeth recollected her saying he was Pemberley's carpenter before she continued. "I saw Mr Utterson riding back from Lambton whilst I was walking; he said he had been to post his letters. You were with him in the portrait gallery this morning, I heard the steward say."

Elizabeth nodded, smiling a little at how fast news spread through a house, and Carew frowned, adding, "I only say this because the master and his sister took an interest in you, but you ought not to set your cap at Mr Utterson."

"Why does everyone assume a walk in the gallery is going to lead to a walk to the altar?"

"Every single lady with no fortune hopes to be married and well-provided for," Carew said as though she thought her a simpleton. The brush in her hair resumed its firm strokes. "His valet says Mr James Utterson does not always have the patience that could be wished for, and I think with that manner he would not make an affectionate husband."

Darcy would be a kind, tender husband. A man who was as good a master, landlord, friend, and brother as Darcy was likely to be a good-hearted man devoted to his wife. He had expected a very warm return of the affections he had professed to her, and then she had told him in the strongest, unkindest possible returns that she did not want him to be her husband.

"Do you not like your hair, Miss Bennet?"

Elizabeth checked her reflection, steadied her emotions, and agreed it was pretty, and Carew kept at work arranging her hair. "What of the other people in the party?" She did not want to hear further talk about Mr Utterson or Darcy. "Can you tell me anything about them?"

Carew's stern expression relaxed. "Miss Darcy said how different you appear from Miss Bingley and Mrs Hurst. Even though your sister only just married Mr Bingley, I expect you needn't me to tell you about them."

Elizabeth nodded. "I met Caroline and Louisa last autumn. And I understand them as much as I need to."

"Miss Darcy also said how highly her brother had spoken of you these past months, and how she wishes to know you better. You shall have to help her on."

She started at the compliment, and Carew had to pin her hair again. "I had feared I would find Miss Darcy to be proud, but from my observations yesterday, I am convinced she is only exceedingly shy."

"She is, ma'am. She has recently suff—she is young and has much to learn, but I have high hopes for her."

Wishing to move quickly from any hint of what happened at Ramsgate—and that she knew about it—Elizabeth asked, "What about Mrs Lanyon and Mr Balfour?"

"Their father is a Scot who made his fortune in the East India Company, and their mother was an Indian. I know what you might be thinking, but they were married properly, Islamic rites in India. But she died, and he came home with their children when they were still young."

"They seem near to one another in age."

"A year between them, I think. He is a lively one; 'tis why the master likes him. But I think him less disciplined than Mr Bingley, although when Mr Balfour settles he shall turn out well enough." Elizabeth held back a smile; Carew was younger than Mr Balfour. "Mrs Lanyon brought ten thousand pounds to her marriage, and got it back when her husband died. She is reserved, modest. We wonder if Mrs Lanyon could be a good match for Mr Darcy."

Elizabeth turned quickly, and Carew dropped her hair. Frowning, she took Elizabeth's head in her hands and turned it back to face the mirror. Her blue eyes narrowed in frustration in the mirror's reflection, and Elizabeth apologised. "I am sorry. You took me by surprise."

"You thought Miss Bingley better suited?" Carew said, her small prim mouth tightening farther.

"No, not at all," she said quickly. "He does not enjoy her flattery."

"He might also know what Miss Bingley truly thinks of Mr Balfour and Mrs Lanyon."

Although the maid was often abrupt, she now appeared positively severe. "How do you mean?"

Carew gave her a knowing look in the mirror. "Miss Bingley does not approve of their origins, and you know I do not mean Scotland."

A wretched realisation struck Elizabeth. Caroline's dislike of Mrs Lanyon was not merely bitterness towards a woman esteemed by Darcy. She called to mind some of Caroline's interactions with the widow: her asking if she preferred Indian muslin to English cloth, her suggestion that she could not afford to appear more tanned. And what had she been about to say when Caroline said why she would not consider Mr Balfour as a husband because he was half . . . what? Indian?

And Mrs Lanyon saw me often in Caroline's company and assumed I share her venomous feelings.

Elizabeth sat in disgusted silence whilst Carew finished her hair.

THE GENTLEMEN LINGERED AROUND THE TABLE AFTER DINNER, BUT Bingley was visibly eager to join the ladies. Darcy suspected that were he a less agreeable man, this besotted newlywed attitude would have been met with taunts and ribaldry. However, he was so earnest in his attachment to so lovely a woman that Hurst, Balfour, and Utterson could not be cruel.

After a few more good-natured compliments, Utterson said, "Darcy, you have been rather silent in admiring the lady. Have you nothing to say?"

Bingley met his eye with an expectant look. Darcy hoped, very much hoped, that Bingley knew how happy he was for him, how—

although it was not needed—he approved of his choice. Trying to affect as serious a manner as he could, Darcy said, "I still say she smiles too much."

This inadvertently led to some coarse talk from the others on why Mrs Bingley might be smiling; but whilst they teased, Darcy smiled at his friend, and Bingley returned it, giving him a grateful nod in acknowledgement.

"We are outnumbered, gentlemen, grossly outnumbered in this party," Balfour said after pushing his glass away. "And three of us five are single, but there are only two single ladies amongst us, and all Bingley's sisters."

Utterson narrowed his eyes. "You forgot Miss Darcy and Mrs Annesley."

Balfour shook his head. "No, Mrs Annesley is too near to forty for my liking, and Miss Darcy too near to fifteen. Some men might like such a young lady, but not me."

Darcy looked around the table. "And none of you is stupid enough to trifle with my sister."

"Certainly not," Balfour answered; Utterson had pulled a face in response to the idea. "So, I shall have to confine my flirting to Bingley's single sisters—if you do not mind, Bingley?"

Before he could answer, Utterson asked, "Why *must* you flirt with them?"

"For practice for when I meet the woman who will actually become Mrs Balfour. She shall be neither of Bingley's sisters since one does not approve of me and the other is too poor for me."

"That is a foolish reason to trifle with either one of them."

"It is not trifling," Balfour cried. "One shall be annoyed by it and not take me seriously, and the other already knows I am not in earnest."

"You do Bingley no favours by requiring him to defend his sisters' dignity when he ought to be enjoying his wife's smiles," Hurst said.

"I think the ladies in question can speak for themselves," Bingley answered. "Besides, Caroline would only notice if one particular man flirted with her." Everyone then looked at Darcy, but had enough sense not to speak.

"I have no design in offending the ladies. Well, that is not true," Balfour added in a lower voice. "I would not mind if I offended Miss Bingley."

"How can you say such a thing about his sister?" Utterson exclaimed.

Darcy met Bingley's eye over the rim of his glass. *He knows that Miss Bingley does not approve of Balfour's race and would never consider him a proper match.*

"Trust me, Utterson, Balfour may amuse himself by trying to charm Caroline if he wishes to," Bingley said darkly. Darcy thought he made an effort to be at ease when he added, "And Lizzy is too clever to be taken in by Balfour."

"I suppose it not worth my time then, and that leaves the pretty but poor Miss Bennet for you, Utterson," Balfour said as he rose. "Shall we join the ladies?"

The question as to why either of them had to flirt with Elizabeth died on Darcy's lips, and the party reunited in the drawing room. Mrs Bingley was at the table with Mrs Hurst whilst Mrs Annesley and his sister made tea and coffee. Mrs Lanyon sat with her fancywork by the fire, and Elizabeth was near Miss Bingley.

Darcy noticed that Elizabeth sat stiffly, with her arms crossed, and he watched Miss Bingley lean towards her now and then to speak softly to her whilst watching Mrs Lanyon.

Elizabeth is looking anywhere but at me. If he did have the chance to speak to Elizabeth alone, to say that he was grateful for her reproofs, he wondered if she would sit silent the whole time they were together.

This thought occupied him as Darcy then moved amongst all the little groups, spending more time with Georgiana to ensure she was happy to pass the evening with his friends. As he walked behind Miss Bingley and Elizabeth, he overheard the former say as an aside, ". . . from *that* part of the world."

As he came around them, he saw that Miss Bingley was staring at Mrs Lanyon. A dismal look darkened Elizabeth's pretty face, and she whispered a harsh "Enough," either to Miss Bingley or merely to herself, he could not be certain. She then rose and strode right past him and sat beside Mrs Lanyon on the sofa. The widow looked up from her sewing in surprise, and Elizabeth began to ask about her work.

Elizabeth decided to show Miss Bingley that she would not listen to her insults.

She did not cause a spectacle in his drawing room against Miss Bingley's prejudice, but not even for her sister-in-law would Elizabeth listen to such talk. Miss Bingley deserved public censure, but that would only make the modest and reserved Mrs Lanyon dreadfully embarrassed. Elizabeth calmly made her principles known, and Darcy felt admiration for her.

"Darcy, shall we play a round game?" Utterson called to him. "Your sister has agreed to perform for us whilst we do."

"You may do as you like," he said quietly, and he left them to arrange their own amusements. After giving a cold look to Miss Bingley, Darcy moved with deliberation to a chair across from Mrs Lanyon and Elizabeth.

Since he did not know what to say to Elizabeth, he asked Mrs Lanyon, "How does your work get on, madam?"

"I could not say with certainty that it would be to the liking of anyone with taste," she replied without looking up.

"I admire your dedication since I cannot do any fine work this late in the evening," said Elizabeth pleasantly. "By candlelight, I make too many mistakes that I have to tear out in the morning."

"Indeed."

"Yes, the shadows cast make it hard for me to see."

Mrs Lanyon nodded to indicate she heard. She was content to sit with her work and have no conversation. Although he always tried, Darcy often found it difficult to get a word from her, and it seemed that Elizabeth had the same trouble.

When Elizabeth realised Mrs Lanyon would not speak, she looked at him, giving a pleasant smile that he returned. Elizabeth gave a little nod, and then looked around the room. Darcy inhaled, but could think of nothing to say to her and exhaled slowly. She then began an investigation of her own fingernails. It appeared neither of them had the heart to speak a word to the other, and the silence stretched.

I shall never learn what she thinks of me if we carry on like this.

"I heard you say, you said at dinner that you walked the park . . ." he began in an awkward manner. She finally looked at him. "Where did you go?"

"We walked a path near a stream that ran near the house amidst a green meadow."

"Yes, that leads into the Derwent. There are other walks bounded by the woods." After a pause, he said, "If you are in as much the habit of walking as you were at Rosings, I am sure you shall see most of it before you go on to Scarborough."

The mention of Rosings was a mistake, for now she looked even less at ease. "I . . . Pemberley appears to be full of walks. I saw the kitchen gardens as well," she added, awkwardly. "I suspect if the weather was better this year you would have had a large quantity of fruit?"

"Yes, it has been too rainy and wet." More silence. "The gardens contain four acres and a half."

Another short silence ensued before Elizabeth said, "Pemberley is delightful, charming—" She stopped, and Darcy saw her change colour, although he did not know why.

His sister's music and the chatter of those playing cards filled the room. Georgiana was smiling as Mrs Annesley turned the pages, and he heard laughter from the card tables; everyone seemed comfortable except for them.

For now, he listened to his sister play, and Elizabeth was at least affecting to do the same. Every so often, he thought Elizabeth might have looked at him, but perhaps he was wrong because she was always turned away when he attempted to catch her eye.

"Mr Darcy?" Mrs Lanyon had decided to speak. "When we stayed at the New Bath Hotel in Matlock Bath, I saw something I meant to ask you about. There was a frame built around one of the springs. It appeared to be embedded with fresh flowers." She turned to Elizabeth. "Have you seen such a thing?" Elizabeth shook her head, and Mrs Lanyon looked back at him. "You should tell Miss Bennet about them."

Darcy smiled. "The custom is well dressing. It is said to have begun in Tissington, but many of the villages in Derbyshire decorate wells, springs, and fountains with flowers." Mrs Lanyon only nodded, but he noticed that Elizabeth was listening with interest. "There is always a festival that accompanies it. They begin in the spring and continue through the summer. Since neither of you have been to Derbyshire, would you like to drive to one of the villages to see them? Matlock has already had their country fête, but Bakewell is to have theirs on Sunday."

"Yes!" Elizabeth cried, smiling. She then blushed and said, more softly, "I would like to go."

Her dark eyes had a lustre to them that all her embarrassment could not stifle. For a long moment, he stared her full in the face, admiring what he saw there, before he recollected himself.

"Madam?" he asked Mrs Lanyon.

"No, thank you."

"It is only five miles to Bakewell—"

"I do not see how you could avoid inviting everyone, and I should prefer to remain here."

"Perhaps you could ride with us and bring your drawing supplies?" Elizabeth asked. "These decorations might be worth putting to paper."

Mrs Lanyon did not look up. "I prefer to draw the natural countryside."

Elizabeth looked towards Miss Bingley. She caught his eye, and then did the same thing again, emphatically, and then tilted her head towards the widow. *Mrs Lanyon does not wish to be in a small group with Miss Bingley if it could be helped.* That was a feeling he could well understand, and he thought of a way to avoid it.

"I shall ask the others if they wish to join us," he said to Elizabeth. "Georgiana might prefer to stay at home rather than spend the day with a large party. Perhaps Miss Bingley and Mrs Hurst would remain behind with her?" In a lower voice he added, "Do you think they would remain with Georgiana if I hinted that was what I wanted?"

Elizabeth struggled to hold back a laugh. "I can almost guarantee it. But I do not think Miss Darcy . . . requires so much company."

He smiled. "Then it is a good thing I told her to ride whenever she feels exhausted by my friends. If I remember correctly, Mrs Hurst and Miss Bingley are not horsewomen?" Elizabeth nodded, returning his smile. "Then, Mrs Lanyon," he said in a louder voice, "since we shall have a small party, perhaps you might like to go after all?"

She kept her eyes on her needle, but said primly, "Thank you. I shall ride with you to Bakewell and find a place to draw rather than attend the festival."

Darcy was relieved that he had discovered a polite solution to please everyone, save perhaps Miss Bingley. It then occurred to him that depending on who joined them—who rode in the carriage or who rode horseback—he might drive to Bakewell in the curricle with Elizabeth.

I shall have five miles there and back in Elizabeth's sole company.

If she was as ill at ease as she was previously, the excursion would be a daunting one. However, if she talked with him, if he could tell her that he did not resent her for what she rightly said to him at Hunsford, the novelty of it was a delightful prospect.

~

WHEN THEY WENT TO BED ON FRIDAY, IT WAS PLAIN THAT THERE WAS A violent storm of rain coming and, to Elizabeth's dismay, it continued all through Friday and into Saturday. There had been a great deal more rain this season than was typical, and although it was August, the wind had roared round the house, and the rain had beat against the windows. Still, as it neared the time to ready for dinner, Elizabeth thought the clouds were parting. It would likely be clear for the excursion to Bakewell the next day to see the wells.

It was cheering to her thoughts to see more of Derbyshire, and just as gladdening was the idea of Darcy's company. At breakfast, it was decided that if the clear weather returned, Jane and Bingley would ride to Bakewell in their chaise, Mrs Lanyon and Mr Balfour would ride with them but not attend the festival, and she and Darcy would ride in the curricle. The others had decided, or had been convinced, to stay behind.

Her heart fluttered at the thought of an hour alone with Darcy. *He deserves to be thanked for what he did for me and my family after Hunsford.* He exposed Wickham's lies not only to her, but to her father to safeguard all of the ladies in her neighbourhood, and he confessed his interference to Bingley and sent him back to Jane, to say nothing of his goodness towards her and Jane since they arrived. His behaviour in general still had its mild gravity and dignified address, but he was making himself pleasant to all. He had improved so much in civility that she was nearly certain that she could be guaranteed of Darcy's friendship once she had spoken with him.

Any other hopes, naturally, are groundless.

Shaking her head, Elizabeth continued her circuit of the house. With the poor weather, the gentlemen had dedicated themselves to beating one another at billiards. The women were left to their work, their music, and their conversation with one another. Naturally, after a day and a half of this, Elizabeth had grown tired of them. She would always want to be with Jane, but her talk about marriage and home with Louisa, and Caroline's petty jealousies, and even Mrs Lanyon's quietude were taxing.

Deciding she had time to take another circuit before dinner, she entered a room to pass through it to the stairs and noticed Miss Darcy standing near the fireplace. Elizabeth would have only curtseyed and passed through, but she heard the unmistakable sound of sniffling.

"Miss Darcy," she said softly, "are you well?"

She started, and Elizabeth saw that she was crying. She drew near and, without saying a word, led Miss Darcy to the sofa. The younger woman's eyes were fixed on the ground for several long moments before she said, "Forgive me. I thought I would be entirely alone here."

"I am sorry to have disturbed you. I only wish there were anything I could do to comfort you."

Miss Darcy shook her head. "I was just thinking over my regrets." She dried her eyes and looked towards the fireplace.

Elizabeth followed her gaze, and then felt a sickness in her heart when she noticed the miniatures suspended over the mantelpiece. One was clearly a young George Wickham.

"Do, do you have regrets regarding . . . that man?"

Miss Darcy lowered her handkerchief from her face. "Fitzwilliam told me that you befriended Mr Wickham, and . . . because you believed his lies, he had to tell you what I—I am so mortified."

Elizabeth took her hand as Miss Darcy started to cry anew. "Then your brother must also have told you that I was blind and prejudiced, and eagerly believed every lie Mr Wickham told. I lacked all discernment. It is shameful, almost criminal, how I favoured that man."

"I am ashamed about my own conduct towards him. You must think me foolish to cry over a worthless man."

"You must regret your imprudence, of course, but you thought the attachment a sincere one. It is natural for you to mourn the loss, even if he is the wickedest young man in the world."

"I am just as ashamed that I consented to an elopement, and with such a man. It was an indulgence to cry over him, over thinking that I had been loved." Miss Darcy dried her eyes one final time and said, still looking cast down, "I am sorry you found me this way."

"I have several younger sisters, and one of them is always having a cry about something," she said to make Miss Darcy smile. "It is an almost daily occurrence at Longbourn, so you have made me feel very much at home at Pemberley."

After a silence, Miss Darcy said, "You will not tell Fitzwilliam, or Mrs Annesley, or Carew, will you? I could not bear it if they assumed I still cared for him."

Elizabeth shook her head. Miss Darcy had only been fifteen, and mourned the loss of her first attachment more than the actual man. "Certainly not. In fact, we shall stay here a little while until you are certain you can dress for dinner without Carew noticing that your eyes were red."

She gave her some privacy and walked around the room. There was a study table, bookcases, and a sofa. There was a rosewood inkstand on the table next to two silver tapersticks. Although it was not as lofty as some of Pemberley's other rooms, it was cosy with a fine view of the gardens. "I was taking a walk around the house—I could walk without fatigue and still not see every room—but I do not think I have done more than walk past this one."

Miss Darcy finished drying her eyes and rose. "I think Reynolds shows it to visitors, but other than that it is rarely used."

Elizabeth approached Wickham's likeness. Next to it was a miniature of Darcy, done around the same age, and she recognised one of

Miss Darcy when still a child. There were other portraits, likely of intimate family, but only Darcy's could hold any interest to her. She heard Miss Darcy come alongside her.

"Why is his picture here?" Elizabeth asked softly whilst looking at Wickham. Why had Darcy not put it to the fire years ago, if not after what happened at Ramsgate?

"This was my father's favourite room, and these miniatures are just as they used to be then. Reynolds says he was very fond of them being all together on the mantelpiece."

"What does your brother say?"

She shrugged. "He is not often in this room. He uses a desk in a room nearer to his bedchamber, and keeps his favourite books there." Elizabeth noticed how Miss Darcy did her best not to look at Wickham's picture. Although she was shy, Elizabeth thought Miss Darcy might say more, and in time her patience was rewarded.

"Fitzwilliam is conscious of Pemberley's legacy, his responsibility to the house, the servants, the tenants, and what he owes to those who came before him. Whilst he might redecorate or make improvements, on the whole he does not want to disrespect my father's memory, and he wants to preserve Pemberley in such a way that, when it is passed to his children and grandchildren, it would be just as recognisable to them as it was to my father and grandfather."

Elizabeth said, "I do not think your father would be so fond of that miniature if he knew the harm that his godson caused his daughter."

Miss Darcy sighed, and Elizabeth wondered if she doubted that she meant as much to her father as had Wickham. "And your brother," she added, "is dedicated to Pemberley, and it is to his credit that he knows what is due to his family as well as to everyone who depends on Pemberley . . ."

Elizabeth picked up Wickham's miniature. "But from what I know of him and what I have seen of his attachment to you, Mr Darcy is equally devoted to *you* and to your happiness." She set the miniature facedown on the mantelpiece, and moved the other family pictures nearer to fill in the space.

Miss Darcy looked at the mantelpiece a long moment, and then nodded in agreement.

"Are you composed now, Miss Darcy?"

"As for tears and regret, I have done with that, as far as *he* is concerned."

"I am very glad, because he is not worth your time or your—"

"Ladies!" They turned to see Mr Balfour enter. "I thought everyone would be dressing for dinner by now."

"Did you return from a ride or a walk? And in this weather?" Elizabeth cried. He must have worn a greatcoat whilst he had been out, and was carrying his hat and gloves, but he still appeared wet through.

"Aye, I had to get out of this house for a wee bit. I rode to Lambton, but there is nothing there. There are only so many times I can beat Bingley at billiards before it becomes dull and, as lofty as Pemberley is, I could not walk it again." Mr Balfour stepped nearer. "Although I do not think I have been in here before. I usually only take a short cut through it to get to the stairs by the picture gallery."

Elizabeth waited for Miss Darcy to reply, but her reticence had returned in the face of Mr Balfour's cheerful temper. He was rather tall, not handsome, but not so plain with his fine figure and pleasing manner. She could see how Miss Darcy's shyness might prevent her from speaking at length with a tall, older man who was so animated.

"I understand this room was a favourite of Mr Darcy's father, and has scarcely been touched since he died."

"Indeed? That makes sense. I met Darcy not long before his father's death; he took it very hard." He came farther into the room and looked around. "'Tis a well-appointed room to be so neglected."

"Miss Darcy was showing me a view of the gardens." At this, Mr Balfour went to the window. Whilst his attention was elsewhere, Elizabeth gave Miss Darcy a look to ask if she was well. She nodded, ducking her head as she did. Miss Darcy was composed enough now to be in company. "I think we shall dress for dinner."

Mr Balfour bowed, and made some compliments about neither of them needing a single alteration to appear before company before allowing them to leave.

CHAPTER SIX

On Sunday morning the wind softened, the clouds were carried off, and the sun appeared. Elizabeth thought that it almost felt like summer, but Carew had still dressed her in her purple pelisse from Kent for the curricle ride. She stood on the sweep with those who were to drive to Bakewell. She took in the house, on its elevated ground with the woods behind it, and turned to see the view of the valley.

The dales of Derbyshire possess true picturesque beauty.

The others were readying themselves to leave and were not as taken by the scenery as Elizabeth. Mr Balfour was assisting his sister onto her saddle, talking about where to place her pencils. Mrs Lanyon intended to find a place to draw near to Bakewell, and her brother simply wished for a diversion whether it was the ride, or the festival, or whatever he found to amuse himself. Jane and Bingley were already in his carriage and smiling at each other; whether they were curious about the excursion or simply happy to be near to one another was impossible to determine.

"Lizzy," Jane called her over whilst they waited for Darcy, "what has Mr Darcy said of these flower decorations?"

"He only mentioned that the wells and fountains were decorated with a profusion of flowers. He did not say why or explain how it was done. Perhaps he will tell me more on the drive."

"If I know Darcy," Bingley said, "you shall have a thorough history of the custom before you have gone a mile! Are you sure you would not rather ride with us?"

"Thank you, Charles," Elizabeth said with a laugh, "but I do not mind hearing about it."

In truth, she hoped Darcy would not spend the entire time talking about the decking of wells, at least not until she had the chance to thank him for what he had done after Hunsford. She had misjudged him and had favoured a contemptible man over a good one. And even though she had thrown unjust accusations against him, Darcy still secured Jane and Bingley's happiness, and preserved everyone from a further acquaintance with Wickham.

"Where is Darcy?" Mr Balfour cried, turning his horse round. Both the animal and its rider seemed eager to be on their way. He pulled out a fine gold watch. "It is quarter to the hour."

As the others assured him Darcy would never be late, Elizabeth walked the road leading from the front of the building towards the stable, trying to take in a better view. Looking down the valley had a very agreeable effect on her spirits: by directing her eye along the edge of the side of the valley, she could see that the country beyond boldly swelled into green hills.

Elizabeth turned the corner and saw two boys throwing a ball near a curricle. There were three men standing behind it, talking, but Elizabeth could only see their hats. As she came nearer, one of the boys threw the ball and it disappeared behind the horses and curricle, only to be thrown back by someone unseen.

"This is bad weather for the hay." Elizabeth recognised Darcy's voice.

"Yes, sir, but it's much worse weather for the wheat. That is a comfort."

All three men chuckled. "Well, that is cheering, Mr Stevenson, thank you," Darcy said drily.

One child overthrew the ball, and it rolled across the cobbles.

"Boys!" the other man cried. "Take the ball somewhere else."

"Your sons may stay," Darcy said.

"You will not say that when they hit one of your horses or break a window," a third voice said good-naturedly.

"Let us not tell Mr Stevenson of the time I broke the window in your father's mill. Old Mr Gabriel was very good to allow me to pay for its repair without ever telling my father."

"Oh, I think old Mr Darcy always knew it was you."

The men all laughed. The younger boy threw the ball again, and it seemed that it was Darcy who caught the ball and tossed it back whilst he spoke with two men, perhaps his steward and a tenant.

The steady sound of the ball hitting their palms continued and the gentlemen's voices resumed, talking about the low yield from the home farm and what that would mean for helping those tenants who also suffered from the poor weather this season. When she heard Darcy thank and dismiss the groom, Elizabeth returned to the others before Darcy drove round.

He is all friendliness and ease with his servants and tenants. He had improved in civility since Hunsford, of course, but Darcy was naturally at ease at home. Elizabeth took in another view of the valley as she rejoined the others. How could he not be at ease in a lovely spot situated by the side of a sparkling stream in a deep valley amongst steep hills covered with foliage and fields?

Darcy then appeared and, after assuring Mr Balfour that he was *not* late—the hour had not struck—he handed Elizabeth into the curricle, and they were on their way to Bakewell. This was the moment for her resolution to be executed. With his cares at home to occupy him, and in such a large party, she might not have the chance again to speak alone with Darcy.

"I can no longer help thanking you for your kindness to my family. You confessed your interference to Bingley, and gave him the courage to return to Jane. You risked his being angry and your very friendship, based solely on what I said."

Darcy shook his head. "You need not thank me. I ought never to have interfered in the first place. I certainly ought not to have concealed Mrs Bingley's being in town last winter. I told him how mistaken I was, and although he was angry, my assurance that she loved him helped him to forgive me."

They rattled on a little farther in silence before Elizabeth said gently, "You know why else I must thank you." She felt his attention, although his eyes were still on the road. "I know you shared your history with Mr Wickham with Bingley, who then told my father. You not only secured Jane's happiness, but you preserved my family and friends from an unworthy acquaintance."

"Did Bingley or your father tell—no, certainly not," he answered his own question. "You are clever enough to have inferred it on your own." Elizabeth saw how he tightened his grip on the reins and set his shoulders.

"I am grateful, very grateful you were willing to sacrifice your privacy, your sister's privacy, for—" She very nearly said *me*, but her heart could not be secure in that. "For the sake of others outside your circle."

"Do not thank me, Miss Bennet," Darcy said through a clenched jaw. "It was my fault that Mr Wickham's worthlessness was not known in your neighbourhood. Correcting that was right to be done. Please do not make it a virtue."

After a moment, Darcy said, in a calmer tone, "My character had to speak for itself. It was my responsibility to see to it that he was not well-received amongst decent people, people who had a right to expect that an acquaintance of theirs, a gentleman, would preserve them from such a man."

"I feel that much good came from barring Mr Wickham from the neighbourhood. *I* dared not disclose what I truly knew of him. What happened to Miss Darcy did not go any farther than Jane by my means, but I did wonder what might happen to other ladies in Meryton who might be . . . ."

"More fond of Mr Wickham than he deserves?" Darcy supplied.

"Yes."

"I feared the same. I feared that if you, with your powers of discernment, were taken in, then what of your sisters and friends? I had to prevent any other young lady being hurt like my sister had been. I trusted Bingley, as well as your father, to be discreet."

70

"You were a good friend to my family."

Darcy only bowed. He said nothing about wanting to continue *their* acquaintance on friendlier terms. Was it strange how strongly she wished to establish a friendship with a man who had said he loved her against his reason? *He could not know how much I regret having misjudged him.* Darcy was not as ungentlemanly as she had presumed him to be.

"Might we," she stammered, "might we talk about Hunsford?"

"A conversation about what happened in Hunsford," said Darcy, in a tone of surprise, "could serve no purpose rather than to produce explanations that are mutually disagreeable."

Elizabeth was filled with the keenest anguish. Did he think she was leading the way to encourage him to propose again? Had the mode of her rejection made it impossible that he could esteem her? *I did make it horribly, painfully clear that his proposals disgusted me; I cannot blame him.*

In a less sharp tone he added, "Let the only thing said on the matter be that I am resolved to be a better man because of your admonishments. Your reproofs of my conduct, my manners, made an impression on me."

"And your letter made me think better of *you!*" The truth burst from her heart, and Darcy started. "Before I am silenced on this subject, you must know that I realise how I misjudged you, that my approval of Mr Wickham was reprehensible, and your letter removed all the unjust prejudices I held."

Even over the sound of the curricle and horses, she heard him sigh, and she watched him swallow thickly. "I was not certain you would believe me, although, I hoped . . . I hoped you would think better of me."

"I believed you if not instantly, then very soon after reading it. I *do* have confidence in your integrity, and your merits. And I was wrong to assume you so . . ."

"So devoid of every proper feeling?" Darcy asked, turning to look her in the eye.

She saw how much her rejection, as well as the manner of it, had hurt him. "I am sorry, exceedingly sorry. I misjudged you, and I am ashamed of myself." She thought back over all that she had said against Darcy in Hunsford parsonage. "I am surprised you do not hate me after that evening."

"Hate you?"

Darcy said nothing else, but the incredulous expression on his face told her how shocked, perhaps even how insulted, he was by the idea. He finally shook his head, saying softly, "I could never hate you, Miss Bennet. After recovering from my surprise at seeing you at Pemberley, I hoped to obtain your forgiveness, to lessen your ill opinion, by letting you see that your reproofs had been attended to."

"I do forgive you," she said. "And you have improved in civility, but you were never as proud or selfish as I presumed. I only hope you can forgive me for abusing you so terribly."

"Your apology is unnecessary. You were acting from ignorance, from mistaken premises."

"And you are being too generous. I would have thought that after Hunsford you would have spurned a friendship—an acquaintance with me," she corrected herself quickly.

Darcy gave her a significant look. "I would be very glad if what happened in Hunsford did not impair a friendship between us." He gave his attention back to the road. "Can we agree to say no more about it?"

Elizabeth agreed, although it felt like something more must be said, but she knew not what. Now that she knew he had no improper pride, that he was not a selfish man, now that he wanted to make himself agreeable, and the shock of learning of his being in love with her had lessened, she now wondered if his feelings for her were unchanged.

They drove some time in silence before he said, "Bingley is happier than I have ever before seen him. I was delighted to learn of their engagement, and to see Mrs Bingley's devotion to my friend is everything I could have hoped for."

This was a safe topic. "Jane is excessively fond of him, and he of her. They are happy in each other."

"I am glad of it. There could be no two young people more deserving of the love and respect of a worthy partner. Although you would know their happiness better than I since you live with them at Netherfield."

"Yes, it has been a beneficial arrangement. However, as they become more settled into their domestic life, I do not serve the same purpose for Jane as I did in the beginning."

Jane and Bingley would insist she stay with them as long as she pleased, but Jane had more in common with married ladies now, and she naturally preferred to spend time with her new husband. Elizabeth's position in their household might not feel like home as the couple grew more accustomed to each other. "They are very mutually and sincerely attached," said Elizabeth with forced brightness.

"I am certain your good humour and cheerfulness will always make you a valuable companion to your sister," Darcy said with a knowing look and a smile.

She blushed in reply, and Darcy said a few more words about the good character of his friend, but soon his attention shifted to the drive. For a long while, with his attention elsewhere, Elizabeth watched him. At first glance, Darcy was handsome with a noble bearing, but perhaps was too ascetic for some people's liking. On closer examination, there was a certain gentleness in his eyes, and often a humour in his look. Had that always been there, or was she now a better observer of him?

I care for his happiness. Darcy deserved to have someone love and respect him, and she wanted him to be as happy as Bingley was. How much of that happiness she wished for him might depend on her? Although Darcy wanted her good opinion, did he still love her? Or would the remembrance of the less just and less gentle sensations of the past, of what happened at Hunsford, always keep them apart?

DARCY DROVE THE CURRICLE TO THE MEWS AT THE RED LION, AND THEN tried not to stare at Elizabeth after he handed her down and she smiled beautifully at him in answer. He could not convince himself that he would eventually grow indifferent to her. He had insulted her, he had not acted honourably or feelingly towards her, and yet Elizabeth seemed to wish a friendship with him. Was it too soon for her to wish for something more than friendship?

If she has any tender regard for me, I will do everything in my power to attach her, to assure her of my continuing affection.

"There is Bingley's chaise," she said, waving to her sister, and then walking towards it. "And there is Mr Balfour."

"Darcy," said Balfour when he dismounted, "Hester has gone to a hill that supposedly has the earthwork remains of some castle?"

"Castle Hill," he said. There were only a few yards of foundation walls left of the castle, and they were covered in verdure and turf. "Perhaps she shall have a view of the village from there if she wishes to draw."

Balfour shrugged, already looking round for the next place to go, the next item to buy, the next person to banter with. "She can sketch where she pleases. You know what it is like"—he gestured to Bingley—"once a sister has married, your role as protector is incredibly lessened. Even a widow like my Hester can come and go as she likes."

Balfour was about to leave when he added, "Miss Bennet, would you care to forgo the church service and fountain decorating frivolities to wander Bakewell with me instead? I shall be more attentive to you than the newlywed couple, and shall be livelier company than Darcy."

Elizabeth gave him a wry smile. "You no doubt have some secret gentlemanly pursuit in your mind, and a single lady under your protection would only put me in your way."

Balfour might have expected a polite demurral or a blush, and briefly looked taken aback before he laughed. "Why, Miss Bennet, you do speak your mind, dinna ye?" He touched his hat and left.

Bingley could not restrain a laugh, but his wife put her arm through his and asked, pointedly, if they ought not to leave. Darcy wondered if Bingley might have become like Balfour had he not married as young as he did, and to as steady a woman as Mrs Bingley. He might otherwise have become all frivolity and carelessness.

Darcy led them to All Saints' Church, thinking that Balfour had been provoking on purpose and that he had not expected Elizabeth to provoke him in return. Women were generally expected to be obliging. Elizabeth's frankness could be objectionable to some people. It may even frighten some gentlemen, but he found it a great attraction. It was a touchstone of honesty, a quality he admired in her.

"Balfour said you would not be lively," Bingley called his attention. "Do not prove him correct."

"Yes," Elizabeth said whilst taking his arm and thereby stopping his heart, "what can you tell us of these decorations?"

"You shall see for yourself during the service, but villages in the Peak have left garlands of flowers at wells and springs for centuries. From there, the custom of well dressing, or well flowering, has stayed in Derbyshire villages. At some point, rather than leaving garlands, we built wooden boards to form a frame about four feet wide. I have seen other villages erect a ten-foot arch over their fountains. The boards are an inch or two deep and covered in soaked river clay where a design is etched, and then flower petals, blossoms, seeds, berries, all manner of natural materials are pressed in to make patterns and pictures."

"Where did the ancient custom come from?" Mrs Bingley asked.

"None can say for certain. In Roman antiquity, there was a festival called Fontinalia in honour of the nymphs of wells with a ceremony to throw nosegays into fountains and put crowns of flowers upon wells."

"But how did such a custom stay so long preserved, and only in Derbyshire?" Elizabeth asked him, her expression curious.

"Was it because the Celts worshiped local water gods, or perhaps Black Death survivors thinking the local water saved them?" Bingley asked.

"Or maybe gratitude for water during a drought?" Mrs Bingley said.

"Some people think so," Darcy agreed. The churchyard was now in view. "Derbyshire is beautiful but remote, and its hills and dales made it a challenge to pass. Perhaps its remoteness kept a Celtic or Roman practice intact even through Saxon, Danish, and Norman invaders."

"What are the designs on the boards?" Elizabeth asked.

"You shall have to see for yourself," he answered with a smile as they entered the church.

His guests were taken aback when the vicar read the service and then left the pulpit, and the congregation followed and listened to him read the psalm at the first well. Bingley and his lady looked bemused by the traipsing around the village to visit each well and spring, but Elizabeth's face was rapt with interest. The procession continued with the epistle, gospel, and then a hymn sung by church singers accompanied by a band at the final well.

"Each well or fountain with its stone surround is covered with a board dressed in flowers pressed into clay?" Mrs Bingley marvelled when the service was ended. She and her sister were looking at the dressing at the well near the churchyard. "Look, Lizzy, they have used violets, daisies, and primroses here."

"The village children spent the last few days gathering flowers, moss, and the like," Darcy said. "Then they are given over to whoever has been deemed the most talented to press into the boards."

Bingley was taking in the crowd in the churchyard. "Why are so many people still here?"

"A fête has followed the service from time immemorial. And those of the village open their doors for strangers, friends, and visitors. Some people have already gone home to put their kettles over their fires for those who brought a picnic on the green."

"How charming!" Mrs Bingley cried.

Darcy saw in Elizabeth's and Mrs Bingley's faces that they wished to attend, so he led them down King Street. Bingley and his wife lagged behind, and he was left to entertain Elizabeth. It seemed he would have the rest of the afternoon in her sole company. If she realised the same, she did not seem to mind going on with him alone. They passed Rutland Square and saw that Bath Garden, with its decorated well, was already full of booths and people.

"There appear to be a great many visitors amongst the villagers," Elizabeth said as a group of children ran past.

"The festivity draws together the rich and the poor for many miles around. All the families in the neighbourhood contribute flowers for the purpose, although the weather this year must have limited their selection. Thank goodness it was dry today. Booths with nuts, gingerbread, and toys shall delight their children whilst their parents roam the village, having a picnic and visiting."

Elizabeth wished for a nearer look at the dressing at this well, and Darcy stood by her whilst she waited her turn amidst the throng to get closer to it. As she took in the happy crowd around her, she said, "At one time I would have been surprised that you would partake in a rural festival that shows gratitude for the gift of water. But I think now that these emblems of faith and benevolence, and of your ties to the community, suit you well."

She spoke with more emotion than he would have expected, and the admiring look she gave him made it difficult to speak. "I hope," he said and then swallowed thickly, "I hope your visit to Derbyshire gives you the opportunity to properly sketch my character."

"I think I already have, and you have my good opinion," she said smilingly.

He might have said more, but then one of his tenants touched his hat in obeisance. This was hardly the place to learn if Elizabeth's good opinion might extend to a more tender emotion. As they waited, Darcy greeted several of his tenants, asking their children which of them would be king of the sports today, and gave his best wishes for a better yield than the cold, wet weather gave them all reason to hope for.

"Oh, look at the tasteful design of it!" Elizabeth cried as she was standing next to the board that surrounded the well. "The vivid colouring and mosaic patterns are beautiful."

"It is no surprise to me that you are awed and charmed by anything having to do with nature. For myself, I have always enjoyed the fellowship in the neighbourhood that accompanies a well dressing."

"All the wells were charmingly decorated, but I think my favourite was the one by the fountain. It was enchanting to see the water flowing from above, surrounded by a mosaic of flowers," she said to him later, once she had insisted on seeing each of the wells a second time. "The daisies and buttercups around the edge gave it the look of a gilded frame, and the foliage arranged into verses from scripture are exquisite!"

The effect of Old and New Testament images and scripture verses, along with the favourite scenes of nature that graced all of Bakewell's well dressings, was beautiful, but seeing them through Elizabeth's eyes made them more fascinating to him. "I am glad you came today, Miss Bennet."

The remainder of the afternoon was spent in rural festivity. They often saw Bingley and his wife, at a booth sampling plain fare or watching the various feats of agility and skill displayed by the village boys, but the majority of the day was happily spent walking Bakewell with Elizabeth and speaking with her.

Upon hearing the cheers and shouts that attended the competitors, Elizabeth's spirits seemed to rise in playfulness when she said, "The athletic rivalry seems quite heightened. Did you compete when you were a boy?"

"I had my share of merry-making when I was young, but I knew well enough not to win whatever the prize effort was."

"You hardly strike me as the sort not to try your best in every endeavour as a matter of principle."

He shrugged good-naturedly. "It would hardly do to have Master Fitzwilliam come into Bakewell and win a prize the sons of my father's tenants wished to win." Elizabeth was looking at him with a soft look in her eyes. "However, I gave my very best to every game of leapfrog and ball."

She laughed, and held his arm a little tighter. The happiness he felt in this moment was clouded only by the realisation that if he had not acted so meanly in the past, had he not been too proud, he might have been walking this festival with his wife rather than his friend's sister-in-law. Still, their conversation in the curricle gave him reason to think Elizabeth could love him. *I ought not to speak of my own attachment yet.* Perhaps her esteem for him was of too recent a date for her to be certain of her own feelings.

As the afternoon grew late, they soon met with Bingley and his wife and, although dancing had begun at Bath Garden, they decided to return to Pemberley. On their way down Bath Street, they saw Balfour riding towards them.

"How d'ye do?" he called. "I have had a dull day. A shame we cannot shoot birds yet, although I am dreadful. I found but one dice game near the green, and only the pawnshop was open today." Balfour brought out his pocket watch, and Darcy saw it was enamel with pearls, with a painting on the case. He noticed Darcy's attention and, as though he had been waiting for it to be admired, said, "Do you like it? This was the only pledged watch she had. I thought I may as well buy it as not since it was finer than mine."

"Why buy it at all when there was nothing wrong with your gold one?" Bingley asked as he handed Mrs Bingley into his chaise.

"Because I am a gentleman, and a gentleman spends his money whenever he can."

Bingley only laughed, but Darcy thought it foolish to spend simply because one had money in his pockets. Balfour would always be careless with his money. It was fortunate he would inherit an estate worth five thousand a year.

The Bingleys began the drive to Pemberley, and Balfour said, "I rode to Ashford, but there was not even a pawnbroker open there today. Do other villages have these well festivals?"

"Yes, Buxton, Matlock, Tissington."

"All today?"

"Between Holy Thursday and Michaelmas," Darcy said whilst handing Elizabeth into the curricle. "Some are later this year because the weather has been so cold and wet."

"Yes, only such a particular, ancient custom of showing thanks for water could continue in a season as wet as this one. These small Peak villages have little to occupy me, my friend."

"Buxton and Matlock are larger and might be more to your liking."

"I shall have to spend my time and my money there. I must find Hester," Balfour said as he touched his hat and was gone.

"Your friend would rather spend freely in town rather than walk freely through the countryside," Elizabeth said when they drove down Bath Street and out of the village.

He thought this an incredibly fitting description of his cheerful friend who spent half the year in London. "Not everyone has your appreciation for beautiful country or the charms of a village festival."

She looked over her shoulder towards Bath Garden and the people near the well and in the garden.

"Thank you for bringing us, Mr Darcy." She turned back around and gave him a beatific smile. "The village looks lovely, does it not?"

At first glance, Elizabeth was tolerably pretty, but he had soon noticed that when emotion moved her, her face came to life, showing all her liveliness and intelligence. Now, Darcy thought her beautiful. Without looking away from her, he said, "It is the most pleasing sight I ever beheld."

CHAPTER SEVEN

A surveyor with some report occupied their host as soon as Darcy entered the house, and since Jane was happy to be alone with Bingley, Elizabeth climbed the stairs to retire to her own room. A new bride wanted a female companion during her early married days, but Elizabeth felt Jane no longer needed her. When Elizabeth was near the top of the stairs, someone with swift steps ascended, and in a moment it gave Mr Utterson to her view.

"I am afraid I alarmed you by running up those stairs," he apologised. "This is the nearest way from the stables to my apartment, and I do not typically see anyone using them this time of day."

"You have had a fine day for your ride."

"Yes, no post today so I rode all over. No field sports yet, either, and Hurst is dull company. I cannot play billiards with him all day and then tolerate his company in the evening as well."

Mr Utterson could be harsh in what he said and how he slighted others. Although she agreed about Mr Hurst, all Elizabeth could politely do in reply was smile.

"Had you a pleasant time looking at wells?" he asked.

She readily agreed and might have said more, but Mr Utterson shrugged and said, "I am not often in the country unless visiting friends. Rural festivities hold little interest to me. I prefer town society and amusements, on the whole."

"You are chiefly in town, then? Is that how you met Mr Darcy?"

"I first met Balfour a few years ago, and through him have slowly come to know Darcy better."

When he added nothing further, Elizabeth said, "You mentioned studying the law."

They stood near the room that had been old Mr Darcy's favourite as they talked. "I am. Twelve terms qualify me to be called to the bar. I am preparing to be examined for my proficiency."

"Are you near to completing your study?"

"I have one year left." Mr Utterson huffed. "My brother shall inherit the baronetcy and has no profession to plan for. He was plucked from the lists at Queen's College for failing his examinations. He could not even handle Euclid, but he shall have the Hall and the title. For my lot, however, I must attend court, study, read in barrister's chambers, and do so on a pittance doled out by my father."

Recognising that he could be an ungracious man or say a severe thing without even realising it, Elizabeth felt she could best tolerate Mr Utterson in a large party, or only after he had aired his grievances to someone else. "I suspect your father fears London life would draw a young man into expensive pursuits, and wishes you to secure a profession so you will be well-provided for."

Mr Utterson looked chagrined. "I am not ungrateful, nor resentful. Sometimes I am more jealous than I have right to lay claim to. It shall all end well enough."

Elizabeth nodded and, not knowing what to say, looked into the room where she had found Miss Darcy yesterday.

"Were there not two candlesticks there?" she said, pointing to the table.

"Likely not. Darcy said it was his father's room, so I presume he cannot bring himself to alter it." Mr Utterson's naturally severe countenance softened. "Darcy was very attached to him, I understand from Balfour. The room is probably just as it was in his father's day." He then checked his watch. "I must go and dress, although there is no theatre, no parties to prepare for. At Pemberley, a quarter of an hour is enough time."

He bowed and left her, and Elizabeth went to her own room to dress for dinner.

She had chosen a gown for the evening, going so far as to lay it on the bed, but when Carew strode in after seeing to Miss Darcy, Elizabeth learnt her opinion did not matter. The maid's deep blue eyes widened, and she gave a shake of her head before putting the green gown back and selecting a yellow one in its stead.

"Your hair is dishevelled, ma'am, and your gown in such disorder," she said as she went through her skilled but rough process of removing Elizabeth's day gown and putting her into an evening one. With every motion, Carew's ring grazed her skin. "I do not know how that is possible since you did, I presume, wear your bonnet and pelisse to Bakewell. I shall have to brush your purple pelisse. It looks as dusty as one of Miss Darcy's riding habits after a long day."

Elizabeth looked to the long-sleeved, full-length, fitted coat, trimmed on the collar, cuffs, and hem with fur. She supposed it did look the worse for wear.

"You need not waste your time. I or one of the upper housemaids can—"

"Certainly not, ma'am. Miss Darcy and the master have put you in my charge whilst you are at Pemberley."

Carew was curiously, charmingly outspoken. Miss Darcy was not the sort to assert her rank, and she did not have much confidence yet, but Carew's authoritative but caring attitude might do Miss Darcy well. It was likely good for Miss Darcy to have the aid of so honest and loyal a creature. Elizabeth found she had grown fond of Carew's manner.

At least whilst she brushes my hair, she is not likely to scrape my skin with her ring.

"Wool does not stand up to frequent washing, you know," Carew was saying as she firmly ran the brush through Elizabeth's hair, tugging her head with every pull. "You are lucky the hem does not touch the ground. I shall brush it best I can with fuller's earth. You likely did not expect to wear it on August walks. I should like to have something so warm when I walk to visit my father."

"If you intend to go to the trouble of cleaning it, you may wear it next." The hairbrush clattered on the ground. When Carew rose with it, Elizabeth saw her shaking her head in the glass's reflection. "I insist. When you next walk to Lambton to visit your father on a cold day, I shall lend it to you."

"Thank you, ma'am, but no."

"I shall tell Miss Darcy to insist that you borrow it. And, if she cannot do that," Elizabeth added, "I shall next take it up with Mr Darcy, and we all know how cross he will be to be put to any trouble. He might dismiss you without character reference if you refuse." She tried to keep her expression stern, but was smiling before she finished.

Carew pursed her lips. "I agree only to save you from troubling Mr Darcy, although he would never act that way. He is a good master and has been civil to me since we were friends as children."

I was completely wrong about Darcy. "Please, borrow it when you visit your father. He is very proud of you, I am sure."

The maid's prim lips now turned into a smile. "Miss Darcy always tells me to take a flower from one of her bonnets to put on my own when I go to see him."

"Then you shall appear lovely when you see him next." Carew's reflection in the mirror showed pink cheeks, and Elizabeth said, to distract her from her embarrassment, "How did Miss Darcy pass her day?"

"She lasted half an hour with Mrs Hurst and Miss Bingley before she rode through the park. And then Mrs Annesley decided that she needed to practise the harp, without an audience. I then needed my mistress to provide me detailed instructions on how to care for her silk gown, so she spent the rest of the afternoon in her apartments."

"I am glad Miss Darcy has good friends who truly care for her happiness. I want to know her better. I think I shall also try to know Mrs Lanyon better."

"Miss Darcy is only shy, but best of luck with Mrs Lanyon, ma'am. She is reserved." Carew bid her to stand to give her a final inspection before sending her to the dining room. "Some of the servants think her good enough for Mr Darcy, but now I wonder if a reticent woman would be attractive to the master. It might be more prudent that a man like him marry someone who might give him a little more liveliness."

Carew curtseyed and was gone before Elizabeth recovered enough to thank her for her help.

AFTER DINNER, WHERE THE TOPIC OF WELL DRESSING WAS DISCUSSED WITH energy, Elizabeth helped Miss Darcy prepare the tea and coffee. They fell into a chat about where best to walk in the park and where to visit in Derbyshire. Although shy, Miss Darcy answered Elizabeth's questions readily, and Elizabeth felt that after a few more conversations, preferably whilst not in a large party, Darcy's sister might be completely comfortable around her.

"I wish her gown had left more to the imagination, and less to the eye," Louisa said quietly as she took her teacup, with Caroline following behind her. "Mrs Lanyon forgets she is a widow."

"Nor is her Titus hair a flattering coiffure," said Caroline, with a look towards Mrs Lanyon. "But, if one has too wide a forehead or crooked eyebrows, one must do what one can to attempt to remedy the defect."

Elizabeth saw Miss Darcy's reddened face. Just like Mrs Lanyon, she also wore her hair cropped, with it crimped prettily around the forehead and temples. Caroline and Louisa quickly realised their error and did their best to repair the damage, complimenting Miss Darcy's fine and regular features and how the short style suited her particularly well.

Between her embarrassment and their fawning, now Miss Darcy might not speak for the rest of the evening.

"You had to spend the day with Mrs Lanyon, Eliza," Caroline said after Miss Darcy had been flattered into mortified silence. "How did you tolerate it?"

Caroline liked nothing more than to speak unkindly about whomever was not present and whomever she feared might form an attachment with Darcy. "I must have been too subtle before when I tried to make it clear how little I like your rude manner of talking about Mrs Lanyon." Elizabeth walked away, and then turned back. "I actually spent the entire day with Mr Darcy, and I tolerated that very well, thank you."

She then left them to sit with Jane and Mrs Lanyon. Elizabeth was tense with anger, and sat silently until Jane included her in their conversation.

"Lizzy, Mrs Lanyon was saying she had great success sketching Bakewell today. She had a lovely view from Castle Hill."

"Have you convinced her to allow us to see her drawings?" Elizabeth asked her whilst looking at Mrs Lanyon.

"You would not need to see them, Miss Bennet. You spent the day there yourself. You saw it with your own eyes."

Elizabeth persevered in friendliness. Since their conversation by the stream, she suspected that once past Mrs Lanyon's reserve and modesty, she might be an interesting acquaintance. "But not from the perspective that you must have had. Unless Mr Darcy is going to take us all to climb that hill, you might, perhaps, let us view them."

"I would like that, but only if Mrs Lanyon is willing," Jane added. "Do not let Lizzy trouble you if you had rather not."

"Jane, dear!" Caroline called. "You must not like your seat. Come tell Miss Darcy about the necklace Charles bought for you."

Jane sighed quietly, and then begged their leave to talk with her sisters.

Elizabeth noticed the anxiety visible on Mrs Lanyon's face. Elizabeth said quietly, "Jane takes all of the good in people, and none of the bad. She *knows* what they are like, but she wishes to be on good terms with her husband's sisters."

The widow's brief look of extreme discomfort was gone. She resumed her needlework in silence, her expression all complaisance.

Elizabeth felt she ought to make it plain what she thought of Caroline's behaviour. "Miss Bingley's dislike originates—"

"I do not need you to describe Miss Bingley's character flaws to me," Mrs Lanyon said shortly without looking up. "I understand her feelings towards me and her motives very well."

"Forgive me." Elizabeth was abashed. "I only meant to say how little I approve of her myself."

She rose to leave when Mrs Lanyon said softly, "I am sorry. I know you do not share her opinion. That is why I helped you on Friday." Elizabeth sat down and thought back to Friday, but only shook her head in confusion. "You and Mr Darcy struggled to speak to one another, although it was plain you wanted to. Had I not asked about the flowers at Matlock's wells, you would have stolen glances at one another but not spoken all evening."

The gentlemen then came in, and she used this opportune distraction to avoid giving an answer.

"It is likely to rain tomorrow," Mrs Lanyon said to her after everyone was settled. "Would you like to join me in my apartments to talk?" Elizabeth's face must have shown surprise, because she then said, "I should like to know you better, and I cannot always be at ease in so large a party."

"Yes, I should like that."

They looked up to see Mr Utterson standing by the sofa. "Pardon me. You were right earlier, Miss Bennet, when we spoke by the stairs. I am sorry I did not have that patience that you might have wished for."

Darcy had likewise come near, but perhaps he was simply warming his hands by the fire and did not come to speak with her. "You owe me no apology," she said kindly. "Although if you speak about your poverty again, I shall have to tell you about what little is left to me on the death of my parents."

He seemed to regret his previous complaints. "Perhaps we can agree that another thousand pounds a year would be a great wealth to both of us? In all seriousness, I was churlish and it was unbecoming of me."

"Let us say no more about it."

He bowed, and was about to leave, and Darcy came closer, but then Mr Utterson turned back. "Your sisters at the tea table were just talking of dancing one evening before you go on to Scarborough. May I have the first dance?"

Mr Utterson must be trying to be more agreeable than was his wont, and she accepted. She had favoured less worthy men than him.

He then left, and she noted Darcy's intent look, and she wondered if he might ask her to dance as well. Instead, he was silent for a long moment before clearing his throat and asking Mrs Lanyon about her horse and was she pleased with her excursion. She answered succinctly, and without any particular interest. It made Elizabeth feel that Caroline's jealousies were ill-founded.

Elizabeth noticed Miss Darcy looked overwhelmed, and she left to talk with her and Mr Balfour until his affability tired even her patience. He was a friendly gentleman, all attention and at ease with everyone, but Miss Darcy was flagging. Elizabeth encouraged her to open the instrument. She turned the pages for her for two songs, and then was relieved by Mrs Annesley, and Elizabeth warmed herself by the fire as she watched Darcy.

According to his custom these evenings at Pemberley, Darcy was making the circle of his guests, and it appeared he was to end with her. As he spoke to his friends, she thought of Darcy's manner at the well dressing festival. He knew the children's names, and with every person who touched their hat to him, Darcy seemed to have something to say: "How many lambs have you had this spring?" or "How many colts are you likely to have?" or "How is your mother faring? Apply to Mrs Reynolds if she has need of anything."

"Half of the people who walked past us in Bakewell acknowledged you," she said to him after he asked how she was. "I expected that in Lambton, but not also in a market town five miles away. Some of them are living under a good landlord, I presume?" she added teasingly.

"Many of them rent land from me, or they or their families work on the estate. I take pleasure in seeing my tenantry thrive," he said.

"I think it more than simply keeping their houses in good repair and hosting a large enough haymaking party. You knew each tenant's principal character and internal circumstance."

"I have always treated them with civility. It is no more than all men are entitled to. I must only be cautious so that growing familiarity does not sink my authority. But I see no reason not to be on friendly terms with any of them." Darcy looked around them, and then lowered his voice to add, in a tender tone, "I see no reason to think meanly of those outside my circle, thanks to you, my dear Miss Bennet."

Mr Balfour and Bingley called him over, and he left her with only a significant look in parting.

She felt her cheeks grow warm. "My dear Miss Bennet" stayed in her mind the rest of the evening. If he were to write a letter to her now, perhaps the salutation would be *My dear*, rather than *Madam*.

~

THERE WAS CLEARLY ANOTHER STORM OF RAIN COMING TODAY. DARCY looked out the window at the foliage bending in the wind, and the sun behind the clouds gave no indication that it was ten o'clock in the morning. Such severe weather all year had led to low yield across his properties. Too much rain and overcast skies delayed planting, would delay harvesting, and would produce little. He wondered if the mowing was too long delayed in hopes of a larger hay crop, and if the whole would then be spoiled.

"You look serious, Mr Darcy," Miss Bingley said from the breakfast table. "Of what are you thinking?"

"I am thinking there was too great an expense incurred in the making of hay this year," he said, turning from the window. "It should cost three shillings per acre, but I fear with this cold, wet weather that when all is said and done, haymaking shall not have been worth it."

"You need not concern yourself with such things, I am sure."

He pierced her with a stern look. "And I assure you, I am very concerned if my tenants' livestock starve this winter."

Miss Bingley turned pink, and Darcy realised he spoke rudely. "Forgive me. The effect of this rain and cold weather weighs heavily on my mind."

"The lady only meant your steward can manage it all," Balfour said, to smooth away the awkward moment. "You meet with him often, and he keeps you apprised."

"Mr Stevenson will keep me informed, but it is I who shall have the worry of it," Darcy said.

"Aye, I suppose. I have no knowledge of such things."

"Maybe you ought to," Utterson drawled from behind his letters. "You do stand to inherit an estate worth five thousand per annum."

"Jealous, my dear Utterson?" Balfour asked with a laugh.

Darcy heard Utterson scoff, but suspected this was the case. Envy was unbecoming, and jealousy over where one falls in order of birth was useless. It could not be changed, so one might as well do what one could to make the most of what talents and choices they did have. Utterson would be happier if he was not so concerned with how much money his older brother will inherit.

"I still say Darcy ought not to stare out the window looking grim when he has all of this." Balfour gestured to the breakfast room. "And I shall continue to spend more than I ought until I have an income to support my tastes."

"Many who know they are apt to inherit a fortune are apt to be lazy and unfocused," Utterson replied, still looking at his post.

"Says you, who avoids Inns at Court whenever he can and wishes for a new desideratum every time he walks down Bond Street."

"Rather like you."

"True, but I spend twice as much. I thought we already established that I am on the high road to ruin, to Hester's and my father's shame. What shall be done to reclaim me?" Balfour asked, laughing, but Utterson merely turned a page of his letter and did not answer.

"You could take an interest in Hyde House so you are not oppressed and ignorant when your father dies," Darcy answered, aware now how they held the attention of the room. He thought of how distressed he had been at his father's death and knew he would have felt adrift had he not already known what Pemberley needed of him.

"But you were instructed from your earliest youth, and it has made you dull, my dear Darcy. Thank goodness you have friends like Bingley and me to draw you out."

"And what a shame it is that my influence has done nothing to improve *you*. What can I say or do to convince you to spend more of your time in Scotland and less of your time parading in town?"

Balfour waved him off. "I shall worry about it when I eventually become a country gentleman."

The conversation ended, and smaller groups began to talk whilst others read their letters or the newspaper. Darcy noticed that Utterson spoke with Elizabeth. It was not the first time he had noticed a short tête-à-tête between them. Last evening, Utterson had apologised for some complaint he had said out of turn and had asked her to reserve a dance. Seeing them talk together made him feel as though Utterson was a rival, even though Elizabeth was not his lover.

I cannot criticise him for talking to a woman I admire. I am not a jealous friend.

He had no right to be jealous, after all. His suit was rejected, rightfully rejected. But the hope of strengthening Elizabeth's affection towards him, the hope of her growing in love with him, would not allow him to look kindly on any man who pursued her. Was Utterson merely enjoying her conversation, or did he have greater expectations?

"What is the matter?" Bingley asked. "You worry for your tenants amidst all this rain?"

It was better to be thought a conscientious landlord than in love with Bingley's sister-in-law. "I do. You cannot sow in heavier, wet soil, then the cold spring and summer and lack of sunshine means harvests are also delayed, with poor yields." Darcy looked up and noticed the butler entered and had a quiet word with Balfour.

"You will almost certainly have a low yield?" Bingley asked.

"Every crop: wheat, drilled beans, turnips. And everything growing in grassland, mown land, and pasture. What shall my tenants' sheep and cows eat this winter if this weather continues? What shall that mean for livestock and planting next season?"

"I suppose it means they won't be able to pay their rent."

"As though Darcy need worry about his income," Balfour interrupted as the butler left. "I will cheer all of you: my new carriage has arrived." He stood from the table. "You must come see it," he said with a grin. "The weather will be averse to outdoor exercise before long."

His enthusiasm was infectious, at least to the men. They strode into the hall and outside to the stable yard to see it; the ladies followed more slowly, as though indulging a child. The wind was strengthening, but it had not yet begun to rain, and they all gathered around Balfour's new equipage.

"It is a travelling chariot!" he said, admiring it and encouraging his sister to look at the upholstery. "You and I can sit just there when we go to Scarborough. Utterson, three shall fit across."

"And I thought you might have me sit with your man on the rumble seat," Utterson muttered, walking round the carriage.

"Why did you not order a chaise if you wanted your own carriage rather than travel post?" Mrs Lanyon softly asked. "It might be more useful to have a carriage that could seat four."

"I wanted something more substantial than a chaise. And to this I can add a box for a coachman whilst in town and remove the rumble seat so a footman can stand on the sideboard for making calls."

Balfour was pointing to this and that whilst Hurst and Bingley looked on with interest. The equipage had looked impressive to Darcy from a distance, but, as he came nearer, he looked at the panels with some concern.

"They did not use seasoned wood, Balfour. You could not have ordered this," Darcy said as he ran his hand across the door.

"Indeed, it is exactly as I asked for. Well worth the price for a man to have something new!"

Bingley bent low and peered at the undercarriage. "I think Darcy could be right," he said.

"If you did not order wood like this, then the carriagemaker cheated you," Darcy said quietly.

Balfour's bright expression darkened, and he looked to be gathering patience. However, he laughed and said, "Aye, you are only jealous that I have something new, my dear Darcy." He turned to the ladies and said, "'Tis a shame he has such a jealous, resentful nature. Must be why he is still single."

Now suspecting that Balfour knew exactly what he paid for, Darcy stayed silent. He who would not ask for seasoned wood was throwing money away to order a carriage from such materials. It was made from wood so green that the panels would slip from their mouldings within three months. *Balfour always thinks he needs what is new, rather than what is lasting.* He would rather have a lower-quality travelling chariot now rather than save to have a more lasting coach in the future.

"Why would Mr Darcy be jealous of your carriage?" Miss Bingley asked. The ladies had admired it politely, and he noticed they all had their arms around themselves to brace against the wind.

"I suspect it is because Darcy's carriage is five years old if it is a day," Utterson murmured, still walking about the new chariot.

"I thought your brother's coach seemed new," Mrs Annesley said to Georgiana.

She seemed to wish to encourage her charge to share an opinion, but when it was clear that his sister was unable or unwilling, Darcy answered. "It was refurbished this spring. Newly varnished, the brass plates replaced, and the cushions newly stuffed, and new carpet, too."

"I thought you had said something or other last year about not bothering, and you would just wait until you married to buy a new one?" Bingley asked.

Darcy kept his attention firmly on Bingley and did not look to the woman who he had hoped would be the one to select that new carriage. "That was unlikely to happen any time soon, and mine needed new carpets and varnish. Nothing else was wrong with it."

"You must wish for a new carriage like mine. I shall let you ride in it," said Balfour, winking at him. Darcy rolled his eyes, and Balfour looked chagrined before he then called Georgiana and Mrs Annesley to sit in it and say what they thought of it.

Darcy noticed the ladies shift their feet, glance at one another, and then collectively come to some decision. A few nodded, and then they all complimented Balfour on his purchase and begged leave to return to the warmth of the house. They left, and when Darcy came to the other side of the chariot, he saw Elizabeth had turned to look over her shoulder. She watched him for a long moment before walking slowly towards the house.

The men continued to admire it, and Darcy stood with them out of politeness rather than interest. He hardly wanted to laud the foolish purchase, and certainly not after Balfour had claimed his warranted concern was rooted in jealousy. *Let us hope that baseless claim does not give Elizabeth a reason to lose her good opinion of me.* That would be a blow after the progress he felt he had made since the well dressing.

Bingley eventually claimed an errand, but Darcy suspected he preferred the private company of his wife. As Bingley hurried towards the hall door, rain drops began falling, but it was not enough to deter Hurst and Utterson from making more remarks about the chariot.

There was a rumble of thunder in the distance, and then the rain fell; finally, they all ran to the entrance nearest the stable yard. As they shook the rain from their hair and coats, when Darcy strode past Balfour, he gestured for Darcy to wait. The others continued into the house, whilst Darcy followed Balfour into the gunroom.

Balfour idly looked round at the rifles and pistol cases before he said, "I hope to go shooting after the twelfth."

Darcy only stared.

"This weather! One needs to be web-footed like a drake to get anywhere."

"Did you call me here for a purpose?"

Balfour sighed at his abrupt reply. "I do hate being on this side of your unyielding temper."

For all his earnestness in conversation, Balfour could say flippant, disrespectful things. His cheerfulness made him a valued friend, but Darcy was hurt by his thoughtless ridicule, and in front of mixed company, no less. He stood with his arms crossed over his chest as Balfour paced.

"How long have we known each other?" Balfour asked.

"Near six years, I would say, not long before my father died."

"I am grateful for whatever lucky circumstance that led to our fathers' meeting. Did you know, after my father met *you*, he said to me, 'There is a fine, straight young fellow. He shall be a good influence on you, Lewis, if you shall let him.' It is no fault of yours that my sprightly nature and being a spirited speaker gets me into trouble."

"You are beyond all hope," Darcy said, unable to help a small smile.

"Aye, *we* know that, but no father wants to believe his wayward son won't ever settle down. I hope you know me enough to know when I am sorry." Balfour held out his hand. "I always know when I have done wrong, and as soon as I called you jealous, I knew it was a damned stupid thing to say, and in front of your sister, too."

Darcy immediately took Balfour's hand. Since Hunsford, he was resolved to be less resentful. "A shame, then, that you never know it before the words leave your mouth."

Balfour gave a relieved laugh, and clasped Darcy's hand with his other in a warm grip before letting go. "Oh, aye, but you typically like how much I talk. It often saves you the trouble." He added quietly, "I *know* you do not have a jealous bone in your body. You were generous to allow me to make sport of you before the others, and I am sorry I did it."

"All is forgiven. I was only worried that you had misspent your money, or had been taken advantage of."

Balfour shook his head, laughed, and clapped a hand on his shoulder. "My dear Darcy, you are a good friend to worry for me." They walked through the door, and had moved to go their separate ways when Balfour called his name. "All these years of friendship, and I know which one of us is the better for it."

CHAPTER EIGHT

Elizabeth crossed Jane's sitting room to look out the window and saw that the gentlemen had only stopped admiring Mr Balfour's travelling chariot once it had begun to rain. *Why is it absolutely necessary that men admire another gentleman's new carriage?* It was always the same with men whether they had a new horse or a new gun. They must all stand around it, admire it, compare it to their own, learn the price paid, and predict how it shall perform.

"Mr Darcy has been very welcoming, Charles dear," Jane said to Bingley after he entered, brushing the damp from his coat sleeves. "And Lizzy, I think there is some alteration in his manner since last autumn."

"How do you mean?" Bingley asked.

Elizabeth turned from the window, and Jane looked embarrassed. Bingley did not know all that had happened at Hunsford. "I mean . . ."

"Jane means there is a new gentleness in Mr Darcy's manner," Elizabeth said, not wanting to illuminate why Darcy might be improved in civility. "His manners are a little softened, perhaps, since when we knew him in Hertfordshire." She gave Jane a look, conscious of Bingley being in the room. "Although, he is not as deficient in goodness, or the appearance of it, as I mistakenly thought."

Jane smiled, and Bingley said, not understanding, "Well, before strangers he generally seldom says a word, but being with his intimate friends he laughs and talks a good deal."

Elizabeth nodded. "It is likely uphill work for him to be talking to those whom he knows so little, but he is an amiable man."

Bingley nodded before sitting next to Jane on the sofa. She was giving him an affectionate look, and Elizabeth wondered if they wanted to retire into each other's arms. "Speaking of that, Mrs Lanyon invited me to talk with her. Excuse me, I shall go now."

She left before they could lie and profess that they wished for her company. It would be good to have another woman to talk to, someone who was not painfully shy, or supercilious, or who talked only of house and home. When she found Mrs Lanyon, it was clear she had been reading but she welcomed her immediately.

"I wish us to be better acquainted, Miss Bennet. I am glad you came."

To Elizabeth, this attention was received with the greatest pleasure, and she thanked Mrs Lanyon and intimated the same.

"What think you of my brother's new carriage?" she asked to begin a conversation.

"I suspect one of the gentlemen would give you a more interested answer than I can give," she said with a laugh. "Providing it has wheels, a comfortable seat, and saves me from walking, it is all the same to me."

Mrs Lanyon laughed. "True. I had wondered if you preferred a new carriage to an older one. You winced when Mr Darcy spoke of refurbishing his carriage rather than waiting for a bride to make her preferences known to order a new one."

Elizabeth kept her pleasant smile in place whilst she thought of all the pain Darcy must have felt following her rejection. The idea of hurting him wounded her more deeply now than it had in April. "Mr Darcy is perhaps more conservative in his spending than Mr Balfour, but I have nothing to say against a young man buying a new carriage if he has the means."

Mrs Lanyon took a breath and said in a rush, "I must apologise again for presuming your opinions coincide with Miss Bingley's."

"There is no need at all," she said earnestly. "I made a foolish assumption about you. You and Miss Bingley are both from trade, fashionably educated women with a fortune who live in the world. I foolishly mistook your reserve for superiority—"

"Let us say no more about it. And whilst we are at Pemberley, we shall have to strive to be polite to your sisters-in-law."

Elizabeth laughed. "That is the most ungenerous speech I have heard you utter."

She looked embarrassed. "What we say about someone can often say more about us than it says about them. And I cannot afford to be too honest around people like Miss Bingley and Mrs Hurst."

"How do you mean?"

"Must I speak plainly? Because those ladies would say of Lewis that he is lively and agreeable but woefully dark. Some have said to me that my complexion must subject me to mortification or that those of a mixed race like me ought to do one thing or not the other."

Elizabeth frowned. "There are Indians and mixed-race Indians in nearly every market town, let alone in London, and most people do not presume—"

"Let me save you the trouble, Miss Bennet. For every person who sees me as another woman on the street, there is one like Miss Bingley who thinks I am inferior."

Mrs Lanyon spoke with a quiet dignity, and Elizabeth was lost for a reply. She was unequal to saying anything that would be a comfort, or that could change how some viewed Mrs Lanyon. Her companion seemed to feel the same awkwardness, and her naturally quiet manner reappeared. Elizabeth allowed her attention to be taken by a miniature of a man in uniform on the dressing table.

"Is that Captain Lanyon? He has a striking countenance, and looks proud to be wearing his uniform. Did you paint it?"

Mrs Lanyon looked at it with a gentle smile before picking it up. "Yes. He was a captain in the 79th Regiment of Foot, the Cameron Highlanders. He joined as a young man when the regiment was raised in 1793."

"When did you marry?"

"We met before he went to Egypt in 1800, and he said if he returned he would marry me." Mrs Lanyon touched the face in the miniature before placing it back on the table. "We married in 1801."

"The only person I know well with an army commission is Colonel Fitzwilliam, Mr Darcy's cousin. His regiment is stationed in London, I believe. Do you know him?"

After a pause, Mrs Lanyon said only, "We have met."

Thinking she might prefer to speak on the subject of her husband, Elizabeth asked, "Did you travel with your husband's regiment?"

"We spent two years in Minorca, and I was briefly in Copenhagen with him. I was often amongst other wives whose husbands were stationed elsewhere, and there was no shortage of company. I saw him often in England until 1808 when the regiment was deployed to Portugal. He did not survive the evacuation after the Battle of Corunna."

Elizabeth expressed her condolences. It pained her to imagine Mrs Lanyon frantically searching the list of names of the evacuees from Spain, hoping her beloved husband had survived.

"What was it like in Minorca?" Elizabeth asked to distract her from the grief that had appeared in her eyes. "This trip to Scarborough will mark the farthest I have travelled. Before now, I had only ever been into Kent and to town."

It became clear that the extensive knowledge Mrs Lanyon had gained in meeting with persons from all parts of the world made her an interesting companion. She had travelled extensively, been in a circle of varied acquaintances, and spoke plainly but with interest about what she had seen and experienced alongside her husband.

"I fear I shall grow jealous of you," Elizabeth said kindly, a quarter of an hour later.

Mrs Lanyon raised an eyebrow. "I suspect the right man will come along at last, if you are willing to love him warmly in return."

"Oh no!" Telling Darcy he could not have made her an offer in any possible way that would have tempted her to accept it ran through her mind. *Is there any reason to hope he might ask me again?* If he were to ask her now, the mode of address would make it likely she would give him a favourable answer. "No, I meant of your travels, in your manifold connexions and acquaintances. I mean, I want to marry, but I—"

"Forgive me for misunderstanding you."

Elizabeth sighed in relief at not having to explain further. "I enjoyed listening to your accounts of Minorca and your friends there. I am surprised you do not speak more in company when you have such fascinating experiences to relate."

"Not everyone wishes to hear, and I wish to avoid bringing undue attention to myself."

"You are an educated woman with—"

"I was educated in fashion, and not improving my mind," she said. "And some might consider me of an inferior race because my skin is tinged with more jet than ivory to listen to what I say."

She could not argue with Mrs Lanyon's own experiences. She wondered if Mrs Lanyon was too used to saying what she thought ought to be said, rather than expressing her true opinions. "I can suppose it is hard to speak with someone who has insulted you because of their own prejudices. But I hope you will not be that way amongst those who would like to be called your friends."

Mrs Lanyon nodded. "How long is your acquaintance with Mr Bingley and his sisters?"

Elizabeth relayed Bingley's visit to Hertfordshire last autumn, and briefly mentioned encountering Darcy again in Kent in April and Bingley's subsequent return to the neighbourhood and his marriage to Jane. "And so we have all met again to travel north and meet Bingley's friends."

"Huh," was uttered with a surprised intonation. "Your acquaintance with Mr Darcy is of a longer standing than I realised."

"We have known each other a ten-month, but only recently am I coming to truly know him better." And she cared for him more deeply than she ever had before.

"I hope you made good use of your afternoon in Bakewell yesterday, then."

Elizabeth was not equal to replying to this, and instead asked if she might see Mrs Lanyon's sketches from Bakewell, and this occupied them until that lady's maid came to dress her for dinner.

∽

THE CLOUDS MUST NOW BE POURING ENOUGH WATER TO DELUGE THE LAND.

The entire heavens were black as ink and lightning flared in sheets of fire as Darcy looked out the window after dinner. The men were still at the table, but Darcy had left to see how much rain had fallen. It was only eight o'clock in the evening on the tenth of August, but it was already too dark to see onto the lawn.

He walked through a door on the other side of the house to better see into the garden. Only when lightning struck could he have a better view, but it was plain they would be flooded by morning. Sandbags had been placed hours ago, but he wondered if they would serve their purpose.

"Darcy, is that you?" a voice called.

He ran back inside, closing the umbrella that had done little to keep him dry, given the wind. Bingley was giving him a concerned look. "Why were you outside in all of this?"

"The gardens at Pemberley lie low, lower than the flood level of the Derwent." He frowned and looked back out the window but, of course, it was too dark to see. He took out a handkerchief to dry his shoes. "The garden is sloped to afford a ready discharge at the surface for storm water, but I fear it is already flooded. I worry what other ravages might be committed on the rest of my land before the storm passes."

Bingley gave him his handkerchief to wipe the rest of the water from his face and sleeves. "Violent storms of rain are not common in the Peak. I suspect it will let up before long."

It did not sound as though it would move on soon, but he allowed Bingley to lead him to join the others in the drawing room.

"Will the Derwent flood?" Bingley asked as they went to where Georgiana and Elizabeth were making tea and pouring coffee.

"It has in the past, but not since I have had charge of Pemberley," he answered, taking a cup of coffee from Elizabeth. He smiled his thanks; she had made it the way he liked. "It flooded in '95, and there was considerable damage when Toadmoor Bridge washed out. And again in '99 at Matlock, it rose to a surprising height."

"Did you say there shall be a flood, Fitzwilliam?" Georgiana asked.

"I cannot see from here. I suspect the stream has already gone over its banks, but perhaps the Derwent will not rise too high. Let us hope none of the weirs break."

"What does it mean if they do?" Elizabeth asked.

"It would worsen a disaster," Darcy muttered.

Elizabeth was looking at him with interest and concern. He had a glimpse of what it might have been like to have a wife to have equal share in all of his concerns at Pemberley. *Is it too late for her to ever have any precious feelings for me?*

Darcy supposed it was natural for him to have hopes on the subject, but he could not yet be secure of her feelings. "Downstream mills have penned-back water by a weir to reduce the fall upstream. The millponds hold water that flows under the wheel. Many in the past thirty years have purchased leases along the rivers and erected water mills. There are two mills at Pemberley alone."

"If the weirs are destroyed, it will not only affect the mills' production . . ."

"If the weirs and gates are carried away by a flood, even more water will come rushing down and the surge would flood the banks and cause more destruction than will come from all the rain."

"It has been a dreadfully wet season," Georgiana said quietly.

"I spoke with Mr Knowlton, the Duke of Devonshire's estate manager, after we came down. He has recorded the rainfall at Chatsworth and says that we have had 135 percent more rain this May, June, and July than is typical."

"Did I hear you mention the Duke of Devonshire?" Balfour said as he brought back his coffee cup. "I was disappointed the rain prevented me from taking the travelling chariot to apply to see Chatsworth. Hester has never been. I missed the party when the duke came of age last May. Did you attend, Darcy?"

He nodded, thinking about how easily the River Wye west of Rowsley, near its junction with the Derwent, could spill over its banks.

"They say the expense of the duke's party was not to be limited, not even in the hundreds of pounds," Balfour said.

"He has sadly inherited properties that are heavily mortgaged," Darcy said, shaking his head. "And he holds them in fee simple." His lordship—and his expensive tastes—had absolute possession of all his estates. "There is no legal restraint to prevent him from increasing his encumbrances."

"All the better," Balfour cried, with a wink. "Chatsworth is splendid."

Darcy gave him a dark look. The idea of mortgaging any of his properties was abhorrent. "Such extravagances must be paid for."

"*You* ought to spend a little more of your—"

"I think Darcy ought to spend a little more time with his friends," interrupted Bingley, clapping a hand on his shoulder. "Let us decide on a game!" he called to the room at large.

"Yes, that should do very well," Elizabeth said. "Won't you join us, Mr Darcy?"

Without waiting for his answer, Elizabeth drew his sister to where the others were gathering to decide what to play.

"Shall we play a game of action? Or a game of intelligence?" asked Mrs Bingley.

"A social game," said Balfour. "Utterson, put down that letter and come near! Mrs Hurst, if you would not mind waking your husband?"

"Very well," said Utterson, standing grudgingly. "But no game of memory because Darcy always wins."

Darcy listened to the rain again, wondering when it would end. "You may play what you like," he said, walking to one of the windows.

"Miss Darcy, what shall we play, since your brother will not choose?" Bingley asked.

During the silence that followed, Darcy listened to the thunder and watched for lightning, judging the storm close by and wondering when it would move on.

"Well, at school, we would play the ribbon game."

"What is that?" Miss Bingley asked.

"Everyone takes hold of a ribbon, and the conductor of sport holds the ends of their ribbons whilst we form a half-circle—"

"Oh, the rule of contrary!" cried Mrs Bingley. "My sisters have played that, but with a large handkerchief."

"I think with so many of us, we shall each need a piece of ribbon," said Mrs Annesley.

Several ladies dispersed to retrieve ribbons from their workbaskets whilst Darcy tried to get a better look of the front lawn through the window.

"Mr Darcy, you cannot stop the rain, for all your glowering," Elizabeth said. He had not noticed that she had drawn near.

He sighed, knowing she was right. "I might just be arrogant and conceited enough to think that I can stand here and argue the rain into stopping," he said in a low voice.

She smiled, as he hoped she would. "No, you are not." After a pause she added, "Your manner is too gentlemanlike." She gave him a quick look and then gazed out the window, likely seeing as little as he could. His heart now resided somewhere in his throat, making it hard to breathe.

Elizabeth seemed equally incapable of speaking further. She esteemed him now, but was there any love there along with it? Could he excite genuine love in her heart?

Elizabeth gave him a more playful smile than the sweet one she gave him a moment ago. "Perhaps you can be an obstinate man, but in the case of the weather, I do not think you will win your point in the end. Come, join the game?"

He bowed, and they joined the others when he had much rather tell all of his guests to go to bed so he could have five more minutes alone at the window with Elizabeth.

Mrs Annesley and Mrs Lanyon were handing out long lengths of coloured ribbons whilst Bingley held the other ends. Elizabeth stood next to him as they collected theirs. It appeared that Bingley had nominated himself to be their conductor of sport.

"Each person being provided with a piece of ribbon holds one end of it in his or her hand," he said. "Now, form a semi-circle around me and I shall tie the ends together and hold them in my hand. When I say 'Hold fast,' let go of your end, and when I say 'Let go,' hold fast."

Darcy looked across the circle at Georgiana. "That is it?"

Georgiana shrugged, but Mrs Bingley said, "We have played at Longbourn, and whilst it is more fun to catch out one who has never played before, it is not so easy."

Utterson, who was holding his end of ribbon between his thumb and first finger with an attitude of the whole being tiresome, said, "This is a great simplicity, and you shall have no forfeits when all is said and done."

"Aye, that is just like you to think of the forfeits!" Balfour cried. "You wish we could play Le Baiser à la Capucine as a forfeit?"

"I think there are too many siblings amongst us for that," Darcy said flatly as Utterson humourlessly sputtered that was not at all what he meant.

"Hold fast!"

All but Hurst dropped their ribbons.

"With no offence to Miss Darcy, this is too simple a game," Utterson said as they gathered up their ribbons.

"Any who harbour such an opinion ought to prove it to be so," said Miss Bingley, with a simpering smile to Georgiana. Darcy hated to see his sister courted for his sake.

"Let go!" Bingley cried. None dropped their ribbon. "I shall add a challenge, then. You must all talk, and I shall at times call out 'let go' or 'hold fast.'"

"Since you are the conductor of the game, give us a topic," Elizabeth said.

"Very well. Since the ladies outnumber the men, and I have recently entered that happy state, you should talk of marriage. Let go!"

Mrs Lanyon let go, and gave an embarrassed laugh before picking her end of ribbon off the floor.

"Louisa," Elizabeth said, taking up the game, "how long have you been married and what advice do you have for Jane?"

"Three years in January. And she ought to establish separate rooms because Charles has snored since he was a child."

The room laughed, and for a while Bingley was too indignant to conduct the game.

"Ladies, what is the proper age a woman ought to marry?" Utterson asked in a grumpy tone to move things along.

"When she is one-and-twenty and needs no permission," Elizabeth said, laughing.

"I have a riddle none of you shall guess," said Hurst. "What are the two rings of marriage?"

"The wedding ring and the suffering," Darcy answered, to Hurst's dismay and to the shaking heads of Mrs Lanyon, Bingley, and Mrs Bingley. He noted that Mrs Hurst showed no opinion.

"Let go!"

Everyone held fast, and Bingley frowned. "None of you are properly distracted. Mrs Annesley, what manner of man would you wish to marry?"

"A single one."

"Caroline, what manner of man do you wish to marry?"

"A gentleman, of course, with a good fortune. A handsome and genteel man, all courtesy and good breeding." She turned to Mrs Lanyon. "What do you think?"

"I would be content with a cheerful manner and an interesting face," Mrs Lanyon finally said.

"Then you do intend to marry again?"

It was an impertinent question, even in the game, especially to one who was not a friend.

When it was clear that Mrs Lanyon would be silent, Elizabeth said to Miss Bingley, "If you ever achieve a happily married state, then I am sure that you could understand if a widow, after properly mourning her husband, may wish to marry again. Or she may keep his memory too close to her heart to allow another man into it."

"Tell us what manner of man you have in mind for Miss Darcy," Balfour said to Darcy, perhaps trying to shift attention from his own sister's distress.

"Let go!"

Balfour did, and then said, "Damn it!" before apologising to the ladies. "You were saying, Darcy?"

"I would wish for her to make a prudent choice," he said softly, with a look to Georgiana that held all the grace he could show her for her mistake at Ramsgate. "There are many considerations that are necessary."

"Hold fast!"

They all let go, and whilst they were collecting their ribbons, Mrs Hurst said, "You must have more to say about the husband you want for your sister."

"Miss Darcy will have an opinion on that as well," Mrs Annesley immediately said, and Darcy admired her for her devotion to Georgiana.

"Of course she will, and her preference will be the most important consideration," Darcy said, giving Georgiana a pointed look. Her smile reassured him that she had recovered from her disappointment at Ramsgate.

"Come now, tell us what you require of a suitor for Miss Darcy," Balfour said.

"I would consider the family and connexions of the young man—which are not the most essential in my eye," he added quickly. "His disposition and frame of mind are important." Darcy turned to Elizabeth, holding her eye and speaking pointedly. "She should consider what prospect there is of his proving kind and affectionate to her, and just and attentive to her children."

"Let go!"

Elizabeth's breath came a little fast as she smiled fondly at him, and Darcy let go of his ribbon.

"You see," Bingley said, "not so simple a contrivance!"

He had kept his passion for Elizabeth within some bounds, but when she smiled at him with such warmth and tenderness, he felt the dawning of particular desires and wishes. Although he had yet to learn for certain if her feelings for him had changed, his blood was boiling in his veins at the hope of it.

Darcy hurriedly picked up his ribbon, trying to settle his racing heart, and they played for a while longer, but no new forfeits were incurred. Hurst, Mrs Lanyon, Balfour, and himself were required to pay penance. Bingley conferred with a few of the others to decide their punishment.

"Well, Hurst, in the spirit of contradiction, you shall do the direct contrary to what everyone in the company asks of you."

They were amused for some time whilst Hurst was bid to be speechless, to not salute his wife, to sing as quietly as he could, and so on. Mrs Lanyon was punished less severely, and had only to attempt to blow out a candle as Bingley passed it back and forth in front of her lips. This feat proved more difficult than imagined, and by the end everyone was laughing.

"I hope you have chosen to award a more interesting punishment to us two forfeits," Balfour said to Bingley whilst drawing Darcy forward with him.

"Indeed? Then, Darcy's quip about siblings notwithstanding, why not Le Baiser à la Religieuse for you both?"

His company cried in amusement, but Darcy worried about his turn. Balfour seemed to have no misgivings about being the Penitent and, to his surprise, chose Georgiana to personate the Nun and Mrs Annesley to be the iron grate. Darcy watched with his lips pressed together, ready to put an end to this nonsense should his sister show the slightest wish of withdrawing.

"As master of our sport, I hope you will order this particular Penitent to only kiss the *hand* and not the Nun's cheek?" Balfour said heavily.

Bingley agreed whilst Mrs Bingley and Elizabeth brought two chairs, and Georgiana sat in one and Mrs Annesley took the other. Georgiana was pink, but she held out her hand. Mrs Annesley put her own hand up in front of it with fingers spread to represent the grate. Balfour knelt by the grate, rather than kneel directly before Georgiana, and said, "Alas, these cruel bars!"

Georgiana looked at Darcy, as though to ask permission. He gave her an encouraging nod, and she said to Balfour, "You may bestow on me a parting kiss."

At the word "kiss," Balfour, as Penitent, tried to kiss the Nun's hand whilst Mrs Annesley, performing the grate, endeavoured to baffle him by closing her fingers. Balfour kissed the bars of the grate, and Mrs Annesley tugged his ear, crying, "Take that. How dare you waste your kisses on iron!"

Everyone laughed as Balfour leant this way and that to attempt to kiss Georgiana's hand, missing and kissing Mrs Annesley's fingers instead and getting his ear pulled every time. It seemed he was not going to win the day, and the grate took pity on him, leaving her fingers open wide on purpose and ending his punishment.

"You may give one parting kiss," Georgiana said, laughing from nervousness, and turning her head away to avoid watching. Balfour leant forward and kissed her hand through Mrs Annesley's fingers, and everyone clapped.

Balfour could say things that would put a proper miss to a blush, but he had behaved gallantly towards Georgiana. He treated her like an adult, but with consideration for her diffident nature. Balfour found a way to include her, whilst kindly remembering that she was sixteen and shy.

Balfour left the chairs and came to Darcy's side. "They say a girl looks best whilst blushing," he whispered, "but I hate to see the lass suffer much or else not join the fun."

Darcy smiled his thanks, and Balfour knowingly touched his forehead in salute.

"Your turn, Darcy!" Bingley called.

Why did it have to be Kiss the Nun?

He would be made to choose again if he picked one of the married ladies, and he would not choose Mrs Annesley and have someone in his employ suffer the master's kiss even in a game. He dared not select Miss Bingley, and if he picked the woman he wanted to kiss, it would embarrass them both. Even if it was just her cheek, he did not want an audience if his lips were going to be anywhere near Elizabeth. Mrs Lanyon, widowed and not inclined to be jealous, was the safest choice.

She and Elizabeth were standing together, and he approached the widow. "Madam, would you be the N—"

"Yes, I shall be the grate," said Mrs Lanyon, linking an arm through Elizabeth's and pulling her towards the chairs. "And you were about to ask this lady to be the Nun."

What the hell do I do now?

If he corrected her, Elizabeth might assume he was reluctant to kiss her. If he cried off, everyone's mood would be ruined and he would spoil the game. He could not press Mrs Lanyon because what if she felt strongly about not being kissed? Elizabeth looked taken aback as she took her seat. She must have seen he had been approaching the widow and not her.

There was nothing for it now. He carefully knelt in front of Elizabeth whilst Mrs Lanyon, to her left, placed her hand against her cheek with fingers splayed.

"Alas, these cruel, cruel bars," he said quietly.

"They are not so narrow." He heard her take in a breath. "You may bestow on me . . . a kiss, one parting kiss."

Darcy stretched up to reach Elizabeth's pink cheek, but he was too slow, and his lips landed on Mrs Lanyon's finger. He winced when she tugged his ear with her other hand, saying, "How dare you waste your kisses on cold iron?"

"Are we not too old for such silly games?" Darcy said after he had been thwarted twice more, and had been heartily laughed at by everyone, save Elizabeth, who was very still.

"This is the point," said Utterson. "Steady, serious people must endure to engage in the ridiculous to amuse the rest of us."

"What is the matter?" asked Balfour. "Do you not want to kiss the pretty Nun?"

"I do," he said under his breath. What only remained to be seen was if Elizabeth ever wanted him to kiss her, on the lips, without an audience.

"The grate shall have compassion on the Penitent," said Mrs Lanyon, straining her fingers wide against Elizabeth's cheek.

"There, Darcy, the Penitent has been sufficiently tantalised," said Bingley. "Kiss her cheek, and your punishment is done."

Mrs Lanyon's open fingers gave him plenty of space. Darcy intended to bring his left hand to the back of Elizabeth's chair, to brace himself to extend up and kiss her, but nature overruled propriety. Instead, he rested his hand against her left cheek, gently holding her still as he kissed the other. At the last moment, Mrs Lanyon removed her hand entirely as she stepped away.

Elizabeth's eyes stayed open until his lips softly made contact with her cheek. He wondered if he lingered there too long. If he had, Elizabeth did not pull back. Darcy rose and held out a hand to help Elizabeth to rise, and the affectionate look she gave made him think that her feelings for him had undergone a material change since April.

CHAPTER NINE

After she awoke, Elizabeth heard from Carew—when she bustled in to deliver her cleaned pelisse—that last night's violent rains were heavy enough to destroy crops and wash away bridges. From her window, she could not see the garden, but she saw how the grounds were a churned mass of earth and rock, and it was strewn with branches and leaves. The sun was shining, but it looked as though it would be days before Pemberley's grounds dried.

She tried to think on what damage the rain might have done, but her thoughts returned to Darcy.

The prospect of Darcy still being in love with her was a constant source of delight. Last night, she knew he had intended to select Mrs Lanyon, but mischance had put Elizabeth in the Nun's seat. Darcy had not insisted on kissing her hand as Mr Balfour had with Miss Darcy, and Darcy hardly looked or sounded composed when he knelt before her and spoke. She would never forget the feel of Darcy's fingertips lightly touching her cheek whilst his warm lips pressed against the other.

His stature was just over six feet, and there was something stirring in the way he had knelt before her, fixing his eyes on her face. He was a handsome man, of course, but now that his manners were softened, now that he showed her more of his humorous nature, she found him still more attractive. Even his decided, commanding air was appealing to her. It was plain from his attitude last night that he was affected by the game.

There had been a sudden, intense gentleness in his eyes before Darcy kissed me.

In order to better understand her own heart, she went to speak with Jane, but she found her in a conversation about gowns with Louisa, and Elizabeth soon left them. Jane likely could not tell her anything she did not already know: that Darcy might still love her, and that Elizabeth was certain now that she loved him. She walked past the stairs near old Mr Darcy's room and entered the room that Miss Darcy had taken a liking to. She found Mrs Lanyon sketching by the fireplace.

"Were you looking for Miss Darcy?" Mrs Lanyon asked. "She was here not three quarters of an hour ago."

"I was in search of company," Elizabeth said, "and I am not disappointed in whom I found."

"I would have thought Mrs Bingley would be your first choice."

"Jane was with Louisa, and I had no interest in interrupting their talk about Caroline's wish for new gowns."

Mrs Lanyon raised an eyebrow. "I hear from the lady who waits on me that Miss Bingley's maid induced her mistress to throw aside all she wore during the last two months—for her benefit, I suspect, because Miss Bingley always appears up to date. Perhaps they were settling the point on whether this was needed or wasteful."

"I doubt Jane's and Louisa's opinions will coincide." Louisa and Caroline were in the habit of spending more than they ought. "At home, my sister sends her lady to me if we go out in the evening. Miss Darcy's maid, Carew, has assisted me at Pemberley. I cannot imagine her to be the sort to influence Miss Darcy for the sake of getting her cast-off gowns."

"That is just as well, since I think Miss Darcy might be persuaded to buy all new gowns if she had such a maid as does Miss Bingley."

"True, but Mrs Annesley would guide her against such foolishness."

That topic seemed to be exhausted, and Mrs Lanyon said, "Did you enjoy the games last evening?" She had not looked up from her sketch, but there was a pointedness in her question.

"You knew Mr Darcy was going to pick you to be the Nun to his Penitent?" Elizabeth asked. "Did you not want him to kiss you?"

"I was educated in London, like my brother. Every movement of the body in entering and quitting a room, in taking a seat and rising from it, was criticised and perfected, but I know nothing about natural sciences. I suspect we are alike, in that way." She frowned at her sketch. "We are also alike in that neither of us is naïve."

Elizabeth wondered what this had to do with anything, and politely said so.

"You might be artless," Mrs Lanyon said as she set aside her pencil, "but you are not foolish. You cannot need me to explain it to you." Elizabeth very much did, and her expression must have said so. "Mr Darcy is only waiting for some encouragement from *you*."

Elizabeth felt a rush of heat in her cheeks. Mrs Lanyon sat silently, an elegant woman who had just told her everything she hoped for whilst mortifying her exceedingly. It was no use to deny it, but she would not admit that she had soundly rejected Darcy in April.

"You mistake the situation," Elizabeth managed to say.

"Then please forgive me. I thought Mr Darcy wanted to kiss you, and that you would welcome such attentions from that quarter."

Elizabeth opened her mouth to demur, but could not find the words. Instead, she said, "We have . . . disagreed with one another in the past, and until—*if* he speaks, I cannot be secure in anything more than my *own* feelings."

"And a man would need to be secure of yours before he speaks."

Not in my experience.

Of course, if Darcy were considering proposing *again*, he would need assurances that her feelings had changed. She needed some opportunity to show him how tenderly she felt for him and give him the encouragement that Mrs Lanyon said he needed. She eagerly wanted to exchange with him those feelings and promises that Darcy's words in April had made impossible.

"I once undervalued his merits—the fault was mine—but he . . . he was not gentlemanlike—" Elizabeth could not confess all that had passed between them. "As I said, you mistake the simplicity of the matter."

"I am sorry to have embarrassed you," Mrs Lanyon said, sounding regretful. "I spoke and acted out of turn."

Elizabeth shook her head. "Not at all."

"It is hardly the behaviour to earn me any friends if I misjudged the attachment between you and Mr Darcy." Mrs Lanyon began to hurriedly pack up her pencils, looking anywhere but at her.

"You are not wrong." There *was* some manner of attachment there; it was only a matter of was it enough to overcome the past. "I ought to show Mr Darcy a stronger hint as to my wishes."

"Well, a man like Mr Darcy has inestimable worth, and you seem to know that." Elizabeth was certain Mrs Lanyon was not speaking of his fortune. "I shall say no more about it," she said firmly, still not meeting her eye, "except to add that you ought to make the most of your remaining days at Pemberley. Shall we go to breakfast?"

Although Elizabeth was not embarrassed, Mrs Lanyon seemed grateful for the distraction. They went to the breakfast parlour, where they were the last to arrive, save for Darcy.

The Hursts and Miss Bingley were settling the details of seeing Chatsworth today, and the Bingleys intended to see Haddon Hall. Mr Utterson and Mr Balfour intended to go to Buxton, but for what purpose Elizabeth had been too late to hear. Rather than take the waters, she thought it more likely the two men were in search of a way to spend more of their money and vary their society. She noticed Miss Darcy looked rather happy as the others sketched their plans.

Miss Darcy would enjoy having the house to herself. As much as she wanted to know Miss Darcy better, Elizabeth resolved to make herself scarce.

"Lizzy, should you like to come with us to Haddon?" Jane asked.

She saw Mrs Lanyon down the table, saying as little as she was known to say. Elizabeth did not want her new acquaintance to feel that she had insulted her by what she had done last night or said this morning. "I would be glad to, but might we ask Mrs Lanyon to join us?"

Jane and Bingley invited her. Mrs Lanyon demurred out of politeness, until Elizabeth added, "Please say yes, Mrs Lanyon. I would enjoy your company." She gave the widow a pointed look, and when she smiled and agreed, Elizabeth knew Mrs Lanyon understood how much she wanted her to come. There should be no awkwardness between them now.

They were nearly finished eating, but Darcy had still not appeared. "Has anyone seen Mr Darcy this morning?" she asked.

Caroline gave her a scathing look. "Why should it matter to *you*?"

Bingley looked askance at his sister. "You asked the same question an hour ago." Elizabeth supposed it was too much to hope that Caroline had thought nothing of Darcy's manner towards her since their visit to Bakewell, or the Kiss the Nun forfeit last night. "I saw him from a window leave at first light. His steward was with him," Bingley said with a sigh.

"He shall be an awful object tonight," Mr Utterson said, turning over a page of his letter.

It soon became clear that half of the group knew something that the other half did not.

"The dreadful storm last night did considerable damage," Bingley said.

"Where?" asked Mrs Lanyon.

"Everywhere," Mr Utterson said. "That is what happens to ground that is already wet when it rains for hours without intermission. I saw it all when I rode to Lambton for my post." He pointed out the window.

"I heard from Miss Darcy's lady that there was damage across the county, but is it truly that bad here?" Elizabeth asked as she rose to the window.

"Apparently, rain inundated Lambton and other lower-lying towns, as well as Darcy's properties, like never before," Bingley said. "The rain caused the Derwent to swell three feet in five minutes."

Those who had not known about the destruction joined Elizabeth at the window. Some of the beautiful oaks and Spanish chestnuts looked as though they had been torn from the earth and tossed about. The stream flooded its banks far enough to drown the land adjacent to it. The floodwater had damaged the paths as well as uprooted and washed away the plants in the garden.

"Thank goodness the house itself is not damaged," Mr Balfour said, leaving the window.

"That is the important thing," Caroline agreed.

Elizabeth was still looking at the grounds. What was not underwater was a mess of mud and debris. The constant heavy rain, falling on already waterlogged ground, must have added volumes of water to all of Pemberley's streams and ponds, and had washed away simply everything.

The house may not have flooded, but what about all of the buildings and land that Darcy owns?

"What effect will this have on the estate?" she asked Bingley, who had come to the window for another look.

He shrugged sadly. "It is too soon to know for certain. No crops, no hay, no livestock . . . then his tenants have nothing to sell and cannot pay their rent, and Darcy has no income. But let us hope it is not as bad as that."

The rest returned to their seats, and Elizabeth reflected on a landowner's responsibility to his tenants. Darcy would be saddled with the expense for every repair, and earn little from the estate this year if the damage was great. *His only income would be off his investments, but that might not be enough to pay for everything.* She felt for him, for the anxiety he must be feeling. She guiltily longed to know what at that moment was passing in his mind, and if affection for her was amongst his more pressing concerns about Pemberley.

DARCY STOOD OUTSIDE THE DRAWING ROOM DOOR, STILL DRESSED IN THE clothes he had worn all day although it was closer to supper than to dinner time. *I want to sleep. Tomorrow will not be easier.* He had not seen his sister or his company since last night, but he could not appear before them as he was: covered in mud to his knees, damp from the splashes of puddles, covered in sweat from riding all day. He had walked through muck and debris, and his gloves, boots, and hat had not been enough to prevent him from being too filthy to appear before even his closest friends.

He did not want to bother changing his clothes to appear before them and knew he would have the utmost difficulty in forcing a little cheerfulness. He was about to leave for the back staircase when the door opened and his sister looked into the hall.

"I thought I heard something as I walked the room," Georgiana said softly. "Were you going to come in?"

"No," he said. "I am too tired, and am not fit to be seen."

"How bad was the flooding? Did the Derwent—"

"Is that Darcy?" he heard Bingley call. "Tell him to come in!"

Georgiana opened the door wider, and they both went into the drawing room.

"Good evening," he said to everyone, not venturing far into the room. He certainly would not sit on any of his furniture.

There were various exclamations about where he had been, and what was the state of the land, and how could he have got so dirty.

"Have you eaten anything today, sir?" asked Mrs Annesley, looking heavily at Georgiana.

"Oh, yes," cried his sister, remembering what she might do in such a situation. "I can have something sent to your room."

He declined. "The steward and I ate in Lambton. Someone brought us . . ." Darcy sighed. Even after half the village washed away, someone thought to bring him something to eat.

"You look like you might use a drink," Balfour said, about to pour, but Darcy waved him off.

"It shall go straight to my head, and I must wake early tomorrow."

"Do you intend to join us in shooting?" Balfour asked. "Your gunroom is one to be envied, and I shall take my pick if you are not there to take the best shotgun for yourself."

Darcy said something or other about being occupied, but the gentlemen certainly knew where they might go to shoot pheasant. He looked at his hands, at the mud on his fingers even though he had worn gloves.

"Mr Darcy?" Elizabeth said. "You must be exhausted. You need not stay with us this evening."

They shared a serious look, and Darcy nodded, saying he would see them at breakfast in the morning.

"No, no, before you go, you must tell us where you have been all day," said Utterson. "You left at dawn, and you have only just returned."

"Where have I been?" he repeated quietly. He was sure he might sink under the oppression of anxiety from what he had seen. "Ten buildings in Lambton are simply destroyed by water. There are nearly thirty farms at Pemberley; not a one did not suffer some damage. Three homes"—he winced, remembering what he had seen—"three are unsalvageable and shall need to be entirely rebuilt."

"I am sorry," said Bingley gently. "I know you can have them rebuilt soon."

Darcy was uncertain if he might laugh. Bingley was so sanguine, and at such a time.

"Did a floodgate end up breaking after all?" Georgiana asked.

He shifted his feet, growing more tired but still unwilling to ruin his carpet and upholstery by sitting. "Yes. The Derwent rose rapidly . . . stone bridges were destroyed and the force of the water . . ." He crossed his arms and looked into the room, but all he saw was the muddy, collapsing devastation of what had once been someone's home. "One of my water mills was clear swept away, without leaving any remains. Trees were torn up by the roots, and whirled away like stubble. I have seen nothing like it in all my life."

"I daresay this will have pressing demands on you," Mrs Bingley said, giving him a sad look.

He had thought of this as he visited each building. "I will have demands upon me for more than a thousand pounds, and that shall only be what I must spend immediately. I may have no harvest this season, then I shall be obliged to buy corn to keep my tenants and their cattle and sheep alive."

"'Tis a great expense," Utterson said, "but your income is considerable."

"Not if they cannot pay me that income this year. If they have nothing to grow and sell, they cannot pay their rent, and they cannot keep their sheep fed this winter." The repercussions would unfold for this season, the season to come, and possibly the one after that. Darcy ran his hand over his eyes.

"If they cannot pay, then you have the right to move them out, do not you?" asked Utterson. "You can move in another family—"

"How can I evict them in such times as this?" He dropped his hand and glared. "Where shall they go, and who could move in and work this land, at this time of year, in these circumstances and yield a harvest that would pay me even half of what is owed?"

"Come now, it shall all be well," said Balfour, with the ease of a man who visited the property he would someday be responsible for once a year. "You may have to borrow. Model after your neighbour, the Duke of Devonshire. I hear the Hursts saw Chatsworth today and—"

"I will not borrow money upon interest." The thought of asking his wealthy uncle to loan him money was nearly as shameful. And Lady Catherine would say he could increase his fortune by marrying Anne. "I suppose to spend money is for now out of the question with me. I shall not run in debt."

"Be careful with that," drawled Utterson. "You have a status to maintain, after all. An unwillingness to spend will harm your reputation."

Darcy closed his eyes. *As if I can think of prestige after what I have seen today.*

"Aye, be sure to spend on parties and visiting," agreed Balfour. "It would be good for your spirits! And your tenants will be borne up by a little ale and some charity from you."

A few chimes of agreement followed Balfour's statement. *They still do not understand.* Darcy felt his patience snap and said sharply, "Instead of ale, I think they would rather have my help with the bodies."

All of the chatter stopped.

"The storm came quickly. Two women were swept away from their own door in Lambton and drowned. One was found near the place; the other body went in the river and was carried three miles off! Some families in the village had to retreat to the upper storeys, and when they came down all of their possessions were gone. I have five members of my tenants' families dead, and more unaccounted for. Some we might only recover once the water recedes."

He had spoken too bluntly, and now everyone gave him a horrified look. Georgiana was crying, Balfour and Utterson appeared mortified, and Bingley had a hand over his mouth. The ladies avoided his eye, except for Elizabeth, who had risen and taken steps towards him but stopped, looking at him with concern. He stood silent, still looking at her, with the fleeting thought of throwing his arms around her.

Darcy blinked and sighed, and ran his hands across his face again. He could not stand here and talk of general subjects after what he had seen, and would see more of in the week ahead. *And neither can I burden my company with my travails.*

"Mr Darcy," Miss Bingley said slowly, and he dropped his hands to look at her. "I am sure that none of us intended to distress you." She glanced at her sister, who was seated by her at the instrument. Mrs Hurst shrugged, not knowing what to say.

What can any of them say? Darcy solemnly protested that they had done anything to offend him, and left.

HE ROSE EARLY THE NEXT MORNING TO SURVEY THE HOME FARM AND THE gardens, and to organise the cleaning up of the grounds nearest to the house: to have the felled trees sawn and chopped if they were not too wet and to salvage what lumber they could, to repair the orchard tree limbs, to replace the glass in the greenhouse. The gardeners were at work before he joined them, but Darcy knew it would take days to clear away the remains of what had been the garden. The fences would have to be fixed before any more sheep were lost; even some stone walls had not been spared.

Now I must join my company for breakfast, and be a better host than I was last evening.

As soon as Darcy entered, he knew by the sudden silence he had been the subject of conversation. "You must allow me to apologise for my manner last evening. There was no reason to speak so bluntly. I had—"

"Darcy, say nothing about it," Balfour interrupted him. All the rest were nodding their heads.

"In fact, we have been talking about how best to help you," added Bingley.

"You need do nothing but enjoy yourselves as—"

"No, no, none of that," Bingley said. He sat beside him and added in a quiet tone, "Utterson, Balfour, and I have it all arranged. Hurst and I shall take Jane, Louisa, Caroline, and Lizzy to Doncaster today and stay in a convenient inn."

Bingley lowered his voice. "We thought you might not want guests at such a time. No," he said as Darcy shook his head, "you won't say we are not welcome, but you cannot want houseguests now. I intend to take my party towards Scarborough from Doncaster. Enfield will welcome us a few days earlier."

"So long as you write to tell him first," Darcy said. Bingley laughed. "I jest, but you need not leave."

"I know, but we were to leave on the fifteenth in any event. Besides, not all of your friends shall leave you. Balfour's party intends to remain as planned, and then we shall all meet at Scarborough later. We know you shall not wish to make pleasant conversation in the evening, but we do not want to leave you entirely alone."

Having three guests rather than nine might be easier in the days ahead. That Bingley was still so good a friend after what he had done to keep him from a woman who loved him struck Darcy with a fresh wave of guilt. "I fear you are right. I shall have much to occupy me in the coming days."

"You must promise that you will take a *little* respite from business. Balfour and even Utterson will ensure you do not run yourself ragged."

Darcy promised, and Bingley smiled. "Then it is settled. If you choose not to go to Scarborough in September, then we shall meet again on our return to Hertfordshire in October. And today, Mrs Lanyon is content to draw whilst Balfour and Utterson will go to Lambton with you to start clearing the damage."

Lambton was an estate village of Pemberley's. It was wholly within the estate, and every residence and shop, the school, the public house were his responsibility. He and his steward had decided yesterday to begin recovery efforts there, and to meet there with his tenants today.

"I cannot have my guests recovering property or chopping wood." *Or recovering bodies.*

Balfour called from his seat, "Darcy, it is decided. Utterson may not be a genius with an axe, but he shall do his best so long as he does not get a callus."

"And what about you, Balfour?" Utterson said from his side of the table, not lowering his letter. "Have you ever exerted yourself beyond buying a shiny new bauble?"

"Aye, that is a proper, gentlemanly exertion, I grant you, but I think rather that sounds more like you?" Balfour turned back to Darcy. "We went yesterday to Buxton where Utterson found nothing to his liking in what they call a jewellery shop—it is nothing to London, let me say —but we found there a pawnshop better than the one in Bakewell. This is what happens when we can find no dice game or horserace to bet on. Do not think less of him for buying some poor fool's pledge. Show the ladies your sleeve buttons, Utterson!"

"You are one to talk. You have often been so hard-pressed for money that your fine clothes might be on your back in the evening, and at the pawnshop in the morning."

Balfour's eyes darkened, but it did not last. "But not today! You are only jealous, I say."

Darcy turned to Bingley and gave him a long-suffering stare. "Must they 'help'?"

Bingley laughed. "Utterson will leave his new sleeve buttons, and Balfour will at the least do what you ask him to." He lowered his voice. "We all want to help you."

Darcy nodded his thanks, then looked down the table. He saw Elizabeth absently staring into her teacup. *If Bingley's party leaves, Elizabeth shall leave also.* He did not want to part from her with a mistaken understanding of his feelings, but everything was in too sorry a state for him to settle anything on that count.

A servant announced the Hurst and Bingley carriages. They all set aside their napkins and rose to part. Utterson and Balfour announced they would change their clothes and meet him at the stables as Georgiana came to his side.

"Shall I come to Lambton today?"

Darcy felt his chest tighten in pride and gratitude. He did not want her to see the early effects of the destruction, but he was cheered by how she wished to help Pemberley's people. "In the coming days, there will be a great deal to do in regard to charity, but not today. Reynolds and I will put you to work before long."

She agreed, kissed his cheek, and parted from his guests. Darcy made his civil goodbyes to the Hursts and the Bingleys, taking care to express to Mrs Bingley how he wished her well and hoped they would stay at Pemberley in October on their way home from Scarborough. After parting from Miss Bingley, he met Elizabeth. He wondered if she was as downcast as he felt at her leaving.

"Miss Bennet, you are always welcome at Pemberley. I—I am sorry to see you leave so soon." He had to be careful what he said; Mrs Lanyon, the Hursts, and the Bingleys were still in the room. The difficulty he felt in parting from her was very great. He wanted her to know that his feelings and wishes were the same as they were in April, but everyone was watching. "I hope . . . I hope this is not your last visit to Pemberley."

"I am exceedingly sorry that this has happened. Your mind must be oppressed with anxious sensations, and I worry for y—" She dropped her eyes. "I hope that when I see you again you shall have not so grave a countenance, and better news of Pemberley."

"You are kind, very kind to take such a concern in m—my interests at Pemberley."

Darcy wished he could give a hint that he welcomed her concern and still wanted her to be Pemberley's mistress. He hoped to leave on the best possible terms, but nothing of her own affections could be certain and they were not alone. He would have to wait until they met again under better circumstances.

She took leave from him, thanking him for his civilities, and Darcy held her hand a little tighter than he ought to have. He would have brought it to his lips, but Miss Bingley's furious glare made him not want to cause Elizabeth any difficulties.

Before he left, Mrs Lanyon asked Elizabeth to speak with her. He was not certain what they talked of on the other side of the room, but Elizabeth often looked over Mrs Lanyon's shoulder at him. Darcy sighed, and readied to meet Balfour and Utterson at the stable. He feared nothing he saw today would soothe his uneasiness about how to manage this disaster.

≈

"BUT LIZZY, I THOUGHT YOU HAD WANTED TO GO TO SCARBOROUGH?" Jane was utterly perplexed by Elizabeth's request to stay at Pemberley with Mrs Lanyon.

"Mrs Lanyon's invitation is generous," she said eagerly. "I would like to accept it and stay at Pemberley with her for the rest of the month."

Elizabeth had already accepted this invitation with pleasure. Darcy had been grave last night, and the idea of leaving Pemberley with so many feelings unsaid was counteractive to her wishes. As much as a house full of guests right now might add to his worries, she disliked the idea of leaving him alone in trying times.

As to any attentions on his side, they might resume once Darcy's mind is not preoccupied with the aftermath of the storm.

"I can well understand Mrs Lanyon—anyone—wishing for your company, but why would you remain here when you could be with us?" Jane asked. "You will see her again in Scarborough in September."

To have the renewal of her acquaintance with Darcy end so soon had been distressing. Her whole happiness seemed at stake until Mrs Lanyon drew her aside. Besides, Mrs Lanyon seemed desirous of her company now that they were more at ease with one another. Jane, whilst professing the opposite, did not need her by her elbow as she once did.

"She prevailed upon me not to quit Pemberley and to instead oblige her with my company whilst her brother and Mr Utterson remain. I know Mrs Lanyon and I could become good friends." Mrs Lanyon was not an easy person to know; there was something aloof and inexpressive about her at first, but Elizabeth had not recognised her goodness as soon as she should have. "I like her very well now that I am knowing her better."

"I was not certain you liked Mrs Lanyon, or that she had any fondness for you. Charles dear"—Jane turned to Bingley—"what say you?"

Bingley shrugged. "I will be sorry to lose Lizzy, but Mrs Lanyon and Mrs Annesley are above reproach. I cannot understand it myself, but if Lizzy wants to stay, I have nothing to say against it, and I cannot imagine that her father would, either."

Jane frowned. "But how shall she get home?"

"She will stay with Mrs Lanyon and then come north with Balfour's party when they come to Scarborough. If she wishes to join us sooner or return to Longbourn, you know that Darcy would put her in his carriage with a man to see her safely wherever she wished to go."

Jane gave her a significant look. "Is this what you want? Charles can tell Mrs Lanyon no for you."

"I want to stay at Pemberley!" Her sister's face showed her surprise. "You shall do well without me, you know. You have Charles, and I think that you have found some common ground with Louisa." She did not mention getting on with Caroline.

Jane pulled her by the hand to the other side of the parlour from Bingley. "You did not even want to enter the house last Wednesday," she whispered. "Why would you stay near to Mr Darcy after all that has passed between you?"

Elizabeth looked at Bingley, who started and pretended to investigate the drapes on the window. "I would admit Mr Darcy's attentions as readily as they were offered," she said into Jane's ear.

"You are joking!" Jane cried. She then lowered her voice. "Do you have reason to believe Mr Darcy will make his attachment public?"

"I do. We have spoken about Hunsford." Elizabeth thought back to the way Darcy kissed her cheek during the game's forfeit. "And I think he has other wishes beyond showing me civility."

"Are you abusing Mrs Lanyon's kindness to use her to stay near to Mr Darcy?"

Elizabeth shook her head. "On the contrary. I think *that* is partly the reason she asked me to stay. She sees our mutual interest and wishes to foster it as much as she wants my company." She gave her sister a pleading look.

"Very well. But you can never mock Caroline for her attentions if you put yourself in Mr Darcy's way like this."

How was it akin to cunning to stay with Mrs Lanyon to be near to Darcy when it was Mrs Lanyon's idea? Somehow, Jane did not see that there was something between her and Darcy when Mrs Lanyon had seen it almost instantly. It felt more wrong to leave Darcy alone now than to do whatever she could to stay near to him.

"The truth is, even if I did not love Darcy as much as I do"—Jane's eyes softened, and Elizabeth felt her throat close and her heart beat fast —"I care for him and his happiness, and this flood is a great worry to him. He ought to have someone near to him who cares for him, who wants to ease his worries."

Jane gave her a quick hug, whispering in her ear, "I hope that you are right about Mr Darcy, because you are apt to get your heart broken if he does not love you with the same devotion, and you shall be here all alone if it does."

CHAPTER TEN

After parting from the Bingleys and Hursts—and suffering
Caroline's jealous glares—Elizabeth had looked from a
window to see Mr Balfour and Mr Utterson riding from the house.
They had gone to Lambton to join Darcy and do what they could to
help the recovery efforts. She wondered how much help those two
might be, but she admired their willingness to aid their friend. Elizabeth then wandered the house in a restless state since Mrs Lanyon
was drawing and Miss Darcy was practising the instrument with Mrs
Annesley.

I cannot remain here idle and feeling dissatisfied.

A disquieting thoughtfulness preoccupied her as she considered
what might be happening in Lambton, and that she was doing nothing
to aid those in need. Elizabeth walked to a window again, looking over
the stable yard, and saw Darcy's steward directing a few men loading
a wagon. She was determined to give what help she could. In a few
hurried moments, she was dressed in walking clothes and in the yard.

"Mr Stevenson," she called before he drove away. "Are you going
to Lambton?"

"Yes, ma'am. Too many in the village are without the bare necessi-
ties of life, and we must give from the house what we have until we

can organise committees to get help from any neighbours who might be able to supply the immediate deficit."

He touched his hat, but Elizabeth said, "I should like to help."

Mr Stevenson shook his head. "It is no place for a lady, ma'am."

Elizabeth refrained from giving him the dark look he deserved. What did he think the women who lived in Lambton were doing? "I did not know you had so many hands to help that you do not need mine."

A cloud passed over his eyes. "Lambton is a devastating sight. Even the men are affected by what they have seen."

"I can, at the least, distribute the supplies you are bringing to free you for other duties."

"Mr Darcy would not want you to—"

"It is about three miles to Lambton, correct? Certainly within five? Do I need to walk, or may I ride in your wagon?" she asked pointedly.

Mr Stevenson pressed his lips together, but gestured to the seat next to him.

"There is substantial wreckage in Lambton, and many tenants' homes and other of Mr Darcy's properties damaged too," Mr Stevenson said after they left the stable yard. "When we get to the village, do not go down Brookside or Church Lane. The water is still ankle-deep in some places, especially near the churchyard and the river. Stay near the smithy or the Pemberley Arms."

When they entered the village, it took Elizabeth a long moment for her mind to comprehend what she was seeing. Wooden joists, fence posts, and tree limbs were strewn like spillikins. They neared the Pemberley Arms, and she saw the flood debris being piled high.

When she alighted, she saw people sorting through the wreckage. Furniture, trunks, bedding, a pianoforte, a clock; whatever was collected was laid out on the street to be claimed. Elizabeth passed by people picking through the muddy piles to find what precious items could be salvaged. They had a haunted, empty look in their eyes.

I was wholly unprepared for this.

Mr Stevenson called a few men to unload the wagon before telling her he was going to the Pemberley Arms. She stood in confusion watching the activity around her. Elizabeth saw Mr Utterson near to the smithy chopping debris with two other men doing the same. She noticed Mr Balfour moving through where household articles had been amassed together, carrying a wooden chair. Farmers were consulting their almanacs, and looking at the sky and feeling the air. They were all concerned that it would rain again tomorrow morning.

Elizabeth turned in a circle, looking at chaos and confusion in every direction. So many people connected to Pemberley were without adequate food, sufficient clothing, or shelter. Her emotions were slipping out of control, and she took a steadying breath.

I help no one by standing in the street crying to myself.

As she walked towards the inn, she overheard flood stories in all the sickening detail. This person was still missing. That family lost everything in their ground floor. This man's business was ruined. The Pemberley Arms had become a manner of committee centre. The smithy had become a gathering place to commiserate. The school, a deadhouse.

The inn's main room was filled with nearly fifty people, mostly men, and their attention was focused on Darcy. He was in front of the bar, trying to listen to one man, whilst being interrupted by everyone pressed around him. Mr Stevenson worked through the crowd and came to his side to talk into his ear. She saw Darcy lean forward to try to better hear him, but all around was a growing din.

I had better ask Mr Stevenson what he wishes me to do. There was no way, and no reason, to talk with Darcy now.

"It was already a wet season," a man said as she moved through the crowd. "What shall be done about the crops—"

"Who can think of that?" another cried. "My wife is still missing! I need men to stop chopping debris and help me to find her!"

"I have two dozen sheep drowned! How am I supposed to pay my rent if—"

The crowd jostled and swayed, and someone knocked into Elizabeth, who pushed him off of her as she reached the front, near a table at the other end of the bar from Darcy. She tried to catch Mr Stevenson's attention, but Darcy was in the way with his back to her. The steward and Darcy were in earnest conversation, and then Mr

Stevenson nodded, left a writing box on the table, and pushed back through the crowd to leave.

Now that everyone had pressed forward, there was no easy way for her to make it back through the crowd. Elizabeth noticed with alarm that someone had marked the height of the water from Monday's storm on the bar. She ran her fingers across it with a distressed sigh.

"Where shall we go if we have no family to take us in until my roof is repaired?" a new voice called.

"Shall you deduct our rent? What am I to do if my pasture is flooded?"

"The great house is not damaged, is it?" This voice was spiteful. "What worry could *he* have?"

"Mr Darcy will not leave us to manage this ourselves."

"*His* sister was not swept away in a river of water down the street!" someone else said. "He has not suffered a thing!"

"You think this is a competition for who has lost the most?"

"What about *my* home and my sheep? How shall I pay my rent?"

"How shall Mr Darcy pay for all of this? He will evict us first."

"Evict us?" another man cried. "Will we be evicted if we cannot pay?"

"What does he care so long as the great house is standing and he can go up to town whenever he likes?"

This man was shoved by another, and calls of outrage followed. *There shall be a riot!* Her stomach twisted with an awful fear. They were all grieving and afraid, and Elizabeth felt how the energy of the crowd shifted and built. It seemed to feed on itself, and the growing force needed an outlet or it was fit to burst. To her surprise, Darcy suddenly stood on a chair and climbed atop a table in front of the bar.

"Do you think I shall abandon you?" he cried.

For a moment Darcy held everyone's attention, and Elizabeth was terrified what might happen—what they might do—if he lost it.

"I can scarcely speak of the awful calamity that has befallen us," he said. "The ruins of your belongings are piled high in the street, the loss of your crops and livestock fills you with fear, and the deaths of your loved ones have broken your hearts."

Some of the rumbling stopped, but there was still an angry energy in the room.

"Are we going to rebuild? Yes. Are we going to take care of one another? Yes. Shall I make allowances on rent day for what has happened? Yes."

Elizabeth watched Darcy look over the crowd, shaking his head sadly. "You cannot think that I am going to sit in the house, idle and work-shy, when you have lost so much. Do you truly expect me to go to town?" he asked incredulously, looking at the man who had made the claim. "Is this your opinion of me?" he asked the group. "Is this the manner of landowner, the manner of *man* you think I am?"

There were a few calls to the contrary, but not enough in Elizabeth's opinion, and the crowd still pressed nearer.

"Have I not always been willing to sacrifice every private consideration and personal enjoyment for the sake of any one of you?" There were approving murmurs as people looked at one another. Elizabeth watched some nod, but many still had their arms folded and were frowning.

"Do you think your losses are not my losses?" Darcy cried, grabbing everyone's attention once more. "I can assure each and every one of you that I am as shocked and affected by what has happened, what has happened to *us*."

It struck her that Darcy was a very young man. Most in this room were ten years his senior, at least. All of his wealth and influence would be disregarded if he could not have the confidence of these frightened people. Had he ever faced such a disaster, such loss, or so madding a crowd in his life?

"We must get to work. Do not be discouraged! A year's hard work will restore the value of your properties, and I promise that none—do you hear me?—*none* shall be evicted for being unable to pay."

He took a moment to pause and let those words settle into everyone's hearts. "I cannot toss provisions into the crowd and have women and children trampled," he said in a calmer voice. "I cannot have a lawless mob roaming about, deciding for themselves what ought to be done. We must organise into committees for every task, just as we have done to clear the streets today.

"I want to hear from one person from every holding. I need to understand your most pressing needs."

The crowd began to rise again in energy and people called out, but when Darcy raised a hand, they fell quiet. "I shall feel obliged if each of you will await your turn, and come and shake my hand, one by one. I shall not leave until I have spoken to everyone. Tell me your greatest concern, and tell me what you are able to do to help your neighbour.

"Form a line, if you will, and Mr Stevenson shall keep an account of all that you ask for as you speak with me."

Mr Stevenson was still outside; through the window Elizabeth saw he was in animated conversation with another man, and he then drove away in the wagon. She saw Darcy turn and notice the same, and their eyes met. He absolutely started at the sight of her, and she saw confusion be swiftly replaced by a powerful look of entreaty.

The throng's restless energy grew as they realised the steward was gone; Darcy lost their attention. *What might happen if we do not begin directly?* It was a sickening feeling, and she was certain in that moment that it was only a fraction of what Darcy must be feeling.

Elizabeth nodded and sat at the table with all the authority she could muster and opened a notebook. No one came forward, and she opened the travelling inkwell set, carefully opened the lid, and dipped the quill in, her hand poised and her gaze steady, overlooking the crowd expectantly.

"Miss Bennet shall keep a record of all that you say, and I promise I will not leave until I have heard from everyone." Darcy climbed down from the table, stood in front of it, and waited. Slowly, the last angry sensations in the room shifted to a calmer energy, and the people formed a rough line.

She might have thought that Darcy was unaccustomed, even reluctant, to have people touch him, but here were fifty tenants, villagers, and half-gentlemen all shaking his hand, some clapping his shoulder; sometimes he grasped an upper arm in sympathy. Darcy remained in close conversation with each man, hearing his concern, his fear, his loss, and promising to do whatever he could for them.

Elizabeth dutifully wrote every name and circumstance, but she could not help but think that if she did not admire and love him before, Darcy certainly now had all the esteem and affection she had to give. He cared deeply about everyone, and he had an innate quality of leadership. She supposed it was so implicit that he rarely had to exert it.

She wondered if it came primarily from the strength of his character.

Two hours passed by the time each man had his time with the master of Pemberley and made his concerns known. When there were only a few men left waiting to speak to Darcy, Mr Stevenson returned, and Elizabeth rose to let him take her place. Darcy looked as though he was about to break away to speak to her, but she shook her head. *This is far more important.* He gave her a grateful look, and then returned his attention to the man before him.

Outside, Mr Utterson was just getting on his horse, looking as though this final effort might exhaust him completely. He appeared to be waiting for Mr Balfour, who was taking a long look at the mass of household items laid out in the street. He bent down to look at a small object, turning it over in his hand.

"Come along, Balfour!" Mr Utterson called. "I want to make it back before I fall off this horse."

"There is ever so much here," his friend said as he joined them and slowly mounted his horse, still looking at the articles on the street. Mr Utterson sighed wearily. Both men seemed affected by the day.

How could anyone not be?

"I see Darcy has put you to use as well," Mr Utterson said to Elizabeth in his dry way. "Do you regret not going to Scarborough with the others?"

"I happily put myself to use," she said, not having the patience for his acerbity today.

Mr Balfour must have noticed because he said, "That is to your credit. And I know that Hester is glad to have your company. She is a little slower to make friends than I am." He smiled. "She is smarter too, but you did not hear me confess it."

"Your secret is safe with me."

He grinned knowingly. "Well, since you are staying at Pemberley, we shall work together to bear up Darcy." Elizabeth nodded, feeling too much on that subject to speak. "I have known him since not long before his father died, and even in those bleak days after his death, I did not see Darcy look so cast down as he was today."

"You have known Mr Darcy a long time."

Mr Balfour nodded. "Aye, and I know from experience he will need friends to cheer him so he does not dwell moodily on all of his trials." He then forced a smile. "How are you getting to the house? Shall I walk with you? Utterson, did you not notice that Miss Bennet has no way back to Pemberley?"

Mr Utterson apparently did not notice, and looked impatient and only just willing to bend for the sake of politeness when he asked, "Should you like us to wait with you until Mr Stevenson is finished so he can bring you back in the wagon?"

Elizabeth firmly declined their offers to wait with her, find her a ride, or walk back with her. She was content to walk the path from Lambton alone, and use the time to pass over all she had heard today. Whilst she had not seen as much destruction as some, she had heard from the mouth of everyone affected by the disaster what pain, and what fear, struck them the deepest.

The sense of grief and woe I feel is nothing to the universal sorrow Darcy's tenants are feeling.

After she arrived at the house, she sat in her room in contemplation for a long while before Carew entered to help her dress.

"I think something simple," she said quietly when Carew opened the clothes press. "None of us shall be in the mood for finery tonight."

Normally not one to have her authority challenged, Carew nodded knowingly and went about the business of helping her out of her gown, and each capable tug grated her ring against Elizabeth's skin.

"You have a fine hoop ring." Elizabeth refrained from asking if she scraped Miss Darcy with it.

"Miss Darcy does not mind my wearing it, and neither does Mr Darcy," Carew said sharply, pulling up her sleeves and then tying the laces tightly. "They know I am not above myself."

"None of us think that." A lady's maid, after all, was a valued and senior position, and she answered only to Miss Darcy. *Unless her brother asks her to let her maid tend to his friend's sister-in-law.* "And none of them would begrudge you for wearing it."

"That may be true, but others might."

To show that she was not such a person, Elizabeth asked, "May I admire it?"

Carew was surprised, but gave a prim little smile and held out her hand. The ring had a delicate split shank and five pieces of pinkish orange coral set very high. That accounted for the light scrapes against her skin whilst Carew worked. The oval coral in the centre was larger than the ones surrounding it. "It is lovely."

"It belonged to my mother. She was a maid at Pemberley as I said, before she married. My father bought this for her, and she wore it every day until she died."

Now that she was dressed, the maid turned her by the shoulders, firmly pushed her forward, and then pressed her into a chair and set to work on her hair. It seemed that whilst Carew was caring, sentimental even, her sternness and efficiency would swiftly overrule any excessive tenderness.

"You said your father lives in the village? How is his home?"

"Hardly any water came in under the door, but his tools were in a shed and many were ruined or washed away. He is better off than many." Elizabeth remembered her saying her father was Pemberley's carpenter. "I shall go to him tomorrow and see how I might help. I suspect he will only want my company. Miss Darcy has said to take as much liberty as I please."

"It is likely to rain in the morning; I heard the farmers talking about it in Lambton. You ought to wear my wool pelisse."

"No, I only just cleaned it for you to wear, ma'am." The hairbrush tugged her head with every pull. At least the coral ring never got tangled in her hair.

"You will get it less dirty than I will." That Carew did not argue spoke to the truth of the matter. "I do not intend to go walking tomorrow, and you already agreed to borrow it. Do not force me to bring the Darcys into it," she added with a laugh.

"Very well, ma'am. For the convenience of the Darcys."

When her hair was dressed, Carew appraised her and said, even whilst wearing her typical stern look, "You will do." She curtseyed and turned to the door.

"Carew," she called, and then went to the wardrobe to take out her pelisse. "You shall need this if it is cool. Take it now, I insist. Enjoy your visit with your father, and thank you for all of your help since I have been at Pemberley."

Elizabeth saw in her large blue eyes that she felt more grateful than the quiet "Thank you" she expressed.

IT WAS TIME TO GO TO THE DINING ROOM, BUT WHEN HE HAD TO DESCEND the stairs, Darcy allowed himself to be distracted and walked into his father's room. It was really an anteroom to a larger space with an arched doorframe at both its entrance and the one into the adjoining room. It was now most often used as a quick passage to get to the stairs. He looked out the window at the gardens. His head gardener had asked him what he wanted done once the ground was cleared and they could replant.

Who could be concerned with an ornamental garden when a mountain of water and debris carried people away? And also household goods, crops, livestock; so much was lost.

He learnt exactly how much was lost as all of his tenants met with him in the Pemberley Arms, with Elizabeth neatly recording everything. He had not known Elizabeth was staying on at Pemberley until Balfour told him in the village that Mrs Lanyon had invited her to stay. As happy as he was to have her company for longer, he had been shocked to see her amidst a crowd equally ready to riot or weep.

Elizabeth is a real and loyal friend.

If he could only have a friendship with her rather than an enamoured love, he would accept that. He wanted that true attachment and constancy from a marriage of equal, and ardent, affection, but if he could not have that with Elizabeth, he would be content with her loyal friendship. He hoped that passion of the romantic order might still be had, but he could not wonder on it now, and her friendship alone was worth preserving.

He looked over the garden, but his mind passed over the food, clothing, and canvas tents to be handed out, how to organise who could stay with relatives and who had nowhere to turn, and who was missing.

The school-turned-deadhouse would have more additions; they would find more bodies when the water receded. *My tenants, the village shopkeepers, my servants' families, the lower gentry; none were spared.* If it rained tomorrow as predicted, it might take even longer to find them.

"Mr Darcy," a voice asked gently, "what are you doing here all alone?"

He turned to see Elizabeth watching him worriedly from the doorway. He wondered how long she had been there.

"Looking at the garden. The rain washed away a stretch of stone wall that stood for a hundred years"—he pointed, and she came next to him to look—"and some big trees gave way because there was so much water around the roots. There was a chestnut tree that was probably one hundred years old and an oak perhaps two hundred."

"Why do you not come downstairs? I know you are of no mind for games or conversation, but you should at least eat."

Darcy agreed and turned from the window. "Thank you for today." He gave a wry laugh. "What a holiday you have had. You have hardly seen anything of Derbyshire. Later this week, you and Mrs Lanyon ought to see Dovedale, or Chatsworth, anything other than flooded streets. I would not have thought it possible, but you shall have a poor opinion of Derbyshire if you only stay at Pemberley."

She shook her head. "Not at all. I have not travelled much, but Derbyshire is unlike any place I have seen. I need only look out a window and I can see light playing on the summits of the peaks. The extensive woods that surround this splendid house are backed with hills that form a beautiful scene." She blushed. "You need not *me* to tell you what you already know. I only meant I am not disappointed. I was glad to help you today, and I offer it again in any capacity you have need of. Do not bother saying it is not a lady's place, or your guest's place."

He saw she was in earnest and knew arguing would be useless. "I have told Reynolds to let the hospitality of the house with respect to the poor be kept up. Georgiana wants to call on all of our tenants, but she is shy and will not know what to say." Elizabeth was already nodding her agreement to go with her. "You need not return to Lambton," he added heavily.

"I do not think there shall be another near riot. You managed their fears and concerns admirably."

Darcy had not shown it, but he had felt a tenuous grasp of control over that desperate group, and he had not been certain he could hold it. He tried to deflect her praise, not wanting to think on it. "Commotions like that sort are like snowballs; they gather in strength as they roll, and I simply stood in opposition to it."

"If we continue the comparison, one must do more than merely stand in its way, otherwise you would have been bowled over. You were strong enough, and empathetic enough, to crumble and divide the snowball before it picked up speed and worsened to become an avalanche."

He still feared that managing this recovery was too much for his abilities; it was already far, far beyond his experience. "Well, let us hope that it shall not happen again and everyone is now assured their needs will be met."

"You might . . ." Elizabeth hesitated, pressing her lips together. "I think anyone in such a position as yours might be in need of a counsellor, another gentleman who would listen."

Darcy felt immutably weary, and he must have looked it because Elizabeth did not press him to reply. He gestured towards the door to hint that they might go down to dinner, but his eyes first passed slowly over the room.

"Is something else the matter?" she asked.

He looked again, from the table, the sofas, to the bookshelves, to the mantelpiece, frowning. "There is something different about my father's room, but I cannot place what it is."

To his surprise, Elizabeth looked embarrassed. "Oh, yes, that is my fault." She pointed to the miniatures. "I did not want Miss Darcy to be distressed, and took it upon myself to redecorate. It is only just turned facedown behind the others if you want to put it to rights."

It took him a moment to realise what she was talking about. Darcy looked back at her and saw she appeared to be expecting a reprimand. If nothing Elizabeth had ever done had excited his admiration, this act alone would be enough to raise her in his esteem. For a moment, he considered asking her again to marry him.

But this is hardly the time to wonder if her friendship and kindness harbours all the tenderness and passion I hope it does.

"I think it is right the way it is, facedown and out of sight," he said. "You must wonder why I had not put it away, or burned it, a long time ago."

"I suppose your father's memory, and the memory of your father's affection for Mr Wickham, was too strong. And everyone knows that you have not used this room since your father died."

"I had been used to keeping silent on Mr Wickham's want of principles," he began slowly, "in order to keep my father from knowing what would only wound him. I learnt at a young age that nothing was going to convince my father that Mr Wickham was not what he appeared to be."

"I am sorry, so sorry that I trusted and believed—"

He turned from the mantelpiece to look at her. "Don't," he said quietly. "He is a practised deceiver, and sowing discord in regard to me is his favourite pastime. Mr Wickham was always resentful of anything I did that was not in his service. And no other man has so convinced himself neglected, slighted, and ill-treated."

"And none, I am sure, has had less cause to entertain such ideas."

She fixed her eyes on him, and Darcy found he loved her even more in that moment. Elizabeth then smiled, and walked past the table. He then realised it was not the missing miniature that he had noticed. "The taperstick," he said quietly.

To his surprise, Elizabeth looked at him sharply. "You are certain there were two candlesticks? I was here a few days ago with Mr Utterson—we met near the stairs—and I thought something was different from when I was in this room with Miss Darcy and Mr Balfour. I thought there had been two, but I did not know the room well enough to be sure."

Darcy picked up the square-based silver candlestick that remained. "They matched and were on either side of the writing box because the inkstand has no taperstick mounted to it. My father would sit here to write because he had a view of the garden there"—he pointed to the window—"and could see out the doorway and watch for my mother leaving her room. He would melt the sealing wax with this one," he said, placing it back, "and the other sat just there."

"Where has the other gone? A servant?"

A servant stealing it was the simplest assumption, but it was not a common occurrence at Pemberley. "They are paid well, given liberty or a reference whenever needed. It is highly irregular, and I have assured everyone that they would be paid at Michaelmas just as always." He ran a hand over his eyes. "I must have Reynolds speak to them."

"As though you do not have enough trials," she said softly. "I suggest again that a confidant might be what you need, a gentleman who understands you and what you are facing."

What he needed was a wife with whom he could live in unbound confidence. He had wanted it before this flood, and he wanted it still in the woman who was looking at him with such concern. He wanted a wife with whom he could have a sincere friendship, in whom he could confide every thought, and who would always be honest with him.

I should not ask her such a question when my mind is oppressed with more anxious sensations.

"I think you are right, Miss Bennet. I am going to write a letter directly. Never did I need the consoling advice of a friend more than now. I shall be down in a moment."

Elizabeth said she was glad of it, and offered to tell the others he would join them shortly. Darcy opened his father's writing box, and sat in his chair, with his view of the garden and the corridor leading to the room that had once been his mother's. Pushing aside the wave of memories, he took out a sheet and sharpened a quill.

Wednesday August 12
My dear sir,

I am now set down to write to you on a subject that fills me with inexpressible concern. You have perhaps read in the papers by now that on Monday a storm unlike any I have seen threatened all of the county. The frequent flashes of lightning coming athwart the darkness and the thunder reverberating through the house had an awful effect. The Derwent rose rapidly to a surprising height, and I have more than one hundred acres of productive farmland destroyed and an estate village ravaged. We are still searching for the dead, but I fear this shall be set back because it is likely to rain again tomorrow. I feel anxiety from toil, loss, and danger, and even the expense of the campaign to recover from this disaster.

CHAPTER ELEVEN

I t was another early morning for him, but it felt better to be tired and active rather than to do nothing. Darcy rode to assess the damage of two buildings, and then visited with a few of his tenants who had not suffered as much as the others. After settling what assistance he could depend on from them, Darcy was riding back to the house when, as predicted, the skies opened.

There is another fine expanse of meadows inundated.

As he came in from the rain and changed his clothes, he wondered at the future expense of everything. He had demands on himself for more than two thousand pounds already, primarily for repairs and for those who now had no crops, and many would be unable to pay their rent. His expenses for the support of his family were manageable, but for visitors, a season in town, travelling, they would now be exceedingly high considering what all else he had to spend for the sake of Pemberley.

Darcy stayed in his apartments as a gloom settled upon his mind. He was lonely, but knew he was in no mind for conversation. Dinner last evening was a sombre affair and everyone retired early, and this morning he ate a very early breakfast alone in his room. He had seen no one since last night and knew he must make an effort to engage with his guests.

The guest he most wanted to engage with was Elizabeth. She had been so expressive in her friendship towards him last night that he considered when he might ask if her feelings for him had strengthened. Darcy looked out the window at all the rain and sighed. He should not be thinking of her sparkling vivacity of wit and humour in times like these. That entire matter of if she loved him had best be put aside for the present.

This second storm settled in for over an hour, during which time Darcy wrote letters asking his neighbours for what help they could give, and to the cabinetmaker in Buxton to be ready for work because they needed coffins quickly. It was a heavy rain, and Darcy saw that it stripped the remaining leaves from most of the trees. Half an hour after it stopped, he was on his way down the stairs to return to Lambton when Mr Stevenson found him.

"I was looking for you," he said, with an air of real regret. "Sir, the gardener has found a body in the stream."

Darcy's shoulders fell. "Where?"

"In the park, about a half of a mile from the house, along the path to Lambton."

He hoped no one connected to Pemberley had walked to the village and been caught in the storm. "Do we know who it is?" Mr Stevenson shook his head. "Maybe they washed down from farther upstream," Darcy wondered aloud. "The poor soul might be my tenant, but it is as likely he is from miles away and the body was dislodged during this morning's storm and swept downstream."

"I don't know yet, only that it's a woman. A boy found her and told the head gardener. I thought you ought to come since she is on your land. Maybe you can identify her."

That will be a gruesome task if she drowned on Monday. The bodies recovered so far had been bloated, fetid, a dreadful sight. A ten-year-old he recognised as a shepherd's boy was on the bank keeping watch; his face was white as a sheet, and Darcy sent him home before he saw any more.

He, his gardener, and his steward stood on the bank peering at what looked like a bundle of water-soaked clothes. The body was face-down half on the bank and half in the water. The feet were encased in good-quality shoes and together with the material of the pelisse seemed to indicate that the woman had been torn from a relatively wealthy home.

I have seen that purple pelisse: walking through Bakewell at the well dressing fête, descending from the Bingley's carriage, in the park at Rosings.

Darcy clamped a hand over his own mouth to stop the exclamation from escaping. The woman with brown hair facedown in the swollen stream was Elizabeth. He felt his throat close and the hot sting of tears in his eyes.

"You ought to go down and see if you know her," Mr Stevenson said quietly, still looking at the body.

Nothing could deaden the fear and shock Darcy felt as his feet refused to walk nearer.

"What is the matter, sir?"

He knew he must be absolutely pale with terror; his stomach was sick in agony. He had never before felt such horror and fright.

When he could not answer, Mr Stevenson turned to the gardener and asked, "Can you bring her up?"

"No!" Darcy cried. "Don't . . . do not touch her." He would be the one to move her; he could not allow a stranger to touch her. "I will do it."

Oh God, she must have gone walking this morning and been caught in the rain. What had happened? Did she slip on mud and fall in? Had she struck her head and then drowned? He swallowed thickly and forced himself down the slick bank. His heart turned over at the thought of the letters he must write to Bingley, and then to Mr Bennet. It would break their hearts; Mrs Bingley would be distraught.

He was now at the water's edge, and he forced his knees to bend. She should not have died here, alone.

He clenched and unclenched his fingers before touching her shoulder. He hated the indignity of her lying in the water and the mud, with strangers staring at her as though she was merely an object.

"I am so sorry, Elizabeth," he whispered.

Darcy exhaled and turned her over; long hair matted with sand and gravel fell away to reveal the agonised face of a woman, her blue eyes stared at nothing. For a moment, he wondered if the water had turned her dark eyes blue, but slowly he comprehended that he was looking at blue eyes, a rounder nose, a small prim mouth.

"Why is she wearing Elizabeth's clothes?" he said softly.

"What did you say, sir?" Mr Stevenson called.

Darcy bent his head to hide his relief, and the guilt he felt for that shameful relief. *Someone's daughter is still dead.* Just because it was not a woman he loved, a woman was still dead, her body still in the cold water. "It is Molly Carew, Mr Carew's daughter, my sister's lady."

As he wiped away the tears from the corner of his eyes, Mr Stevenson and the gardener came down with the litter and Darcy helped to place her on. The gardener was about to pull the sheet over her face when Darcy stopped his hand. "Look," he said, pointing, and Mr Stevenson leant over. "Her temple is crushed. There is blood in her hair."

"Did she slip and hit her head, and was knocked unconscious and then drowned?"

Darcy looked back to where they found her, and then farther upstream. "I cannot see where she might have struck her head near the water's edge."

They carried her back up to the path, Darcy following behind, deep in thought. *Was she dead before she fell into the stream?* "Mr Stevenson, will you send a few men to walk the path along the stream as it leads from the house to Lambton? I want them to try to find where Carew fell in or where she hit her head, since she did not hit it here."

Mr Stevenson agreed and then asked, "Shall we take her to the house, or her father's? Or to the makeshift deadhouse in Lambton? The other drowned souls did not need an inquest and a verdict, but if she hit her head . . ."

"Pemberley," he said with authority. "If her father wants her home then we shall bring her, but I am not arriving on his doorstep with his daughter's body." He could not think on a coroner's inquest now. "Miss Darcy and I—" He cleared his throat. *Georgiana will be devastated.* "We must tell him first. Can you send a man to the farm where her brother works and tell him to come home to his father?"

"Yes. Shall you go to him directly, sir?"

Darcy felt a wave of exhaustion and nausea hit him, and for a moment he thought the receding terror from standing over what he had thought was Elizabeth's corpse might make him vomit. He took a deep breath and tried to flex his numb fingers. "Soon. I must . . . I have to . . . There is something I must do first, but once it is done, Miss Darcy and I will call on poor Mr Carew."

ELIZABETH HAD HEARD FROM MANY QUARTERS THAT MISS DARCY PLAYED and sang well, and by her own admission she was fond of music, but this was the first time Elizabeth had the opportunity to listen to her without any distractions. Miss Darcy's performance, both vocal and instrumental, was infinitely superior to her own. Even if she practised as much as Lady Catherine suggested, she would never match Miss Darcy's skill and natural talent.

After she had performed two or three songs, Mrs Lanyon and Elizabeth shared an amazed look before applauding and complimenting Miss Darcy's voice and taste. Mrs Annesley encouraged her to accept their compliments with words rather than by only turning pink.

"Shall you play another?" Mrs Lanyon asked gently. "You are a true proficient."

"Yes, that was beautiful," Elizabeth added.

Miss Darcy begged to be allowed to perform for them another time. Mrs Annesley then suggested that the ladies might like to enjoy the library or use the instrument themselves whilst Miss Darcy tended to other matters. Elizabeth supposed that her companion knew that her young charge was overwhelmed and, after they were gone, she suggested so to Mrs Lanyon.

"Yes, she is shy, but age and confidence will improve that."

"It was an enjoyable way to pass a rainy morning. Should you like to keep me company whilst I write my letters?"

"If you want my company," Mrs Lanyon said cautiously, "I am happy to give it to you."

Elizabeth sensed that both of the ladies in the house wanted to be alone, one from shyness and the other from her reserved nature. She had her own desire for inwardly contemplative moments, and told Mrs Lanyon to find her later. Elizabeth, upon finding a maid at work in her own room, took her writing box to the library.

On her way, she passed a servant who wore a black armband. She suspected black would be the general dress throughout the neighbourhood. *If what Darcy said about recovering bodies is true, then almost every family has lost a friend.*

She kept these melancholy thoughts to a minimum as she wrote to her father to tell him about remaining at Pemberley and to second all of Bingley's assurances that Mrs Lanyon was a respectable woman. She cautiously wrote how pleased she was with both Pemberley and its master. However much she fixed her heart on Darcy, it would not do to be effusive with her praise.

But in case his feelings equal mine, it might help to lay the ground if I write to my father that I no longer hate the man.

One of the doors was then thrown open, and Darcy entered, slamming it behind him. His expression was almost desperate as he charged into the centre of the room and turned in a full circle.

"Miss Bennet?" he called, shattering the stillness of the library.

She had risen when he entered, and he looked absolutely pale when his eyes finally fixed on her.

It was impossible to observe the expressive singularity in his eyes and not be struck by the alarm in them. After staring at her for a moment, he marched towards her. She gave a little start of surprise and instinctively stepped back, and he stopped. Darcy raised his hands in surrender, even going so far as to take a step back himself. He had surprised her—not frightened her—but when she tried to tell him so, he would not hear her.

"I am sorry. Exceedingly sorry." His breath came in quick rasps as he looked her up and down before closing his eyes.

"What is the matter?"

"There is nothing the matter with me. Forgive me for alarming you." A shudder seemed to pass through him. He then looked around the library as though he was surprised to find himself there. "I simply had to—I am going now. It is nothing."

"It is not nothing!" He was agitated and his hands were shaking. "You are not well; sit down."

Darcy complied, but said again, "It is nothing. I cannot stay."

"Whatever is causing you to act this way is not an imaginary trouble. Please, take one moment to collect yourself before you leave. Can I get you something?"

He shook his head, then rested his elbows on his knees and pressed his palms against his eyes. What could explain his strange behaviour? She could only observe him in compassionate silence.

"I am distressed by some dreadful news," he said, finally raising his head.

She wanted to tell him she would do everything in her power to make him happy and ease any suffering he had. Darcy was staring at her intently. He had entered near to trembling, calling out her name as though he did not expect her to be in the room. "Has it anything to do with me?"

"Carew, my sister's maid, is dead." Elizabeth felt her stomach drop, and her mouth fell open. "She was found in the stream this morning after the rain stopped."

"Good God! She drowned?"

"No . . . possibly?" He seemed to be wondering what to say. "I think she hit her head, somehow, and died and only fell into the water. Or hit her head and drowned soon after? I do not know what happened yet."

Elizabeth was grieved, for she had admired Carew very much. "What a terrible accident! She spoke of visiting her father in Lambton this morning. Did she make it there?"

"I shall learn soon enough. Georgiana and I . . ." he sighed, but was beginning to look and act more like himself. "I must tell my sister, and then we will both call on Mr Carew. I have already sent for his son to come home."

His face was grim, full of pity so deep that she could see how it hurt him to think about Carew's death and the distress it would cause her family. "How dreadful for you. I am so sorry. I know she grew up on the estate, and even though she had a stern manner, she showed me how fond she was of both you and Miss Darcy."

He thanked her quietly. Of course Darcy would feel grief over the sudden death of one who had shared some of his childhood experiences and who took care of his sister. But he had entered in such a fear.

"Is there anything else?" she led.

He rose and shook his head. "I must find Georgiana." He bowed and turned to the door.

"Mr Darcy, wait." She rose and called after him. "Your pale face and impetuous manner tell me there is more to this sad story."

He came back to stand in front of her, not saying a word. He seemed to be settling some point in his own mind.

"Did you give Carew some of your clothes?"

What a strange thing for him to ask. "Oh, I let her borrow my pelisse. She had been kind to me since I arrived—in her own way— and I wanted her to have something fine to wear when she called on her father. She said Miss Darcy would give her a flower to wear in her bonnet." She smiled sadly. "I thought it sweet of her to want to look pretty for her father. I know he must have been proud of her."

"She wore your purple pelisse today."

Comprehension slowly occurred, and she fixed on him in astonishment. "She was wearing it when you found her?" He nodded. "You recognised it as mine?" she asked, disbelieving.

"You wore it almost daily in Kent, and it has been so cold and wet that you wore it here, even when we went to Bakewell. Carew has— had—light brown hair, but it was wet and appeared darker." He briefly closed his eyes, and she knew he was remembering the sight. *He thought I was dead!* "She was facedown in the water and wearing your purple pelisse. I had not seen you, nor anyone, since last evening."

What anguish had he felt when he thought she was dead? Even if Darcy had no romantic love for the woman who had refused him, he was not so heartless a man as to not be affected. She felt tears in her eyes at what he must have suffered in those moments. She brought a hand to her mouth, shaking her head.

"I did not mean to make you uneasy."

If she judged by his complexion now, no longer deathly pale, he was embarrassed. "I am not distressed for my own sake, but for *yours*. The shock must have been terrible."

He looked at her with his whole attention. "The horror of that moment . . . I was absolutely sick with horror, Elizabeth."

She was astonished to hear her name, and scarcely dared to lift her eyes to his face. *Had I not been wanting to give him encouragement?* "If our roles were reversed, and I thought you were—" Her voice broke at the thought. "I could not bear it." She felt heat in her cheeks and said no more.

What could be construed by her saying that if she had mistakenly thought Darcy was dead, she would be unable to utter a single word until she threw her arms around him to feel for herself that he was alive? *I would not mind him taking it to mean that I love him, but if his feelings are not the same it would be the worst mortification.*

"Miss Bennet," he spoke softly, "now that the shock is over, and I have assured myself that you are safe, I must go. I have to tell Georgiana, and we must tell Mr Carew without the delay of another minute."

She agreed he ought to go at once, but he took a gentle hold of her hand. "I have much to manage in the days ahead. There is something strange about Molly Carew's death, I have to organise the committees to recover and rebuild, and the needs of everyone who depends on Pemberley must come first."

"Of course, you have many responsibilities; it is a trying time. I wish I could—" She gave him an earnest look that she hoped said more than she could find the words for. "You must remember that your friends wish to help you."

Darcy gave a half-smile, her hand still in his. "Will you . . . will you speak with me soon?" He spoke low and tremulously. "Now is hardly the time, but I want to talk with you alone in the coming days."

Elizabeth's heart beat unusually high at the hope of being secure of Darcy's affections. "I will give you a private meeting whenever you ask me for one."

Now he gave a genuine smile, and his relief showed in his face. He kissed her hand eagerly, gave her a significant parting look, and was gone.

· · ·

WHEN SHE AND MRS LANYON REMOVED AFTER DINNER, ELIZABETH RAN UP to Miss Darcy. She had been too upset for company after learning about Carew, and having to share the sad news with Mr Carew. Elizabeth would have stayed with her to offer what comfort she could, but Miss Darcy was tearful and silent, and seemed on the verge of falling asleep from weariness. Mrs Annesley stayed with her, and she encouraged Elizabeth to return to the others.

"Miss Darcy's spirits are still unequal to company?" Mrs Lanyon asked when she returned.

"They are. I think she has nearly cried herself to sleep."

"Her brother must be as distressed, but he has a naturally calmer temperament, although that is no slight against Miss Darcy."

Elizabeth did not disagree about his strength of mind, but the memory of how shaken Darcy had appeared in the library contrasted sharply against how calm and cool he had appeared at the dinner table. Rather than betray her thoughts on any such subject, Elizabeth said, "Brothers and sisters often have different temperaments even though their first associations are the same. Look at Charles and Caroline, or yourself and Mr Balfour. You are reserved, whilst he—"

"Is anything but?" she interrupted with a smile.

"I was going to say talkative," Elizabeth said, laughing. "For a man born in India and who enjoys talking, I would have thought he would have stories to share about life there."

"He would rather be playful, and put everyone around him at their ease." Mrs Lanyon hesitated. "Truthfully, Lewis can scarcely remember my mother or living in India. He sees himself more as a Scot than half of each."

She looked as if she did not know what to say next. It was often uphill work to get Mrs Lanyon to speak, but Elizabeth was determined to know her better. "Northern Britain is well represented in India through the East India Company," she said conversationally.

"Yes. So many of my countrymen have been in India that my father every now and then is meeting with an acquaintance who was there, and many of them bring word of the city we once lived in."

"Was he disappointed to leave India?"

Mrs Lanyon frowned and looked away. Elizabeth thought she was going to change the subject, but she then said, "The truth is there was conflict between my father and the East India Company because he had married my mother in Islamic rites, and they feared he had embraced the religion along with the dress and customs. But also, many of the Hyderabad court could not fully accept my noble mother's mixed-race children. However, both of my parents feared the injurious consequences resulting from bringing up certain children in Britain."

Elizabeth shook her head, not understanding. "*Certain* children?"

"Neither of us has a complexion that could escape detection."

Although it was more obvious with Mrs Lanyon than with Mr Balfour, one might guess by sight that their forebears had come from somewhere far from Britain. "My dear Mrs Lanyon, I hope that the majority of people take you on your own merits."

"I am not ashamed of my affinity to my mother's race," she said plainly, "even if I choose to speak less often in company to spare myself needless confrontations with those like your sister-in-law."

"Indians are not as well represented here as Scots are there, but there are ladies from India who accompanied their husbands home, and Indians who were born here."

"I find that is so more often in London or Edinburgh," Mrs Lanyon said. "Wherever we lived, India or Scotland, our complexion would subject us to scrutiny."

"And neither side trusted the other when your father served with the East India Company? Is that why he left?"

"No, my parents were devoted to one another, and my mother did not wish to leave home. My father spent nearly twenty years in Hyderabad before we were born. He hated the climate, but loved his wife, and it was only after she died that he returned to Scotland."

"What do you remember about living in India?"

"Only a child's memories. I can remember the veranda. I correspond with my grandmother, and I think her stories mix with my memories," she added softly. "I was five when we left; Lewis was three. I remember being called Nur, named for my mother's sister. My father will sometimes slip and call me Nur at home, but Lewis has no memory of ayahs calling him Sahib Allum or me Sahib Begum."

"It is a shame you cannot share those memories with Mr Balfour."

Mrs Lanyon shrugged. "Not every experience can be shared with a sibling, especially as our interests, or business, or friends take us in opposite directions."

Elizabeth thought of how Jane had found new companionship with her husband and would find closer connexions with young married women like her. "Yes, that is the way of things."

Mrs Lanyon gave her a soft look. "Of course, brother and sister have a different relationship from the bond between sisters. I am certain you will always be dear to Mrs Bingley." Elizabeth smiled politely, thinking again of how little Jane had seen of her growing attachment to Darcy. "Perhaps when you marry, you will find an intimate and trustworthy companion in your husband."

This was said heavily, and Elizabeth blushed. Darcy would be the sort of man with whom she could talk about anything, or nothing. Before either of them could speak, Mr Balfour and Mr Utterson entered in the midst of some conversation with Darcy.

"No, I cannot spend heavily now. I must consult my means rather than my wishes," Darcy said wearily.

Mr Utterson threw himself into a chair near to Elizabeth. "Since the flood, you are a gloomy, stiff creature."

Everyone looked askance at Mr Utterson's ill-breeding.

"No, not at all," said Mrs Lanyon politely. "In fact, Mr Darcy is particularly interesting in conversation lately since he has so much to think on."

Mr Utterson gave a grimace that Elizabeth supposed was his attempt at a gracious smile. "Of course, madam. The subject of Darcy not being able to spend merely took me by surprise."

Elizabeth wondered if a woman like Mrs Lanyon, someone with her own wealth, would be a better match for Darcy. *My lack of fortune would not have mattered to him a week ago, but he is now in a situation where a marriage that brought him wealth would be to his immediate advantage.* Elizabeth took solace in remembering Darcy's words in the library from earlier today, but that did not make her less eager for his trials to be over so they could have the private conversation he promised.

~

"I SHALL BE ABLE TO MAKE BOTH ENDS MEET THIS YEAR," DARCY SAID, HIS arms folded across his chest, "but I will have a real want of money in the future." To distract the others from such further talk, Darcy asked, "How did you gentlemen spend your day?"

"Not in as trying a manner as you," Balfour said, giving a strained laugh. "It must have been wretched for you to find that woman in the stream."

From the look on Utterson's face, Darcy suspected Utterson found the subject tiresome. The subject of Carew's death had been well canvassed at dinner. When he and his sister had broken the news to Mr Carew, he learnt she had visited her father and was returning to Pemberley when she died.

When Darcy made no reply other than a quiet sigh, Utterson said, "Well, I rode early to Tissington where I had some sport with Lord Poole."

Balfour muttered an aside that sounded like "Fine sport with Poole's daughter."

Utterson turned red but said nothing. Mrs Lanyon gave her brother a scathing look and then asked him what he had done today that had him leave so early. "I went to Buxton where I played cards in the Assembly Room of the Great Hotel with any gentleman who wandered in. I am up, Utterson, so you need not tease me about needing to pawn my clothes."

"I am sorry for so often leaving you alone," Darcy said quickly before Utterson could respond.

"You have done nothing wrong by your guests," Balfour said firmly. "In fact, it is us who have not done enough by you, to try to bear you up and distract you. You cannot spend your evenings dwelling over what passed during the afternoon. Now, what shall we do in Derbyshire? I intend to force you into some amusement."

Darcy said his participation would be impossible, and his guests talked on of finding their own amusements, with Darcy offering his opinions here and there. It seemed as though none of his guests had been to Dovedale, and the hope of seeing it was talked of.

Utterson had put on a more pleasant face, and he now turned to Elizabeth. "Would you be willing to give us some music?"

Darcy was at that moment reminded of Rosings and watching Elizabeth sit with Fitzwilliam at the instrument. It was not that he had been jealous of his cousin—he knew Fitzwilliam had no romantic interest in Elizabeth—but rather that he too wanted that ease with her. As Darcy watched Utterson stand beside the instrument to turn the pages, he felt an unaccountable rush of envy.

Utterson was not tall, but he was a well-made man with sandy-coloured hair and freckles that caught a lady's attention so long as Utterson was not scowling. For all of his complaining about not having much of an allowance, he would soon be called to the bar, and Darcy suspected the Honourable James Utterson, barrister, might then receive more money from his father than as a young man spending freely in town when he ought to be studying.

There was no reason for him to turn a jealous eye on the irascible Utterson. Simply because Darcy feared his heart would be torn asunder if she refused him a second time, it did not mean she would. He could not forget how Elizabeth spoke to him in the library, how every look and word spoke to her affection for him. It was easier to think on matters of the heart rather than think about Mr Carew's devastation when he had to break to him the terrible news. The pain and grief in Mr Carew's voice and sobs surpassed anything he had ever had to witness.

"No, that is hardly enough," he heard Utterson call to Balfour and Mrs Lanyon. Utterson left the instrument to join Balfour's conversation with his sister. Darcy noticed the wry smile on Elizabeth's lips as their eyes met and she turned the page herself.

"You disagree with me?" Mrs Lanyon asked.

"Aye, he does," Balfour answered for Utterson. "He sides with me. A man in London with only five thousand a year cannot be distinguished above a tradesman!"

"And you do not even have five thousand a year yet," Utterson said in his acerbic way.

Balfour looked indignant before saying, "Aye. And you, like me, subsist on whatever money your father allows you."

Elizabeth finished her song and joined them. "What were you saying about living in London?"

"That a certain income is necessary to live there," Mrs Lanyon said.

"And Utterson and I can scarcely afford it," Balfour added, giving a rueful smile. "Thank goodness I manage to scart together enough funds for a season. Utterson's father at least pays for him to live in town, if not enough for him to enjoy it. But," he said, turning to Darcy, "that is not a concern of *yours.*"

"I will not be in town this winter," Darcy said, knowing what exclamations would follow.

"What? Not at all? But you have a house, leased for generations," Balfour cried.

"Under my present scarcity of cash, I shall find it difficult to collect the rent to answer this emergency, let alone to fund a season."

"You cannot tell me that you have no funds in reserve," said Utterson, his expression one of disbelief.

"Of course not. But complying with my engagements in town when I have a single tenant without a roof or without enough to eat is impossible. Any extra money must be spent on their well-being. I will spend my last shilling to preserve their welfare."

Utterson only shrugged but Balfour shook his head and said, "My friend, you will be missed. You have had a disaster here, but a lively winter in town will be a reward for all you will deal with this autumn. You deserve some diversions, and I daresay you will need them."

Darcy shook his head.

"You must spend *some* money on society, on travelling with your friends, on your own enjoyment."

"I will sublet the house in town." He was all out of patience, and rose to leave, pleading that he had to check on his sister. The door opened suddenly, and a footman let a harried-looking Mr Stevenson enter.

His steward gave an apologetic look to his assembled company before hurrying to his side. "I did not think it could wait, sir," he said quietly.

"No matter," Darcy said quickly. "What is it?"

He lifted a heavy object wrapped in cloth. "I sent men along the path between the house and Lambton, along the stream, to find where Molly Carew hit her head and fell in. One brought a dog, and he ran into the grass on the other side of the walk, about twenty feet from the path, near to where we found her." He spoke faster. "He kept barking, and they found this."

Mr Stevenson folded back the cloth to reveal a small silver candle-stick. Darcy narrowed his eyes, tilting his head as he took it. "It is from my father's desk." He turned it, looking at it from all sides before seeing what had so discomposed Mr Stevenson. On the bottom was a large reddish-brown smear of what could only be blood.

CHAPTER TWELVE

Holme Hall was on rising ground near the River Wye outside the village of Bakewell. Darcy looked at the south-facing entrance and had an easy view of the crenellations on the parapet and the mullioned and transomed windows. Ten years ago, it was purchased by Robert Birch when it was sold under order of Chancery to pay the debts of its previous owner. Mr Birch not only purchased a Jacobean manor, but he had sufficient wealth and influence to become the parish magistrate.

Last night, the appearance in Pemberley's drawing room of what was possibly a murder weapon had ended the evening. There had been no shrieks, no cries of disbelief. It was rather that a melancholy fell over the party, and then everyone drifted silently to their own chamber. When they were gone, Darcy had written a hasty note to Mr Birch to ask that he call for a coroner's inquest into the death of Molly Carew.

Darcy had received Mr Birch's refusal late last night, and set out immediately upon waking to persuade him that her death might not have been an accident. He was about to ring the bell when the door opened and the magistrate himself came from the house with a little girl of about ten years old. Mr Birch frowned when he recognised him, but touched his hat before saying, "Play by the trees, Harriet. Papa needs to speak to Mr Darcy before we take our walk."

He led them a little farther from the house, and then said, "I suppose you disagree and are here to rant and storm?"

"Let us hope that it does not come to that. Only a peace officer of the parish may ask for a coroner's inquest, and it must be done without delay."

"You expect me to impanel a jury, take twelve men from their own concerns—after the week we have had—just to view a drowning victim and examine you, Mr Stevenson, your gardener, and a shepherd boy?" The magistrate shook his head. "Not all deaths are investigated, Mr Darcy, not if it is an obvious accident."

"But this victim was found near a silver taperstick with blood on it, and Carew's temple bone was fractured."

Mr Birch barked a laugh. "Are you a surgeon? Maybe the body hit a rock in the stream after death."

Darcy struggled to keep his patience. "I am not, but James Mander, the coroner of the High Peak, could tell us if you let him take an inquisition of the body."

"None of the drowning victims from Monday's storm needed an inquest."

"This victim may not have drowned," Darcy cried. Mr Birch's eyes widened, and Darcy took a calming breath. "Any medical man could determine if Carew's body was submersed whilst alive, and examine the wound on her head to see if it was received during life or after death. The blow might have killed her."

"And it might not. I cannot unequivocally justify an inquest. Is that even blood on the candlestick? Was the candlestick already in the grass before she died? For all you know, Miss Carew stole your candlestick, had a seizure, dropped the candlestick, hid her head on it during a fit, and rolled into your stream."

"But the candlestick was on the other side of—"

"Mr Darcy, for every scenario you create, anyone else could create another. Besides, there is no suspect, no one heard any screams, and no woman would stand silent and allow a villain to hit her on the head."

"If her body was examined by the coroner, we could know for certain if she was wounded in a struggle."

Mr Birch shrugged. "If a coroner's inquest is held, they might bring in a verdict of accidental death, and for what? To tell us what we already know, with no one to hold responsible, and at what cost to the county?"

"I shall pay Mr Mander's fee," Darcy said. "And it is also possible the jury will return a verdict of murder."

"The county would still have to pay if a murder case is referred to the assizes in Derby. Shall you pay for that as well, after the expenses of this storm? Oh wait," Mr Birch answered his own question, "it does not matter because we have no suspect. And a parish constable, who usually deals with drunkards, fisticuffs, and petty thefts, shall never find a culprit with no evidence."

The responsibility for securing justice lay with the injured party, or their friends. If someone was accused, the next step was to appear before the magistrate and lodge a formal complaint. Local constables would then be instructed to seek out and arrest the accused and bring him or her before the court to answer the charge.

There is no one at present to accuse of the crime, and Mr Birch believes there never will be.

"Simply because there are no witnesses, no suspect *yet*, it does not mean that her death was an accident," Darcy said earnestly. "And she was wearing borrowed clothes when she died; what if she was mistaken for someone else? You must let the coroner decide if her death was an accident."

"There is no evidence to support calling an inquest," Mr Birch said firmly. "You seem to be struggling to accept this point. *I* decide whether the evidence supports an inquest, or a trial. Another woman drowned during a heavy rain. At some point before, during, or after drowning, she *might* have hit her head. None of this warrants an inquest."

"You are a Justice of the Peace, with a responsibility—"

"A responsibility to maintain public order," Mr Birch interrupted in a low voice. "We are in the midst of a crisis in this parish due to a cold, wet season, and now this disastrous storm. What riots shall we have if it is feared there is a murderer amongst us and we have no suspect?"

Darcy's thoughts flew back to the inn in Lambton and the angry crowd growing more fearful, pressing closer, getting louder. Still, he said plaintively, "Mr Birch, Justices of the Peace administer both criminal and civil justice; you must keep the peace even if there is outrage following an inquest or trial."

Mr Birch counted on his fingers. "There is no one who has acted suspiciously, no lover, no one who threatened to harm her, no one has fled the area, no witnesses who saw her after she left her father's house. What if a constable, an unpaid volunteer, decides that the shepherd boy must have killed her since he found the body? In strained times, an innocent boy could be tried and executed like that." Mr Birch gave Darcy a serious look before growling, "I *am* keeping the peace."

"You cannot fear that the entire parish would riot or act irrationally."

"I do fear it, Mr Darcy." Mr Birch looked at him with entreaty. "The community are still drying out their belongings and wondering if their landlords will evict them or what will they grow next year. The landowners are all worried about having no income this year or next, losing tenants, affording repairs, having to sell land."

"And if they fear there was a murder and we have no suspect, you are afraid that an innocent person might be accused from a wish to find someone to blame, regardless of guilt?"

Mr Birch's voice fell. "Some are burying their loved ones who drowned. What if they fear *their* loved one was murdered also? Anyone might be targeted, and they might even try to exact their own justice. A crowd could turn, and then what? I shall have to read the riot act, but does that ever convince an agitated crowd to disperse?"

Darcy knew the next step would be to arrest and punish half the parish, and call in the militia to do it. *And then how many more would be dead?* One look at Mr Birch's face made it clear that the magistrate would not yield, not when he thought he was acting for the greater good. Darcy might have said more about living with the possibility of letting a murderer go free, but Mr Birch's daughter came skipping back towards them.

"I see that there is nothing more I can say to convince you," he said, putting on a pleasant expression for the sake of the little girl, "but I feel that not calling in His Majesty's Coroner is a mistake."

"And I feel that calling one is." Mr Birch bowed, and Darcy touched his hat. "Mr Darcy"—he turned back—"until you have experienced the role of an acting Justice, you cannot conceive of the fatigue I feel," he said solemnly. "My head is full of parish rates, surveyors' accounts, vagrants, runaway husbands, assaults, petty larcenies, militia lists and substitutes, and distress warrants. The welfare of the parish is a heavy burden. Molly Carew's death could have been an accident, and we have no suspect if it was not. I shall not add to anyone's troubles without certain cause."

Mr Birch touched his hat, gave him a firm look, and then put on a smiling expression for his daughter before taking her hand and walking away.

∾

Elizabeth entered the cool wine cellar where she had been told Carew's body was kept and was surprised to see Miss Darcy standing at the foot of the table. The space was dim, but the ceiling was not very low, the floor was paved, the stone bins neatly filled with bottles and casks, and many candles had been lit. She was on the point of going away again to leave her in privacy, but Miss Darcy asked her to stay.

"I just sent away the maid keeping vigil," she said, sniffing into a handkerchief, "but I find that I would like company after all."

"Certainly," Elizabeth said quietly.

"You are always coming upon me when I am overwhelmed," Miss Darcy said, trying to smile.

"I only came to pay my respects. Carew had a solemness to her that was surprising in someone so young, but I liked her. It was clear that she was kind and caring in her way." She ventured to put an arm around Miss Darcy's shoulders and gave a tight squeeze. "I know she admired you."

Miss Darcy nodded and dried her eyes. "She was not a gentle person, not open and motherly like Mrs Annesley, but I was never in doubt that she had my best interests at heart, that she cared for my happiness."

"Of course she did. Is Carew being buried from this house?"

"No, she will be laid out at her father's. He said yesterday that he would build the coffin himself. Fitzwilliam offered to hire a cabinet-maker, to take care of everything, but Mr Carew insisted." Miss Darcy turned from the body and asked, "Do you . . . what think you of the missing candlestick?"

Her eyes were wide, and Elizabeth wondered if it was better to assuage Miss Darcy's fears or admit that she shared them. Carew's death had the appearance of an unfortunate accident, but Darcy's pale face and grim manner last evening made it clear he thought that she had suffered a hideous violence. In her opinion, the reappearance of the taperstick, near to the body and with what looked like blood on it, could not be ignored. "It might be a coincidence. I suppose we shall know if there is an inquest into her death."

The door then opened and Darcy entered, stopping short at the sight of them. Looking at his sister, he said, "I am sorry to disturb you. How are you bearing up?"

"I miss her." Miss Darcy tried to put on a brave face, but Darcy came near and took her in his arms. After a moment when Elizabeth wondered if she ought to leave the siblings alone, Miss Darcy asked, "What did Mr Birch say?"

"He said that there is no cause for an inquest, that her death was a tragic drowning."

"Oh! I am so relieved!" Miss Darcy cried. "I hate to think what fear she would have suffered—and who might have done so horrible a— oh, it is a tragedy, but I am relieved there was no crime."

Miss Darcy rested against her brother's shoulder, her whole body exuding relief, and Darcy met Elizabeth's eye over her head. One look at Darcy's face was enough to show that he did not agree. *He is not reassured at all.*

"Would you send the maid back in, Georgiana? After she has warmed up, I would like her to stay with Carew until the men take her to her father's soon."

Miss Darcy nodded and, with a parting look at what remained of her devoted maid, left the cellar. Darcy took her place and bowed his head. Elizabeth wondered if he wished to have a moment alone, but the expression that had been in his eyes when he said there would be no inquest made her stay.

When Darcy finished and turned around, she asked, "You do not agree that it was an accident, do you?"

"I do not. The magistrate said that the candlestick is not conclusive reason to call an inquest, that there are other ways to explain it, and there is no indisputable evidence that a crime took place."

"Then perhaps it was an accidental death," she said weakly.

Darcy scoffed. "Mr Birch fears upheaval in the neighbourhood if the coroner finds murder, but we have no witness and no suspect to accuse. He wants the parish to take it as a drowning like the others from the first storm to avoid a riot or a scapegoat being sent to the gallows." He gave her an earnest look. "You saw how frayed everyone's nerves are when you took notes at the Pemberley Arms, but how can that justify letting a potential crime be ignored?"

She ached to have something useful to tell him, but there was nothing.

He looked at Carew. "I fear someone struck her, and she rolled into the water and drowned, or she was struck dead as soon as the base of that taperstick touched her."

"There is no proof," she said gently, "and the magistrate has put an end to the matter."

"There might be proof if there was an inquest," he muttered. In a thoughtful voice, and still looking at the body, he said, "With no inquest to see if she has water in her lungs, let alone if she was bruised from a struggle or if she was alive when she hit her head, we will never know."

Elizabeth thought for a moment, and came nearer to the body, looking at the hands folded across the chest. "Have you ever seen women quarrelling over a man in the village square, or a woman defending herself from her ne'er-do-well husband?"

He gave her a confused look. "What?"

"Hair is pulled, faces are scratched, shins are kicked. Carew's clothes do not appear dishevelled. Look at her hands," she said, pointing. "They are not scratched, and her nails are not broken."

Darcy nodded slowly. "She would not stand there and let someone hit her." He sighed heavily. "I had wondered if someone mistook her for you . . . Well, perhaps she was not attacked after all and I am worried for nothing." It was as though he wanted to convince himself the magistrate was right, and she did not want to take that hope from him.

"It is possible it was an accident," she said, looking back at poor Carew. She heard Darcy moving away as she looked at the folded hands. "Darcy, wait!"

Elizabeth realised her mistake after the name passed her lips. That he was surprised was evident, and she waited for the expected, the deserved polite correction to come. He came to her side, still not asking her to not address him so informally. She was about to apologise when he asked, "What is it?"

This brought her attention back to where it belonged. "Her ring is missing."

"Perhaps she took it off that day."

"No, absolutely not," she cried. "Carew dressed finely to visit her father; he was proud of her. She would often borrow a flower from your sister to put in her hat when she went to see him. I loaned her my pelisse to make the call." Her voice rose and she spoke faster. "She wore that coral ring every day—it was her mother's—and it scraped my skin whenever she fastened a tie or pulled down a sleeve. Miss Darcy would have noticed the same. It is missing!"

He looked pensive and began to pace. "If it was stolen after she was dead . . ." He shook his head in disgust at the thought. "She was not wearing gloves when we pulled her out, but would normally. Did someone take them off? How would anyone have seen the ring beneath her gloves?"

"If the gloves got wet whilst walking to Lambton and had not dried before it was time to return to Pemberley, she would have put them in her reticule. She was only walking home. Someone might have seen the ring on her finger and . . ." It was too horrible to think on.

"What did it look like? Was it expensive?"

"No, its value was more sentimental than monetary. It had five pieces of coral that sat very high in a thin gold band."

"That makes no sense," he said, frowning. "Who would steal a silver candlestick, kill someone with it, then throw away all of that silver just to steal a few ounces of gold and coral?"

"It is worse than that," Elizabeth whispered.

He gave her a concerned look. "I agree that it is sickeningly awful, but what do you mean?"

She felt her heart beating faster. "I walked that path from the village, and there is no place near the stream to hide to take someone unaware. She would have seen this person, possibly walked past him. If they were that near to one another, out in the open, he would have known it was Carew and not me. She has no wounds from defending herself. Darcy, Carew might have known her murderer, and she had no reason to be afraid of him."

THERE WAS A PECULIAR, DREAMLIKE QUALITY TO HAVING TO MEET DARCY'S guests across the breakfast table. Elizabeth struggled to smile as she buttered her toast and pretended to listen to Miss Darcy and Mrs Annesley. Not an hour ago she had been standing over a woman's body and thinking about who killed her, and now she had to make polite conversation and choke down toast and chocolate. Darcy, she saw, was not even attempting to be engaged as his coffee cup sat untouched and he read his letters and looked at no one.

"Darcy," Mr Balfour called, "you left us early again this morning. Utterson and I went back to your village and sorted through debris." He heaved a great sigh, pretending as though he had been terribly imposed upon. "Utterson had to get his hands dirty, and you were not even there to see us being benevolent. Although I think Utterson only went to send his post."

Darcy gave them a small smile that did not reach his eyes. "Forgive me for neglecting you, and thank you for helping. I was surveying land that was flooded on Monday, and then had to ride to Bakewell." Rather than wait for a reply, Darcy looked back at his post. Elizabeth watched his jaw tighten as he set one down and opened another.

Mr Balfour seemed to realise his friend did not want to speak, but Mr Utterson did not. "I suppose you spoke with a magistrate about . . . that matter."

All conversation stopped, and Elizabeth watched Darcy slowly set down his letter. In the silence that followed, Mr Balfour looked round the table and then said, "Not in front of the ladies, Utterson. Think of Miss Darcy. Sometimes I wonder at your good sense."

Mr Utterson glared at Mr Balfour and then, with a little bow to Miss Darcy, noisily picked up his newspaper and hid behind it.

"You may as well know, seeing as my sister already does," Darcy began. "The magistrate sees no cause for an inquest into what he is certain was an accidental drowning. The circumstances surrounding the missing candlestick are unrelated, or at least not certainly related, according to Mr Birch."

"That is reassuring," cried Mr Balfour. "You seemed to be of another mind last night."

Darcy hesitated before answering. "My opinion does not matter. As far as the Justice of the Peace is concerned, the matter of her death is closed."

"Quite right," Mr Utterson said, lowering his newspaper. "It is not for every gentleman to go round deciding for himself what ought to be investigated."

"You would have more to occupy you as a prosecutor if that were true," Mr Balfour said, laughing. "Think of the money you would earn if everyone decided for themselves what was brought to trial."

Mr Utterson did not notice his friend's humour. "One must trust the process, trust in law and order. The magistrate sees no evidence of such an atrocity. Therefore"—he gave Mr Balfour a heavy look—"there is no cause for an inquest."

"Oh well, then, be rational when I wanted to amuse Darcy by being playful." Mr Balfour shrugged and took a long drink of his coffee.

"That must be a consolation, Miss Darcy, certainly, to have that fear put to rest," Mrs Lanyon said after everyone had shifted in their seat, taken a sip from a cup, or pushed their food around. "Small consolation though it may be, your dear maid was not the victim of a crime, only a tragic accident." Miss Darcy nodded her agreement.

"It still does not explain how that candlestick got outside," Mrs Annesley said quietly.

"I am sure none of the servants took it," Miss Darcy said quickly. "Reynolds spoke to all of them, and no one came forward, not even with a suspicion."

"I suppose then you think one of your guests' servants did," said Mr Balfour, with a teasing smile. However, rather than meeting him in his humour, Miss Darcy took him at his word and stammered that she would never presume such a thing about her friends' servants.

"Vagrants, I suppose," Mrs Lanyon said, nodding to herself. "Someone wandered into the house and stole it, and then, for whatever reason, threw it aside. Perhaps he saw someone approaching, and he did not wish to be caught with it."

The others nodded and murmured their ready agreement. *A vagrant trespassing, stealing it, and then tossing it into the grass does not account for the blood on it.* Elizabeth noticed that Darcy did not contribute to the discussion. Everyone else was trying to convince themselves not only that a murder could not have happened, but that not even the theft of one candlestick could have been done by anyone they knew.

She thought about where everyone was yesterday when Carew died. Mrs Lanyon had been with her and Mrs Annesley listening to Miss Darcy play. Elizabeth would swear that none of the ladies had left the house that morning. Darcy had been examining tenants' homes and then was in the house whilst it rained. Mr Balfour said he had gone to Buxton and played cards, and Mr Utterson was shooting in Tissington at his friend's estate, but she had not actually seen any of the men that morning.

She had seen the ladies herself, and it could not have been Darcy. Not only could she not believe it of him, but his terror when she saw him in the library was too genuine. That left Mr Utterson or Mr Balfour —who lied about where they were—unless it was a servant or a vagrant. A cold shudder rippled down her spine. She did not want to think that anyone around the table was capable of such a crime.

I am no different from the others, trying to tell myself whatever I must so as to not face that someone has been murdered.

"What are you glowering at now, my dear Darcy?" Mr Balfour asked. "You need a respite from business or you shall go mad. Please, set the letters aside for a moment and talk with us."

He did, although Darcy kept the scowl on his face. "You cannot want me to talk about how the second storm, so soon after Monday's and with the ground already so wet, dislodged coffins from Lambton's graveyard and that half a dozen additional bodies will now have to be identified and reinterred." Everyone around the table drew back. Darcy pushed one letter aside and picked up another. "We must construct a temporary bridge over the Derwent." This letter was dropped and he picked up another. "And apparently there was looting in Lambton both Wednesday and Thursday evening."

"Looting?" Mrs Annesley cried.

Darcy's expression was severe. "Deserted residences and damaged shops were entered, and articles not destroyed by the flood were taken by some . . . some marauders," he said, his mouth twisting in distaste.

"I hardly see how," said Mr Balfour. "Utterson and I have twice been in the village, and the items we recovered are too large for someone to steal undetected."

"That is true," Elizabeth said. "When I was there on Wednesday, most of the items in the street were things like baby cradles, broken sofas, a pianoforte."

"The account is that smaller items discovered later are now missing." Darcy looked back at the letter and frowned.

Those around the table looked at one another, wondering what they might say. Elizabeth suspected Darcy would prefer it if everyone left him alone, but Mr Balfour said, "You seem incredibly angry over a few missing trifles."

"It is not trifling!" Darcy cried, looking up. "This plundering, it shames me. I had not thought my tenants and villagers capable of such an outrage against their own neighbours. They seemed in better spirits since I spoke with them all on Wednesday, but clearly I had not moved them nor encouraged them as much as I had assumed."

Mr Balfour waved his hand. "One or two rotten apples, is all. They shall not infect all their neighbours. You do not have bands of marauders roaming Pemberley's land."

Darcy gave a pained smile, as though knowing there were not many looters was no consolation for only having a few. "There is unaccountable stupidity in these looters, however many there are."

"How do you mean?" Mr Utterson asked. "A few are taking advantage of a wretched situation. Although it is a crime, I do not think them stupid for thinking of it."

"Because they must know that I will find them," Darcy said in a low, firm voice. "I will find them, and I will show them no quarter."

"That does not sound like your usual generous manner," Elizabeth said.

"If they were stealing food, clothing, I would not feel this way," Darcy said quickly. "They are not desperate, but selfish. They are stealing silverware, coin purses, jewel—"

He stopped, and shared an intense, knowing look with her. Elizabeth felt the air drain from her lungs. Valuables were being stolen in the village, silver had been taken from the house, and someone had stolen Carew's ring from her body. What if it was the same person or persons?

"You were saying, Darcy?" Mr Utterson led.

Darcy looked a little pale as he continued his thought. "Their actions are actions of cruelty against those who have lost so much, their own friends and neighbours. I can hardly believe anyone would act so low." He looked at her again, both of them comprehending that someone connected to Pemberley might be capable of killing. "And this looter or looters shall be better off if *I* find them before the villagers do, because they might demand revenge rather than justice."

"Organising a committee to keep watch overnight until everyone is resettled may deter more looting," Elizabeth said.

"You are not going to send Utterson and me to take first watch, are you?" Mr Balfour drawled with a teasing smile. "Utterson would fall asleep within an hour, and, in truth, I am not a good shot. If you ever allowed yourself to stop working and went shooting with us, you would know that for yourself."

Elizabeth watched as the anxious and furious Pemberley landlord changed his demeanour, and all the dignity and ease she had seen from him with his guests returned. Darcy was once again the charming

169

host of a group of friends, not one managing a heinous situation. He gave a friendly, complacent smile to everyone.

"You have been kind to remain with me and my sister at such a time. My trials are no excuse to speak about such business in company, or ignore you for days. I promise to say as little as possible about the state of affairs at Pemberley, and you are all to silence me on the subject should I forget and introduce it myself."

Everyone murmured expressions of their friendship and their agreement, including Elizabeth, but she did not think it wise. Refusing to talk about the storm, the damage, the loss, and now the death of Carew might do Darcy harm. This forced complacency for the sake of his friends could not be maintained for long.

Elizabeth could not suppose that Darcy would mention again what they had spoken of earlier. He seemed determined to keep the matter of Carew's death from his guests. *If I was not his friend's sister-in-law but rather his betrothed or his wife, he might confide his fears and anxieties.*

Did he have any idea how much she had fixed her heart on him still loving her? She had thought it possible yesterday, when he had charged into the library to find her, still shaking with fear that she had died, that Darcy might have then asked her again to marry him. But what a mode of attachment would there be if it was the murder of his servant that spurred him to speak? It would be unlike him to be dying to kiss her whilst a murder victim lay in his house, whilst people under his care were suffering.

Whilst she wondered what could she do to engage his attentions at so trying a time, and whether she even should, the door to the breakfast room opened. Looking as though he had just alighted his horse, Colonel Fitzwilliam strode into the room.

CHAPTER THIRTEEN

Darcy's forced composure and cheerfulness for the sake of his guests' feelings had been near to the breaking point when his cousin suddenly appeared in his breakfast room, coming right up to his side of the table saying, "Darcy, how are you?"

He rose, astounded. "How d'ye do, Fitzwilliam?"

His cousin gripped his hand, concealing in that handshake his friendship to such a degree that it might have convinced his guests of their indifference. Darcy knew, however, that it held all the closeness that would have led either cousin to do anything for the good of the other.

"I did not expect you to come all this way when I—" Darcy narrowed his eyes. "But I only wrote to you Wednesday evening! There is no way you could have received my letter, let alone come here by Friday."

Fitzwilliam gave him a surprised look. "I read of the storms and floods in Derbyshire in Tuesday evening's newspapers. They said the area near Bakewell and Matlock were underwater and that the Derwent rose three feet. I left London first thing Wednesday morning to see of what use I might be, long before you ever put pen to paper."

Proof of his cousin's genuine attachment moved him, and Darcy turned away to hide a grateful smile. He quickly gestured to his friends, saying, "You know everyone here, of course."

Fitzwilliam had by this time kissed Georgiana's cheek and greeted Balfour and Utterson.

"I am glad you are here, Fitzwilliam," Balfour added. "I need another cheerful friend to help me force Darcy into taking a respite from his concerns now and then."

"Have you had any luck so far?" his cousin asked kindly.

"Not at all, but perhaps together we can influence him. I worry for his peace of mind."

Darcy heard Fitzwilliam give an audible swallow before addressing Balfour's sister. "Mrs Lanyon, always a pleasure to see you." Mrs Lanyon bowed her head. He then turned to Elizabeth with a bemused smile. "And I trust you will not misunderstand me when I ask how *you* came to be here."

"My friends abandoned me here to go to Scarborough without me." She gave a little laugh. "In truth, I chose to remain in Mrs Lanyon's care until she and her brother see fit to return me to them."

Fitzwilliam gave Mrs Lanyon a smile that she did not see since she was staring into her lap. "You could not be left with a better companion than Mrs Lanyon."

Balfour then said, "Miss Bennet has kindly glossed over how she would rather spend her time with Hester instead of with Bingley's haughty sisters."

"Miss Bennet's good manners are to her credit," he said, "and I agree that anyone of sense would prefer Mrs Lanyon's company to Miss Bingley's or Mrs Hurst's, but if you tell Bingley I said that I shall deny it." Everyone laughed good-naturedly. "How came you to be travelling with Bingley's family, Miss Bennet?"

"I am now *in* Bingley's family; in fact, I live with them. My eldest sister resumed her acquaintance with Bingley this spring, and they married this summer. We all travelled north together, and I will reunite with them when Mrs Lanyon, Mr Balfour, and Mr Utterson go to Scarborough in September. For the present, I have the pleasure of Mrs Lanyon's company and the chance to further my acquaintance with her and Miss Darcy."

"Did you say that Bingley resumed an earlier acquaintance with your sister?" Fitzwilliam asked.

Elizabeth nodded, but her attention was gained by Mrs Lanyon who asked to hear all about her sister's romance. Georgiana, under Mrs Annesley's prompting, brought Fitzwilliam a plate and encouraged him to sit. As Fitzwilliam took his seat and other conversations began, his cousin lowered his voice and leant towards Darcy. "Was her sister the woman you had strong objections to last winter?"

The look on his own face must have been answer enough. Fitzwilliam's eyes widened, and he whispered, "I think I accidentally told her about your efforts to separate them."

There was another reason for Elizabeth to be furious with me during my proposal in April. Of course, it would have ended about the same even if he had not nearly ruined her sister's happiness.

"I confessed to Bingley after we left Kent. He has forgiven me," Darcy murmured, "and so has Miss Bennet."

"There must be a story there," Fitzwilliam said, quietly laughing.

"I have plenty to tell you when we are alone," he said. Bingley's marriage was the least important thing he had to tell Fitzwilliam. Perhaps he could help him make sense of the missing candlestick and the death of Molly Carew. *I hardly know what to make of it, and my mind revolts at the idea that anyone in this house is capable of murder.*

Soon, Mrs Lanyon set aside her napkin and stood. "Miss Darcy, did you not say that you wished to ride before it grew late? Are you and Mrs Annesley ready to leave?"

Fitzwilliam opened his mouth, but Mrs Lanyon was not done. "I suspect Colonel Fitzwilliam shall be too tired to join us, since he has travelled so far today." Darcy looked at his cousin to see how he bore being dismissed, and he thought that his polite nod hid disappointment. "Another time," she added, linking an arm through Georgiana's. "It shall be just us ladies today."

"Then what about Miss Bennet?" Georgiana asked. "She is not a horsewoman, you know."

Mrs Lanyon looked embarrassed by her misstep, but Elizabeth did not look as though she felt slighted. "I am perfectly capable of finding my own amusements. You must enjoy yourselves whilst the weather is fair. I am happy to walk the park."

"I think," Darcy said, and the ladies all turned to look at him, "that until the looting in Lambton is certain to be stopped, none of you ought to go far from the house alone."

He felt his cousin's sharp attention, but Mrs Lanyon and Georgiana agreed as they left. Elizabeth turned pale before his eyes. She alone understood there might be more to fear than her jewellery being taken. Whilst it was not likely Carew had been murdered for appearing like Elizabeth, there was still reason for caution.

Is she frightened to stay at Pemberley? Darcy wondered if he had been wrong to talk with her so plainly about his thoughts on Carew's death. Her observations about Carew's hands and her ring were astute, but he would rather not distress her by talking over the matter with her again.

"I promise to stay near the house," she said.

"Perhaps, Miss Bennet, you would permit me to join you?" Utterson asked, with more pleasantness than he typically demonstrated. "I am willing to be of use and escort you anywhere you wish to walk."

"Certainly," she said brightly, "thank you."

"I shall go along too," Balfour added, "since Darcy said he did not need further help today. Besides, I cannot go to Buxton to gamble away my fortune *every* day."

"What fortune?" Utterson drawled. "As far as I know, your father is still alive and well."

"Aye, as is yours, but at least on my father's death, I expect an *increase* in fortune." Utterson looked away.

Elizabeth gave them a long-suffering glance before laughing. "So long as your quarrelling over fortunes and inheritance are left in the house, you may join me. Let me run upstairs to change my shoes."

They all rose as she left, with Utterson, nearest to the door, opening it for her. She smiled her thanks as she passed, and he returned her gesture. It was odd to see an open smile on Utterson's face. He often looked upon everyone with impatience.

But who could not be charmed by Elizabeth's good nature and friendly manner?

"Utterson, do you admire Miss Bennet?" The jealousy Darcy had begun to feel on Wednesday, that had been building whenever he saw Utterson and Elizabeth in conversation, overrode his good judgment, and he immediately wished the question unspoken.

Utterson looked at him askance. "Why do you ask?"

"Because she is a pretty, sprightly woman," Balfour answered for him.

"She is good company," Utterson said with a shrug. "And I would never single out your or Balfour's sister."

"Quite right," Darcy and Balfour muttered. Darcy noticed Fitzwilliam pointedly avoided looking at Balfour.

"Then," Darcy said after a pause, "then you do admire her?"

Utterson wrinkled his nose in distaste. "She is too poor, and rather all in one straight line from head to foot for my liking."

Darcy was unsure how to respond because to argue against these criticisms would show his own feelings. He felt half about to strike Utterson, and half ready to thank him for his reassurance. It ought to make him happy to hear that Utterson could not admire her, but as far as he was concerned, Elizabeth was the handsomest woman of his acquaintance.

"I made *my* situation clear to her our first evening at Pemberley," Balfour said, to Darcy's surprise. "I must marry with attention to money, like most of us. Miss Bennet seems sensible; she would not expect a proposal because of a conversation or a walk."

"I think," said Fitzwilliam slowly, "that any man in this room could afford to marry wherever they liked if they better managed their expenses."

Balfour laughed. "Miss Bennet *is* pretty, but not worth the effort in my own case. I prefer to spend and act as I have always done."

"Which is spending a lot and acting very little," said Utterson, smirking.

"And you are right there alongside me, my dear Utterson."

"You will sink into unmanly sloth if you are not careful, Balfour," Darcy said, now in a lighter mood.

"Oh, nae, I have a desire to prove myself," Balfour said in mock seriousness.

"A desire to prove that you can spend as freely as you like?"

"And that desire is little restrained by prudence," Utterson added wryly before Balfour could speak.

Elizabeth's return spared them from further banter, or a sharp retort from Balfour. As lively and amiable as he was, Balfour had no talent or inclination for serious study, public life, or the responsibilities of a great landowner. Utterson was no better, and he lacked even the amiable nature. Balfour and Utterson both had great inclination for expense and none for profession. The question if either of them were capable of theft or violence pressed uncomfortably, painfully, on Darcy's mind, and he pushed it away.

As the other men rose to leave with Elizabeth, she said, giving him a tender look, "I suppose you have too much to do today, with organising watches and rebuilding bridges, to walk with me?"

She knew his answer even as she asked the question, but as she stood by the door, giving him a hopeful smile and looking into his eyes, Darcy was certain that Utterson was a fool. Elizabeth had more perfection of form, of expression, of intelligence than he had ever seen before. He was certain he saw the same longing in her expression that was at this moment cutting his heart to pieces.

"I am exceedingly sorry," he said softly, "that my responsibilities must keep me from your company."

"Do you need us?" Balfour asked, surprised. "I am not certain if I would be a good watchman, but I can help in the village again."

Utterson had been walking to the door, but upon hearing this, he turned back and gave a little bow.

Darcy shook his head. "There are enough men in the village to take turns keeping watch for a few days. I shall take my own turn tonight or perhaps tomorrow. I insist that your time at Pemberley is your own from now on."

"If you truly have no need for us," Balfour said in a questioning way, and Darcy iterated that he did not, "and since Fitzwilliam shall be here in the evening to draw you out"—he turned to his friend—"Utterson, shall we go to Tissington to visit Lord Poole after we walk with Miss Bennet? My travelling coach ought to be shown off."

Utterson agreed quickly. "It is only fifteen miles, and Poole is always eager for company."

"Is the Honourable Miss Newcomen equally eager for company?" Balfour asked, with a sly smile. Utterson threw him a dark look, and Darcy was certain it was only Elizabeth's blush that ended a more ribald line of discussion. "We might go this afternoon and shoot there tomorrow morning." He turned to Darcy. "We could return on Sunday in time for dinner?"

Darcy nodded. "As you like."

He felt an ache of loneliness closing in on seeing Elizabeth go. She cast him a lingering look as she left, and the hope of commanding her attention for five minutes struck him before the guilt that quickly followed. *How can I think of securing a lovely woman when death, destruction, and possibly murder have happened to those under my protection?*

"I suppose I was lucky you came home to eat," Fitzwilliam said, jolting into his thoughts. "Otherwise, I might not have seen you today." He gave him a serious look. "You look worn down by all you must do in the wake of this storm. The expense, the anxiety of it, the cares of the people who live here, it all must be very great."

Darcy shifted his weight and looked away. "No, it is not so bad as that." He rose quickly. "I must set up a watch in the village to deter looters, and then I must organise the burning and clearing of the rest of the debris, and then meet with my steward about how best to pay for . . . for simply everything." He gave his cousin a smile. "I shall see you before I take first watch in Lambton, though. The house is yours, of course. I shall return—"

"Stop, stop, Darcy," his cousin said, rising and throwing aside his napkin. "Let me organise the men into shifts to guard the village. I am not in the army for nothing. You can take care of the rest."

"There is nothing for you to do that I cannot do myself. All I ask of you is to keep the ladies company tonight whilst I am keeping watch— no great trial for you." Darcy suspected Mrs Lanyon would be the recipient of most of his cousin's good will and friendliness.

Fitzwilliam gave him a look as though he were stupid. "Do you think I came here to play cards and drink your claret? Stop acting as though I was some noble guest you have to impress!"

Darcy quietly apologised, and his cousin's angry glare softened. Fitzwilliam clapped a hand onto his shoulder. "*I* am going to set up a night watch in the village whilst you meet with your steward and see to whatever else has to be done today. And I doubt that you will be needed to keep watch yourself." He only let go of his shoulder when Darcy agreed. "Besides, if you had your way, you would go to bed at candlelight. I suspect you would fall asleep and whatever that is left of value in Lambton would be taken under your watch."

"Thank you," he said, meaning it more than he could say with two simple words.

"What has happened here, my dear Darcy?" Fitzwilliam asked quietly.

Darcy threw up his hands. "Only a season of wet, cold weather that nearly ruined every crop before a storm on Monday finished the job. I have hundreds of people affected who are afraid they will be evicted or will starve and who doubt I can afford to repair their homes and shops, and I share the same fears. Scarcely an hour passes in which an application of some kind or another does not arrive, and . . . and I wonder how I shall manage it all."

His cousin crossed his arms and gave him a searching look. "You may be the sort to hide away every concern you feel—hell, maybe *every*thing you feel—but you cannot deceive someone who truly knows you. I am trying to decide if you look haunted or are merely exhausted."

Darcy closed his eyes and saw Carew's body in the water.

"I have much to tell you, but it shall have to wait. There is more to this storm than the loss of crops and most of my income. Now there is looting, a theft of silver from the house, and, although there is no conclusive proof or a witness, I fear a murder as well." Fitzwilliam's face drained of colour. "I do not know what is happening, but I think the plot thickens fast."

~

DINNER THAT EVENING WAS A QUIET AFFAIR OF MOSTLY FAMILY TOPICS THAT Elizabeth had little to contribute to, and Mrs Lanyon left early, claiming a headache. Elizabeth spent the hour apart from the men coaxing Miss Darcy to talk with her, and had admirable success, and when the gentlemen came in, they all played cards. After another hour, Elizabeth went upstairs to check on Mrs Lanyon. Rather than finding her abed, she was reading.

"Forgive me for intruding," Elizabeth said, a little embarrassed. "I thought you were feeling unwell and might need something."

Mrs Lanyon turned pink; she set aside her book and invited her to sit. "I am better now. I stayed away because I thought the Darcy family might want an evening to themselves since Colonel Fitzwilliam is here."

Elizabeth thought that this bore little resemblance to the colonel's wishes, since he looked crushed when Mrs Lanyon left the table. "Then you might have let me into your plan," she said, smiling. "If they want a family evening, I would only ruin their peace. May I stay for a while to let them enjoy their time alone?"

"Of course. How was your walk with Lewis and Mr Utterson?"

It had been pleasant more for the scenery than the company. The stream's course ran through the secluded dale that surrounded Pemberley, and its banks bent through dark woods, imposing rocks, and slopes of sunny verdure. Despite what had happened to Darcy's land, and the troubling crimes committed on it, Derbyshire was the most beautiful place she had ever seen.

The company, however, tried her patience. Mr Balfour incessantly talked about his new travelling coach and other purchases he wished to make, and Mr Utterson often checked his watch and seemed impatient to leave for Lord Poole's. She had not been sorry to see them go.

"Pemberley is beautiful. I could never tire of it." She thought about what she felt whenever she had the chance to be out of doors in Derbyshire. "I would go so far as to say that the natural beauty of the scenery here moves my heart."

When Mrs Lanyon only smiled, she added, "I am sorry that your ride this afternoon caused a headache." Elizabeth suspected there was no such headache, but went along with her new friend's claim. She seemed to wish to avoid the colonel, which was unfortunate given how he seemed eager to spend time with her. "I would be surprised to learn that Miss Darcy's company caused it."

"Not at all. I enjoy riding with either of the Darcy siblings." She smiled. "They are both quiet, and I can enjoy the ride and the scenery without any chatter."

Elizabeth laughed along with her. When their laughter faded, she said quietly, "Colonel Fitzwilliam mentioned he had looked forward to your company after you left the dining room."

Mrs Lanyon looked away. "I am sure he will enjoy your company when you return."

"He might enjoy mine well enough, but I think he will *miss* yours." Mrs Lanyon did not so much as look at her. "I am sorry," Elizabeth said gently, "that you do not feel comfortable at Pemberley any longer."

"You met Colonel Fitzwilliam in Kent, I understand?" Mrs Lanyon was determined to pretend not to hear. "You are easy and cheerful in mixed company, just like he is, and you each speak with the men or the women with equal ease."

Mrs Lanyon did not sound jealous, but wistful. "But you do not?"

"I often find women tiresome," she said after a moment's pause. "The hour in the drawing room after dinner with a large party is a trial to me. Women are always in competition. Oh, perhaps not always, but I feel it nonetheless. They are rarely truthful, always comparing and judging."

Elizabeth thought on this for a while. "They are often in competition with one another, and I suppose they often say one thing when they believe another, but you cannot have those fears with Miss Darcy, and I am sorry if I ever gave you an indication of being insincere."

"No, not at all, my dear Miss Bennet," she said warmly. "You must not let my unsocial nature allow you to believe I do not admire you. I am truly glad that you stayed at Pemberley with me. Miss Darcy is sweet, but she is young and too shy to be good company yet." Elizabeth gave her a reassuring smile. "In some ways, the gentlemen are easier to talk to, but of course one must be cautious in cultivating friendships with a man too."

"I do not think that in this small group of friends it is a problem. But it is not as potentially damaging to your reputation. In your case, as a widow, you can have a gentleman friend and no one will raise a critical eye."

She shrugged and looked over her shoulder at the miniature of her late husband. "I must be above reproach always, and that is best done with silence."

Elizabeth now felt she had a better understanding of Mrs Lanyon's behaviour today. "No one here would reproach you." She paused. "Colonel Fitzwilliam looked surprised and happy when he arrived and saw you at the breakfast table."

Mrs Lanyon only nodded, and Elizabeth tried again. "Did Colonel Fitzwilliam know Captain Lanyon?"

"Slightly; we had the same group of friends whilst my husband was alive. He was always kind to remember me, to include me, after Captain Lanyon died." She gave a small smile. "The colonel is an amiable man, he listens well . . . easy for me to talk to . . ."

When she said nothing else, Elizabeth said, "He makes a better first impression than his cousin does."

Mrs Lanyon laughed and in that moment appeared much younger. "I suppose so. Although most would say that Mr Darcy is the more handsome man."

"Colonel Fitzwilliam might be considered plain by comparison," Elizabeth led, wondering if Mrs Lanyon might contradict her.

"Yes, but he has so much countenance! And he is tall and well-made and has an engaging smile. I defy anyone who has spent time with him to call him plain."

Elizabeth smiled, and Mrs Lanyon blushed and looked again at the miniature. Elizabeth said gently, "Captain Lanyon has been gone three years, and everyone deserves to be loved by someone."

"No," Mrs Lanyon said sharply, "everyone deserves to at least know what it is to be loved. I have already had that once."

"Do you feel as though you are being disloyal to Captain Lanyon if you love a second time?"

"To love again, to marry again, some would call it a betrayal."

Having never loved and lost a husband, Elizabeth sat silent for a long moment. "I cannot speak from experience, but I feel that a worthy man would understand that you have room in your heart for both your first husband and a second. Was Captain Lanyon not such a man?"

Mrs Lanyon reached over to pick up the miniature. "He always said that if he died in battle that I ought to find whatever happiness in life that I could."

"Are you avoiding Colonel Fitzwilliam because he is not the type of man to understand you will always have an affection for your first husband?" She did not believe it of him, but Mrs Lanyon appeared to know the colonel better than she did.

"Oh no, my dear Miss Bennet," she answered softly. "I avoid him because he *is* a good man, one who might be devoted to me if I let him, and I do not know my own mind. Many believe that a widowed woman who was happily married does not deserve to marry a second time, after all."

"I think what matters is what you and Colonel Fitzwilliam have to say on that point."

Mrs Lanyon struggled with what to say. "Well, as I said, I do not know my own mind enough, and I should not raise his hopes. I have had lapses in judgment with him over the past year, and it ought not to happen again."

"Lapses?" Elizabeth blushed as she realised her meaning. "And how far did these lapses tend?" she asked with a playful look. "You fluttered a fan in his direction?"

Mrs Lanyon smiled knowingly and shook her head. "A lapse as in the consequence of our every private interview leads to an increase in passion. Must I speak more plainly?"

"Oh no, I simply wanted to hear you admit it! You grinned at the memory of these passionate lapses after all." Mrs Lanyon covered her red cheeks with her hands. In a more serious voice, Elizabeth added, "I hope you will not allow your first love to prevent you from finding a happiness that you richly deserve."

"We have spoken enough about me," she said primly, forcing herself back into composure. She clearly did not wish her affection for the colonel to be universally known. "Have you had any *lapses* yourself?"

"Me?" Elizabeth asked, surprised. "I am a proper maid; no lovers for me. I can boast a few stolen kisses from curiosity, but most of my embraces are chaste kisses from forfeits in games. In general, they convinced me I really ought to try harder to win."

"You did not mind the forfeit during Kiss the Nun earlier this week."

That felt so very long ago, but it was only four days. Elizabeth thought of the game and Darcy's surprised expression when Mrs Lanyon agreed to be the grate. "It was clever of you to change places with me so Darcy would have to kiss me rather than you."

Mrs Lanyon did not look embarrassed. "Is it so wrong for someone who was once very happy in love to wish to form her friends into a happy couple? It is clear that there is something between you and Mr Darcy."

Elizabeth refrained from making any similar remark about her new friend and Darcy's cousin. "How did you know?" Elizabeth shook her head in disbelief. "Even Jane could scarcely believe I had a reason to hope Mr Darcy might love me, let alone how much I want that to be true."

"I knew for certain when we played the ribbon game on Monday." At seeing her questioning stare, Mrs Lanyon said, "Whilst Mr Bingley distracted us, Mr Darcy answered to the type of man he wished for his sister, and you looked at him with absorbed attention." Elizabeth remembered what he had said about an affectionate husband and an attentive father. "And he looked right at you. He wanted *you* to know what manner of partner he would be."

"I think," Elizabeth said slowly, "that anyone fortunate enough to be Mr Darcy's partner in life would have extraordinary sources of happiness attached to her situation."

"I had at first thought yours was an instant attraction, but now I realise on both sides it is a stronger affection." Mrs Lanyon leant forward in earnest. "It is a shame that this storm has occupied Mr Darcy's attention, although I suppose you are not so selfish as to blame him for it."

"Not at all. But I confess that the continuance of his preference feels more uncertain now than it did a few days ago." The reservedness of Darcy's manner towards her contradicted one moment what a more animated look had intimated in the preceding one. *When will he ask me again?*

"His mind is oppressed, that is all," Mrs Lanyon said firmly.

"You are right that one must make allowances for all the trials he is facing." With so much to occupy him, she wished there was something she could do or say to convince Darcy to take her into his confidence.

"He will come to the point before we must meet your sister in Scarborough."

"Perhaps all we need is to convince Mr Darcy to play a parlour game and make certain that I lose? If I pay a kissing forfeit to him with enough enthusiasm, maybe he will make his intentions known."

"And then you and he could have as many lapses in judgment as you wish!"

They both laughed, and Elizabeth kept secret her own curiosity and enthusiasm for committing such a lapse with Darcy. She had reason, of course, to believe that his admiration included a desire that matched her own. Despite every insulting word he had said during his proposal, Darcy had expressed how ardently he admired and loved her. To think on it now made her blood run hot and her body ache with wanting.

What remains is for him to make me those offers and commitments that would guarantee the right to satisfy the love and restless passion I feel for him that has been intensifying since I arrived at Pemberley.

Mrs Lanyon's smile faded, and she set aside the miniature of her late husband and joined Elizabeth on the sofa. "Please forgive me if I have overstepped. I simply want you to be as deeply and as happily in love as I—as I once was, Miss Bennet."

Rather than mention her equal hopes for her friend's happiness with Colonel Fitzwilliam, she said, "My friends call me Lizzy."

Mrs Lanyon looked surprised, and then bowed her head trying to hide a large smile. "Hester, if you please."

CHAPTER FOURTEEN

W hen Darcy and Colonel Fitzwilliam first left Pemberley Saturday morning, they had a dismal ride of it to Lambton, for it drizzled the whole way. It was a brief and lighter rain than the previous storms, but it was still an annoyance. Darcy met with tenants in the public house to arrange buying corn to feed their livestock whilst Fitzwilliam oversaw the committee to get rid of all the refuse and broken wood. They had found a meadow for the fire, and once the wood was dried out, the fire would rage through the night.

Thank goodness Fitzwilliam is here; his efforts are self-sufficient, and reliable, and he does not complain about his boots being covered in mud.

"What were the final casualties?" Fitzwilliam asked as their horses walked back to Pemberley that afternoon.

"One hundred sheep, six cattle, and one horse were drowned," Darcy recited. He sighed. "Now that most of the water has receded, it was discovered that in total three men, three women—four, if one counts Carew—and two children connected to Pemberley were drowned. Plus the bodies from Lambton's graveyard that must be reinterred."

The River Derwent bent very near to Lambton's churchyard, and the second storm, with the heavy volume of water already in the ground, had forced out of the earth and broke open several coffins. They too had been taken to the makeshift deadhouse until they could be identified and buried again.

"'Tis a gruesome task to have their families suffer at seeing their bodies, and to have to bury them again," Fitzwilliam said grimly. "If they are even recent enough to have any family now living to do it."

"Each hour reveals some new and horrible story of outrage as a result of these storms and the whole wet season."

He had already told Fitzwilliam about Carew, the missing candlestick, and his fear that his sister's maid had not drowned after all.

"I have been thinking about the looting," his cousin said, "and that your father's room is known to be not often used. It must have been someone who was familiar with the house."

"You agree that the person who was searching for plunder in Lambton is likely the same who stole the taperstick off my father's desk?"

"And if so, then that same person might have hit Carew over the head and stole her ring."

Darcy knew it was likely, but the pain of that realisation was difficult to face. "I cannot believe that one of my servants stole from me, let alone murdered Carew, one of their own. I know theft happens," he cried when Fitzwilliam threw him a look. "Before you call me easily deceived, there is nothing else missing, no servant has pointed a finger, and Mrs Reynolds has neither heard nor seen anything suspicious. You know how quickly rumours spread through a house."

Fitzwilliam was silent for a moment. "If you are so certain it is not a servant—"

"I am," he answered firmly. "I am not naïve, but not one of my servants is suspicious of another; no one appears to suddenly have more money. Nothing else is missing." Fitzwilliam gave him an expectant look. "What?"

"There was no looting last night, and it might have been the same person . . ."

Darcy blew out a breath. "Then perhaps I am wrong, and the looting and Carew's death are not related."

"Darcy!" Fitzwilliam shook his head, giving him an exasperated look as they rode towards the house. "Do all people tend to believe the world is what they thought it was, even clever men like you? Even when evidence to the contrary is presented to them?"

"What are you implying? I *want* to find out what happened. I hardly care about who stole from me, but if Molly Carew was murdered, then I want her murderer punished."

"Then think!" Fitzwilliam spat. "If it is not a servant, not a villager, and there was no looting last night, and it was someone who knew the house, knew the room was not often used, and was someone who Carew would not have fled from, then you know who to suspect."

The truth was a twisting knife in his heart. "Balfour or Utterson."

Rather than boast at having seen the matter so clearly himself, or mock him for not admitting it aloud sooner, Fitzwilliam said gently, "A man believes what he must to sleep at night."

"I no longer care about my peace of mind." Darcy saw that they were now coming near to the place where Carew's body was discovered. "She borrowed Miss Bennet's pelisse, and her hat had a flower in it that belonged to Georgiana, but I think that is unrelated to her death."

Fitzwilliam agreed. "Whoever killed her was near enough to know that it was Carew."

"I have known Balfour for six years, Utterson for three, although not as well . . . how do I determine if either one killed her?"

"You cannot be objective."

"Then help me," he said, just short of pleading.

Fitzwilliam stopped his horse and turned to look at him. "Where were they on Thursday?"

"Both men were away from Pemberley on the morning Carew died. I did not see any of my guests from Wednesday night until I came back to the house Thursday afternoon and saw Miss Bennet and then Georgiana after finding the body. Miss Bennet, Mrs Lanyon, and Mrs Annesley were with Georgiana that morning. Utterson said he was in Tissington shooting at Lord Poole's, and Balfour was at Buxton playing cards."

"That is not easy for you to verify, since their friends might lie for them, or an employee is bribed."

"You know both of them; you are above bowing acquaintances at the least. They are well-connected young men, and your circles have crossed many times. What do you think of each of them?"

"Balfour is a lazy, harmless sort of man. Nothing to like or dislike about him. The sort of man you would shoot with in the morning and play cards with in the evening without growing tired of him."

Darcy agreed. "He is of good family; respectable connexions. He did spend his early years gaming, horse racing."

"And spending."

"Yes, high spending, but he was not wild or reckless, then or now."

"Hester—" Fitzwilliam coughed. "Mrs Lanyon says Balfour enjoys dice and cards, but no more so than any other young, single man waiting to inherit."

"Utterson is no different in his habits," Darcy said, overlooking his cousin's error, "though he shall have to make his own way in the world. His father tries to control his behaviour by controlling his purse."

"I do not know Utterson as well. He appears gentlemanlike, but he is not as easy and affable as Balfour. He does not want abilities, though."

"He can be a pleasant companion when he thinks it worth his while," Darcy agreed.

"Rather like someone I know," Fitzwilliam muttered with a wink as he cued his horse and they resumed riding.

"Utterson is the younger son of a baronet, a few years younger than Balfour and me. His father is paying his fees and expenses to enter the law, but has reduced his allowance to keep him from spending too much and not studying enough. Utterson complains of his wants and distresses, if not in direct terms, then at least by strong innuendo," Darcy said slowly. "He might have a greater want of money than I realised. And he prefers London life, and all of the expenses that go along with that. He has to live on whatever his father allows him until he completes his studies."

"But Balfour also complains about living on a father's meagre allowance."

"He will inherit. Utterson will not, and he is jealous."

"Utterson is the poorer man, certainly, but does he spend as much as Balfour? I doubt it."

"Would either of them have sunk to such depths, to steal from me and from those poorer than them, to maintain a London style of living?"

Fitzwilliam shook his head. "It would be a selfish desperation I can hardly comprehend, especially if one of them killed for it."

The idea of either of them killing Carew burned him. "I would have helped either of them," Darcy cried angrily. "If either man had a real distress of funds, or wanted advice on how to better manage their expenses, I would have helped him!"

His cousin gave a sad laugh. "You are labouring under the idea that whoever killed Carew shares your sense of gentlemanly honour. If a man feels entitled to an expensive manner of living and is willing to steal, he would never turn to someone for advice and admit he did not have the funds. If Balfour or Utterson did this, and did it in order to appear as though they have more money than they truly do, then he is not the man you thought he was."

Darcy was about to say something about such a betrayal of friend-ship, but then he thought of Molly Carew. He had to close his eyes to put aside the memory of her father's weeping. Her murder outweighed any sense of betrayal or disappointment he felt.

"Fitzwilliam, what shall I do? I have no support from the magis-trate. Can I accost them directly? Search their belongings for stolen goods?"

His cousin thought for a long while before answering. They were nearly at the stable when he said, "If you stole things to gain funds to spend and gamble, would you not sell them quickly? You should look, but I doubt the items remain at Pemberley."

"They have been very much on their own since they arrived, and more so this week since I have been occupied with recovering from the storm, but where could they have quickly and easily sold them?"

Fitzwilliam thought for a moment. "There are pawnbrokers in every town. Bakewell, Buxton, Matlock, all across the Peak are towns large enough to boast a pawnshop. And for someone desperate enough to kill to have more money to throw around in full view of his friends, the idea of turning in a piece of silver for ready cash is tempting."

"Pawnbrokers will not accept stolen goods, and one must give a name to leave a pledge."

"Not every pawnbroker is reputable," he said, scoffing, "and whoever is behind this will not admit to where his items came from or even use his own name."

Darcy ignored this slight on his worldliness. "If it is true, then how weak and desperate he must be," he said quietly. "To steal, to kill, and to sell those items below value to have money quickly."

Fitzwilliam gave him a stern look. "Like I said, whoever is behind this is not the man you thought he was."

It was a chilling realisation, and yesterday both men walked alone with Elizabeth. What if she had mentioned her suspicions about Carew's death or noticing her missing ring? "I expect them to return on Sunday. I will search their rooms before then, and then watch to see if either of them leaves the house to plunder Lambton again."

"And I will ride to Matlock and Buxton on Monday to see if anything of note was pawned this week. Someone who is not the usual weekly pawner might stand out."

They were now in the stable yard, and made their way inside where they were told that Miss Bennet and Mrs Lanyon had accompanied Miss Darcy and Mrs Annesley to distribute clothing and food to his tenants. Even though Balfour and Utterson were fifteen miles away, he was glad to know that his steward was accompanying them.

Upon realising the women were still gone and there was an hour yet until they had to dress for dinner, Fitzwilliam asked, "Cues or maces?" and turned towards the billiard room.

"Cues," he answered, and they settled on the rules and that they would play to only six.

They played in companionable silence for five minutes before Fitzwilliam said, "Why did Miss Bennet leave her newlywed sister to stay here a few weeks longer? I would have thought she would be unhappy with you after she learnt how you disapprove of her sister's match."

"Disapprov*ed*," he corrected, hitting the red ball. "Past tense. I heartily approve now that I know she loves Bingley." Darcy struck another ball. "And my former objections had nothing to do with *her*, but rather her connexions, the behaviour of her family, and my mistaken belief of her indifference to Bingley."

"Still, even after what you did, Miss Bennet left her sister to stay here . . . with you."

"With Mrs Lanyon," he corrected.

"With her new friend of scarcely a week? A strange reason to leave her family."

Darcy thought Fitzwilliam was the last person to imply anything wanting in Mrs Lanyon's friendship, but he stayed silent on that point. "Miss Bennet could be drawn to Mrs Lanyon's intelligence and dignity, and Mrs Lanyon must enjoy Miss Bennet's friendly manner. You have said yourself that Mrs Lanyon does not make friends easily," he added, stepping rather close to his cousin's friendship with the widow.

"After what I inadvertently told Miss Bennet about your part in separating Bingley from her sister, I would not have been surprised to learn that Miss Bennet hates you." Fitzwilliam aimed at the white ball but missed. "Would that have distressed you?"

"Yes, in general I am loathe to have houseguests who hate me." *What about houseguests who might be thieves or murderers?*

"In Kent, I thought you might have found her pretty, and that lively manner of hers was an attraction too."

"Hmm," Darcy said as he aimed and missed also. "Perhaps."

"I think your interest is more than a passing admiration." Darcy said nothing. "If Miss Bennet visited Pemberley even after you nearly ruined her sister's chance of happiness, if she extended her visit, if she really did forgive you . . ."

"Yes?"

"Must I speak plainly? You ought to think about what that says of her feelings for you."

"You think that Miss Bennet admires me?" he said, turning his head to hide a smile.

"I do," he said simply. "I would not have said so in Kent, but her manner towards you was less satirical yesterday than I had seen before. I do not think she would have stayed at Pemberley if she did not like you. I always thought you might have admired her. You ought to seriously consider the subject."

Darcy barked a dry laugh. "My marrying Miss Bennet has been the subject of many contemplative hours, I assure you."

This made Fitzwilliam miss again. He looked up sharply and asked, "What did you decide?"

"I decided at Hunsford to ask her to marry me." Fitzwilliam's mouth gaped open. "I think it obvious what Miss Bennet decided. I would not wish that this matter should be made a parade of," he added, pointing at his cousin.

"She refused you? Because of what you did to Bingley and her sister?"

Darcy set down the cue and ran a hand over his eyes. "Yes . . . no, not only because of that. My behaviour to her at the time merited the severest reproof. It was unpardonable, and she was right to reject me."

Fitzwilliam set aside his own cue and crossed his arms, giving him a stare. "It looks like it *was* pardonable, given how you said she forgave you and she stayed at your house when any other woman would have left at the soonest possible hour."

He gave a weak smile. "I have reason to hope. We have spoken about what happened at Hunsford, and she forgives me for . . . everything."

His cousin gave him an expectant, wide-eyed look. "Then why have you not asked her a second time? Your family would not desire the connexion, save for Georgiana and me, but you were already willing to cast away every family obstacle on your side and overlook her family's behaviour and connexions. What keeps you silent now?"

Darcy walked to a window that overlooked the ruined garden. "Because of this," he said, pointing. "The storm has occupied my every waking moment this week. There is much to be done, so much to pay for, everyone else's fears to placate. The livelihoods of hundreds of people under my protection have been threatened; it is not a responsibility I take lightly. And," he added drily, "let us not forget Carew's death, and the plundering in Lambton, and the unhappy possibility that one of my friends might be behind both."

His cousin gave him a gentle look. "I know of no person who, in my judgment, could better execute the duties of restoring Pemberley than yourself."

"My father—"

"Is dead," Fitzwilliam said kindly. "*You* are Mr Darcy."

He nodded, collecting himself. He would manage this disaster, he would safeguard the well-being of everyone at Pemberley, and he would find and punish whomever was behind Carew's death.

"You need a little respite from business, Darcy," Fitzwilliam said.

"You sound like Balfour. Moderate exercise and books are a good restorative."

Fitzwilliam glared. "That is not what I mean."

"Many people's happiness is in my guardianship, and that happiness and stability has been threatened. Until they are secure, I can hardly think on securing my own happiness."

"Do not squander the opportunity you have. Miss Bennet is right here," he added, pointing to the door.

"Very soon we will have a conversation, once this matter of Carew's death is resolved and I can think clearly."

Fitzwilliam shook his head. "You are not just a landlord and master. Despite your chaste history"—his voice lilted in a tease—"you *are* a man first."

Darcy was tempted to remind his cousin of *his* unchaste history with Mrs Lanyon, but that would only prolong a conversation that was fast becoming too personal. It was bad enough that his heart beat faster at the thought of holding Elizabeth against him, feeling her arms around him and her lips moving over his, preferably whilst they were lying in his bed. *I long to know for certain in what manner she thinks of me, if she loves me.* "I shall manage it in my own time, and in my own way, thank you."

"Does the uncertainty of her affections not weigh on you just the same as all the rest of your concerns?"

Darcy suspected his face expressed the truth of that. "Of course it does. But how do I think of my own happiness, of courting a woman, when the people here are suffering? When one of my friends is possibly a murderer?" He shook his head. "Soon I will have a conversation with Miss Bennet," he repeated.

Fitzwilliam nodded once. "Leave it with me."

Darcy knew that look. "No, no, I shall speak to her in my own time—"

"Balfour and Utterson return tomorrow night and our acting as sleuth-hounds begins in earnest. You need to leave Pemberley for a few hours tomorrow, and you need to throw yourself at Miss Bennet's feet." Fitzwilliam walked away, ignoring his plea to not interfere. "Leave it with me," he called over his shoulder as he left.

To Elizabeth, it felt almost like a family party, although she and Hester were outsiders. The conversation at dinner was quick and lively. It could not help but touch on Pemberley's concerns, but it did not feel as heavy a presence as it had been. The talk between the cousins recurred to their younger days, and they supplied anecdotes in abundance to occupy and entertain the rest of them. Colonel Fitzwilliam's presence added a levity that had been missing since the first storm, and his presence made Darcy exert himself more than he had recently.

After the gentlemen rejoined them in the drawing room, she realised that Hester was also more at ease, but it was because Colonel Fitzwilliam did not distinguish her with any particular attention. He was engaging and polite, but he never singled her out, and Hester was calmer than she had been yesterday.

He respects the boundary Hester has placed around him.

Elizabeth was playing—content that no one was truly listening to her performance—when she heard the sudden sound of Darcy's laughter. He was on the other side of the room with his cousin, and Colonel Fitzwilliam had said something that stirred Darcy's face into mirth. His laughter was more melodic and joyful than she would have expected from one so guarded.

She watched Darcy playfully shove his cousin—making the colonel laugh—and then walk away, still smiling. The mirth slowly faded from his face as he sat with Miss Darcy, admiring her work and likely saying all the things an attentive older brother ought to say. Colonel

Fitzwilliam, now by himself, noticed Elizabeth's attention and joined her at the instrument.

"No, Miss Bennet, I cannot tell you what I said to him. Men must have their secrets, you know," he said with a wink.

She laughed. "I hardly care what you said to him." At his disbelieving look, she added in a lower voice, "There is a sadness now that overshadows Mr Darcy's countenance. I am simply happy to see it lifted."

Colonel Fitzwilliam looked at his cousin, with a sad little smile. "Darcy has a more sorrowing heart than one might expect. Not for his own affairs," he added quickly, "but for those dear to him."

"He has scarcely smiled this week, let alone laughed. I understand it, of course, but I see a weariness in him, and I worry for his equanimity."

Elizabeth felt Colonel Fitzwilliam's attention and busied herself with looking through the sheet music. To him, she must sound strangely protective of an independent man, who had lived in the world, who had every advantage. *I sound too affectionate for his friend's sister-in-law.*

"Darcy feels these things more than any other person I have met with," he said quietly. "I am exceedingly sorry to see him so. It is more than responsibility or duty towards the people here. I cannot quite describe it," he said, shaking his head.

"He is extremely affected by their suffering," Elizabeth said softly, still looking at Darcy.

He noticed their attention and left his sister to come nearer. "You two have been looking at me," Darcy said with an air of nervousness she was surprised to see. "What have you been talking of?"

"We were noticing how dull you look," Colonel Fitzwilliam said quickly, "and it must be because there are so few women here to shower you with attention, hoping to engage in a flirtation. You must be terribly lonely without half a dozen single women trying to make you fall a little bit in love with them."

The look Darcy was giving his cousin was thunderous. "Yes, a commonplace flirtation with any woman breathing sounds very like me."

Colonel Fitzwilliam pretended to look around the room. "Where are the ladies breaking their hearts over you? Where is there a woman for you to flirt with?"

This was said heavily, and Elizabeth blushed. Darcy did not look half as amused as his cousin, and Elizabeth decided to spare him this unwanted teasing. "I suppose it is because Mr Darcy put out mantraps, or should I say womantraps, around his grounds to discourage the hordes of women who seek his perfection."

Colonel Fitzwilliam barked a laugh whilst Darcy gave her a little smile. "Indeed. It is the only reason I can sleep peacefully at night, knowing that I am safe from senseless chatter and empty flirtations."

There was a moment of silence where Colonel Fitzwilliam looked expectantly between them, but she and Darcy only smiled shyly and said nothing. The colonel huffed. "Well, if there are traps across the park, for your safety Darcy must have taken you touring elsewhere in the Peak?"

"Hester and I went to Haddon Hall with the Bingleys, and Mr Darcy brought us to a charming well dressing festival in Bakewell"— she gave Darcy a smile—"but all I have seen of Derbyshire has been this park. Whilst avoiding the womantraps, of course."

"That will not do. Mrs Lanyon," Colonel Fitzwilliam called across the room, interrupting Hester's conversation with Mrs Annesley, "this is your first time in Derbyshire also, is it not?" She nodded. "Darcy, we ought to take the ladies to see some of the picturesque beauties of the Peak. Where ought we to go?"

"Oh, we could take them to Dovedale," Miss Darcy cried.

The proposal was caught by delight. Miss Darcy, Mrs Annesley, Colonel Fitzwilliam, and Hester all talked on of exploring the dale, and a picnic, and it was only a morning's ride—fifteen miles—and would the views not be well worth it, and they could have it all arranged to leave in the morning.

Elizabeth had nothing to say against it, but Darcy had not joined in everyone's enthusiasm. Colonel Fitzwilliam was still seated by her at the instrument, and he rose upon seeing a rather emphatic look in Darcy's eyes. Darcy led him a little apart and behind her. They spoke quietly, but were not as far away from her as they suspected.

"If I leave, my concerns at Pemberley are left as a body without a head," she heard Darcy whisper harshly.

"It is one day! Your steward can oversee matters for *one* day."

"You know that is not the only—"

"And you cannot accuse Balfour or Utterson until they return, and until I investigate the pawnshops," Colonel Fitzwilliam said sharply. "Search their rooms before we leave, but you won't solve anything else tomorrow, so you may as well amuse your guests with an exploring party to Dovedale."

Realisation struck Elizabeth. Darcy and his cousin suspected that either Mr Balfour or Mr Utterson were behind the looting in Lambton. They thought one of them stole items from the village and then pawned them for money. One of them must have taken the candlestick from old Mr Darcy's room as well. What a deception from a man she had thought was a gentleman, and poor Darcy, to be deceived by a friend.

Her breath came faster, and she felt a sickening coldness creep over her. *Darcy thinks one of them killed Carew.*

She brought a hand to her mouth to stifle a cry of surprise. Every feeling revolted against it, but she could not allow her reason to falter. Both men had a want of money, they both liked to spend beyond their means, they both had the opportunity to loot the village, and they both were known to be away from the house when Carew died. She blew out a breath and forced her shaking fingers into fists on her lap. One of Darcy's friends might be a murderer. It was little wonder acute sorrow seemed to have settled in his eyes.

"I *intend* to!" she heard Darcy cry.

"Yes, well, a smile, half-bow, and a wish that she has a good morning whilst you do not see each other for the next eight hours, and then spend the evening in mixed company will hardly get the desired result!" Colonel Fitzwilliam's voice had raised too, and she turned to learn what it meant. They noticed her, and the effect was immediate: Darcy's expression softened, and Colonel Fitzwilliam bowed and walked away.

"You, you did not hear much, did you?" Darcy asked in a low voice. "I mean . . . nothing to distress you, I hope?"

He does not want to worry me because I already suspect that Carew's death was not an accident. To see the man she loved distressed, and to be unable to relieve him, was a painful affliction she would not wish on anyone. The least she could do was pretend that she was not terrified as her mind jumped from wondering if it was Mr Balfour or Mr Utterson who was a killer.

"No, not at all," she said, but from Darcy's troubled expression, he did not believe her. She ought to try to bring back some of the smiles he had worn earlier. "What think you of the visit to Dovedale tomorrow? I should like it very much."

"It is one of the most pleasing scenes of the Peak," he said, but with no enthusiasm.

She would not now mention the horrid idea that one of his friends might be behind the death of one of his servants. "Hearing and answering applications for help leaves you no hours for recreation. I hope you can enjoy one sightseeing afternoon without feeling guilty."

She could see in his face that was precisely how he felt. "I *will* feel guilty, but you and Fitzwilliam are determined to see me go." Darcy smiled, and she could see him putting in the effort to be agreeable. "For your sake, I shall show you all the beauties of the valley and the River Dove."

"I hope you can enjoy it, Darcy. I know"—she placed a hand on his arm—"I know you have much to worry you, and how much you care for the people here." She dropped her voice and gave him an earnest look. "You can be honest, you know, with me. You need not pretend you are not afflicted for my sake."

She had drawn her hand down his arm before removing it, and he grasped her hand, lightly, giving her fingers a squeeze before letting go.

"I do," he said slowly, "I do feel a duty, a responsibility that weighs heavily on me, more so than anything I have ever felt." He looked her full in the face, and for a moment she thought he might mention his fears about Carew's death but, in the end, he only said, "Miss Bennet, I dare not say more about it, but if I were to wish a bitter curse on an enemy, I should put him in my place with my feelings."

She tried to imagine his loss in knowing that one of his friends was a killer—his strain, his fear—but she knew what she imagined could never match Darcy's reality. If she could not share his concerns, she would try to raise his spirits. "That would put Mr Wickham as Pemberley's master, and that would gall you more." She smiled at his surprised expression, and he laughed a little. "So I think it best if you remain Pemberley's caretaker."

"You intend to tease me?"

"Absolutely, if you will let me."

The look Darcy gave her was so tender she wondered if he was about to declare all of the sentiments she hoped he would confess. Elizabeth then noticed how the rest of the room was watching, and she took a small step away from him.

"Shall we enjoy ourselves tomorrow?" she said in a more conversational tone. "Can you suffer a few hours with your friends, as a reward for the effort you have already put forth for Pemberley?"

Darcy too noticed that they had gained the attention of everyone else. He lowered his voice, and even bent a little lower to look directly into her eyes. "I shall suffer ten times more if I am not with you."

CHAPTER FIFTEEN

The ladies were comfortably settled in Darcy's barouche to drive to Dovedale. Elizabeth and Hester rode with Mrs Annesley as Darcy drove and his sister joined him in the box. It was pleasant to see brother and sister full of conversation. She often saw Darcy's handsome face in profile when he turned to speak to or smile at Miss Darcy. She seemed to have forgotten that there were three people seated behind her; Miss Darcy talked more freely than Elizabeth had previously seen.

"We are fortunate the weather is fair, and it is unlikely to rain," Mrs Annesley mused happily.

Their road was through a pleasant country and the sun was shining, and Elizabeth was happy in admiring the beauties before her. Hester often looked back after Colonel Fitzwilliam, who decided to ride rather than crowd the barouche. Elizabeth suspected he did not want to force Hester into his company. She smiled to herself when Hester appeared to be admiring some scenic beauty and, when Colonel Fitzwilliam gained on them whilst ascending a hill, would whisper, "There he is."

After this happened a third time, Elizabeth did not hide her smile fast enough, and Hester blushed. "I am content with our friendship as it is," she said softly.

When Mrs Annesley was admiring the rising hills, Elizabeth said to Hester, "You could be more than *content*, you know."

Hester simply bowed her head. She was swift to listen, but cautious with her tongue. Elizabeth felt that Hester loved Colonel Fitzwilliam, but she held too firmly to the edict that a widow who had happily married once did not deserve a second love match. *I hope she does not hold out against what her heart wants, if her longing glances are any indication.*

Miss Darcy was enjoying her brother's undivided attention without any guests around to make her nervous, and Elizabeth was certain that Hester would soon settle the point as to what manner of relationship she wanted with Darcy's cousin. Even amidst trials, even amidst the possibility that one's friend might have committed a horrible crime, there were moments of joy. That gave her hope that perhaps soon she might command enough of Darcy's attention to remind him that he had asked for a private conversation with her.

I would be nearly as happy to just feel his arms around me and his lips on mine.

"I was thinking that we might join Lewis and Mr Utterson on our return," Hester said. "Tissington and Lord Poole's house are only a few miles from Dovedale. Why do we not meet Lewis and Mr Utterson and ride back together? Lewis would be proud to let some of us ride in his new carriage."

A sickening feeling settled in Elizabeth's stomach. This must be how Darcy felt every moment. Her emotions were now deeply oppressed at the thought of looking at either Mr Utterson or Mr Balfour. There was no true escape from the anxious sensations, and it was little wonder that Darcy had been reluctant to go to Dovedale. Even a few hours of rural pleasure would be interrupted by thoughts about which one of them had possibly killed Carew and taken a ring off her body.

Hester was still looking at her. "Certainly," Elizabeth said, and then left Mrs Annesley to say all the necessary things about being eager to see the absent gentlemen.

Who was likely to have committed the crime? Was it Mr Balfour, who bought his new carriage for the sake of impressing his friends, or Mr Utterson, who envied it even with its imperfections because he had no carriage of his own?

The road through the small village of Thorpe was along open pastures winding around the base of a mount that seemed to guard the entrance to Dovedale. Elizabeth raised her eyes to the perpendicular rocks across its summit. *That would give a fine view of the Dove through the dale below.*

"I was in hopes the road would be passable, but they tell me we cannot ford the river near Bunster Hill," Darcy said by way of apology when they alighted. "The late flood carried away the bridge over which we were to drive and left a great hole in the bank in its place."

Everyone declared that they had nothing to say against walking the last mile. They fell into pairs to walk along the margin of the river, with the Darcys insisting that she and Hester take the lead. The valley left room for little more than a channel of the river with a footpath along its banks. The wet season had caused the water to rise, flooding the Staffordshire side and leaving only a small space to walk on the Derbyshire side.

The character of Elizabeth's first view of Dovedale was pure grandeur. The hills swelled boldly from both sides of the river, and their majestic summits seemed to be amongst the clouds. The river was still high, and they walked past a few intrepid anglers. It was a splendid scene, with water breaking over fragments of stone and trees framing the river.

Near the same high hill she had seen from the carriage, they found themselves enclosed in a narrow and deep dale where the river bent sharply. Elizabeth and Hester stopped and raised their eyes to observe on one side many craggy rocks above one another to a vast height, and on the other an almost perpendicular ascent covered with grass and a few sheep.

"What do you think?" Miss Darcy asked her and Hester. "The area is celebrated for its wild and fantastic appearance."

"Derbyshire is beautiful," Hester said, breathlessly, turning to look to the other side of the Dove.

Elizabeth saw Darcy hiding a smile. Colonel Fitzwilliam laughed and stepped nearer to Hester. "It certainly is—but that is Staffordshire." He took her by the shoulders and turned her to face the other side. "*This* is the Derbyshire side of the river."

They all laughed, even Hester, and Elizabeth noticed that she did not shrug off Colonel Fitzwilliam's hands or step away after he removed them.

The others talked of the rock formations farther upstream that they must see, but Elizabeth's attention returned to the grand limestone hill.

"That is Thorpe Cloud," Darcy said, coming away from the river to stand near her.

"Is it so named because it seems high enough to touch the clouds?"

He smiled. "No, sadly. Your reason would be more fitting for such a location. 'Cloud' is simply a corruption of 'clud,' an Anglo-Saxon word for a large rock or hill."

"That is dull," she said, turning to face him, "but we cannot blame it for its name." She craned her neck to take it in again. "How high is it?"

"'Tis a moderate-sized hill." He shrugged, looking at it with her. "Nearly a thousand feet?"

"Those of us from Hertfordshire would call that a mountain," she cried.

Darcy laughed. "Then it is a shame you do not live in Derbyshire."

He turned from looking at Thorpe Cloud to look at her, still with a smile on his face. Elizabeth thought of the unintended meaning behind his words. "Yes," she said, looking into his eyes, "it is." Comprehension seemed to strike him, and his amused expression turned tender. "I think," she added softly so no one else could hear, "I could enjoy living here very much."

Elizabeth dearly wished everyone away whilst Darcy looked at her with such dark eyes, hopefully full of the meaning she thought they held, but she was not to be so lucky. Hester and Miss Darcy called their attention, and they rejoined the others near the riverbank.

"Mr Darcy," Hester said, "I was earlier suggesting to Miss Bennet that since Dovedale is so near Lord Poole's that we meet up with Lewis and Mr Utterson and ride back together."

Elizabeth saw the flicker of unease in Darcy's eyes and was sorry that he was reminded of his cares when they had only just arrived. *He is deeply distressed.*

"Certainly," he said with a curt bow. "I can send one of the servants ahead with a note for Poole when we are ready to leave."

"Mrs Annesley has said that she and I can ride in Mr Balfour's new travelling chariot," Miss Darcy added, "if you and he approve, of course."

Darcy's voice was cold when he said, "No."

He is afraid to leave his sister alone with Mr Balfour or Mr Utterson. How was he to put Miss Darcy in a carriage with someone he fears murdered his servant for a coral ring? Elizabeth saw the startled expressions on Mrs Lanyon's and Miss Darcy's faces. His being unduly protective of his sister, along with his abruptness, was out of character. She felt certain that had they been less reserved or less shy, both ladies would have remarked upon it.

"Come now," Colonel Fitzwilliam said, giving Darcy an emphatic look, "what could be said against respectable young men and women driving in the country together? Mrs Annesley would be with her."

"Mr Darcy must decide if it would be indecorous or not," Hester said primly. "You must not press him."

Colonel Fitzwilliam gripped Darcy's arm and spoke directly into his ear. Darcy clenched his jaw and nodded once. Whatever the colonel said made an impression; although he still looked a little pained, he said that he could have no objection if Georgiana wanted to ride in the new coach so long as Mrs Annesley accompanied her.

Darcy would make a terrible actor.

After he had assured his sister that he had no reservations, she said, "Fitzwilliam, shall we take your friends towards Milldale?" Miss Darcy turned to Elizabeth and Hester. "There are many interesting rocks and caves along the way."

"Yes," Colonel Fitzwilliam agreed. "You must walk the steps at Lover's Leap, and we must show you Reynard's Cave and all the rest."

"How far is it?" Hester asked.

"Perhaps three miles to Milldale, a mile to Lover's Leap."

Whilst they discussed the distances and what they might see along the way, Elizabeth looked at Thorpe Cloud again.

"Are you ready to press on, Miss Bennet?" Darcy asked.

"Yes, I suppose so."

He looked at her for a moment and then said, "Would you rather climb Thorpe Cloud instead and see the view?"

Elizabeth smiled sheepishly and said that she would. "But I do not want to take anyone away from a walk along the river."

"I shall climb with you," he said. In a louder voice he said to the others, "Are any of you intrepid enough to join us?"

"If you prefer to climb Thorpe Cloud," began Miss Darcy, "we could all—"

Colonel Fitzwilliam put a hand on her arm and then looked pointedly at Hester.

"It shall be too much for any of us," Hester said, "but you must climb it with Mr Darcy."

"We shall go ahead to Lover's Leap," said Colonel Fitzwilliam, already leading Miss Darcy away, "and you can meet us back here when you have seen all there is to see."

The others followed the river, and she was left only with Darcy. She had been wanting to engage a moment of his attention all week, but it was clear from his pensive look that his mind was still on other matters. *How much can I cheer a person whose income this year is not guaranteed and whose friend might be a killer?*

Forcing a smile, she said, "Thank you for bringing us. I know you have a great deal on your mind." She wondered if he wanted to talk more about Carew's death and what it would mean if one of his friends had caused it. "What occupies you now?"

"A variety of important occurrences, continually interposing to distract my mind and withdraw my attention, must explain my seeming neglect of–of my friends."

Elizabeth did not see how she could force him to speak about his suspicion that his friend killed someone. "I know you did not wish to come today, so you need not pretend for my sake, but you can speak of those demands and occurrences if you like."

Darcy was silent so long that she wondered if he was going to answer. "I have many demands on me, and my tenants seem to think it is but for them to ask and everything they want is done, and when it is not done directly, they grow frustrated. And I grow frustrated when I am powerless to do more."

He paused to gesture where they ought to ascend the hill. "The sides of this valley are in almost every part steep and craggy; however, there is a tolerably good ascent this way." After a moment he added, "I am afraid I shall not appear to my advantage if it is known that I spent a day sightseeing whilst my tenants are rebuilding."

His honesty both surprised her and flattered her. "None blame you for this tragedy, you know," she said.

"Yes, I know it was the misfortune of weather and chance, but the end result will still prevent us from making tolerable crops this year. I shall be in arrears; it is only a matter of how much. I did not have debt before this and refuse to run to debt now. I can weather the—" Darcy winced. "I can help my tenants and remain solvent if I retrench."

They left the shallow section beneath Thorpe Cloud and were now climbing higher. "You are unused to financial travails, that is clear," she said. "But you appear to have a plan to manage the disaster, and so long as you meet your tenants' immediate needs, I do not think they will begrudge you a moment of recreation now and then."

Darcy nodded as though determined to believe this. "I will endeavour to not act so afflicted, at least when I am enjoying your company."

This made her heart beat a little faster. *If only good manners allowed the woman to speak first.* She was half ready to disregard all propriety and tell him that she had come to love him, to put her arms around him and finally kiss him as she had wanted to do since they played the parlour game before the storm. "Affliction is the good man's shining time, so it is said."

"At one point you did not think I was a good man, or a gentlemanly one."

This was said with an uncertainty that surprised her. He only needed to believe that she wanted him to repeat the sentiments and renew the offers she rejected in April. Perhaps she really ought to consider speaking first.

"My dear Darcy, now I think you are everything that is benevolent and good."

~

To all appearances, he was sure he had looked perfectly composed when Elizabeth called him "my dear Darcy." But it still felt like his heart was beating so violently that his pulse could be seen from a distance.

Since the storm on Monday, he had an ever-present feeling of woe, as well as an urgent need to fix everything directly and to do much of it himself. Add to that the pain and grief of Utterson or Balfour being capable of murder, and Darcy knew he was hardly fit to be in company. The guilt he felt whenever he was not acting on behalf of his tenants must be discernible if Elizabeth was prompting him to talk of his cares.

When he returned to Pemberley, he would immediately have demands upon him. There would be letters to answer, his steward to meet with, his banker to write to. Balfour and Utterson would return, and he would somehow find the wherewithal to behave no differently towards them whilst he and Fitzwilliam gathered what evidence against the guilty party that they could find.

And, fool that I am, here I am alone with the only woman I have ever loved, and I am talking about the demands upon my time and my purse.

He would ask her to marry him when they reached the summit. The hope of feeling her heart beating against his chest as he kissed her was now crowding out thoughts of Pemberley and storms and destruction as they ascended Thorpe Cloud. The thought of soon indulging in every possible passion with her made his heart race. He was certain that Elizabeth admired him more than the last time he asked, but he felt far more anxiety than he had at Hunsford parsonage.

"Your sister was right to suggest our seeing this place," she said, looking all round as the incline grew steeper.

"Do you think Dovedale and Derbyshire beautiful?"

She smiled as though this were a foolish question. "There is a character of wildness to Derbyshire rather than a straightforward beauty, but I like it very much."

Never had the exquisite sight, smell, sensation of nature—tranquil, enlivening, warm—been more attractive to him as seeing Derbyshire through Elizabeth's eyes. "The view of Dovedale from the top is said to be one of the most pleasing scenes of the Peak."

She nodded, but the exertion required now made it a little harder to climb and speak at the same time. When they reached a flatter, grassy bank, Elizabeth exhaled loudly and stopped. "This is quite the excursion!" she cried, looking up at Thorpe Cloud that, from this vantage point, blocked most of the sun. "It looks so steep I fear I shall have to crawl on my hands and knees to reach the top."

Darcy silently thought that would be pretty near to the truth, but he did not want to discourage her. Instead, he pointed in the other direction for her to take in the view. "There is an immensity to it," he said quietly.

"There is. It is too magnificent, too interesting a landscape for quiet contemplation." She seemed to catch her breath, but rather than begin again, she stared at him with deep interest.

"What is the matter?"

"Do you still love me?"

He had never before been simultaneously shocked and made so happy. Elizabeth dropped her gaze and her cheeks were pink, but there was no doubt in his mind that she wanted an answer.

"With all my soul, my heart, and my strength. Do you love me?"

She could not look him in the eye, but her voice was unhesitating when she said, "I do not have words strong enough to tell you with what ardency I love you."

"Elizabeth," he said, raising a hand to her chin to lift her gaze to his, "I want to turn to you for consolation when I am melancholy, consult with you when I need advice, make a friend of you to share every experience." Although she was smiling, he still felt real apprehension and anxiety when he asked, "Will you do me the honour of marrying me?"

"Yes, happily and eagerly, yes," she said, giving a little laugh before putting her arms around him and laying her head against him. Darcy put his arms around her waist and felt a delight at knowing for certain that Elizabeth loved him. Of all the burdens now facing him, to have this uncertainty resolved, this important matter settled in the way that he had long hoped for, was a profound relief.

As he was recognising how wonderful it felt to hold and touch Elizabeth, she pulled away, smiling. Darcy captured both of her hands, unwilling to lose contact with her so soon.

She gave another shy laugh. "I have wanted you to offer yourself again for so long!"

"You cannot have had such feelings when you first learnt that you would be staying in my house," he said with a laugh of his own. "Part of me wonders if you wanted to hide in Bingley's carriage for the entire fortnight."

She blushed, and he suspected that might have been the case. "My first feelings of esteem and attachment were formed *not long* after arriving, and have grown steadily and swiftly to a perfect admiration and love."

Their amusement faded, and a tender look appeared in Elizabeth's eyes. He was about to ask if he could kiss her when her gaze dropped to his mouth. He gently pulled on her hands to bring her near and leant down to place a delicate kiss on her lips. It was fleeting, but the warmth of it, the meaning of it, made his pulse drum in his ears.

"You are not upset that I spoke first?" she whispered after, still holding his hands.

"Not at all. Although, once we had reached the summit I was determined to ask if your feelings for me had changed."

"I had wondered if you might rebuff me, but at other times I was certain your affections were what they had been in April."

"I have been distracted these past few days, and foolishly thought that I could not speak until every other pressing concern was resolved. I am glad you did not give up on my being constant."

"Oh no, I think until you said otherwise there would have always been a flame of hope alight in my heart."

There was a hitch in her breath, and Darcy pulled her close again to bring his mouth to hers. The press of her lips against his sent a wave of longing through him. She wrapped her arms around his neck and held him tightly, pressing herself against him as he deepened the kiss. His arm went around her waist and he held her in his embrace, their breath coming in short, panting breaths as Elizabeth welcomed his tongue into her mouth.

What she was doing with her warm lips and tongue set his heart racing at a furious pace. His thoughts ran to wanting to untie her bonnet and throw it aside so he could kiss a path down her neck and tangle his hand in her hair. The truth of their circumstances intruded, and he reluctantly stopped doing what was fast becoming his favourite activity.

When she looked at him questioningly, Darcy cleared his throat and gestured to the countryside. "As secluded a spot as this is now, at any moment a carriage might drive past the hill or a shepherd might come in search of his sheep or other tourists might ascend." He tried to apologise for kissing her so thoroughly where they might be seen, but she refused to hear him.

"You were distracted by passion and love, and I cannot fault you for that."

"I did not think I had a heart susceptible to tender passion, dearest Elizabeth, but you unknowingly put love's torch to it." He could not help but kiss her again, and she made a satisfied hum against his lips that nearly drove him mad with desire. "And every smile, every lively expression, every clever quip fans the flame."

"And every kiss?" she asked in a low voice.

He tried to look stern when he said, "I could not say. I have not been so lucky as to have enough of your kisses to be certain. It is poss—"

Elizabeth swiftly took his face in her hands and pressed her lips against his, and he kissed her again with slow and thorough attention. He trembled when her nails scraped along the back of his neck, and she stroked her tongue along his lips before tasting his mouth again. It took all of his effort to keep his hands firmly on her hips and not allow them to wander. She gave him a self-satisfied smile when she pulled back, and he was rather pleased to see how swollen her lips were.

Let us hope that lessens before we reach the others.

"We should keep walking," he said, still breathing heavily. "Do you still wish to reach the summit?"

She shook her head. "I am already breathless, and I am unwilling to chance making it worse for anything less than your kissing me again."

They decided to wind around the hill and descend the other side to await their friends. This introduced a discussion of the intimacy between Fitzwilliam and Mrs Lanyon.

"I am not unconscious of their fond attachment," Elizabeth said after he first made the hint.

"Is it fond on both sides? I could not say for certain what Mrs Lanyon feels for him." She was a quiet woman, and so scrupulously polite that he found it difficult to discern her true thoughts.

"The lady would have to answer to their level of acquaintance," she said, avoiding his eye.

From her tone, he thought Elizabeth had a stronger idea of Mrs Lanyon's feelings than she was willing to admit. "He loves her." She looked at him in surprise. "He has not said so, but I know him; he must." Fitzwilliam would not waste the energy on a woman who gave him no encouragement if he did not have feelings for her.

"I think," she said hesitatingly, "in general, Hester is afraid of opening herself to ridicule for any reason, including marrying a second time. She has to decide not if she loves him, but if Colonel Fitzwilliam is worth the risk of possibly being judged harshly. She is sometimes judged unfairly simply by walking into the room."

Darcy shook his head at people like Caroline Bingley. "The world is moving forward. One day we shall neither be favoured nor hindered because of the colour of our skin."

"That may be true, but I think the degree feels small to a reserved, serious, private person like Hester, particularly as a woman, for women are always judged more severely than men." After a while, she added, "Given their . . . slips, she cannot be indifferent to your cousin."

He was astonished that Elizabeth knew that they were, or, at least, that they had been lovers. "I am amazed Mrs Lanyon admitted to an intrigue."

"I am sure a woman can be a good wife even after having an

intrigue. A woman ought not to be assumed to be immoral for taking a lover when men do the same." He looked at her, both wanting to ask the question and dreading the answer, when she cried, "Oh, not me. I meant Hester. She is widowed, after all."

"And I did not mean to imply that Mrs Lanyon and Fitzwilliam have loose morals," he said in earnest. "I was only surprised she admitted it freely since she is so reserved."

Elizabeth was now blushing fiercely. "Well, both of them are free, after all. What harm is there really to a single person?" She looked about to ask him a question, and then turned away.

"For myself," he said slowly, "the harm would come from the emotions of the entanglement, the possible disappointment when it ended. That, and the possibility that I could suffer a thousand pains for a pleasure," he added drily.

"What do you mean?"

How to explain it without being coarse? "I did not want to risk a lifetime of mercury." Her quiet "Oh" showed she understood him. "But I always thought the emotions required to engage in an affair would be too great a burden after the tryst was over."

She stopped walking and looked at him intently. "So you . . . you have never . . .?"

He could hardly believe they were having this conversation. It was likely to be discussed, but he had not thought it would take place five minutes after they became engaged. Darcy shook his head.

Rather than appearing mortified by the topic, Elizabeth was looking at him as though she thought him the finest man in the world. "I have not had any intrigues either." Her eyes dwelt on his with an ardour he had been unused to behold. "I hardly think it an intrigue or an indication of loose morals if . . . if said lapse is with the person you intend to marry."

The idle thought of what Elizabeth might be like as a lover had certainly crossed his mind, but the idea that she was aching to begin stole his breath. *Could I take Elizabeth to my bed without every guest and servant at Pemberley learning of it in the morning?*

"You were not silent when I asked if you loved me," she said archly. "Has my boldness silenced you now? Shall we pretend it all unsaid?"

Her natural, very frank manner produced in him a satisfying, delighted feeling. "Oh, no. In fact, whenever we are certain to have absolute privacy, you ought to tell me every bold thought and secret wish you have. But we must be circumspect, especially as our friends do not know of our engagement."

"How annoying for us both for you to be so sensible and conscious of propriety," she said teasingly as she resumed walking.

"When do you want to tell them?"

"I could run down this hill crying it out at the top of my lungs, but I also would not mind time to enjoy my newfound happiness before we share it."

Darcy saw the wisdom of it and agreed to wait another day or two. His own mind was now relieved from a heavy weight of uncertainty, and after quiet reflection, and perhaps more time in private with Elizabeth, he would be able to speak of his engagement with tolerable composure. Everything felt too recent to be shared. "We still ought to write to your father tomorrow," he said.

"I can tell him how much I have come to esteem and admire you since my mother told him how shockingly rude you were on our first meeting. I will assure him that I can be happy with a man who thought me not handsome enough to dance with."

He resigned himself to being laughed at with a rueful smile and a quiet apology.

"I know you have much to occupy you," she said when they rounded Thorpe Cloud and made their descent, the river in sight again, "but are *you* happy, my dear Darcy?"

"I would be happier if you gave me my name when we are alone," he said, and she nodded whilst a grin threatened to pull at her lips. "I am happy. And I hope thrice happy shall we be in three weeks."

"So soon?" Elizabeth laughed and put her arm through his and tugged him closer. "I do want to return to Hertfordshire first, to part from my parents. You are eager considering how long it felt waiting for you to come to the point."

"Perhaps four or five weeks, then, so you have time to travel home," he said stiffly, "but I see no reason for a long engagement, do you?"

Elizabeth tilted her head to look directly at him. "Fitzwilliam?" Her voice sounded heavy, as though his name itself was weighty on her lips. His heart was now pounding a little too fast. "I am as eager to marry as you are."

CHAPTER SIXTEEN

"Have you enjoyed your day at Dovedale, Miss Bennet?"

Elizabeth was seated next to Miss Darcy and had been in pleasant conversation with her as they finished their picnic under the shade of the alder trees skirting the river. Hester went to a small hill to sketch, Mrs Annesley was reading, and Darcy and his cousin were fishing. She could hear them muttering to themselves about grayling and trout, but their baskets were empty.

She could not keep her eyes from admiring the brother when she answered the sister. "My happiness certainly has been promoted by the excursion."

Darcy must have felt her attention; he turned from the water to give her a smile. His features in general were under control, but she knew now that they could be expressive of deep feeling when moved by his emotions. A rush of heat passed through her at the thought of his words, his look, the feeling of his being pressed against her. There had been unparalleled tenderness in all of Darcy's actions towards her today, but she felt that tenderness was only a breath away from an unconquerable passion.

She turned from Miss Darcy as a joyful grin threatened to burst from her lips. She had only secured his affections two hours ago, but now that they had admitted to every feeling, she was eager to embrace him as a lover. Darcy had admitted to never having one before, but he had not shied away when she suggested it was not too early for them to begin.

She was certain she would never forget the look in his eye when he bent to kiss her, the way he wrapped his arms around her. She had felt the heat of him, the barely contained strength, when he held her against him on Thorpe Cloud. She wanted to see all that strength without any clothes covering it up.

"I hope this is not your last visit to Pemberley," Miss Darcy went on, and Elizabeth pushed her immodest thoughts away to be the friend that Miss Darcy deserved. Soon she could call her Georgiana and profess all the affections of a sister.

"I know that you cannot always want guests about when you are at home, so I am grateful that you have made me feel so welcome. I hope that we shall be dear friends."

Miss Darcy blushed, but nodded eagerly. The men then came from the river and set down their tackle in such a manner as to tell everyone that they did not have any sport. She exchanged an amused smile with Miss Darcy as Hester came from the hill and packed her pencils and paper.

"I do not think the anglers were successful," Miss Darcy whispered.

"Will your brother and cousin be in a poor temper today because of it?"

Miss Darcy shrugged. Elizabeth gave her a small smile and decided to hint at their soon-to-be nearer relationship. "Shall I practise to improve my powers of consoling your brother and charming away his worries?" Miss Darcy smiled, her expression amused.

"You are not going to be in a fit of bad temper for the rest of the day, are you?" Elizabeth called to them both, but looked expressively at Darcy. "I would hate for there not to be a single thing for you to enjoy about our excursion to Dovedale."

Darcy frowned, saying something or other about "the damned wrong-sized flies" as he put away his tackle.

"Maybe you should get married," Colonel Fitzwilliam said to him.

"You need a wife to tease you into better humour. Do you not agree, Mrs Lanyon?"

"Certainly. His lady ought to be of a friendly disposition to counteract his gravity," added Hester.

Elizabeth exchanged a look with Darcy, who turned slightly pink and clenched his jaw. *They are determined to see us engaged.* Elizabeth wished that Darcy could find amusement in their charmingly awkward attempts to forward his interest in her, at their help being entirely unneeded, but he was either mortified or too genuinely annoyed at not having caught anything.

"And his chosen lady ought to be a good-humoured woman who has the courage to stand up to him," said Colonel Fitzwilliam. "Miss Bennet, where shall we find such a woman to esteem Darcy?"

For such a conversational man, one who was in general at ease, he was anything but subtle. "It cannot be difficult, I am sure, to find such a woman. It is impossible to know Mr Darcy without esteeming him."

"You did not always think so," Darcy said, standing from the tackle box.

"I did not always know you as I do now."

She hoped he saw in her brief look all the affection and esteem he could wish for. At least it seemed his annoyance over the angling was gone.

"What say you, Georgiana?" The colonel was determined to keep on the topic. "What manner of woman do you want to be your sister?"

"That is entirely up to Fitzwilliam," she said quickly. "But . . ." She looked at Elizabeth, but not into her eyes. "I am sure Fitzwilliam would make an affectionate husband. And he is remarkably clever."

"You have all said quite enough," Darcy said firmly.

The conversation ended, and everyone saw to gathering their own things to walk back to the carriage. Darcy and Elizabeth, by unspoken agreement, let the others outstrip them on the path along the river. When they had fallen far behind, he said, "If we had not come to the point earlier, I would not have had patience for their hints. As it is, I am too happy with my good fortune to be resentful."

"They did lay it on with a trowel"—Darcy laughed—"but they love you and they think marrying me will make you happy. And Hester knows that I have been desperate to command five minutes of your time to learn if you loved me."

"At least now I know that Georgiana desires the connexion as much as Fitzwilliam does."

"Yes, and now because of her I know that you would be a fond and kind husband and that you are clever. Thank goodness for your sister's good information, otherwise I would not know what manner of man I promised myself to."

He laughed again. It was quiet and restrained, but the amusement was genuine. Elizabeth said, "Why, I had no idea that you had such beautiful teeth. I shall have to keep you smiling and laughing so you show them more often."

"You intend to keep me in perpetual drollery, then. Are you up to such a task?" he asked, leaning down to kiss her cheek since no one was near.

"I ought to say that I expect you to make the chore worth my while," she said, linking her arm through his, "but the truth is I want to sport with you and make you smile as often as I can."

They continued in this manner, walking slowly, leaning against one another, teasing and laughing, until they arrived at the carriage. As they approached the others, Elizabeth dropped his arm, and he reined in his smiles so they would lead to no suspicion. Colonel Fitzwilliam gave a pointed look at Darcy and mouthed the word "Well?" and he returned his look very innocently and whispered, "What?"

His cousin huffed, and Elizabeth shared an amused glance with Darcy as Hester came near.

"Mr Darcy, I sent your man ahead to Lord Poole's for Lewis and Mr Utterson to travel back with us."

Immediately, Darcy looked like the sort of man who could frighten away another's speech with a haughty glance. His posture changed, and Elizabeth could feel the tension rolling off of him.

How will he ever keep from showing his suspicion until he can prove if one of them killed Carew?

"Capital!" Colonel Fitzwilliam cried, coming beside them. "Darcy, if you intend to drive, lead on." He gestured to the box with a hard look in his eye. Darcy took the hint, and Elizabeth was grateful his cousin was here to help manage Darcy's behaviour. "Mrs Lanyon, may I?"

Colonel Fitzwilliam assisted the ladies into the barouche, and they made the short, but sometimes steep, drive to Tissington to meet Mr Balfour and Mr Utterson. She could understand Darcy's feelings; in Meryton he could scarcely touch his hat to Wickham and now he would have to act the gracious host to someone who might be a killer. Her own stomach twisted at the thought of bantering with Mr Balfour or walking the gallery with Mr Utterson.

I will have to overcome my revulsion if I am to help ease Darcy's manner in front of the others.

They arrived at Lord Poole's seat and saw Mr Balfour and another man on the sweep by his travelling coach. Everyone alighted and Lord Poole met them graciously. He was a polite man satisfied with his consequence and was about as old as her father.

"How are you, Hester?" Mr Balfour said, greeting his sister with a kiss. He then turned to Miss Darcy. "I understand you want to return home in the finest travelling chariot in the Peak. Will your brother allow you and Mrs Annesley to ride home with me? I promise to not upset them, my dear Darcy."

Darcy gave a restrained smile.

"I see Fitzwilliam managed to do what I could not," he went on. "He was able to convince you to have a few hours of recreation. I am glad of it! Shall I have the same luck and convince you to shoot with me before we leave Pemberley?"

Darcy touched his hat but said not a word as Lord Poole joined them.

"My lord, where is Mr Utterson?" Elizabeth asked whilst Mr Balfour assisted Miss Darcy and Mrs Annesley into his carriage and asked their opinions on the upholstery.

"He said his man forgot something and ran back inside," his lordship answered. "He ought to be here by now. Darcy"—he turned—"I am glad you are enjoying yourself with your friends. I understand your estate village suffered losses last week."

Darcy chatted easily enough with his fellow landowner about the storm and their tenants, but then Mr Utterson ran down the steps. The effect was immediate. A shade of hauteur overspread Darcy's features.

"Did you find whatever it was, Utterson?" Lord Poole asked, and Mr Utterson gave a polite assent and thanked him for his hospitality. Whatever Mr Utterson had forgotten inside must have been small enough to fit in his pockets because he carried nothing.

"Say a fond farewell?" Elizabeth heard Mr Balfour whisper to his friend before he took leave from his lordship. Mr Utterson gave him a scathing look and then threw himself into Darcy's barouche.

"How d'ye do?" he muttered with a careless wave towards the box. He nodded to her and Hester, and then angled his body away from them. *He really is an unpleasant sort of man.*

They would have to look at a surly and silent Mr Utterson for the ride home. From the chatter that she heard from Mr Balfour's carriage, Mrs Annesley and Miss Darcy were sure to be better entertained.

She watched Darcy as he cued the horses. The set of his shoulders, the tight grip on the reins, the silence. They would have to prove soon which man killed Carew because Darcy was not going to manage a complaisant attitude towards them for long.

I have to tell him that I know he suspects one of his friends. Darcy should know that he need not hide anything from her. She wanted to enjoy her newfound happiness with him, to move towards the ease and familiarity that was growing between them, to enjoy a season of courtship before they married. But she knew Carew's death would weigh on him until he found her killer.

Soon she would leave Pemberley to marry from Longbourn. It was not that she would be long parted from him, but Derbyshire already felt more like home, and right now Darcy's sanctuary was under siege. She was certain he felt absolutely wretched.

I cannot leave until we prove who killed Carew.

"I thought I would find you here."

Darcy looked up and saw that Fitzwilliam stood in the doorway to his father's favourite room. Everyone else was abed, but Darcy had been sitting at his father's desk to view the stairs, and to think. He was in his shirtsleeves, his cravat loosened, but he was no more relaxed now than he was when he first sat down.

"No one left the house tonight," Darcy said whilst his cousin entered to sit near the empty grate. "After the party broke up, I sat here to catch anyone who tried to sneak away, but . . ."

"I know, I checked that the doors were still locked myself," Fitzwilliam said. "Both of their servants said their masters were abed. Perhaps they might try tomorrow, but I think there is nothing unattended left in Lambton to take. Did you search Balfour's and Utterson's rooms this morning?"

He said this as though invading someone's privacy was such an easy thing to do. Darcy might have the right to enter any room in Pemberley whenever he pleased, but it still felt wrong. He nodded, and there was nothing else to say. He had seen nothing that did not belong.

"Well, my dear Darcy, then I shall check the pawnshops in the largest neighbouring towns and hope to turn up a stolen item and a name or a description, something that you can take to the magistrate."

Darcy clenched his fists. "I want to haul them into a room, lock the door, and refuse to let them leave until one of them confesses to killing Carew."

Fitzwilliam scoffed. "Balfour and Utterson are from influential and well-connected families. You do not accuse the son of a rich Scottish member of parliament or the son of a baronet of stealing and killing without proof."

Darcy exhaled loudly. The pain of the betrayal and the anxiety of who had done it was almost too much to bear. *I had been happy today.* He ought to have come home delighted after having proposed and been accepted. But the reality of Carew's death came roaring back with the return of Balfour and Utterson. He could scarcely make it through the evening with a pleasant face.

"Go to bed. No one is leaving tonight."

Darcy started. He had forgotten his cousin was there. "Soon."

"You know, now that you have met their immediate needs," Fitzwilliam said, rising, "your villagers and tenants might be glad to know the master is going to marry. That might be reassuring to anyone concerned about Pemberley's future."

"You ought to go to bed too."

"You ought to ask Miss Bennet again. It is plain that she admires you."

He did not want to discuss Elizabeth now or have to explain why he was not showing the happiness he ought to feel now that he was finally engaged to the woman he loved. "Since we are dispensing advice, why do you not ask Mrs Lanyon to marry you?"

"You know why." Darcy regretted the question, but before he could apologise, Fitzwilliam said, teasingly, "I shall overlook your rudeness since you said that out of jealousy when you still have not performed to the hilt. You could solve that problem too, you know."

Darcy did not so much as raise his eyes. "Go away." Under his breath, he muttered, "And I am not untouched."

"Not entirely, but there are pleasures you are yet ignorant of. It is about time; you are nearly thirty."

"My not being married had more to do with it than my age."

"How romantic. I feel for Miss Bennet, though. If you ever end up—"

"Good night, Fitzwilliam!"

Darcy leant on the desk, resting his head in his hands as he listened to the footsteps move away. This manner of sporting with him was common, but he had no patience for it now.

Balfour or Utterson killed someone.

Pemberley was silent and he was alone, but he felt the oppressive agony of despair as though it was a presence in the room screaming at him. Both men had been his friend, and the deception, the dishonesty, the falseness of that friendship burned him. *I brought a man into my home who is capable of killing someone and dumping her body in a stream.* The guilt was excruciating.

He heard footsteps re-enter the doorway. "Damn it, I told you to go to bed."

"You did not."

Darcy snapped his head up and saw Elizabeth come near and set a chamberstick on the desk. "After the way you acted in the drawing room, I thought you might need company. I have waited a long time for everyone else to go to bed so I could talk with you."

She came around the desk and reached out a hand. Darcy said a quiet apology as he pressed a kiss to it, then held a loose grip on it. "I am perfectly well, dearest Elizabeth."

"This is you well?" She raised her eyebrows. "It is a good thing we did not announce our engagement, otherwise all of your friends would think you a reluctant groom. They would think that you were being forced to the altar with a knife at your back."

He smiled. "On the contrary. I know I am the last man in the world you could be prevailed on to marry. If anyone knew our history, they would think it was *you* who had to be coerced down the aisle."

She perched at the edge of the desk. "Now that you think Jane is worthy of Charles, I am willing to accept you to have your house, your purse, and your protection at my command."

"So you are not one bit in love with me?"

"I fell madly in love with you, but for now it is a great secret."

He laughed softly, enjoying having Elizabeth here with him.

"Fitzwilliam, why are you up so late, and all alone, in the dark?"

I was considering the heartless behaviour of someone I trusted, someone capable of murder. "I was distracted by unpleasant thoughts, and I thought an interval of serious meditation was the best corrective."

"You had your cousin set up a watch in the village." He looked at her in surprise at her wanting to talk about that. "It is astonishing that a tenant would raid the debris and damaged houses of their own neighbours for valuables, especially since you have done so well in assuaging their fears and in meeting their immediate needs."

"Yes," he said shortly, not wanting to worry her with it, "the conduct of the looter astonishes me beyond measure."

She waited as though she expected him to say more before saying, "The same person might have broken into Pemberley to steal the candlestick that matches this one," she said, pointing to the one still on the desk.

He let go of her hand, leant back in his chair, and nodded, wondering what her point was.

"It was likely the same person who stole it, who looted the village, and who killed Carew." She took a breath. "But we both know that the person who took the taperstick from this desk did not have to break anything to gain entry to this house"—she gave him such a sad look—"because it was one of your guests. One of your friends probably killed her."

He did not so much as blink, shift his weight, or look away. Despite shielding her from it, Elizabeth had observed, assessed, and came to the same conclusion Fitzwilliam had. He had to throw off all reserve and speak to her with the confidence of a husband who loves and trusts his wife.

"I did not want to worry you," he whispered.

"Thank you for wanting to spare me the pain of knowing, but what about you?"

"Me?"

"You must feel pain at this, this breach of trust—"

"I am only angry," he said quickly, "and determined to prove who is guilty and haul him before Mr Birch." The truth of the murder was one thing, but he did not want to confess his feelings about it, even if he had little hope of concealing them.

"If we found Carew's ring amongst their things, would that be enough for the magistrate?"

He noticed her use of "we" and found it a relief. "I searched their rooms this morning before we left for Dovedale." He had the right to search any room in his house, so long as he did not break open anything that was locked. "Balfour has a lockbox, Utterson a trunk, but there was nothing I saw that was out of place to my eye."

"And nothing was stolen from the village since Colonel Fitzwilliam set up a night watch?"

He shook his head, running a hand across his eyes. "No one stole anything last night whilst they were at Lord Poole's, and no one left the house tonight. I think we need not continue the watch. Fitzwilliam intends to check the pawnshops in Matlock and Buxton tomorrow for anything recognisable and ask if new pawners have been in."

Elizabeth frowned in thought. "They both were gone from Pemberley the morning Carew died. Someone must have seen them."

"They both *claimed* to be gone, but everything had been in

disarray here, and I and the servants were always going in and out of the house. His gaming friends in Buxton might lie for Balfour or Lord Poole might lie for Utterson. I cannot rely on that." He felt the agitation, the frustration, building in his chest again. "Once I have anything to bring before the magistrate, then he can compel witnesses to testify in court. Until then"—he sighed and took her hand again—"I need proof, something specific, before I go back to Mr Birch."

She traced her thumb along the back of his hand. "Who do you think it was?" she whispered.

"It is hard to accept either of them stole valuables and"—he swallowed—"killed someone over them. Money must be the motive, but both men still receive some monies from their fathers. Balfour will inherit, and Utterson will become a barrister."

"I wonder if Mr Utterson is best qualified for that species of business."

Darcy considered it. "He might know that he is not, and might be in want of money so he can spend like he thinks the son of a baronet should since he cannot earn a great income by his profession."

"Mr Utterson seems to have clearness and quickness of mind, but he can sometimes be unjust or unkind."

"And Balfour talks a great deal, and always with animation. But does being affable make him less likely to be guilty? Does Utterson's resentful and ungracious nature make him more likely to be guilty?"

Elizabeth looked as though she wished so much that this was a question she could answer.

"Balfour cares deeply about reputation and appearances," he finally said, "and wants to spend, but his father limits him."

"That sounds like Mr Utterson as well."

He nodded, staring at the space on the desk where the other taperstick should be. "This is why I need proof."

"I know we shall find it." She forced him to meet her eye and gave him an earnest look. "You will either catch them in the act when they are tempted again, or the pawnbroker will have information you can take to the magistrate."

Darcy pressed a kiss to her hand as a thank you, and she surprised him by slowly lifting off the desk and settling gently on his lap. "Is this good?" she whispered.

He rested his hands on her hips, and she gradually brought hers to his shoulders. He nodded as she pressed her forehead to his, and he closed his eyes. Before he could enjoy the sweet, tight tension that was threatening to overtake him, she said, "I wish you would talk about it with me."

"What more is there to say?" he asked, opening his eyes. "I need proof, and I will soon have it."

Those large dark eyes of hers, that often judged so well, were giving him an expectant look. "One of your friends stole from your tenants and killed someone. You might not have the words to explain it, but you cannot hide from me how hurt you are."

One of her hands had moved behind his neck and was brushing through his hair. It was such an intimate gesture, with her sitting in his lap and looking at him as though nothing in the world mattered more than what he was about to say. "I have plenty of words—sorrow, regret, rage, grief—but none of them properly express my feelings about this sickening betrayal."

"It is a betrayal you could never have expected."

He exhaled and looked directly into her eyes. "It is my fault. Whoever it was, they were my friend. I invited him into my home, trusted him, introduced him to my sister. It is my fault Molly Carew is dead, my fault that her father broke down in his parlour and had to build her coffin, my fault that—"

"It is not!"

"I am responsible for a killer being welcomed at Pemberley."

Elizabeth shook her head. "You were deceived, everyone was deceived, and no one could have known Mr Balfour or Mr Utterson was capable of such a thing. It is a betrayal of trust, of the bonds of friendship." Her fingertips were still absently stroking his neck. "You must be suffering so much."

"I had to drive home with Balfour with my sister and Utterson with you with the knowledge that one of them could murder you."

"That was not going to happen in an open carriage—"

"And I am sure Carew felt safe walking in Pemberley's park, even as she approached whoever it was who murdered her!"

She flinched, and he winced at having raised his voice. "I am sorry, my dear. It is simply a horrible thought, that she knew her attacker but had not known to be afraid of him. She might not have even run or defended herself because he was supposed to be a gentleman, the master's friend." He gripped her a little tighter. "I brought this into my home, Elizabeth."

"Oh, Fitzwilliam, it is not your fault." She pressed a kiss to his cheek, lingering there. "Guilt is a terrible taskmaster."

"Yes," he whispered. "Yes, it is."

"You have a responsibility to everyone at Pemberley, of course, for their safety, their happiness—but you did not kill Carew. You cannot take on all of this guilt. Leave some for Mr Balfour or Mr Utterson. They are to blame, not you."

He nodded and gave a half-smile. She was not wrong, of course, but that did not lessen his self-reproach.

"I am torturing myself thinking of what Carew's final moments must have been like," he said, remembering turning over her body in the stream, the blood on the side of her head. "Of what her father suffers now and will suffer further when I tell him that my friend, the friend of the man who employs him and employed his daughter, who he had a right to expect would keep his daughter safe . . ." He shook his head.

"You cannot carry the pain of someone else's loss."

"In this case, I think I can."

She brought a hand to his cheek and gave him a sad smile. "Then you shall have to let me help you carry the burden."

Darcy brought his hands to her face and pressed a soft kiss against her mouth. He tried to draw back and thank her, but Elizabeth increased the pressure of her lips and coaxed his lips apart, slipping her tongue deep into his mouth. The intensity in her kiss set his mind whirling and gave him the courage to let his hands move up from her hips.

Elizabeth moaned softly into his mouth, and rather than tensing under his touch, she pressed into his hands, making desperate little sounds that spurred him on. He could have kissed her and touched her like this for hours, but Elizabeth pulled away to kiss his jaw and neck. Darcy sighed at this calmer feeling after such a passionate exchange, but then she moved her hand from around his shoulder to down between them to touch him.

The air in his lungs escaped in a rush, his voice low due to his tightening throat. "You don't have—"

"I want to," she murmured into his ear.

He could hardly argue with such a reasonable answer. It was a foreign sensation to feel someone else's fingers drawing him to life. Even through his clothes, he shuddered at the gentle contact. After enjoying it for longer than he should, he moved her hand away and wrapped his arms around her, pulling her tighter against him, seeking her lips. She relaxed into him, parting her lips and offering her tongue, but this time both of their hands stayed in one place.

"Will you come to bed with me?" she asked after this exchange ended.

His heart raced along with his ardour even as he shook his head. "This . . . this pain, this grief about what happened—it is a terrible reason to go to bed with you."

"Only if it was the only reason." Her eyes were dark and full of meaning. "If Hester, or Caroline, or any other woman came in here looking to comfort you, would you have let them this far into the room?" He shook his head. "There is nothing wrong with your finding solace with me." She shifted in his lap and gave a quick downward glance, her lips parted. "If you said yes, it would be because you love me, and have loved me for months, and because I have promised to marry you."

What had before been only transient desires, Elizabeth inspired in him a rising passion, and thoughts of her as his wife began to take a more settled hold in his imagination. He had never felt the calm satisfaction of being loved, and certainly not by someone who so well understood him. Darcy brought a hand to her cheek, running his thumb across her lips until she gave it a firm kiss. "I have been a fool. I should have asked you to marry me a week ago, and I should have said yes the moment the invitation left your lips."

Her brow creased in sympathy. "Not a fool, Fitzwilliam. Perhaps you have been . . . rather too much of a gentleman."

"Then ask me again."

"If I were to invite you to come to my room in ten minutes and"—she blushed prettily but did not look away—"and stay for the rest of the night, would you?"

"Of course."

CHAPTER SEVENTEEN

Elizabeth dressed for bed and paced with a mixture of tension and excitement. She was ending the day with a complete reversal of her situation, and at various moments was certain she would laugh from happiness at finally being assured of Darcy's love or laugh from nerves at knowing what was to happen now.

She had to appear at least outwardly composed before Darcy entered. She knew enough of his character that if she appeared unsettled, he was certain to not spend the night with her.

She tried to remember what Jane had told her, and almost wished she had asked Hester if she had any helpful advice. What was slyly spoken of at weddings and christenings were perhaps the most useful hints she had. But they were two intelligent, curious people who loved each other; how difficult could it be?

There was a soft knock, and the door opened. Darcy entered with a hurried air, and she saw him bend and flex his fingers as though his hand had shaken whilst he closed the door.

"You are here," she said, rather dumbly, she realised.

He tilted his head. "Did your heart prophecise some mischance? Did you think I would get lost?" He smiled. "You cannot have thought that I would change my mind."

Elizabeth shook her head as he came nearer, noticing that he had also dressed for bed. She wondered if she ought to unfasten his wrapping gown or let him do it. Should she take her dressing gown off first? He gave her a long, conscious look; she hoped he was as eager as she was. Darcy might be able to hear how loudly her heart was beating.

"You seem thoughtful," Darcy said quietly. "What are you feeling?"

"I feel overpowering happiness." He did not appear to believe her. "Perhaps some trepidation too."

"We don't have—"

"I want to," she said quickly. "I am simply wondering what it will be like. But I won't have an answer if we only stand here looking at one another."

She smiled and stepped closer, but he did not open his arms as she expected.

"Before, there was a self-imposed line beyond which I would not go," he said haltingly. "That does not matter now because we are going to marry. But all of my love and respect for you will remain exactly the same no matter what you decide."

"I already decided," she said firmly. "I am not confused about what I want." *Only about how to do it.*

"*I* need not retract or qualify anything," he said in a tone of sincere tenderness, "but I leave it entirely to you to decide what will happen now."

"Then I have decided," she said slowly, "that we are overdressed." Elizabeth unfastened each button on his wrapping gown. His breath came out in a rush, and he untied hers and slipped it off before tossing his to the chair. Darcy's fingers came back to her shoulders, delicately brushing along her skin at the edge of her shift. He wore only a long nightshirt, and she had a thought of how soon would it be before they were wearing nothing at all.

Darcy was still silent and unmoving aside from his fingertips tracing back and forth. *He must have meant it when he said I had to decide what would happen.* She smiled before bringing her hands to his face and kissing him. He wrapped an arm around her waist to pull her against him. It was a tender kiss that quickly changed into a more passionate meeting of tongues and an ardent pressure of lips.

She let out a whimper when he moved his palm to her breast, and he pulled back abruptly.

"I am sorry." Darcy would not look her in the eye and had even held up his hand in surrender.

Elizabeth shook her head and took his hand to move it back. "Only be sorry if you stop."

His eyes darkened and an alertness came into them. He nodded slightly before tugging her body flush with his again. He kissed her roughly and palmed her breast harder, this time not stopping or slowing when she moaned. It was as though he had finally accepted that she was willing and eager.

She closed her eyes until she felt the soft pressure of his lips against her neck. She had never felt anything like this, his teeth nipping behind her ear, one hand slowly twisting in her hair, the other tugging open the drawing string at her bodice to touch her breasts.

He brought his gaze to her eyes before tracing his hands down to gather the fabric of her shift in his hand. "May I take this off?"

When she nodded, he pulled it up and over her head. As he stared at her, a small sound came from his throat that she had never heard before, and Elizabeth wanted to hear him make it over and over. She wanted to kiss and touch every part of him, but her mouth was incapable of forming words when Darcy looked at her like that. Instead, she gestured vaguely to his nightshirt to show how she wanted that last piece of linen gone.

Darcy took it off far too slowly for her liking, but at least by the time he pulled it over his head and tossed it aside, she already had a satisfying glimpse of him before he wrapped her in his arms again and kissed her feverishly.

He wants me as much as I want him.

She ran her hands across his shoulders and then pressed kisses down his chest. He started, and she pulled back, surprised. Darcy shook his head, smiling. "Don't stop—only, no one has ever—" He swallowed thickly and gave her a heated look. "No one has stroked their fingers or kissed me there."

She kissed his chest a few more times, tracing her fingers across him before putting her arms around him. Although they had just seen each other naked for the first time, there was something just as intimate about her bare breasts pressed against his chest. He kissed her over and over, flicking his tongue against hers, tentatively at first, but then with a passion that made her moan and rock her hips against him.

Darcy then pulled away to look into her eyes. "I love you."

She whispered, "I love you too," and kissed the side of his neck, which earned her a tremor. It made her wonder how Darcy might react if she kissed the inside of his thighs in the same way. His breath came faster when she softly touched him there, and he brought a hand to her jaw to draw her back to his lips. Their tongues were stroking against each other, teeth nipping, when he shuddered at the tight grip of her hand around him.

"We can stop with this," he said in a rasp that made her never want to stop touching him this way.

"Do you want to stop?" She would not believe him if he said yes.

"No," he said through a moan, "but I want you to be happy both tonight and when you wake up tomorrow."

"I *am* eager . . ."

Darcy heard something in her voice and drew back, and she dropped her hand. He pushed the hair back from her face and gave her a sympathetic look, waiting for her to speak.

"Just . . . inexperienced, I guess."

"So am I. I think we will understand everything quickly enough." He pressed a kiss to her temple and lightly ran his hands down her body to rest on her hips. "Besides," he said in a low voice, "we seem to be doing well so far."

"Jane said—"

"Don't tell me," he said seriously. When she frowned, he added, "Anything you learnt from Jane is intrinsically tied to Bingley, and I will live happier without knowing what he is like behind closed doors."

She laughed, and he laughed along with her, and the rest of her tension dissolved and left her only with wanting the first object of her warmest, devoted love. Elizabeth laced her fingers together at his neck, and when she opened her mouth to his, Darcy drew his hands low beneath her backside and squeezed. When he nibbled at her bottom lip, they were soon kissing again the way she wanted, all tongue and teeth and unrestrained passion.

"I want to take you to bed."

His voice was rougher than before, heavy with desire for something more. She felt him against her, hot and insistent. It made her faint with pleasure as she nodded. His expression was more expectant, more confident now as he walked her backward to the bed, kissing her hard along the way.

The back of her legs hit the bed and she ran her hands across his bare chest, saying, "I have wanted this all week."

Elizabeth was flat on her back before she could take a breath, and the look on Darcy's face sent a rush of heat down her body. He joined her on the bed and lowered his mouth to one breast whilst bringing his hand to stroke the other. When that hand moved lower, she arched into him with a sigh.

It was both blissful and strange to be touched where she had never been touched by anyone else. He was too slow at first, or maybe a little uneasy, to fully satisfy her, but that did nothing to quell the desire that had been building since Darcy entered her room. She wondered if she should tell him exactly what to do, but there was an aspect to it that was intuitive. She could tell he focused on the subtle changes in her breathing or the way that she shifted her hips when he touched her.

"Like that?" Darcy's voice was low in her ear before kissing along her neck.

She tried to speak, but all that she managed was a nod and a long moan. Soon she was in a frenzy of passion that was unlike anything she had felt before. Elizabeth answered him more fully by throwing an arm around him and kissing him, their kisses fervent until she gave a deep cry.

"Elizabeth," Darcy whispered, tracing his thumb across her lips. Her eyes fluttered open to see him looking intently at her. His eyes were wonderfully dark, and full of an open warmth. "You are beautiful."

The compliment took her aback, and she gave a nervous laugh. "You sound surprised." She doubted she looked beautiful since she was certain her face was flushed, she was covered in sweat, and she knew her hair was plastered about her face.

His mouth twitched, but his voice was low and serious when he said, "Surprised that I get to see you like this."

Darcy's breathing was a little uneven. She pressed a kiss to his lips and put enough pressure on his shoulders to show that she wanted him on top of her. He braced two hands on either side of her, and he looked down intently between them.

His gaze blinked to hers, long enough to gauge that she was willing. Gently, and ever so slowly, he pushed into her. He kissed her softly across her face, whispering apologies and endearments as she winced. Eventually, it was easier to arch towards him, allowing him to enter farther.

He exhaled loudly and then hung his head. "Oh God, Elizabeth."

This made her kiss him again, slowly and lazily as she basked in what was finally happening. She thought she wanted him to move, but she was unused to this build, only the release he had given her before. His mouth trailed away from her lips and nudged her chin up to get to her neck. She surrendered immediately, tilting her head back as he sucked at the ragged pulse in her throat.

"I need—Please, Elizabeth, I need to move."

She nodded, not realising that he had been waiting for her. His slow rhythm built the same desire in her that she had thought was satisfied only a few moments ago. He continued to glance down, watching her body envelop him over and over as he slowly moved. Darcy seemed as roused by what he was seeing as much as by what he was feeling.

As he moved over her, his breathing more pronounced with building passion, she wished he would move faster. *How is he supposed to know what I want?* "Fitzwilliam?" He stopped moving entirely and she whimpered in frustration. "No, don't stop. Can you move faster?"

He leant down to give her a fierce kiss before complying, moving not only faster but harder. He was now laid out more fully atop her and she hooked a leg around his hip. She started to move in counterpoint to him, her fingernails scraping into his shoulders and down his back as he moved with more fervour. She felt the same ecstasy as before come on at length, and she was fairly certain she felt the same symptoms from Darcy.

She could only make out some of what he was saying. He might have been swearing, or praying, but she often heard her own name. This time, she cried out his name at the last. Darcy was now still and quiet, except for his pounding heart that she could feel beating against her own chest. For a while, they were both silent, perhaps tongue-tied, with joy and rapture.

"Was it worth the wait?" she asked, running her fingertips through his hair.

He hummed happily against her neck, and she held him a little tighter. There was a stronger and more satisfied intimacy between them now.

"I could ask you the same question, dearest Elizabeth." He pressed a long kiss against her throat.

"Oh, yes. I hope you won't make me wait long to do it again."

Darcy was not a man given to broad smiles. More often his lips just turned up and a hint of humour shone in his eyes, but now he looked radiant. He then gave her an ardent kiss that seemed to express all of his satisfied desires and enduring love.

"I am at your command."

Darcy was startled awake when something landed roughly on his face. He flinched and sat bolt upright, not knowing where he was. His alarm fell away as he realised he was still in Elizabeth's bed, and she was facing him with her arm outstretched. He rubbed his nose where her hand had hit him and, looking at the light coming in through the curtain, guessed it must be near five o'clock in the morning. He had not meant to stay this long.

He dimly remembered blowing out the candles and Elizabeth insisting he stay for "a little while longer," and they must have both fallen asleep.

Darcy leant against the headboard and pushed back a strand of hair that had fallen over her cheek. She had a beautifully expressive face, even whilst she was sleeping. *Here is the person who has made me so happy.* This lovely woman was going to be his wife. An intelligent companion he could trust in, confide in. For a while, he watched her sleep, stroking his fingers through her hair until she began to stir.

"Good morning," she said thickly. "Why are you awake already?"

"I can tell you are not used to sleeping with anyone," he said, lying back down next to her. "You turned in your sleep and threw out your hand, striking me in the face."

He laughed, and there was just enough light to tell that she blushed. "Well, you must have been on my side." Elizabeth ran her hand up and down his arm. "I hope this does not put you off wanting to share a bed with me."

Her voice had raised in question, and Darcy caught her hand and kissed it before putting an arm around her. "I should have told you: one of the conditions of marrying me is that we share a bed every night."

She gave a happy sigh. "I am glad you were not too proud to ask me again to marry you."

Good God, so am I. "Are you glad for anything else?" he asked, hoping that she was as content this morning as she had been last night.

"Yes, but I think I have forgotten the finer points. Would you be so good as to remind me?" She gave a smile of the tenderest satisfaction, and he met the kiss she leant forward to give him.

"I want to, but a maid will be in shortly, and I am already likely to pass a footman in the corridor as it is." He sighed as his mind fully appreciated that today was a new day. "Besides, I must find out what happened at the pawnshops in the nearest towns, and try to—"

"No, none of that when we are stark naked." She leant up and rested her head on her hand. "I am happy to talk with you about all things, including *that* matter, but not now. I will not have my happy memories ruined."

She was serious, and he could not blame her. He nodded and kissed her lightly before leaving the bed to find his clothes.

As he drew on his nightshirt, he said, "Am I allowed to speak about business related to you? I intend to write to your father today, if you want to include your own letter, and we can arrange your return to

Hertfordshire to say goodbye to your parents." He put on his dressing gown. "I would like to marry you before October, and I think everything can be settled within a month."

"I will allow that discussion only because you are dressed, but all other business must wait until we are both clothed."

He fastened his dressing gown and came back to the bed. "That is perfectly fair."

She sat up to kiss him, not caring at all that the bedclothes had fallen away and she was naked. It was a natural development of the intimacy of their relationship. He looked at her as she settled herself back on the pillow, smiling up at him. He would never again be able to look at her without knowing all of this, all of her.

"I love you, Elizabeth."

DARCY BURNED WITH IMPATIENCE TO FINISH HIS BUSINESS WITH HIS distressed steward and finish meeting with the worried tenants who called during his early hours. Once these tasks were complete, he could write to Elizabeth's father, and then hopefully spend half an hour in her company before he had to meet everyone at breakfast.

However, his letter to Mr Bennet did not come to him as easily as he thought it would. He had to convince this gentleman of his undying regard for his daughter in terms that would not offend him, but also convince Mr Bennet to grant his blessing. Whilst they were in Dovedale, Elizabeth had indulged him to write whatever account of their history he deemed appropriate, and Darcy struggled with what to confess that would both convince Mr Bennet of his long-standing attachment, but would also paint him in an amiable light.

He thought he could make Mr Bennet respect and approve of him in two sheets of paper.

Mr Bennet could not be deeply impressed with his merits based on what he had known of him in Hertfordshire, but Darcy hoped he would not be displeased thus to have him for a son-in-law. At the least, Elizabeth's letter expressing her own convictions might reconcile him to the idea until Darcy could meet with Mr Bennet in person.

After Balfour or Utterson is hauled before the magistrate, and the rest of the flood recovery planned for, then I can be in a carriage to Longbourn.

It was now time to take breakfast with his guests, and Darcy knew he would have to make an effort to behave better towards both Utterson and Balfour to rouse no suspicion. When he entered, he received an affectionate look from Elizabeth, but no other outward indication that they had awoken in the same bed. She was talking with Mrs Annesley and Mrs Lanyon, and so Darcy listened to Georgiana's quiet talk about what she wanted to organise for the village children since their school was currently a deadhouse.

When she asked if he approved, with such a hopeful look in her eyes, Darcy said proudly, "I think that is an excellent idea." After he married Elizabeth, Pemberley could be Georgiana's home too.

He heard Fitzwilliam and the other men before the door opened, and Darcy took a steadying breath. Whilst they settled themselves at the table, Elizabeth gave him a small encouraging nod.

"You must have had a pretty piece of business to keep you locked away on such a fine morning," Utterson said as he sat. "It is finally not raining or too wet to shoot, and you missed it."

"Aye, your man said you were working all morning," Balfour said whilst pouring himself coffee.

"You ought to have come with us," Utterson said. "A shame to let that fine gunroom go to waste. What could have kept you occupied again?"

"Mind your business," Darcy said, "and I shall mind mine."

His sharpness earned him a few surprised stares. *It is so difficult to put on an agreeable face.*

"Yes, we ought to leave off teasing Mr Darcy," Elizabeth said pleasantly. "He has a disaster to manage, lest you all have forgot."

She gave Balfour and Utterson each a pointed look and then set to buttering her thick piece of toast with absorbed attention.

"It is well he did not join us because Darcy is a tolerably good shot and he would have left no birds for us," Fitzwilliam said, smiling round the table.

They began to tell the ladies, who Darcy could tell did not care at all, about how they went out with a dog and Utterson brought back one brace of partridges and Fitzwilliam two, and one of them nearly stepped on a nest.

"How did you shoot, Lewis?" Mrs Lanyon asked Balfour.

"As I always do," he cried, laughing. "I am a terrible shot, but I do enjoy it."

"You are not as bad as you say," Fitzwilliam told him. "There was one time when I thought you had a chance."

"Nae, but you are kind to humour me," Balfour said. "But where I could outshine both Utterson and you, Darcy, is fishing."

Darcy was not equal to a reply beyond a polite smile, so Fitzwilliam said, "I suppose that is because you need not aim, and the fish come to you."

Everyone laughed, and Darcy was amazed at how his cousin could take his friends shooting and keep up a course of friendly conversation. Even Elizabeth was talking with them through the course of her conversation with Mrs Lanyon and Georgiana.

When breakfast was nearly over, Fitzwilliam answered Mrs Lanyon's question as to how he intended to pass the day. "I have business in Buxton and then in Matlock."

Darcy wondered if the small movements of the widow's lips and eyes showed disappointment that his cousin would be busy across the Peak, or if he only hoped to see that attachment there.

"Buxton *and* Matlock?" Balfour cried. "It will fill your entire day!"

Fitzwilliam only gave a rueful smile.

"You won't return before dinner. Let me or Utterson take care of some of the business for you. One of us can go to either Buxton or to Matlock."

Utterson folded down his newspaper enough to narrow his eyes at Balfour. "I will thank you not to put me forward without asking me first."

"Oh, are you much occupied today?" Balfour said, drawing back. "Plan to return to Tissington, do you? Feel the need to call on Poole again?"

"What if I was?"

"I would call you a fool, but it seems to be the day for lengthy and indulgent travels."

Utterson's glare softened. "I am not visiting Lord Poole. I have only to go for my post in Lambton"—he turned to Fitzwilliam—"so if you want me to go anywhere for you, I shall."

"I am afraid my business must be done myself, not by an agent."

This satisfied Utterson, who gave a little nod and returned to his paper. Balfour, however, would not let it go.

"It is fifteen miles east to Buxton; it shall take you over two hours to get there, and then you must pass Pemberley to go on to Matlock. That is twenty miles in all! Then the five miles back to Pemberley from Matlock." Balfour checked his new watch, and it struck something in Darcy's memory. "It is now half past ten. Can I at least go to Matlock for you so you can come right back after Buxton?"

"If only you could, but I have just learnt of an errand I must do for my father before I return to town."

Darcy watched Balfour and Fitzwilliam share a commiserating headshake, as though both understood doing the bidding of one's father. Balfour pocketed his watch and said, "You were good to take us shooting and put off your business, but it shall make you very late tonight."

"It is no matter," Fitzwilliam said, and he directly asked the ladies what they had planned.

"I had hoped to ride," Mrs Lanyon said whilst giving Fitzwilliam a long look, before turning to her brother. "Perhaps you might like to join me?"

"Aye, so long as you don't stop and draw," he said with a teasing smile. "Miss Darcy, Mrs Annesley, shall you join us?"

"What about Miss Bennet?" Georgiana asked before turning to her. "I do not wish to leave you alone."

"I have letters to write," Elizabeth said cheerfully. "Maybe I shall practise the instrument and we can play a duet soon."

Balfour and some of the others rose. "We might still be in the drawing room when you return this evening," he said to Fitzwilliam, "but I doubt it." He then turned to Utterson and asked, "Are you riding with us, then, since you have nothing else to do but get your post?"

"No, I shall find my own amusements," Utterson said before giving

Darcy a little bow and saying something about seeing them all at dinner.

Slowly, the group slipped from the room, with Elizabeth giving him a pointed look and saying clearly that since the maid was sure to be at work in her room, she would write in the library. Fitzwilliam remained, and Darcy dismissed the servants.

He leant back from the table, throwing his napkin onto it. "Thank you for being a charming host to my guests. I cannot dissemble for my life."

Fitzwilliam laughed. "That is the truth. We must find something for the magistrate soon." He too stretched his legs from the table and tilted back, looking up as he thought. "Housebreaking or burglary might be impossible to prove. It shall be grand larceny, I think."

"I am more interested in proving murder."

Fitzwilliam gave him a pitying look. "We may not be able to prove the thief is the same as the killer. You will have proof of theft if we discover items of yours or from Lambton in the pawnshops, and you might have to content yourself with that."

The look on his face must have shown how little he liked this because Fitzwilliam threw open his hands. "Well, unless we find stolen items amongst their things—"

"Mr Birch will never issue a search warrant for their belongings," Darcy said, running a hand across his eyes. "Unless the killer confesses, or we catch him in the act of stealing again, it all depends on us finding Carew's missing ring."

"He would be a fool to keep it on him," Fitzwilliam said grimly.

"Then it is as you say: our best hope to connect him is to find her ring in a pawnshop and have the broker identify him. That would satisfy the magistrate that someone was connected to her death, and Carew will get her coroner's inquest."

"Or you might only prove that Utterson or Balfour stole a ring off a dead woman. He could claim that he saw her body, and in a moment of weakness stole the ring."

"Her temple bone was fractured, and a bloody candlestick was found nearby!" Fitzwilliam gave him a stern look, and Darcy took a calming breath. "Even Mr Birch will not be able to deny an inquest is needed if I can prove my houseguest pried a ring off her finger as she lay half-submerged in my stream."

"But not that Balfour or Utterson was the one who killed her."

"The coroner's inquest will prove she was murdered," he said firmly, "that she was struck with something like the candlestick that was stolen from this house. Utterson and Balfour were both gone that morning, and if the coroner agrees she was murdered, the magistrate will interview their friends to see who lied about their whereabouts. Their friends might lie to me, but they are less likely to lie when called to testify in court when the charge is murder."

"They might only find manslaughter, or a miscellaneous killing. Her death may not have been planned—"

"I want to know who did it and *why*!" Darcy stood from the table with restless energy. "And I want Molly Carew's father to know that even though I brought a villain to Pemberley, I did not protect him. I will drag whomever it was in front of Mr Birch myself."

"It is not your fault."

Darcy nodded once, thinking of Elizabeth's words from last night. "I know that now, but I still have to do what I can to make it right. I shall go to Bakewell before I must oversee the rebuilding planned for today."

Fitzwilliam raised an eyebrow to silently ask the question.

"Did you see Balfour's watch this morning?" His cousin nodded. "He bought it at a pawnshop in Bakewell last Sunday whilst the rest of us were at a well dressing, only because it looked finer than the one he had."

Fitzwilliam pursed his lips. "He might not have gone back to the same pawnshop. It makes more sense to go farther."

"Matlock is only five miles, and you intend to go there for the same purpose."

"Only to be certain, and because it is a larger town. You said Utterson bought cufflinks last Tuesday in Buxton from a pawnshop. I think that is most likely to lead us to a solution."

"You do not want it to be Balfour," he said gently, "because you love his sister."

His cousin rose. "And you want it to be Utterson since he is not as dear to you as is Balfour, but what we want does not matter, does it?"

Darcy shook his head. "What matters is that Molly Carew's killer is found. I may as well check the Bakewell pawnshop whilst you check the ones farther away."

His cousin touched his forehead in salute. "I am always happy to oblige."

"Yes, you are," Darcy said seriously, "and I am more grateful to you than I can possibly say."

Fitzwilliam's pleased look faded, and he gave a wry smile. "If you will thank me, why don't you go to the library on your way to Bakewell? Miss Bennet said something about writing there. Let me help you: she was hinting that she wanted your company."

"Was she?" he said with a straight face. "Are you certain?"

Fitzwilliam closed his eyes in disappointment whilst squeezing his hands into fists. "You need *so much* help. I shall be back very late, but hopefully with something useful." He walked towards the door. Over his shoulder he called, "Go to the library. Remember, faint heart ne'er won fair lady."

CHAPTER EIGHTEEN

Elizabeth had already written to her father, and was as affectionate in her tenor on what she thought due to him in asking for his consent as much as she was on her tender sentiments for Darcy. Her announcement in the breakfast room regarding the library was only a ploy for Darcy to seek her out for a moment of privacy. Expecting him, she was surprised when a quarter of an hour brought Hester instead, dressed in her riding habit.

"Lizzy, I wanted to speak with you before I rode with the others." For a moment, she needlessly smoothed her long skirt. "I had to ask—apologise, I suppose."

"Whatever for?"

"I worry that I have left you too often alone." Hester looked unsure of herself. "I wanted to give you every chance to spend time with Mr Darcy, but it occurred to me that I—well, I am unused to having a young lady under my charge. Have I pressed too hard to forward a match with Mr Darcy? Would you have been more often with Mrs Bingley, or as much with Mrs Annesley if you were Miss Darcy?"

She smiled and squeezed Hester's hand. "You have been above reproach as a chaperon." Elizabeth paused, thinking that perhaps her father might have something to say against that if he knew Darcy had slept in her bed. Hester was now giving her a concerned look. "I have no complaints about our friendship, and no one would expect you to follow me all day and always sit at my elbow."

Hester's shoulders lowered to their normal place, and she smiled. "Mr Darcy seemed attentive to you yesterday at Dovedale. I would not be surprised if he sought you out here."

Elizabeth tried to keep her expression bland when she said, "I am certain Mr Darcy will come to the point before I return home, and I will help him on, of course."

Hester tilted her head. "Home? Are you not going to Scarborough with us in September?"

"I mean . . . I am only more confident that the matter will be resolved as I wish."

"You assume you will need to go home to prepare to be married?" Hester asked, with an excited little smile. She nodded, and Hester gave her a thoughtful look. "I could travel with you, and then return to town. Then you need not travel with one of Mr Darcy's servants. I suspect it will be a while before he can follow you."

"I would like that above anything else," Elizabeth cried. "But do you not want to go to Scarborough? You intended to meet friends there before returning to Haddingtonshire."

"I will still return home—to Scotland, I mean—for Christmas, but they are mostly Lewis's friends." Hester grew nervous again, and Elizabeth waited for her to speak. "Colonel Fitzwilliam will not stay long in Derbyshire. He must return to his regiment in London."

"And if you are in town, your paths would cross?" Hester nodded, and Elizabeth felt happy. "I had noticed you more at ease with him these past two days."

Hester blushed. "I have thought about what you said, about deciding what I want. I should give him, give us, a chance . . . but I worry what society would say about my marrying again."

When she said nothing else, Elizabeth asked, "Have you decided you want to marry him?"

"No . . . but I live in dread of his marrying somebody else."

"How natural!"

They both laughed, and then Hester's smile faded. "I fear that if I do not choose soon, choose to have him myself, he will give up and take comfort where he can."

Elizabeth did not believe for a moment that Colonel Fitzwilliam was ready to abandon Hester. "He must be wishing to attach you. It would be too stupid and too shameful of him to be otherwise, and we know he is not a stupid man."

Hester only laughed, but she did look relieved.

"You have some of the same friends," Elizabeth said, "so they might be wishing for the connexion too. Does Mr Balfour know about your relationship?"

"I doubt it," she said whilst pulling a face. "The colonel and I have kept it a secret. Besides, Lewis is more of a friend than a brother, and we are too near in age, with me being the elder, for him to have ever acted as a guardian to me. He does not understand my fear of being treated unfairly. He is not a woman with a reputation to consider, who is judged more unfairly than a man."

"He does not appear to share those concerns that you have," Elizabeth agreed.

Hester shrugged. "It is because I am more betwixt and between than he is. He is a lively man with business that takes him into the world, and he is not immediately seen as one with an Indian parent. One would look and listen to him and think him Scottish through and through."

"It is how he sees himself?"

Hester nodded. "Whereas I am proudly both Scottish and Indian. Regardless, he does not know about Fitzwilliam and me. I do not think he would be bothered by any romantic entanglement I had, provided it was discreet."

Hester would be devastated if her brother was the killer. If money was the motive, Mr Utterson seemed more likely to be the culprit since he would be the poorer man in the end. It was impossible not to speculate, but they could not act on conjectures. She and Darcy needed proof to connect one of them to Carew's death.

They both turned when one of the library doors opened and Darcy entered. He stopped short at the sight of them both and gave a proper bow. Elizabeth watched his eager expression slide back into a calmer look of the gracious host. "Ladies. I came to see if Miss Bennet has had a letter from the Bingleys."

Elizabeth suspected he had come here to kiss her senseless, and admired how quickly he shifted his behaviour for public view. "I had a letter from Jane yesterday. She wrote about the extreme badness of the roads and tempestuous weather along the way."

Darcy made a thoughtful sound. "The roads are normally choked with dust in summer."

"She writes that all was ankle-deep in mud, but they are safely arrived now."

"I am glad to hear it."

After a stretch of silence where she and Darcy looked on each other intently, Hester gathered the skirt of her riding habit with great purpose.

"I ought to find the others so we can make the most of this dry day." Hester scarcely kept from smiling, and gave her an emphatic, private look before she left.

The door shut, and Darcy gave a small smile. "Now that the topics of weather and our friends have been addressed . . ."

He said not another word. What his lips concealed, his intent gaze betrayed as he came near, put both hands around her hips to pull her against him, and walked her backward until she hit a bookcase. The shelves pressed into her back, and Elizabeth stared at Darcy's lips, feeling his warm breath with every exhale. He was more confident than he had been last night, and it made her heart beat fast.

Darcy brought his hands to rest against the bookcase on either side of her head, keeping his hips pressed against hers. He brushed his lips across her neck before slowly moving them up. When he flicked his tongue over the sensitive skin behind her ear before biting softly, her body trembled.

"Kiss me," she said.

He did, more passionately than she anticipated, and when her tongue swept against his, a raw sound escaped his throat. Elizabeth kept her hands at his waist, holding back from unfastening every button on his trousers until she knew how far he wanted to take this encounter.

Meanwhile, Darcy kissed her with a feverish desire that made her grateful the furniture was supporting her. He rocked his hips against hers whilst tasting every corner of her mouth, nipping at her bottom lip, before moving to her throat, and then to tug her earlobe between his teeth. All of the tentativeness he had shown last night was now replaced by a confident urgency.

She shuddered in pleasure, and then Darcy took her mouth again, their tongues swirling together until she pulled away long enough to ask, "Sleep with me again tonight?"

He made a sound of approval before kissing her again even harder. She ran one finger down his chest, enjoying the way he panted against her lips. She went to unfasten his trouser buttons, but Darcy grasped both of her hands and firmly lifted them both above her head, holding her wrists against the bookcase in one of his hands. She gave an eager gasp of surprise, and Darcy looked into her eyes.

He must have been encouraged by what he saw because after he kissed her again, his free hand wandered over her breasts with touches and pressures that made her moan. He stroked his thumb across them, and Elizabeth wished he would press his mouth to them, sucking and biting them as he had last night. When she gripped the shelf above her to arch her back, pressing herself harder against his hand, he let go of her wrists.

Darcy was breathing heavily. "I was run away with . . ." He blinked a few times and looked from side to side. "We might be interrupted here in the library."

He was resting his weight comfortably against her, still trapping her happily against the bookcase. She felt the certainty that he wanted her, and it lessened her disappointment at stopping. "Maybe we won't be."

He brought his hands to the shelf on either side of her head again and exhaled, giving her a longing look. "If we were seen, every servant would know by the end of the day," he said, frustration clear in his tone, "and none of them would respect either of us—you for seducing the master or me for taking advantage of a single woman."

Elizabeth tucked her hands beneath his coat and linked them

around him. "Maybe your family would catch us rather than a servant, and they would keep the secret?"

He pressed a quick kiss to her lips. "Most assuredly. Georgiana would run from the room and never look me in the eye again, let alone speak."

"And what would your cousin do?"

"If he feared you were unwilling, he would throw me through that window." He gestured with his chin and smiled.

She tugged her hands to make him lean into her harder as she pressed her hips against him. "Oh, it would be plain that I am willing."

"Then Fitzwilliam would probably wait in the corridor to congratulate me after, and use it to embarrass me for the rest of my life."

She had been about to kiss him, but she laughed, and he did too. Elizabeth rested her head against his shoulder as he wrapped her in an embrace, pressing a kiss to her temple before stepping away from the bookcase.

"He told me, in fact," Darcy said as he led her to a sofa, "to come in here to offer myself to you."

"Hester suspected that you had come for that purpose. We shall have to tell everyone their hints are no longer needed."

She settled next to him, and he raised an arm to put around her shoulder to tuck her into his side as though they had sat this way together a hundred times before. "I wrote to your father, and if you have your own letter ready to post, then it ought not to be put off."

Elizabeth leant into him with a sigh. "I shall leave Pemberley soon."

She felt him nod. "Only for a month. It is right for you to want to see your parents first. And in a fortnight, I will follow you into Hertfordshire. I can send you ahead with—"

"Hester has hinted that rather than go on to Scarborough, she would escort me home and then return to town."

Darcy was silent for a moment. "Fitzwilliam must return to his regiment. She hopes to see more of him, in the hopes it could lead to matrimony?" She nodded. "I would be glad of it, for his sake. He will need her encouragement."

"I would think the disappointed look on her face when she learnt Colonel Fitzwilliam was to be gone all day would help him on."

"I am leaving soon myself. I only came in to see you—"

"To kiss me, you mean?"

He gave a quiet laugh before giving her a gentle kiss. "I hoped for both, but I did find you to tell you I am leaving and to ask for your letter to include with mine to your father. I will put it in the post when I am there."

Something in his voice made her shift in his arms to look at him. "Where are you going?"

"To Bakewell," he said in a low voice. "I want to know if Utterson or Balfour went to the pawnshop to sell Carew's ring. Fitzwilliam is going to Buxton and Matlock to check for the same."

"I have nothing at all to do today; you must let me come with you."

The worry lines around his eyes and mouth deepened. "The last time we rode alone in an open carriage together, we were in a large party and your sister was with us."

"Who would dare to say anything against me in Bakewell? Besides," she said playfully, "I appear so innocent, as if I had never had a wicked thought in my life."

Darcy's lips turned into a wry little smile. "And what would those who remember the events of last evening say, or of five minutes ago against that bookcase?"

Elizabeth gave a mock pout, but Darcy only laughed. "Well, if you will not allow my virtue to be compromised in your library, then I shall have to settle for raising a few eyebrows by riding with you to Bakewell. And it will give everyone a hint that I mean more to you than only being the sister-in-law of your friend."

He still did not look convinced, so she added, "I saw Carew's ring, and would recognise it if I saw it again."

"It is not as though I could take it from the broker even if you did. It would be up to the constable and the magistrate. I described it for Fitzwilliam, based on what you said, and I would know it if I saw one near enough like it to justify sending for Mr Birch. I am only gathering information to convince the magistrate to call for a coroner's inquest."

"Please, please let me help," she said, putting her hands on either side of his face. "It is a very small thing, but I must feel like I am doing something for Carew."

A pained look flashed across his face. He took one of her hands from his cheek, turned his head, and pressed a kiss into her palm. He held her hand for a long moment before squeezing it. "Meet me in the stable yard in half an hour."

He had not wanted to be seen escorting a single woman into a market town—into a pawnshop, no less—but he had seen in Elizabeth's eyes the same feeling that had settled into his own heart last week. He would do whatever he must to see justice rendered for Carew, and the need to see her killer punished, even if it was one of his friends, built stronger in him with each passing day.

Elizabeth, however much she wanted the same justice, also seemed determined to tease him into good humour before they arrived in Bakewell.

"No, that is not what happened," he said, trying to suppress a smile as he drove into the inn yard. "You continue to wilfully misunderstand me."

"You are the one who refused me. Was it a punishment of sorts, for what happened in April?"

"I was only unwilling to let matters progress to their natural conclusion *in the library*."

"I can concede that Miss Bennet ought not to be caught being pressed against a bookcase beneath Mr Darcy, but I wonder if Mrs Darcy would be allowed a little more margin."

She flashed him a bright smile that threatened to send all the blood in his body straight down. He exhaled through his nose and closed his eyes before climbing down from the curricle.

"My dearest," he said quietly as he came around to hand her down, "if you swear not to say such tempting things in public, I promise that Mrs Darcy can have her way in any room she pleases."

A satisfied feeling filled his chest when he watched her eyes darken. "I shall be perfectly dull and proper, I swear it."

They left the curricle and turned onto Bath Street, and she added, "I hope you will not find me dull after we have been married twenty years." She grew thoughtful, and he wondered if she was thinking about someone's unhappy marriage. "I hope you shall never grow tired of me."

"Never." Darcy took her hand and tucked it under his arm. "Besides, I am certain your play of mind will be the same as it ever was even after you are settled down in conjugal and maternal affections."

"I have much more to say—and do—regarding those conjugal affections, but I just promised to be dull and proper in public."

He gave her a heated look before they entered the post office. When they left, he felt Elizabeth shiver as the wind picked up, and he asked if she was cold.

"A little. I have not had another pelisse made"—her voice caught—"and this spencer is not warm enough for a windy day."

They shared a sad look, and he was no longer in the mood for playful hints about their happy future. He felt Elizabeth give his arm a squeeze, and knew she felt the same.

"Who do you think it was?" The question seemed to burst out from her lips.

"I could guess. Utterson does not know me as well as Balfour does, and it might be easier for him to steal from me than it would be for Balfour."

"But who is capable of killing Carew?" she whispered.

"Utterson is more short-tempered . . ."

"Yes. I remember Carew saying that she had heard from his man that he did not always have patience, and we have all seen how abrupt he can be."

"But always being impatient will not be enough for a magistrate. As far as who is capable of using a pawnbroker, it could be either of them. Utterson bought cufflinks at a pawnshop in Buxton simply because he saw them in the window."

"And Mr Balfour bought a new watch here in Bakewell because he wanted to spend." After a little farther, she added, "Did you notice at Lord Poole's that Mr Utterson was not ready to join us when it was time to go?" He nodded. "His lordship said he had forgotten something, but when he came out, Mr Utterson carried nothing with him."

"Or he had hidden in his pockets something small, something he took from the house to pawn? That is quite a conjecture, but if he stole from me, he would not scruple to steal from anyone else." Utterson was appearing to be the likely culprit, but suspicions would not be enough for Mr Birch. "It might be him, but what you observed means nothing unless we find proof that connects Utterson to Carew."

Elizabeth nodded sadly, and they crossed the street. "How many people borrow money on the security of pledges? What kind of rate is charged?"

"I could not say to the former, but an act was passed that set it at one and two-thirds percent a month."

"That is still twenty percent a year," she cried. "Who would accept such a rate?"

Darcy shrugged. "If one has no credit and is so far from a bank, where else are they to get cash, and quickly?"

Elizabeth's lips turned down. "But are the brokers predators or providing an essential service?"

"Pawnshops are a place shunned by the pious and the wealthy, but I know they support those of limited means, those out of work, and widows."

"Why would people not appeal to you or another landowner if they need help?"

"Because the labouring poor want dignity, and whilst I give food or clothes or medicine or a deduction from rent due, that is not the same as needing cash after an illness has prevented you from working or your husband has gambled away his earnings again. I think them necessary in some cases."

"Then why do many cast judgment on those who use them?"

Darcy felt her confusion and looked at her. "Think of it this way: the Duke of Devonshire would mortgage every property he owns and spend to excess, and no one would think ill of him, but I am sure he and his friends would assume one who used a pawnshop to pay their rent when money was tight was as shameful as a gin drinker."

Elizabeth nodded. "And who is the one truly guilty of vice?"

He gave no answer as he saw the shop on the corner, and the pawn-brokers' symbol of three gold balls hung by one of the doors. A sign read "Money advanced on plate, jewels, and every description of property." When they entered, he could tell it was not so much plate and jewels but china cups, chessmen, carpenters' tools, and bed linen that was pledged in return for cash.

"What is that for?" Elizabeth asked quietly, pointing to the walls erected at the end of the counter to form a tiny room with a door at the back and open only to the counter.

"It is for those who wish to pawn without being recognised by their neighbours."

There was an older woman behind the counter who wore a fine bracelet and necklace, neatly attired, looking respectable but not high above the station of her typical patron. She was about to greet him when awareness crossed her eyes.

"I did not think the storm caused so much damage that you needed my services, Mr Darcy."

"No, madam. I am here to learn if you took a pledge for a coral ring last week."

The proprietor's eyes narrowed. "I am not in the habit of receiving stolen goods." She pointed to the door. "You may—"

"We would never suspect you of that," Elizabeth said, stepping up to the counter. "That is not at all what Mr Darcy meant. In fact, I know he has respect for the service you provide."

The proprietor's shoulders settled back down, although she still looked at him warily. "So long as you know I am also not an informer, and you had best not bring any false accusations of my receiving stolen goods before the magistrate."

"That is not Mr Darcy's intention at all, I assure you."

Thank goodness Elizabeth was here, otherwise he would have been dismissed for accusing the broker of compromising her integrity and he would learn nothing. *Let us hope that Fitzwilliam's easier manner serves him better in Buxton and Matlock.*

"Do you ever have suspicions about what items are brought before you?" Elizabeth asked.

"I know enough to question a servant from Pemberley or the other great houses, but I do not know everyone. Still, if one of my regulars came with a watch chain without the watch, or a housemaid came with an ornate clock, I would be on my guard."

"Was there anyone in your shop recently who was not one of your usual weekly pawners?" Darcy asked politely. "May I see your pledge book, madam?"

She shook her head. "These people trust me, and not just with their goods, but with their privacy and their good name."

"I am not here to judge. I fear that stolen goods were pawned here."

The broker was unwilling to agree. "You cannot compel me to break that trust based on your fear that a trinket is missing from Pemberley."

"The pawner is guilty of another crime," Elizabeth said earnestly, "a far worse crime, but if Mr Darcy can prove that pawner stole goods, it could connect him to that greater evil."

"I promise, madam," Darcy pressed, "that your business and your pledgers' business are not my concern. I am interested only in convincing the magistrate that the thief committed a worse crime." She looked ready to refuse him, so he said in a rush, "You can keep your investment if I discover anything that was stolen. Whatever sum you laid out on the pledge, I shall match once the matter is resolved by the court."

The proprietor pursed her lips, and then reached under the counter to pull out a ledger. "You may look at only the last week's entries." She turned the book around and opened it.

Down the page were dates, names, addresses, the items pledged, and the amounts loaned.

"Neither of their names are here," Elizabeth muttered, running her finger down the page.

"But Balfour was here last Sunday. He wandered the village whilst we attended the well dressing, and he bought a gold watch."

"If your friend only bought and did not pledge an item, I would have no reason to issue him a ticket and take his name," the pawn-broker said. "But I remember that man, more for what he bought than for himself. That gold watch had been here fifteen months, but the pledger will still be sorry when he sobers up and cannot get it back. I have to keep every item for a year, you know, but I always stretch the time for my regulars."

Darcy tapped his fingers against the book, thinking. "Has that man been back again?" She shook her head. "Did anyone this week pledge or sell a gold ring with five oval pieces of coral, the centre one slightly larger than the others?"

"No. I am not like a city pawnshop or goldsmith, you know. Aside from the gold watch your friend bought, I do not have much finery here, mostly tools and clothes. They pledge their tools on Saturday to redeem their Sunday best, and come back on Monday to do the reverse."

Darcy turned to Elizabeth, feeling frustration building in his chest. "Neither of them fenced goods here. We know nothing more than we did before."

She reached to lay a consoling hand on his arm, before closing her fingers and remembering where she was. "He might still have gone to another broker farther away. Your cousin could return with the proof you need."

He kept his irritation from his face as he thanked and parted from the pawnbroker. When they were near the door, Elizabeth turned back. "Would you tell me what one might get upon a coral ring like that?"

The proprietor thought a moment. "Five shillings, up to one guinea perhaps."

One pound and one shilling at the most. How could he remain composed? Carew was killed for something worth no more than a single coin. He felt Elizabeth's hand on his arm, and he went through the motions of opening the door and guiding her outside, and then walking towards the curricle.

After they were back on the street, he turned quickly to Elizabeth, who said sadly, "I know, it is horrible."

"He killed her and wrenched a ring from her hand whilst it was still warm for a guinea!"

"Not now," she whispered, looking round the street. "It is terrible to think about it in such stark terms, but we cannot talk here." She put her arm through his and held tightly. He kept his silence, but all the frustration and anger that had been steadily growing since he realised

Carew had been murdered came rushing back to twist his stomach and squeeze the air from his chest.

Having Elizabeth's warmth against him as they walked was a small comfort, the only one he had. *I had been happy yesterday, last night, this morning.* More than happy, delighted, but until this dreadful matter was resolved, until the murderer was out of his house, until he could tell Mr Carew that his daughter's killer was apprehended, how could he rest easy?

When they were in the curricle, Elizabeth said to him gently, "Your cousin will find the ring in another shop, or maybe you will catch them stealing again in Lambton." She gave a weak smile. "You shall have to put on a pleasant face for just a little while longer."

"Carew deserves justice, Elizabeth," he said. "But I . . . I do not know how to live with never knowing what happened to her, and why."

"I think," she said slowly, "that even if we learn the why, the answer will only disappoint you."

She was right; whatever the motive, it could never be justified. He cued the horses, setting his shoulders and forcing himself to stop clenching his jaw. "Then I shall have to settle for finding whoever is guilty and doing all that I can to see him punished as richly as he deserves."

CHAPTER NINETEEN

On account of the riders being hungry after their long excursion, they sat to dinner at five, but it was a dull affair. Elizabeth thought that Miss Darcy had already exerted her social energies for the day, Hester looked often at the empty seat that Colonel Fitzwilliam had previously occupied, and that gentleman was still in search of a coral ring in a pawnshop somewhere in the Peak.

And Darcy is looking between Mr Utterson and Mr Balfour, as though trying to guess by their outward appearance which one might be a murderer.

Elizabeth was not surprised when the men did not linger at the table after dinner, Miss Darcy pleaded to be excused, and Mrs Annesley went with her.

"It shall be a quiet evening," Hester said as she made the tea. "I can make myself scarce as well . . . unless Mr Darcy put his time to good use after I left the library?"

Elizabeth could not keep the secret from her any longer, even if it was not time to make it a general concern. She dropped her voice to a whisper. "Darcy made me an offer when we were at Dovedale. We wanted to wait to tell everyone, until we both wrote to my father, but I cannot keep it from you."

To her pleasant surprise, Hester pulled her into her arms and said everything about her happiness for them both and wishing them all the joy they deserved. Elizabeth looked over her shoulder and caught Darcy's eye. He gave a little smile—the first she had seen this evening.

"I will keep the news to myself," Hester said into Elizabeth's ear, "but you must know how happy Miss Darcy and Fitzwilliam will be. And Lewis is always one to enjoy another's good fortune." She laughed. "Even Mr Utterson might force out a smile on your behalf."

Elizabeth politely agreed, and Hester gave her another congratulations before the gentlemen joined them at the tea table.

"Well, upon the whole we have had a very good frisk at Pemberley," Mr Balfour said to Darcy as they settled themselves with their coffee. "But a few more days shall see your guests go on to Scarborough. I hope you and Miss Darcy decide to come for at least part of September."

This was an obvious invitation to conversation about travelling, about having guests, about friendship and visiting, about nearly anything, but Darcy only bowed.

When the silence stretched too long, Hester said, "Lewis, I am returning to town and will join you in Haddingtonshire this winter instead."

"Hester!" Mr Balfour cried. "What about our friends in Scarborough?"

She shook her head. "Most of them are *your* friends. My friends are in town, near St James's Street, you know."

"Aye, you have liked the wives of the army men since you were on the Married Roll." He gave a fond smile. "If you marry again, I daresay it would be to a military man, and you would hope to travel with him. Unless," he said slowly, "he was in a fashionable regiment and likely to remain in London."

Mr Balfour gave her a wink and turned to Darcy. Elizabeth and Hester shared an amazed look at his comprehending more about Hester and her wishes than they realised.

"I heard in the stable yard that whilst we were riding," Mr Balfour said to Darcy, "you raised a new house today. Did your tenants applaud you?"

Darcy gave a wry smile. "They are happy with the progress, but in fact they had criticisms on where the new building will stand."

"Why do you tolerate any criticism?" Mr Utterson asked him. "You are the master."

"A man who wishes to stand well in the opinion of others must accept fair criticism, because he is thereby able to correct his faults or remove the prejudices against him."

Darcy had answered his friend, but he gave Elizabeth a serious look as he did so. She immediately wished them all away so she could show him how proud she was of him, for what improvements he had made since Hunsford and for what he had accomplished in Pemberley's recovery so far.

"I do not believe there was a single criticism," Mr Balfour teased, clapping Darcy on the shoulder. "The dignity of Darcy's presence produces reverence in his grateful tenants."

"If they did revere Darcy, it is because of his great fortune," Mr Utterson quipped as he rose to return his coffee cup.

"No, it is because he is a complete gentleman: sensible, amiable, virtuous, generous," Elizabeth said.

Darcy's cheeks actually turned pink. Elizabeth knew she had spoken too warmly, but the truth about their engagement would come out soon. She added in a calmer tone, "It is because they trust Mr Darcy to help them."

Mr Utterson shrugged. "Darcy was left a great fortune to start his life with, and his tenants can at least trust in that."

The desire to defend Darcy rose before she could sensibly silence it. "Do you not feel that your father gave you enough to start with in life? Your education and career have been well-provided for."

"And in return I promised my father to become an impressive lawyer, to do him credit. Whilst my foolish brother inherits everything and earns nothing."

His resentful tone made her angry. "Unfortunately for your father, you appear to prefer a lively evening in town, being seen, and spending to excess to making him proud."

"Like I said to you once before, I am not ungrateful and it shall all end well enough. I will be called to the bar next year, and I suspect my father will supplement my income so I can live as a son of a baronet ought." Mr Utterson bowed slightly before stalking away.

Other conversations resumed, and now that everyone had been served tea or coffee, she and Hester left the table to join the three men.

"You will wear yourself down unless you take a small break from all of this," Mr Balfour said gently to Darcy.

"Under my present scarcity of cash, I shall find it difficult to collect rent to answer this emergency, let alone travel."

Mr Utterson shook his head. "We shall miss you if you do not come to Scarborough."

"Complying with my previous engagements is now impossible. And as I said, I shall even sublet the house in town next season."

"You are a dead bore," Mr Balfour said, with a smile.

His friends could not see that any decadence would contrast with his tenants' suffering, and Darcy could never tolerate that. Luxurious life at a house party or resort would give Darcy infinitely more pain than pleasure now. "His tenants might fear he has not their best interests at heart if Mr Darcy is gone for long and so soon after the storm on any matter other than business," Elizabeth said.

Mr Balfour shook his head. "We must disagree, Miss Bennet, because I think Darcy's tenants and servants think so well of him no matter where he is that they would storm hell for him if he made the plans."

"I think I had better try rebuilding the mill first," Darcy answered. He shared a look with her, and she wondered if he was remembering the near riot in Lambton.

"Still, our visit has been a pleasant one, has it not?" Mr Balfour asked the party in a tone of cheer. "We all seem disposed to be pleased and are endeavouring to be agreeable, and I hope we succeed, for your sake," Mr Balfour said to Darcy. "I know you have had a difficult time, but difficult times pass."

"He still ought to come to Scarborough," Mr Utterson said. "It would show his friends, society as well, that he can manage the disaster with his fortune intact."

"I may instead tell my friends that I am engaged in raising houses," Darcy said, "which, I think, goes on better whilst I am present."

Mr Utterson and Mr Balfour went on about the importance of maintaining a gentleman's reputation and the good opinion of society, and that there was no shame in borrowing a little if the need arose. Darcy frowned and stalked away to return his coffee cup to the tea table; Elizabeth rose to stand near to him.

"You must keep your forbearance and command of countenance for a little while longer, Fitzwilliam," she whispered when they both had their backs to the others.

He set his saucer down with a clatter. "The thief and the killer are likely the same, and I must bring the guilty man before Mr Birch. I am near to demanding one of them confess now."

Elizabeth stroked the back of his hand, which rested on the table. "It will be finding Carew's stolen ring in a pawnshop—that is how we will solve the puzzle."

Darcy turned his hand over to squeeze hers. She knew that pretending to be at ease, that not knowing the truth, was driving him to distraction.

"I cannot rely on that," he whispered, looking at their joined hands. "They shall leave any day, and the ring might never be found. And once they leave the parish, it shall be harder to get a warrant if we ever do find proof." He gave her a look she could not comprehend. "I am very sorry you and Mrs Lanyon must hear this."

Before she could ask what he meant, he returned to the others.

"At least I do not need a night watch in Lambton any longer," Darcy said as he joined them. "It is just as well, since if I were to take my turn, I would be asleep within an hour."

"Aye, that does sound like you," Mr Balfour said. "If you did not have coffee, you would be asleep within an hour of candlelight."

"Your cousin organised a watch, did he not?" Mr Utterson asked.

"Yes, but it is not needed now since the streets are cleared and any valuables that survived are secured." He gave a thoughtful pause. "It is only the deadhouse that might have anything of value now, but Fitzwilliam did not organise men to protect that. Perhaps it is of no consequence," he added with a shrug.

"Why do you even need the deadhouse a week after the storm?"

Mr Balfour asked. "Were not the flood victims identified and returned to their homes to be buried?"

"A few did not have homes left to be buried from, but most who remain are the disinterred bodies from the second storm that pushed the coffins out of the soaked earth."

Elizabeth's stomach turned over as she watched Hester cringe and set down her plate.

Darcy looked at both Mr Balfour and Mr Utterson. "Is it worth it to keep watch over the possible desecration of the dead, especially those long dead? The ground is dry enough to reinter them soon, now that they all have new coffins."

"It is hardly worth it to have anyone lose sleep keeping watch over a few waterlogged bodies," Mr Utterson agreed, nodding his head. Both Hester and Mr Balfour looked rather ill.

Elizabeth watched their conversation, thinking how unlike Darcy it was to mention such harsh truths in mixed company.

"Is there no one to claim the unearthed dead?" she asked.

"Most are older, since they are from the section of the churchyard nearest to the river, and there are no relations still living to reinter them. The parish shall take on the expense to rebury them in the next day or two, along with the last flood victims who could not be taken home."

"Do many bodies remain in the deadhouse?" asked Mr Utterson.

Darcy seemed to think, but Elizabeth suspected he knew exactly how many, as well as their names. "Oh, maybe four or five disinterred bodies, and only two left from the storm." He looked round at everyone. "Ought I to send a man to make sure no one takes their trinkets or shoes?"

"Oh my," Hester said, paling.

"No," Mr Balfour said firmly, with a worried look at his sister. "I cannot imagine anyone stealthily picking their way along the lined-up corpses. Now, some music? Hester, I think we all wish for an early night after our long ride, but perhaps you could give us one song?"

Hester all but ran to the instrument, and Mr Balfour and Mr Utterson decided to play cribbage before going to bed.

"Miss Bennet, a turn around the room?" Darcy said pointedly. "It seems it shall be an early night."

She rose and took his arm, and he asked quietly, "I need you to retire early and convince Mrs Lanyon to do the same. Then we can see if this will work."

In conversation, Darcy looked a person full in the face; he was deliberate in action and in words. She realised all of that was said with a purpose. "You are encouraging him to steal," she whispered, "to catch him in the act."

He nodded. "Like you said earlier, maybe I will catch the murderer stealing again in Lambton."

"When I said *you*, I meant a constable in the village, and I never considered anyone stealing from the dead."

"The clothes, the jewellery on the bodies, all of it would earn a few guineas from a pawnbroker."

"But your cousin might return from Buxton or Matlock late tonight with evidence."

"And he might return with nothing," Darcy muttered. "If someone is caught stealing from the dead, and we go to Mr Birch with the belief that Carew's ring was stolen from her body, it will strengthen the cause to hold an inquest and connect the theft to the death."

"Finding her stolen ring in a pawnshop would be better," she said when they were farther away.

"Both would help us, do you not think?"

Elizabeth sighed. "Yes, it would. What shall we do?"

"You and Mrs Lanyon retire, and I shall claim to do the same," he whispered. "Balfour and Utterson will finish their game. Before that, I shall wait in the deadhouse to catch him in the act."

"Why not just follow him from Pemberley?"

"There is nothing against the law in leaving a house at night. And if he notices me following and gives up? I need to see him commit a crime."

"You are certain one of them will go forth in the shadows of the night to plunder the dead?" She shuddered. "That is heinous."

"So is stealing from people who have lost their homes. So is striking a woman with a candlestick."

When their turn around the room brought them farther from the others, she asked, "You still feel that it is Mr Utterson?"

"My feelings do not matter," he said, "but yes, I think he did it, and I intend to catch him."

"Shall you bring a few men with you?"

"How could I without alerting everyone? If there is a hint of a group coming from Pemberley, he will know it, and it might put him off from trying." He dropped his voice. "The villagers would know it too. Remember what nearly happened at the Pemberley Arms. What will a crowd do if they discover a man looting their dead?"

"They will drag him before the magistrate, which is what you want."

"And I want him to be alive when he gets there. A resentful crowd may be tempted to carry out their own justice. I will go alone and wait for him." Elizabeth gave him a worried look. "He is not going to murder me, my dear."

"Carew undoubtedly thought the same," she muttered.

Darcy looked pensive as they walked. "I shall bring a pistol to ease your mind. I need only catch Utterson in the act so I can be a witness and convince the magistrate. When we recover Carew's stolen ring, it will all be enough for an inquest."

"Fitzwilliam," she whispered, and took both of his hands in hers. If anyone on the other side of the room saw them, they might think they were lovers offering endearments and promises. "You must be careful. Someone *killed* Carew."

Darcy did not tell her she had nothing to worry about. He only nodded before kissing her hand and pointedly telling everyone he was rather tired and to have a pleasant evening. Elizabeth put on a smile for the others. Darcy had asked her to be certain Hester was out of the way for the evening, and she would do that.

But he is mistaken if he thinks I am going to hide in my room until morning.

~

To avoid anyone noticing him leaving, Darcy bypassed the stable and walked to the village. Twilight had faded and, although it was too dark to bring out his watch, Darcy knew it must be ten o'clock. He walked to Lambton by memory, skirting along the stream for most of the way. His guests would travel north soon, and if the thief was tempted to steal a few jewels that none would notice missing, he had to act now.

As he neared the village, he checked the carriage pistol he took from the gunroom. He had at first thought to bring the smaller pistol he carried when he rode alone a great distance, but for Elizabeth's sake he took this larger one. It usually sat under his seat in the coach, and its pair in its case with the coachman. It scarcely fit in his frock coat pocket, but he had promised. He did not expect to need it; all he had to do was observe Utterson and then report what he had seen to the magistrate.

But could I observe him and not confront him?

His father had instructed him not to draw a weapon unless he had sufficient firmness and self-possession to fire it. To preserve his family's safety, for Elizabeth's, he could certainly use it. He felt its weight. An eight-inch, single-barrelled pistol, long enough to be moderately accurate, and relatively stable; he had never once had to draw it.

The village was silent as he passed the Pemberley Arms to the school that housed the coffins. Darcy collected himself before opening the door. Three large blocks of ice packed in straw had been delivered, and there was a noticeable difference in temperature. The tables were pushed to the centre of the room and six coffins lay across them.

The bodies awaiting burial or reinterment had been arranged by size, from a stalwart man to the body of one helpless child. He had seen them when they were first brought in. Some had been mostly bone and tattered outdated dress, and those faces had been much easier to look upon than the recent victims. There were labourers with plain dress and coarse shoes, and the finer clothes of a gentlemanly man, and two women shopkeepers who had drowned during the storm.

He was doing more than protecting their jewellery from being pawned for spending money. He was protecting their dignity, and protecting anyone else from suffering the same degradation.

Darcy looked at his pistol again, half-cocked, as he leant on the same wall with the only door in the corner, so whoever entered must pass him unseen to begin his ghoulish work. He could not stop the villain before he began; he had to witness him in the act.

Whilst he waited in the dark, all he could think on was what if the thief did not yield. He had the right to defend his property and his person, but that did not make it easy to fully cock his pistol and fire it. The courts would find that whomever he shot had been the aggressor, and that he acted in self-defence. He certainly had the skill to fire and hit his mark, but could he use it? What if Utterson refused to cooperate, or threatened him, or said he was leaving and taking what he had stolen?

Do I have sufficient nerve to aim at my friend and pull the trigger?

ELIZABETH WAS CERTAIN THAT BY NOW DARCY HAD LEFT FOR WHAT HAD become a temporary *la morgue*. Every moment of taking no action brought her fresh agitation, and only by going to Lambton herself would she have any tranquillity. Even as she changed her shoes and put on her spencer, she knew Darcy would be angry if she walked the same path alone, at night, that Carew had been murdered on in broad daylight.

Mr Utterson had struck Carew down with a candlestick. A shudder passed over her. If Darcy listened to her and brought a pistol to the village, she ought to do the same.

The gunroom was about twelve feet square, had a fireplace, and cases and drawers along two walls for every item related to fishing and hunting. The room smelled faintly of leather and the tallow for oiling weapons. Several double-barrelled shotguns hung near to fishing rods, and two pistol cases were open on a table next to an Argand lamp.

Two coat-pocket pistols were in one case, and a larger pistol was missing from the other. Each case had its powder flask, bullet pliers and screwdriver, flints, and an oil bottle. Two of the pistols were stored with their hammers down, the frizzen up, oiled and cleaned, and the flint wrapped in leather. But one of the small pocket pistols was loaded and half-cocked.

How strange to leave one loaded.

Darcy must have loaded the smaller one, and then changed his mind and chosen a larger pistol. At least he took her seriously; it would be easier to aim one with a longer barrel. Elizabeth felt the greatest dread of the consequences of his meeting come over her. Darcy was alone with only one shot to defend himself.

Was it foolish to leave the house alone, or foolish to let the man she loved face a murderer alone? Elizabeth lifted the small pistol; it was scarcely longer than the palm of her hand. She was going to be Mrs Darcy; Pemberley was to be *her* home, her tenants, her servants, her family to protect.

She filled the pan about halfway from the small horn on the table, just as she had seen her father do, then snapped the frizzen in place over the primed pan. Elizabeth tugged open her long sleeve and tucked the tiny pistol inside. Her spencer sleeve was fitted, but hung loose as it passed her wrist. The pistol fit, and no one would see it if she kept her arm mostly straight and her fingers curled. Darcy would be angry when he saw her—and that was a shame—but he would forgive her.

As long as I do not trip and shoot myself.

What would she have to do if the situation in the deadhouse became untenable? Fully cock the hammer and pull the trigger. *And hope that Mr Utterson is only a few feet away.* Elizabeth moved her arm to see if the pistol would stay in its place and tried to steady her breathing. She was more agitated than she had ever before felt, but she could face whatever was necessary with self-command, certainly if it was for Darcy's sake.

As she passed through the hall, she saw light through the drawing room keyhole. Darcy had asked her to make sure Hester was abed, so Elizabeth entered to be certain that someone had only left the candles burning.

She felt fresh confusion when she saw a man at the writing table, folding up a letter with great haste.

"What are you doing here?" she cried.

"I might ask you the same," Mr Utterson drawled. "I cannot imagine Darcy would be pleased to find you alone with another man." At her shocked silence, he added, "If you will give me leave to hint as to what I think your wishes are."

"What?" She was completely astounded. Mr Utterson was supposed to be in the village by now.

"If you do not understand me, then never mind," he said, rising. He approached the door, and she still stood in front of it. "Pardon me."

"Why are you here at this hour?" Was he about to go to the village, or had Darcy's hints not tempted him?

"I do not need to explain my actions. Good evening," he said firmly, gesturing to the door.

Elizabeth stepped back to block the door, putting one hand on the lock. She was not willing to draw the pistol—at least, not yet.

"Have you lost your senses? Let me pass!"

She shook her head, but was ready to scream if Mr Utterson advanced on her.

"Damn it, I am writing a letter because the candles are still lit here and I can hardly see a thing in my room by the light of one candle. Are you satisfied?"

She would have to let him go to plunder the dead, and it made her sick. He noticed her looking at the letter in his hand, and quickly tucked it into his pocket.

"Are you hiding something?" she asked shakily.

"Not at all," he said quickly. "Were *you* hoping to importune Darcy? As you see, he is not here, and if you are wanting advice, I do not think that he appreciates cunning." He pressed a hand to the pocket that held the letter. "Now, may I pass?"

"No!" she cried. "You are hiding something, and we are trying to catch a killer!"

That was a mistake, a dreadful, impulsive mistake. Mr Utterson stared a moment before asking, "Killer? Who died?" He thought a moment and asked, "Miss Darcy's maid?"

Elizabeth let go of the handle and inched to the side. *My fear has made me extremely foolish.* She had wanted to help, and now she had gone and made it worse. It was best to let Mr Utterson pass if Darcy's plan was to work. If Mr Utterson believed she knew nothing about it, he might let her go. The pistol's wood handle was warm against her wrist, the steel barrel just touching her palm.

"Does Darcy think it was me?" he said angrily as he took a few steps closer.

She put her hands behind her back and slid the pistol into her palm. "He—I do not know." Her heart pounded, and she readied herself to raise the pistol if she had to.

Mr Utterson's features twisted. "All he said in the drawing room . . . Did he go to Lambton to witness a villain stealing from the dead?"

"No, of course not," she whispered.

"And he suspects *I* would do such a thing?" He cursed under his breath. "Darcy thinks whoever killed the maid will plunder the dead? He thinks me a thief and a murderer?"

She said nothing, and her fingers were shaking. Being red in the face was not reason enough to bring the gun from behind her back.

"Why on earth would Darcy suspect *me*?"

He was angry, and Elizabeth wondered if he was genuinely insulted. Hints of doubt crept into her mind. "Carew was killed with a candlestick taken from old Mr Darcy's room. The thief had to be someone who knew the house, who could easily enter it and leave it . . ."

"And?" he asked in a low voice.

"And you and Mr Balfour are unaccounted for on the morning she died." At the look of confusion on his face, she added, "Last Thursday."

"I left early for Tissington, to see—to spend the day with Lord Poole." Mr Utterson began to pace. He was no longer near enough to harm her. She could flee now, but he then asked softly, more to himself, "Why me any more than Balfour?"

Elizabeth had to swallow and take a breath before the words came. "You are jealous of Darcy, jealous of Mr Balfour, of your older brother because you will not inherit." He looked sharply at her. "You complain of not having the money you deserve—"

"It was not me!"

"Would Lord Poole say in court that you were there?"

He blanched, and Elizabeth's finger moved to be ready to fully cock the pistol after all. "His servants could account for my presence, and so could his daughter."

She saw the way his hand moved over his coat pocket again. Mr Utterson was always going to the post or reading a letter, and Mr Balfour's rude asides came to mind. "You were here writing to Miss . . .?"

"Miss Newcomen," he said. "I want to marry Lord Poole's daughter, but he does not think me wealthy enough. I will do what I must to show him that I can provide for a baron's daughter. I was here writing to Margaret—we write every day—and are secretly engaged."

That was all the more reason to suspect him. "A man may be propelled to do much by the impulse of illimitable ardour."

"I did not steal to make myself look like I have enough money to marry on!" he cried. "And I certainly did not kill over it." He shook his head in disgust. "You and Darcy must trust in the law and those who carry it out. The magistrate did not call for a coroner so—"

"Only because he feared there was no suspect, but then we saw Carew's ring was stolen from her body and you were gone from Pemberley that day. Someone took a candlestick from the house and struck her!"

He narrowed his eyes. "You truly think I killed someone? For a *ring*? I assure you, I am not so sadly involved as that! A few debts of honour over cards and a bill to my tailor are what I have outstanding. I shall be called to the bar and enter my profession, and will make my fortune by it."

The doubt that Mr Utterson was the killer gained more ground against the certainty that he had committed the crime. "When Darcy convinces the magistrate to investigate, when they ask Miss Newcomen if you were there . . ."

"Of course I was there! Lord Poole did not see me, but Margaret did and so did her lady and a servant in the stable."

"And you went back on Saturday for the chance to see Miss Newcomen again?"

A fond smile spread over Mr Utterson's face, displacing his anger. "I would take every opportunity to see her." His expression darkened again. "And to show her father I can afford to marry a baron's daughter—when I become a barrister. Of course I would like a greater fortune, but I would not steal or kill to get it."

She edged the pistol back up into her sleeve. He was angry and offended, but he was not a murderer.

Mr Utterson approached her again, but she did not feel the same fear this time. "Is that why Darcy has been abjectly miserable? He thinks I killed a maid for spending money and was waiting for a way to prove it?"

"You and Mr Balfour were the ones with the opportunity—"

"Stupid!" he cried, showing all that impatience he was capable of. "It is even more laughable if he suspects Balfour. Balfour will inherit Hyde House! Darcy will return from Lambton with a desperate villager, or a servant, or with no one because the idea is ridiculous!"

Darcy would be shocked when he saw who entered the deadhouse. "I fear Darcy shall need your help with Mr Balfour, to go for the magistrate and a constable—"

"No, I am going to Balfour's room. He is there, and he will laugh heartily at this foolishness. I need his good humour to improve my temper after all I have suffered to hear you say."

She was still near to the door, and although she was no longer afraid of him, she flinched to see the hard look in his eye.

"I will make a fortune by my profession," he repeated, "not by stealing trinkets for gaming money or to make it easier to impress anyone with my spending. Now step out of my way, or so help me, I will move you myself."

Elizabeth sidled away, not able to look him in the eye, and Mr Utterson went through, slamming the door behind him.

CHAPTER TWENTY

D arcy had never been so outraged in his whole life as he felt when he watched Balfour enter and pry open one of the coffin lids with a crowbar. Balfour wrested off both shoes from the body and put them in a sack, and then came to the head to pick up a hand that was mostly bone to slide off a ring. He replaced the lid and proceeded to do the same with a woman in the next coffin.

His surprise to witness Balfour, not Utterson, mingled with a disgust that made it hard to speak or act. He watched Balfour move to the next victim to open the lid and remove the shoes, and then he tugged to try to remove a diamond ring. Balfour pulled harder before huffing in frustration. Darcy saw him pull a knife from his pocket, and his stomach roiled horribly as he realised what Balfour was about to do.

"Stop."

Balfour cried out, and his knife clattered onto the table.

"Darcy! You nearly stopped my heart!" Balfour brought a hand to his chest and exhaled loudly. "What the hell are you doing here?"

"What am I—" He gave a hollow laugh at the absurdity of Balfour's question. "I am keeping watch against the desecration of the dead."

"Aye, well, I am sorry." Balfour rubbed the back of his neck. "You see, it was tempting to take a few trinkets no one would miss."

"How dare you?" he whispered angrily. Thank heaven he did not bring any tenants with him, because their fury would outweigh his. He had to get Balfour to Pemberley and send for the magistrate before his people learnt they were here. "How can you steal from the bodies of wives and daughters of men who have already been robbed of what they hold most dear?"

"There was no harm done." He gave a placating smile. "I can put it all back."

"No harm? Balfour, the knowledge of what you have done would be a torture to those who survived the storm."

Balfour threw him a look. "Come now, most of these bodies are not drowning victims. Most are long-dead people whose coffins were pushed out of waterlogged graves."

"As though that makes it better!" Darcy cried. He took a breath and lowered his voice. "We need to return to Pemberley before anyone in Lambton knows we are here." The memory of the near riot in the aftermath of the storm came surging back to him. The villagers might mete out swift punishment to someone who dared to desecrate the corpses of their loved ones.

"Very well, I shall put everything back, and it can all be forgot." He returned the shoes and replaced the ring whilst Darcy watched in sickening disbelief.

It would be so much less painful to tell his friend it could all be forgotten. But then he could never look at Mr Carew again, and he would see Molly Carew's corpse every time he closed his eyes. *I am responsible for what I do, and also for what I could have done but chose not to.*

"This can never be forgot, you know. We have much to deal with, and we are returning to the house."

Darcy had been ready to draw the pistol if he had to, but Balfour pocketed his knife and took up the bag with the crowbar. He was remarkably at ease. Perhaps he was chagrined at having been caught, but he showed no fear of the consequences. For his part, Darcy felt horror-struck, and thoroughly ashamed that he had not known what his supposed friend was capable of.

His anger and disappointment built during the long, quiet walk back to Pemberley. When they passed near to where they had found Carew's body, Darcy asked coldly, "Were you going to wrench the gold teeth from their jaws as well?"

He laughed, and said, "Nae! Good heavens, Darcy, the things you say."

Balfour showed no consciousness of guilt that gave one look of embarrassment, and that burned a righteous fury deeper into Darcy's chest. With one hand in his frock coat pocket, around the pistol handle, Darcy gestured with the other for Balfour to enter through the stable yard and go into the gunroom. It seemed the servants were asleep since this part of the house was quiet. The lamp was still lit, and Balfour set down the sack with the crowbar next to it before leaning against the table with his arms crossed over his chest.

Darcy stared at him for a long moment, waiting for Balfour to confess, to show regret, to plead for forgiveness, but he only waited silently. When he felt the chains of patience about to snap, Darcy asked, "For how long have you been so hard-pressed for money that you have taken to stealing and pawning?"

Balfour gave his usual carefree smile. "I had a small legacy from my mother. She was from a noble family in India, you know."

"But you spent it all."

"Aye, I cast up my accounts a year or so ago and saw that I had spent near three times my income."

Income was earned from work or from investments. Darcy thought of every single family who worked Pemberley's land, and of the pain of their recent losses, and how much work they would all need to do together to restore the value of their properties. "You mean you spent three times the allowance your father gives you."

Balfour's expression darkened. "A man needs money to show to the world he is a proper gentleman. And because of all I still owe, it is near impossible for anyone in town to extend me credit. You know the fortune my father earned in India, and what does he give to me? A few hundred pounds a year. I am the son of a wealthy and influential member of parliament, a *gentleman*. Appearances matter." In a calmer voice, he added, "As I said, my mother's inheritance was gone, and I could hardly say where it all went."

"I suspect that whatever was not spent on amusements or baubles, you lost at play and the turf."

Balfour shrugged. "You know how a gentleman must appear to be above the concerns of debts and expenses. If I cannot wager and spend freely, I am likely to lose friends."

Darcy felt a vise squeezing his heart. "*My* friendship, far from being diminished, could only increase in the ratio to your misfortunes."

"I am not a beggar, my dear Darcy."

"No, you became a thief instead!" He pursed his lips and tried to stay calm. "Do you do this often? Do you steal items from where you think they shall not be missed to sell for ready cash? So you can look to be a man of means before your friends and acquaintances, be able to wager what you like or spend on an impulse?"

"Yes, items here and there from homes and clubs and what have you. I do not expect you to understand. You are fortunate that your father is dead and you already have all of this."

Darcy shook his head, staggered. "I would trade it all to still have my father with me."

Balfour gave him a pained look. "I am sorry, that was unkind of me. I know what your father meant to you, and I remember how hard his death was on you." He sighed. "Let me try again. You inherited when you were two-and-twenty, and have ten thousand a year. I need to accumulate sufficient income—"

"What you steal and pawn," Darcy cried, disgusted, "is not income."

"Capital, then, sufficient capital to maintain the gentlemanly style of life in which I had been brought up. You do not know how humiliating it is to have a father exert financial pressure on you. I pawn baubles that no one would miss to make it easier to sit at the same table with my friends. Once I inherit Hyde House, I shall have no need of that."

"You are lost to all sense of shame," Darcy said sadly, "and to every feeling that ought to govern an honest man."

"Enough with the lecture!" Balfour cried. "I usually take from those who are not so dear to me as you are. I shall not steal from your house, or your villagers. It was badly done, and I am sorry." He bowed his head. "I have lost your respect, and am justly chastised, and can only hope to earn back your good opinion. Now, may I go to bed?"

Darcy was certain his mouth hung open. Balfour thought he was here for a morality lesson, like a recalcitrant child. He was incredulous that Balfour thought his crimes would go unpunished. "I am sending for a constable and the magistrate."

Balfour uncrossed his arms to set them on the table behind him, bracing himself. "You cannot mean it. Over a few pairs of shoes and jewellery? I put them back! Once the nails are hammered back into the lids, no one will ever know."

"I might have overlooked that, I truly think I"—his voice broke—"I could have, but you know why I must see this through." Balfour stared like he had no idea what could be the matter. "You killed someone!"

Balfour paled, and his shoulders tensed as he gripped the table's edge. "That would be impossible to prove."

"Do you deny it? Were you truly in Buxton playing cards on Thursday?" When Balfour said nothing, Darcy said, "You struck Molly Carew with a candlestick that you stole from my house, and then you pried a ring from her finger. That appears to be a habit of yours," he added when Balfour was still silent. "Did you pawn the ring, along with whatever else you pilfered in Lambton?"

"You cannot prove any of that."

"And if someone checked the pawnbrokers across the Peak, would he find a gold ring with five pieces of coral, and a name and description of the man who pledged it?"

Balfour's pale face turned red. "You are my *friend*. You won't send for a constable to arrest your friend. I shall leave in the morning, and I can only hope that someday you forgive me for this little transgression in the village."

As Balfour pushed himself from the table, Darcy said, "You are not leaving. You will be arrested, and you will stand trial."

"Trial!" he cried. "You would see your own friend in a gaol? What about loyalty above all else?"

"Except above honour," he said quietly.

"I am a gentleman—"

"By blood rather than behaviour! You ought to relinquish that title to a man more deserving."

Balfour pointed a finger. "I am walking out that door, and we will never talk about this again."

Darcy pulled the pistol from his pocket and levelled it at Balfour. "No. I am sending for Mr Birch."

His eyes turned to saucers at the sight of the pistol. "How could you present evidence against *me*?"

"Because you murdered a woman."

Balfour shifted his weight and looked at the pistol. "*If* I could explain, would you look the other way?"

He could not threaten him, or promise him any favour if Balfour confessed; it would only harm the case in court. Darcy wanted desperately to know why Carew died, but not at the expense of her justice. "Say nothing."

"No, no, you must hear. You think it was done on purpose." He exhaled loudly. "Yes, I can see how that would affect your judgment if you thought I had planned to kill her."

Balfour fidgeted nervously before bringing his hands back to the table behind him as he leant against it. "I took the taperstick from your father's desk on Saturday after Miss Darcy and Miss Bennet left me there. They said the room was not used, so I took one candlestick and intended to go back for the other if no one noticed it missing." Darcy heard Balfour tapping his fingers against the table behind him. "Everyone was at liberty that morning, you were gone from the house, the weather was poor, and I decided to sell it, along with my own gold watch.

"I was riding the path towards Lambton to go on to Matlock, riding along the stream, and she was coming from the village. I had the sack with the candlestick, my old watch, and a few small items I took from Lambton, if you must know. I could hear the stick clanging against the watch, so I dismounted to put the watch back into my pocket and wrap the other items in a handkerchief, and there was the candlestick sticking up out of the sack plain as day as she came near.

"'Is that from the house?' cries she as she runs closer. I said it was not, that she had best not concern herself. 'No, 'tis of a pair, from old Mr Darcy's desk. Reynolds said it was taken.' I told her again she was mistaken, and she said in this stern little voice, 'I shall check for myself, and then tell the master.'"

Balfour now looked as though he had explained it all satisfactorily. The pistol felt heavy in Darcy's hand, and it took him a moment to find his voice. "You insist on my knowing, so you may as well finish."

Balfour's shoulders fell. "She was going to tell you!" He blew out a breath and said more calmly, "I realise now I ought to have let her. You would have understood, and I would have returned the items. But she just primly walked away, and I dinna want the truth to come out." Balfour held out his hand, looked at it, and closed his palm. "She was walking away, I grabbed the candlestick, came up behind her and—" Balfour swung his closed fist across his body at about shoulder height. "She fell right over, and rolled down the bank, and then I tossed the candlestick away."

"Why not take it?" he asked softly. "After you hit her, why did you throw it into the grass?"

"It had blood on it, and there was no way to then clean it without blood getting on me. I decided it too riskful to fence it that day. And I could not be seen with the candlestick before she was found. I planned to go back for it," he said plainly. "I could not recover it from the stream, but if I tossed the candlestick into the tall grass, I could still sell it later after the maid was found, and after I cleaned it."

Darcy acutely felt the effects of this shocking narrative. He felt physically sick, his heart was racing, and he was thoroughly exhausted. "And instead of running for help when you realised what you had done, after assuring yourself you had murdered her, you plundered her jewellery." He waited for Balfour to speak, but he only shrugged. Darcy's disgust twisted his stomach. "How convenient for you to find something extra to pawn for your trouble."

"Yes, I took the ring because it was there, but her death was an accident! I did not plan to kill her."

Balfour seemed to think that a miscellaneous killing or manslaughter was more forgivable than wilful murder. That Darcy would now put down the pistol and invite him to his private study for a friendly drink.

"You will be tried at the assizes in Derby. Utterson and I will ensure you have—"

"No! I might be transported, or imprisoned, or executed," Balfour pleaded.

This was the man who kindly included his shy sister, who sought to put everyone at ease, who insisted on everyone participating in an evening's entertainment. His friend of six years, who had been with him after his father died, who teased him until he smiled. Darcy felt near to breaking down. "And I will be there to see it happen."

"Damn you, Darcy." Balfour turned from him, facing the table with his head bent.

He had to send for the magistrate. He edged around Balfour, to back towards the door to call for someone whilst still keeping the pistol aimed on him. Darcy had taken three steps when Balfour turned suddenly—holding the sack with the crowbar—and swung it. It struck the barrel, and the pistol was dashed from his hand.

Darcy cried out in surprise and was knocked off his balance. Rather than run for the door, Balfour dropped the sack with the crowbar and surged past him to gain the pistol. Darcy grabbed him by the shoulder, but Balfour threw back his elbow with a sharp blow that split open his lip. The impact sent him staggering, but not before he gained a grip on Balfour's sleeve to slow his progress towards the pistol. Darcy drew back and struck him in the eye with a closed fist. This sent Balfour to the floor, and they scrambled for the pistol, but Balfour, already being on the floor, reached it first.

The sound of Balfour fully cocking the hammer was loud over their laboured breathing. Balfour jumped to his feet, pointing it at him. Darcy rose more slowly, wiping the blood from his lip.

"What shall you do now?" he asked, spitting out the blood in his mouth. "The first death might have been manslaughter, but shooting me will be murder."

He heard quick footsteps approach the door, and when it flung open Elizabeth charged into the gunroom. Balfour started and swung the pistol straight at her. She gave a gasp of astonishment and stepped backward in alarm until she tripped against the door's edge, shutting it behind her.

Darcy cursed quietly. A cold sweat broke out across him. Every muscle in his body felt tense, and he had to decide if he could convince Balfour to let Elizabeth go, or if he must rush forward to stand between them.

"Balfour," he said quietly, and, thankfully, as Balfour's attention turned back to him, he aimed the pistol at him as well, "we had best tell Miss Bennet there is nothing to be concerned about, and let her get to bed."

"I dinna think she should leave. She will raise an alarm!"

"No, no of course she won't," he said as gently as he could. "She heard a noise and came to check, but there is nothing the matter. Miss Bennet will say good night and leave us to finish our conversation, won't you?" he added, looking directly at her and imploring her with his eyes to run from here as fast as she could.

Elizabeth shook her head slightly, but she brought her hands behind her back to reach for the door. He heard what must have been the latch click and felt a surge of relief. But Balfour aimed the pistol at Elizabeth again, his fingers shaking. She started and dropped her hands at her sides.

"She is only opening the door!" Darcy cried. "She can leave. Miss Bennet knows nothing about any of this."

Balfour's left eye was rapidly swelling shut, and he seemed on the verge of angry tears. "She may not, but you cannot say she will be quiet about what she has seen here."

"Listen to me!" he cried, and the pistol moved back to him. "You can leave. I shall say nothing about this or the other matter. Let Miss Bennet go, and she will go straight to bed. Then you can take a horse and leave. The stable yard is right there."

Balfour might shoot him before he fled, but it would keep Elizabeth safe. Balfour would only have time to fire one shot before the whole house came running. *And I cannot allow that single shot to be fired at Elizabeth.* Besides, the ring might still be found, and Elizabeth and Fitzwilliam knew the truth. If Balfour murdered him, Carew would still have her justice.

"If I leave, you won't stay silent about that maid, will you?" Balfour asked, his voice raising. "You would see me hang! Me, your friend!"

Elizabeth appeared to be wringing her hands or nervously adjusting her sleeves. He hoped she had the presence of mind to run as soon as she had the opportunity. Balfour was growing frantic. The more certain he was that he was not going to escape justice, the more desperate he would likely become.

And the more likely it will be that someone gets shot.

"What matters to me now is that Miss Bennet remains unharmed," he said softly, not looking at her in case Balfour followed his attention with the pistol.

"She will say that I shot you. I shall have to kill both of you and flee!"

"You have one shot. Shoot me if you must, but Miss Bennet is leaving now," he said, taking a step closer.

He heard Elizabeth give a little whimper, and Balfour's pistol moved towards the sound.

"Balfour! Look at me!" he cried, hating the desperation that surged into his voice. The pistol jerked back to him, and that was what mattered. "She is walking away, and then you may leave as well. Elizabeth," he said without looking from Balfour, "go upstairs."

"But you will still go to the magistrate if I leave the parish." Balfour gestured angrily at him with the pistol, but with only eight feet between them, he was certain to hit him. "You will get a warrant from the King's Bench, and put a notice in the *Hue and Cry* to make them pursue me across Great Britain!"

"No, I won't."

"Damn your soul, Darcy," Balfour said, with a sad smile and levelling the gun, "you truly cannot lie to save your life."

The sudden crack of gunfire filled the small room, and he heard the dull thud of an impact against the wall.

Balfour flinched, and he lowered his pistol arm. Darcy rushed forward and grabbed the barrel with his left hand, forcing it down, whilst drawing back with his right to punch Balfour a second time. When he fell, Darcy pried the pistol from his hand; it was still loaded and fully cocked. Balfour stayed on the ground, his face filled with abject despair, and only then did Darcy look at Elizabeth.

Somehow, she had got a hold of the pistol he had left behind, and distracted Balfour by firing it. She took a few steps into the room, alternating her shocked gaze between Balfour and the hole on the opposite wall above their heads. The horrified look on her face made it hard for him to determine if she was about to faint or scream.

"Are you well?" he asked, keeping the pistol aimed at Balfour.

Elizabeth dropped her pistol onto the table and nodded.

"Would you go into the hall and call for—"

Before he could finish, Mrs Reynolds ran into the room wearing her dressing gown, followed by a footman out of his livery. Colonel Fitzwilliam, who looked like he had just arrived, hurried in behind them. He watched his cousin's eyes take in the scene—Darcy's bloodied lip, the pistol in his hand, and Balfour on the floor—and began to shout orders.

In the noise and activity that followed, the arrival of the constable and the magistrate, the raised voices, the confusion of many questions, the tying of Balfour to a chair, Elizabeth took his hand for a moment before slipping from the room. It was a simple gesture, but it made all the difference to him.

CHAPTER TWENTY-ONE

"Miss Bennet will hardly want to kiss you now, looking like that."

Darcy was sprawled across his bed in his shirtsleeves, pressing a soaked flannel against his swollen lip, staring unseeing at the dimity bed hangings above him. Fitzwilliam was in a chair, his arms hanging down over its sides, and he sounded exhausted. Darcy pulled the cloth away and saw the cut was closed. He rolled the cloth into a ball and threw it at his cousin, but it only made it two-thirds of the way to the chair.

"I missed what you said to Mr Birch about the pawnbroker in Matlock Bath whilst I was speaking to the constable," Darcy led, not in the mood for teasing now.

"The pawnbroker had the coral ring; it was just as you described. Mr Birch is sending a constable tomorrow to retrieve it and take his statement." His cousin hesitated, and Darcy lifted his head enough to see Fitzwilliam rub his eyes. "The entry in the pledge book was 'Bingley, residing at Pemberley House,' but the description the pawnbroker gave was definitely Balfour."

"He used a nom de guerre to fence his ill-gotten trinkets like some sort of spy?" Darcy cried.

Fitzwilliam lifted his eyes in disgust. "The pawnbroker will be called to testify, as will you, and those who found Carew and the candlestick."

Darcy sat up all the way and leant against the headboard, toeing off his shoes and letting them fall to the floor. He had thought what he experienced the day after the storm was the weariest a man could feel. "It is possible that Miss Bennet may not need to testify. Mr Birch thinks his confession in the gunroom would be admissible in court. And the results of the coroner's inquest and the ring in the pawn-shop are the most critical evidence in proving that Carew was murdered."

His cousin yawned. "He is returning in the morning to take official statements from all of us?"

Darcy nodded. "After he calls on Mr Carew and explains the sad truth behind his daughter's death." It was close to morning now; hopefully Mr Birch would call very late. "The coroner will examine the body, and the case will go to the assizes next Lent." He paused. "Unless Balfour's father can get him out of it."

Fitzwilliam made a disagreeing sound. "The most his father might be able to influence is not having him executed. But if Balfour's drawing a gun on you and Miss Bennet comes out in court . . ." He blew out a breath and shook his head. "I do not see how anyone could overlook that."

Darcy had been utterly shocked when her gun went off and was grateful that he had not been too stunned to act during the brief moment Elizabeth had given him. He might have been seconds away from being murdered himself. Elizabeth must have primed the pistol and taken it before he and Balfour returned from Lambton. "Do you think she meant to follow me to the village, or was she waiting in the house to help me detain the prisoner?"

"I hardly know," his cousin said, throwing up his hands. "I am just thankful your lady had a pistol. It was a good thing she startled Balfour. From what you said, I am convinced he would have shot you in his panic."

"Balfour simply could not comprehend that I would turn him over to the authorities," Darcy said slowly. "He showed no regret, no remorse for Molly Carew at all. He thought our friendship would triumph over all of his dishonesty, his violence."

Fitzwilliam sat up in his chair and looked at him sharply. "Some friendship if he drew a gun on you!" He rubbed his eyes wearily. "I know it could have been Balfour or Utterson, but I was genuinely surprised when the pawnbroker described the man as tall with black hair and amber eyes rather than short with sandy-coloured hair."

They had both wanted it to be Utterson because it would have been easier to bear, because although he had become a friend, he did not mean as much to them as did Balfour. Darcy glanced at the clock and saw it was close to four in the morning. All of the energy he had felt in the midst of the confrontation, and in realising he and Elizabeth were safe, was long gone.

"It was Balfour, but Utterson acted like he loathes me now too," he said quietly.

Utterson had come down when he discovered Balfour was gone from his room to find a group of men by the gunroom in complete confusion. "Well, about that." Fitzwilliam yawned again. "To begin with, whilst you talked with Mr Birch, Utterson said to me that Balfour was alternately rich and poor, but Utterson had assumed it was from spending beyond his means that Balfour was obliged to surrender to pawnbrokers the plunder he culled from the gaming table, not sundries from his friends' homes," Fitzwilliam added drily. "I sincerely doubt Utterson knew Balfour was stealing; his shock seemed genuine."

"No one knew, and that adds to how frightening this entire situation is." For all of Balfour's love of money, Darcy and everyone else had still seen Balfour's amiability and liveliness. He had faults, but nothing that hinted to the cruelty he had shown tonight. He had appeared the same as any other man, but was capable of such immoral acts. How did Balfour get to such a place in his own heart and mind where he could not only steal, but also strike a woman dead from fear of his thievery becoming known?

Darcy shook his head sadly. "I don't understand, Fitzwilliam. It is not as though Balfour was addicted to the cards or the dice and could not help himself. He chose to spend to excess to make it appear as though he had unlimited funds and not a care in the world. He might even have asked his sister for funds, but he would rather everyone think him a wealthy man." Darcy yawned. "But that does not explain why Utterson was so curt with me, even for him."

"Ah, well." Fitzwilliam cleared his throat. "From what he said amidst all the activity, it seems that whilst Miss Bennet awaited you, she came upon Utterson and hinted to him that he was your first suspect. What he said to her about where he had been the day Carew died cleared him of suspicion as far as she was concerned."

"He went to Lord Poole's after all?"

Fitzwilliam smirked. "Well, he was there, but his attentions were exclusively focused on Poole's daughter." Darcy's eyes widened in surprise. "Utterson was not pleased to have to admit that they are secretly engaged."

"I am sure he was also not pleased to be accused of murdering Carew." Darcy suspected Elizabeth bore the full brunt of Utterson's impatience and irascibility. "That explains why he was angry with me; he is a short-tempered man."

"Utterson does not have a mild or patient temper," Fitzwilliam agreed, "but I think when the whole story came out, he felt for you."

Darcy had nothing to say. Fitzwilliam was quiet for a long moment before he said, "Damn it, that was terrifying. I was in the stable yard, bone-tired from a day on horseback, and I heard the pistol shot." Fitzwilliam squeezed his eyes shut before blowing out a breath. "I was afraid I would have to put you to rest with your forefathers."

"I might have felt worse in the deadhouse than in the gunroom. The agony of that moment, seeing Balfour steal those items, seeing the depth of his heartless, unfeeling behaviour"—he sighed as the feelings washed over him again—"it was horrible."

"Not as horrible as him aiming a pistol at your gut!"

"That was nothing to what I felt when he turned the gun on Elizabeth." Darcy closed his eyes.

What he had felt when Balfour aimed at Elizabeth beggared description. It was near to what he had felt when he saw the body in the stream and thought it was her, but a thousand times more intense, a terror that nearly cut him to pieces from the inside out. "Good God, Fitzwilliam, what might Balfour have done if he knew I love her?"

Might Balfour have held her hostage? Used her to bargain against his seeking justice for Carew? Shot her to distract him whilst he fled?

A more gruesome possibility occurred to him. "He might have been able to take both guns, kill us both, and with his charming manner convince everyone that it had been a lovers' quarrel and that she and I killed each other."

When Darcy blew out a breath and lifted his eyes, Fitzwilliam gave him a sympathetic look. He then rose with a weary sigh. "I must get to bed. Mrs Lanyon is still asleep, and when she wakes . . . well, there will be a great deal for her to hear."

"Mrs Lanyon will need you," Darcy said gently.

His cousin gave a little nod. "It will break her heart. She cannot have known about it, I am certain of it."

"None of us knew." How horrifying was that, that someone capable of murdering without remorse appeared the same as any other person in their circle?

"Whilst you are making statements to the magistrate, I shall comfort her as best I can. I suspect she shall want to leave—"

The door opened, and Elizabeth rushed in. He ought to have stood to greet her, but he could not summon the strength. She was dressed for bed, and her lips were pressed tightly together, and she seemed to be thrumming with desperate energy.

Has she been waiting up all this time to see me alone, but could not wait a moment longer?

Darcy instinctively knew that what they both needed was to wrap their arms around one another. Whilst still looking at Elizabeth, he said to Fitzwilliam in a low voice, "Get out."

"Now, a moment, Darcy. I am sure she only wanted to see for herself that you were well. Let me first make certain the corridor is empty so no one sees her leave your—"

"Not her," he said shortly, now looking at him. "You. Get out."

His cousin tilted his head, then looked between him and Elizabeth, made a thoughtful sound before giving an embarrassed laugh, and gave Elizabeth a slight bow. When the latch clicked, Elizabeth ran across the room, leaving her wrapping gown and slippers on the floor as she climbed onto him, and tried to give him a passionate kiss. He winced, and Elizabeth gave his swollen lip a worried look before moving to kiss along his neck.

Weariness sapped his strength and fatigue dulled his senses, and for a long while he was passive as she kissed him and lifted off his shirt. Then he saw her eyes were filled with tears. Her whole expression, as she tossed his shirt to the floor, was anguished.

Even as she sat astride him to unfasten his trouser buttons, she was sniffling.

"Stop," he said as she tried to push them down his hips. "Stop," he said, more forcefully.

"Why?" Elizabeth dropped her hands and her shoulders fell. Tears were running down her cheeks.

"Because you are crying."

She sniffed again, and Darcy brought his hands to either side of her face to wipe away her tears with his thumbs. "Come here." He pulled her by her shoulders to rest her head against him. He could smell the sulphur of the black powder in her hair.

He held her tightly until her crying slowed. "I thought he would kill you," she said into his neck. "He was angry and desperate and—" She broke off with another sob. "And you were going to let him shoot you!"

"I could not let him shoot *you*." He ran his fingers through her hair. "I was afraid Balfour would kill you in his despair." He had been absolutely sick with fear, and she had clearly felt the same. "What must you have felt when you ran into the gunroom!"

"I heard a noise and assumed that you had returned with Mr Balfour," she said, still lying against him, "but I had no idea that you had fought over the gun and that I would see him aiming it at you."

"You looked anxious, but you acted calmly the entire time," he said, wanting to know what she had thought.

He felt her warm breath against him as she sighed. "I did not feel calm," she said slowly, "and certainly not after I had only ten minutes before faced Mr Utterson in the drawing room. But I was resolved not to leave you, certainly not when I had a way to protect you."

"Did you take the pistol from the gunroom earlier to follow me to Lambton?" He felt her nod.

"I knew you would be angry if I followed you, but it was foolish of you to confront him alone. I never should have let you go by yourself."

He had been too worried that a crowd of outraged servants, tenants, and villagers would take justice into their own hands. "I ought to have guessed Balfour might become violent against me, considering what he had done to Carew. I just—I just could not comprehend the depths he had sunk to. You were very quick in the gunroom, dearest. I had not even noticed you had the small pistol up your sleeve. It was clever of you to distract him."

"Clever!" she cried, sitting up to look at him. "I was not trying to be clever. I was trying to shoot him."

Darcy thought of the lead ball embedded in the wall a foot higher and to the left of where Balfour had been standing. He was only spared further mischance because Elizabeth fired a pistol badly.

He dried her tears again and said, "Next time you ought to just take it by the barrel and throw it." As he hoped, she laughed. "You might have better luck."

"It had a very short barrel!" she said, smiling. "And it recoiled more than I expected." She gave him a mock scowl and playfully pushed his chest. "And it is not as though I know how to aim one."

"I can teach you." She shook her head. "Neither Balfour nor I suspected you would take any action tonight. I promise not to under-value your mettle in the future."

"I cannot make myself appear weak simply because gentlemen are supposed to be strong."

He felt so weary, nothing at all like the strength he normally felt with her. "I lost a friend today, Elizabeth, as though he had died." He had expected to see Utterson, a man who had just moved from an acquaintance to friendship. He had not truly prepared himself to see Balfour plunder the dead.

"Oh, Fitzwilliam, it must hurt terribly."

"The pain of betrayal is real, like a knife wound."

Elizabeth gave a small smile. "Or a blow to the face. Does your mouth hurt very much?"

"My fingers hurt more." He bent and flexed the fingers of his right hand. "I have not punched anyone since I was thirteen, and I hit Balfour twice tonight."

"Was Mr Wickham the last person you struck?"

He nodded. "Mr Wickham's insults and offences were never a betrayal because he was never my friend. Mr Wickham betrayed my father, not me, and my father never even knew it," he added. "Balfour . . . I can hardly stand to think of him at the end of a rope."

"He killed someone. He stole, he killed, and he threatened both of us."

Elizabeth's eyes were now dry, and although she gave him a stern look, Darcy began to appreciate that she was astride him. It brought to mind all the pleasures she had given him last night. He brought his hands to her hips, brushing his fingertips back and forth. "I know it, and my conviction to see him prosecuted will not change. I only wish I did not care so much."

"When you care about people, it makes you vulnerable. You care so deeply about your friends, your family, everyone who relies on Pemberley."

"You make it sound like being vulnerable is an asset," he said, scoffing.

Elizabeth looked thoughtful and said slowly, "I think if you were unable to be hurt, you would be unable to love, and then you would hardly be alive at all."

She pressed a gentle kiss to the corner of his mouth. By now, she had a manifest sign of his amorous intentions, and she gave a little knowing smile and started to stroke him with the same eager curiosity she had shown last night. After years of tending to himself, the novelty of her light, steady touch made him fear their encounter would be over before it had properly begun.

Darcy gently moved her hand away. "Too distracting," he whispered, as he lifted off her nightshift. He could not kiss her mouth as he wanted, so he trailed his lips down her neck, softly sucking and biting at her throat, his tongue against her collarbone and his hand kneading her breast. He knew he would never forget how good his name sounded on her lips, intermingled with moans and breathy sighs.

The moan that escaped her after he had moved his hand lower, stroking faster, sent another surge of desire through him.

"You have become good at that," she said breathlessly.

"A new skill," he murmured before chancing a firm kiss to her lips. "I should practise to be proficient." He focused on every response of her body to guide him until the pleasure rising in her made her wild with the sensations of it. Before it overtook her, Darcy laid down on the bed and watched Elizabeth close her eyes as she pushed herself all the way on to him.

She rested her hands behind her on his legs and, when she gave him an uncertain look, he gripped her hips to encourage her to move. She leant back farther, and he moved his hands to her breasts, caressing them as she began to move faster, arching against him until her broken murmurs gave way to a strangled cry.

Elizabeth fell forward and rested her head on his shoulder, panting heavily. "Fitzwilliam," she breathed into his ear, "we had better do that again in the morning."

Although she was satisfied, Darcy still needed to feel that release he had never found anywhere else. He rocked against her as a hint, and she gave a ragged gasp. She pushed herself up onto her hands and began moving slowly over him, taking him deeper and watching him intently. Soon, her enthralled gaze fell away from his, and Elizabeth started making small, needy sounds.

He wanted to know if he could bring on for her that critical ecstasy again, and how she wanted him to do it, but all he managed to ask was a breathless, "Again?"

Harsh, uneven breathing was her answer. It was all too much, and not enough, a building ache of need he wanted to surrender to but not before he satisfied her again. Darcy sat them up, bracing an arm behind him, and together they picked up the languid pace. The muscles in his back and arm were flaring at having never been used this way. But her gripping his shoulder and the headboard behind him, urging him on with murmurs of "oh God" and "harder" made it impossible to stop or slow.

Elizabeth's naturally brilliant eyes darted flames until they rolled upward, her fingernails dug into him, and she cried out, tightening around him. Every thrust came harder and faster now, and the sound that ripped from his throat at the final moment was one he had not known he was capable of making.

After a while, they found their way to their sides, with Elizabeth's back cuddled against his chest. "Wake me when you want to do that again," she said sleepily, linking her fingers through his.

"I would like to, but you ought to leave before my valet comes in." After a moment, he added, "I could look like a villain, you know, if anyone learnt of your being here."

"How do you mean?"

"Your sister is absent, and you are in a single man's house with a chaperon who encourages us to be alone." He kissed her neck and tightened his arms around her. "And I was taken with you, I solicited your chastity, and obtained my desire."

"You left out the part about having several times committed sin with me, and at my urging."

"You know that women cannot be trusted to know their own minds on such matters," he said, laughing before he could finish the sentence.

"Oh, yes, I had no notion at all as to what was happening." She was quiet for a moment, and then said, "We ought to marry soon to prevent you from appearing like a complete dissolute."

He sighed at the necessity of her leaving Derbyshire, however temporary it would be. "If it is Wednesday by now, then I can send you to Longbourn on Thursday, along with another letter for your father for the banns to be read."

"And when shall you come to claim me?" she asked, yawning.

"A week, ten days maybe. As soon as matters with the magistrate are arranged, I will leave. I shall have everything resolved with papers and settlements for your father, and if your mother will have me, I can stay at Longbourn."

"I shall leave a ladder outside my window in case you find Longbourn intolerable and have to abscond with me to Scotland."

Darcy laughed. "I will do what I must to return you to Derbyshire as Mrs Darcy and not lose your parents' good opinion."

"Maybe Charles will let you stay at Netherfield until our wedding day."

He wondered if she was thinking of all that he had said and written when they were at Hunsford about the inferiority and impropriety of her family. "I respect your family. I do not mind staying at Longbourn."

"I have lived at Netherfield since Jane and Charles married. I have many reasons to go into that house before my wedding day. And I would not mind your being in a nearly empty house three miles away from where my parents are."

All the stirrings of desire that he had thought were satisfied came rushing back. Elizabeth noticed, and turned around in his arms, saying playfully, "Are you reconsidering that I retire to my own rooms?"

"Since I already believe myself your husband"—Darcy moved them both so she was underneath him—"I should usurp part of the prerogative of that office once more before you leave."

EPILOGUE

October 1813

E lizabeth still had her love of a solitary walk, and now she had a park ten miles round that was hers to explore. Although she had more demands on her time than she did when she had last signed her name Elizabeth Bennet a year ago, Pemberley's mistress could still do things for her own interest and enjoyment, and admiring Derbyshire's landscape was high on her list.

Her pleasure came from the scenery as much as the exercise. In the park there were woods, hills, streams, rocks, and only Pemberley House itself could be equal to anything amidst such grandeur. She had scaled every height, and from each summit seen every tranquil dale. Many delightful hours could be spent in contemplation of wood-crowned hills and immense rocks, and all within her own home.

She was now returning to the house, crossing mown meadows and waving to labourers, when she saw a rider make its way towards her.

"Lizzy, I did not know you were walking this morning," Georgiana said as soon as she was within hearing. "I would have gone with you."

"I know how you enjoy to ride, and I hate to take you from it.

Besides, you were kind enough to ride with me last week, slow as it was."

Georgiana gave an indulgent smile. "You have gotten much better."

"Thanks to your brother's lessons and a very gentle mare, I hope that *next* year you and I can put a biscuit in our pockets and enjoy a long excursion together, but for now I shall have to settle for a ramble on my own feet."

Darcy had patiently presided over the whole of her riding lessons, but thus far she had only managed to rise into a canter. She was a long way from being shown Derbyshire on horseback with her newest sister.

Georgiana and her groom set off for another part of the park, and Elizabeth ascended a small hill, taking a winding route back to Pemberley. This higher ground gave her eye power to wander, and there were many charming views of the valley, the hills opposite, and part of the stream. But it was the sight of Darcy approaching her, and at no great distance, that made her heart beat fast rather than the lovely scene.

"You are not an easy woman to find, dearest Elizabeth," he called with a smile.

"Had I known you were wanting to join me, I would have waited for you," she said as she descended the hill to meet him. "You were very much occupied in how many barrels of beer were to be brought up from the cellar when I left."

Now that the hard work between midsummer and Michaelmas was over, and the winter grains sown, Darcy had organised a larger harvest festival than was typical. There was usually a party after harvests were in and the grass mown, but after the travails of the last year, he had thought it best to celebrate with more attention to lifting his tenants' spirits.

"That was the only discussion I needed to have with Mr Stevenson. You managed everything else splendidly."

"I think your idea for a grander celebration was a good one. If there are any games, shall you compete to win? I think you have a very good chance at taking the prize."

Darcy laughed and shook his head. His deportment was still typically firm and often imposing, but she knew he would drink from the same glass of ale passed around amongst the men and he would start the dancing too. "I am merely glad that this season's yield was as good as it was, all matters considered. We are not where we once were, of course, but it was better than I expected."

"And next year's shall be even better," she added. "Certainly, everyone is in better spirits than a year ago."

Darcy nodded and looked down the valley with a pensive look on his face. Gleams of light illuminated various aspects of the landscape. This year had been warmer and drier in comparison to the last. It was still a year of rebuilding, but the hopes for next year's season held everything promising.

She gently linked her arm through his. "Why are you not at ease?"

"How could I not be at ease in a lovely spot, with you, near a sparkling stream in a valley covered with foliage and fields?"

"That sounds like something I would say," she said with an emphatic look that he ought to begin again.

He shrugged before taking her hands in his. "I am glad of that. You know, I had wondered last year, before I proposed to you at Dovedale, if you could be happy in Derbyshire after all of the terrible things you had seen." After another long look at the valley, he said quietly, "I was thinking about the near riot in Lambton last year. How quickly the situation with my tenants might have fallen apart if we could not band together."

"They banded together with you because they trusted you." Since the storm, Darcy had been sure in his decisions, cautious in his spending, and generous to his tenants. "You managed the disaster well."

"I also managed the tragedy of the murder of my servant, and the looting of my villagers, and the need to retrench."

Lewis Balfour was still a painful subject, and she avoided it by saying, "General economies were made, but you still possess a good and clear estate, and you have not had to sell part of it to answer the purpose."

They now walked through the valley towards the house. "Was it," he asked cautiously, "was it difficult for the new bride? You had to forsake a new carriage, a house in town for two seasons, and seeing the

Gardiners, as well as travelling to Staffordshire to see Bingley and Jane settled in their new home."

"We shall see them all here at Christmas. What was sacrificed was done out of necessity, and it was temporary."

"I think next summer I can take you to any watering place you wish to go. Bingley has written of returning to Scarborough if you want to join them."

"Jane and Charles told me enough about the balls, theatre, and public teas." Elizabeth gripped his arm a little tighter. "I am happy here." After a while she said, "Now, as much as you long for my conversation, surely you did not walk two miles to find me simply because I am witty and charming."

He did not even try to deny it and flatter her, not that she would expect him to. "I received some letters, and wanted a walk to clear my head. And then I needed to find you to talk it over with you. One was from Utterson; he says that he has nearly completed his terms at the Inn of Court."

His was a name that had not been mentioned in some time. "I remember you commenting that Mr Utterson had been saying that he was nearing the end of his study for years."

She felt Darcy shrug. "An inactive state is exceedingly disagreeable, so unlike my own, and I feared that Utterson was addicted to ease and pleasure, as much as he is assumed to have sound judgment. I wondered if he would ever complete his degree or if he would waste whatever talents he has."

"Perhaps he only needs a patron, some reason to stay encouraged to focus on his study of the law."

"He found that in Miss Margaret Newcomen, who by now has become Mrs James Utterson." He smiled at her gasp of surprise. "It seems the couple grew tired of waiting for her father to approve and went to Scotland to make Lord Poole's approval unnecessary. Utterson writes that he is now back in London, will be called to the bar soon, and, wishing to provide for his wife properly, asks for my help to promote his career in the law."

"I would have thought he was asking for a place to stay in Derbyshire since he will not be welcomed at Lord Poole's."

Darcy smiled. "No, quite unlikely, at least until there is someone to call Poole 'grandpapa.'"

"Shall you help Mr Utterson? I feel sorry that my interference let him know we suspected him and it caused a rift in your relationship."

"Do not feel sorry. His fault is that he is a resentful man, and he admitted in his letter that he ought not to have been unyielding towards me for our suspicions. My own temper is not as forgiving as it could be, after all, and I can show him a little grace."

"Especially because he admitted that he was wrong to hold it against you."

Darcy nodded. "Still, I am not reluctant to engage on his behalf, not when he wants to make amends."

After walking in silence, she led, "You said letters . . ."

"I was surprised to learn that Fitzwilliam is selling his commission in the Foot Guard."

"What?" she cried. "That would bring him a few thousand pounds, but not enough to live on."

"More like eight or nine."

"Still, what strange scheme is this?"

"At first I thought like you, but the more I think on it, I see he is prudent, not a schemer."

"What is he thinking? He would still have only three hundred or so pounds to live on if he sells his commission."

"He intends to marry well."

Comprehension dawned. "Hester has not said a word!" Elizabeth and Hester were faithful correspondents, but they had not seen each other since she married Darcy. "When did he ask her?"

"His letter was sly, but I suspect your friend did the asking. Aside from hinting strongly as to his wishes and proving his constancy over the past year, I think Fitzwilliam left the choice entirely in her hands. If you do not approve of him selling his commission, I know you at least heartily approve of the match. I do, since it is what Fitzwilliam has wanted for two years."

"She is sensible, full of information, and without a particle of affectation, and will devote herself to making him happy." With her talents, Hester could be a brilliant leader in the fashionable world, but that was not in her nature. "But why did he leave the Foot Guard? He loved his career, and Hester loves the army and the officer's wives, and has friends amongst them all."

Darcy gave her a sad look. "*Had* friends, you know. She cannot bear to return to London, Fitzwilliam says. They will live a more retired life, and so he resigned his commission. She gave up her house after the Lent assizes and intends to stay in Haddingtonshire. Hyde House is hers, after all," he added quietly.

Darcy had gone to the Derby assizes, given evidence, and was there when the verdict returned guilty. It was the judge's duty to pass a sentence of death, and Mr Balfour's father influenced him to recommend a reprieve to the King and Privy Council. Darcy had waited in Derby until they learnt if it might be transportation or imprisonment instead of execution. He had intended to remain until the last, but when it was time to stand in front of Friar Gate and await the prisoners being led to the gallows, Darcy had been unable to bear it and came home.

"Fitzwilliam wants to come next month," Darcy was saying, drawing her back from her reflections.

"Your cousin need never ask," she cried. "He ought to know he is always welcome."

"He wants Mrs Lanyon to join him here, to marry from Pemberley." His voice raised in uncertainty. "Her father is dead from grief, and his father does not approve of her family. My uncle—indeed, most people —believe that after what Balfour did, every person of character must be divided from Mrs Lanyon forever."

"They certainly can come," she said firmly, "but why did Hester not write to me to ask?"

"Fitzwilliam wrote that she wanted to know for certain if she was welcome—if *I* would welcome her," he corrected. "She did not want to put you in an awkward situation if I refused, which of course I would not."

Elizabeth thought back to the morning after the incident in the gunroom. "She did not mean the things she said to you, Fitzwilliam." Hester had not believed her brother was guilty, and had railed and cried, and rather than face the truth—and the pain—of what her brother had done, had finally insisted that Darcy must have made it up.

"I know," he said softly, "and there is nothing to forgive on that score, but you know her manner." He was quiet for a long time. "She will need assurances that I do not hold it against her, and I hope I can give them in person, but . . . Elizabeth, how do I look her in the eye?" His expression was pained. "She is marrying my cousin, my closest friend, but how can I face her? Her father dead from grief, and her brother—" He lowered his eyes and swallowed. "I did right in having charges brought against him, he murdered someone, but—"

"It is not your fault he was guilty," she said quickly, "or that the punishment had to be death, or that the hanging cabinet chose not to reprieve it." When the whole truth was laid bare in court, the stealing, the murder, what happened in the gunroom, it was too much to expect that mercy would be granted. Three other men guilty of only robbery were also hung that day. "It was plain to anyone who knows you, anyone who saw you this spring, that there was no triumph for you in what happened at the Derby gaol."

Darcy's public demeanour was at all times dignified. Even his movements and gestures seemed composed, but still graceful. But when he had returned from Derby, Elizabeth could see that he was not himself for a long while. To know that nothing but time could improve his situation, that there was nothing she could do for him, was a trial to her.

Although she doubted that Darcy realised it, as the truth of his actions for Carew became generally known, Elizabeth saw that the respect and admiration that the neighbourhood felt for Darcy intensified. He might have not been like himself, but everyone at Pemberley knew he had seen his friend hang for what Balfour had done to Molly Carew. Between that and how he had managed the tragedy of the flood, none could say they doubted Darcy's dedication to Pemberley.

After a long silence, he said, "I spoke to Balfour, briefly, before . . . before I left."

"You never said that," she said slowly.

"It was after the verdict but before a reply was returned from London, and I convinced a guard to let me have a few moments with him. I hardly know what I expected, or what he could say for himself. Elizabeth, we stood in that small, brick, windowless cell, and Balfour was his usual, engaging self." He sighed heavily. "I could not say if he was putting me at ease because he harboured me no ill will, or if he thought he would be reprieved and it was all a joke. But as I left, he said, 'My dear Darcy, I die hard, but I am not afraid to go.'"

Darcy was a man whose decisions were seldom if ever shaken, but she still asked, "Do you regret pursuing Carew's death?"

"No," he said firmly. "In contempt of all decency, Balfour murdered someone he feared would expose him, he pillaged the dead"—he stopped walking and looked at her—"he threatened you. But then why do I regret that I could not save his neck from the noose?" His voice broke, and he scoffed, shaking his head. "How is that rational, Elizabeth?"

"Because he was your friend," she whispered, blinking away a tear.

He shook his head again and resumed walking. "It is unacceptable."

"It is acceptable to admit that he hurt you."

"He betrayed my trust, my friendship, but he killed Molly Carew, and I could never have let him go unpunished."

"You have had a difficult year or so, but are now happier?" she asked, trying to cheer him. "Bingley now lives twenty miles away, you shall mend your friendship with Mr Utterson, and your cousin is uniting with a woman he has long loved, one you respect highly, and your tenants are recovered from a disaster."

Darcy laughed wryly. "Whilst you are accounting for my year and a half, you may also add a rejection to a terrible marriage proposal, a complete change of my self-belief, and the disquiet that goes along with wondering if the woman I love might ever admire me after all."

Any one of those things—the uncertainty of her regard, the storm, the burden of how to provide for hundreds of people, the murder of his servant, the betrayal by his friend, the financial travails—would have distressed the spirits of any man. "It was enough to break anyone's heart to pieces."

He gave her a significant look. "If it was, then it is a good thing I found someone to help me put it back together again even stronger than it was."

A surge of tenderness towards him overcame her. A season after the flooding, Darcy's contracted, pensive face that spoke of his deep worry was done away with. She more often saw expressive touches of humour in Darcy's eyes and at the corners of his mouth than she had a few months ago.

I have the certainty of knowing that his pleasant smiles come not only from a surcease of his sorrows but from his domestic happiness.

They were now near to the house, crossing the lawn where preparations were being made for tomorrow's celebrations. There were about a dozen men putting out tables, marking a field for games, hauling barrels from the cellar, and for a while Pemberley's master talked with everyone.

"How do you do? What have you been about? Four hundred heaped bushels is very good. How does your mother amuse herself? If your son wants work, I can hire him out as a timber feller. You chose a good location for the principal weir in the stream. Have you begun to take up potatoes yet?"

Elizabeth would normally have joined him, but today she hung back and listened to all that passed between them, and admired Darcy in every expression, every sentence, that marked his concern, his interest, and his good manners.

"I shall have to make a speech to please them all tomorrow," he said after he rejoined her, "to thank them for their dedication this season."

She thought of how well he had managed their fears in the days after the storm last year. "I wager that before the dancing begins tomorrow your tenants will obey the genuine dictates of their hearts and salute you with three cheers."

"They will when they see how many barrels of beer Mr Stevenson has brought up."

They were now near the stable yard, and Elizabeth left the road to walk away to better admire the winding of the valley.

"Every time the carriage returns us home, you are distracted by this view," Darcy said, coming up behind her and wrapping his arms around her waist.

"I did marry you only for the landscape and the grounds."

Darcy bent to kiss her neck. "I am lucky, then, that there is unparalleled beauty in Derbyshire, and that your heart thrills at every sight of it."

She smiled as she leant against him, assured that he knew very well what truly thrilled her heart. Still, the beautiful scenery, the noble mansion, and the distinguished master all felt as belonging to one another, as being part of the whole. *But as much as I love Derbyshire, I would take the man wherever he was with whatever he had.*

After looking down the valley a little longer, she said, "We shall have a grand festival tomorrow, and then a wedding in six weeks, and at that point Hester and Fitzwilliam might as well stay for Christmas with the Bingleys and the Gardiners. You know that they would share in their happiness without any judgment."

"I shall be glad to have the people we love around us, and that my cousin will stop sighing and casting many a longing glance at Mrs Lanyon."

"Hester and Fitzwilliam shall be happy in each other, even if their circle will be much smaller now. They were friends first, after all, before falling in love."

"We were not friends first," he said into her ear, and Elizabeth took his hands in hers and wrapped them around herself. "We did not become friends until you came to Pemberley with Jane."

"True. You loved me first," she said, "so maybe love could also produce that tender friendship and closeness that I think should always be the cement of such a union."

"But you did not then love me in return," he said quickly.

"Oh, I loved you before I thought of you as a friend, or at the least, love and friendship grew steadily and quickly last summer until I could hardly tell one from the other." She turned in his arms and brought her hands to his neck. "I certainly love you now, and very deeply."

"I was never in doubt of that."

She pretended to think. "No, you seem insecure and uncertain. I could show you how much I love you." She leant into him and gave him an emphatic look he was sure to understand. "In fact, I cannot wait until tonight to show you, or even until we return to the house."

"Mrs Darcy," he said in a low voice, shaking his head.

"We have a companionship of mind and spirit. Is it not natural that a companionship of the body should follow?"

"Perfectly natural," he said roughly, "but hardly a thing to mention, or enjoy, here." Nothing was so brilliant as Darcy's smile. "I am surprised at you."

"What? You cannot be surprised at my warm feelings for you, or my lively spirits."

"Even if there were not a dozen people fifty feet away—"

"That would be scandalous! I would lead us into those trees over there first."

His smile widened, and although she now had a strong hint that he was not opposed to such an idea, he said, "Since I intend to return the favour, I would prefer the privacy of our rooms and the comfort of some furniture."

Elizabeth gave him a long, ardent kiss that she rarely dared to give him outside of their chambers. "Pemberley is a large house, and it will take too long to walk there." She continued to tease him. "It is a beautiful day, and I remember you once promised that Mrs Darcy could have her way with you wherever she wanted."

"I think I promised you could do so in any *room* you wanted."

"Well, the whenever I wanted was implied, and I choose now."

"Whenever may have been implied but indoors, in a room with a locked door, was also implied." Darcy let go of her waist to take a firm grip on her hand, tugging on her to lead them into the house, both of them laughing as they went.

THE END

AVAILABLE NOW

Mr Darcy's Valentine

Will an exchange of secret valentines lead to love?

After her aunt notices her partiality for Mr Wickham, Elizabeth Bennet is invited to town for the winter along with her sister Jane, and February in London gives Elizabeth the chance to become better acquainted with the Gardiners' young and single friend.

When Mr Darcy and Elizabeth meet by chance at a concert, Darcy must account for how Bingley left Hertfordshire as he considers his deepening feelings for Elizabeth. Bingley is determined to renew his attentions to Jane, and an evening's diversion of writing valentines leads to disastrous results for Darcy. Darcy doubts he has a reason to hope but, as she comes to know Darcy better, Elizabeth has to consider who is best suited to make her happy.

When Valentine's Day arrives, who will Elizabeth want to receive a valentine from: the lively man she just met or the man whose proposal she already refused?

NEWSLETTER

Receive the *Persuasion*-inspired short story *That Voice* when you sign up for my monthly newsletter. It imagines what might have happened if Captain Wentworth fell on the Cobb instead of Louisa Musgrove.

Subscribe for sales info and new release updates, exclusive excerpts, contests, giveaways, and more!

www.HeatherMollAuthor.com

ACKNOWLEDGMENTS

Thank you, as ever, to my amazing editor, Sarah Pesce, and also my fabulous proofreader, Katie Jackson. I rely on both of them to keep me on track and I would never put out a book without them.

Special thanks to my author friends, especially Cathie Smith, who understand the ups and downs of the journey.

I'd like to thank all the readers who have enjoyed my books. I love connecting with you on social media and you don't know how much I appreciate you, especially on the days when being a writer is hard.

Love and thanks always to my husband and son, even though they've never read *Pride and Prejudice* and probably never will.

ABOUT THE AUTHOR

Heather Moll is an avid reader of mysteries and biographies with a masters in information science. She found Jane Austen later than she should have and made up for lost time by devouring her letters and unpublished works, joining JASNA, and spending too much time researching the Regency era. She is the author of *An Affectionate Heart, Nine Ladies, His Choice of a Wife,* and *A Hopeful Holiday.* She lives with her husband and son, and struggles to balance all of the important things, like whether or not to buy groceries or stay home and write.

Connect with her on social media or on her blog, and subscribe to her newsletter for updates and free stories.

facebook.com / HeatherMollAuthor
twitter.com / HMollAuthor
instagram.com / HeatherMollAuthor
goodreads.com / HeatherMoll
bookbub.com / authors / heather-moll

ALSO BY HEATHER MOLL

An Affectionate Heart

Are love and affection enough to overcome the pain of grief and anger?

Nine Ladies

How can Darcy and Elizabeth overcome 200 years of differences in this time-travel love story?

His Choice of a Wife

When a man's honor is at stake, what is he willing to risk for the woman he loves?

Two More Days at Netherfield

How would spending a few extra days in each other's company affect the relationship between Elizabeth Bennet and Mr. Darcy?

A Hopeful Holiday

Is the holiday season a perfect setting for a second chance at love?

The Gentlemen Are Detained

"Will Elizabeth welcome the renewal of our acquaintance or will she draw back from me?"

Made in United States
Orlando, FL
08 September 2024

51298177R00193